The Rising at Roxbury Crossing

The Rising at Roxbury Crossing

— A NOVEL —

JAMES G. REDFEARN

Olde Stoney Brook Publishing
Wrentham, Massachusetts

Olde Stoney Brook Publishing
P.O. Box 851
Wrentham, MA 02093
www.therisingatroxburycrossing.com

Grateful Acknowledgment is made to the Driscoll Family for permission to reprint the photograph of Patrolman William J. Driscoll on page iv.

Photograph credits: page 98, Eamon de Valera at Fenway Park and page 340, State Guard Rounds up Hoodlums at Boston Common, "Courtesy of the Trustees of the Boston Public Library, Print Department"; page 294, Roster Card, "Boston Police Department Archives"; page 410, Eamon de Valera Inspects I.R.A. Troops, © Hulton-Deutsch Collection/CORBIS.

The Rising at Roxbury Crossing may be purchased for educational use. For information, please write Olde Stoney Brook Publishing, P.O. Box 851, Wrentham, MA 02093.

Cover design by Dunn+Associates, Inc., dunn-design.com
Interior design by Dorie McClelland, springbookdesign.com

P: ISBN 978-0-9839960-5-7
E: ISBN 978-0-9839960-6-4

Library of Congress Preassigned Control Number has been applied for.

First Trade Paperback Printing
10 9 8 7 6 5 4 3 2 1

Printed in the United States of America.

Always Gail

CAST OF CHARACTERS
IN ORDER OF APPEARANCE
Historical Persons Designated by *

March 1909

Sean Cahill	Ballinasloe youth, seventeen years
Matthew Cahill	Sean's younger brother, fifteen years
William Dwyer	Cousin to Cahill brothers, fifteen years
Bernie McLean	Son of local bank manager, seventeen years
Mr. Keegan	Elderly farmer
Sledge	I.R.B. (Irish Republican Brotherhood) battalion leader, identified as Peter Quinn
Whippet	Unnamed I.R.B. man

May 1919

Patrolman William Dwyer	Boston police officer, Station 10
Patrolman Albert Coppenrath	Boston police officer, Station 10
Captain Hugh Lee*	Boston police officer, Commander Station 9
Alex Sturgis	Russian Bolshevik, Lettish Workmen's Association
Martha Foley*	Irish Socialist
Louis Fraina*	Socialist, Lettish Workmen's Association
Frank Bradley	Middle Bradley brother, fourteen years
Johnny Bradley	Youngest Bradley brother, ten years
Joe Dalton	WWI veteran
Joseph Kursh	Socialist, twenty-year old prodigy and Harvard graduate
Patrolman Fulton Quigley	Boston police officer, Station 10
Wesley Ferguson/Parker Ellis	Boston police livery boys
Carlo Venezia	Owner of local tailor shop
Catherine Loftus	Waitress at the Switch
Charlie Bradley	Oldest Bradley brother
Sergeant Philip McGuiness	Boston police officer, Station 10
Patrolman George Nolan	Boston police officer, Station 10 detective
Emily Coppenrath	Albert's wife and daughter of Jim Rankin
James Rankin	Dandy Jim, Roxbury Ward Boss, State Senator, President of Boston Central Labor Union (BCLU), father of Emily Coppenrath, father-in-law of Albert Coppenrath

Virginia Rankin	James' wife
Martin Lomasney*	West End Ward Boss

June 1919

Mildred Healey	Victim at Mission Church
Alice	Mildred's friend
Peter Carlucci	New York anarchist

July 1919

Edwin Upton Curtis*	Boston police commissioner
Miss Harris	Secretary to Commissioner Curtis
John McInnes*	President of Boston Police Union
Michael Lynch*	Chairmen of Boston Police Union's Bargaining Committee
Bradford Henshaw	Owner of Patriot Realty and Management
Andrew J. Peters*	Mayor of Boston
Maximilian Henshaw	Harvard student, captain of football team, Bradford's son
Kevin Farrell	Irish farmer
Colum Farrell	Kevin's son
Graves O'Brien	R.I.C. (Royal Irish Constabulary) Constable/inspector, Ballinasloe barracks

August 1919

C. Tucker Appleton	President of the First National Bank of Boston, chairman of the Downtown Club Association
Pearl Brodsky	Owner, Brodsky Investigation & Security
Eamon de Valera*	President of political party, Sinn Féin, and newly elected president of the Dáil Éireann
Peter Quinn	I.R.B. Battalion leader, de Valera bodyguard
Aiden Fahey	De Valera bodyguard
Valerie (NLN)	Waitress at the Switch
Dr. Mary McKeigue	Doctor of forensic medicine, Trinity College Ireland
Michael Crowley*	Superintendent of Boston police
J.J. Connarty	Ballinasloe postmaster
A. Lawrence Lowell*	Harvard University president
William Pierce*	Retired superintendent of Boston police
Bob Fisher*	Harvard football coach

September 1919

Herbert Parker*	Counsel for Commissioner Curtis, advisor to Calvin Coolidge, former attorney general of Massachusetts
(John) Calvin Coolidge*	Governor of Massachusetts
Salvatore Rossini	Number One noble of Pearl Brodsky
Michael Dwyer	Willie's younger brother
Darren NLN	Ballinasloe postman
Stewart Chipman	Owner of Necco Street warehouse
Reginald (Hump) Schultz	Brodsky noble
Jack McCarthy	Brodsky noble
Captain George Keveney	Boston police officer, commander, Station 10
Patrolman Timothy Mulvey	Boston police officer, Station 1 detective
Patrolman Malcolm Byrne	Boston Police officer, Station 1 detective
Tenants at 45 Leroy St	Old woman and her son, Gordon
Patrolman Fred Cratty	Boston police officer, Station 10
Mrs. Gerhardt	Landlady of Willie's rooming house
Doctor Shutt	Boston City Hospital, emergency ward

September 1919

Lefty the houseman	Boston police officer, Station 10
Samuel D. Parker*	Brigadier General, commander, Massachusetts State Guard
Francis O'Neil	Owner, O'Neil's tavern, Roxbury Crossing

The Last Word

Frank Stearns*	Coolidge confidant, businessman, Amherst Alumnus
Boston Police Appeals Board	Unnamed chairman, Captain Jeremiah Sullivan and Captain (NFN) Howell
Catherine Malone	Pseudonym for Catherine Loftus
Dudley Malone	Pseudonym for Eamon de Valera

Prologue

~

Ballinasloe, Ireland
March 1909

In the purgatory grey of morning, three boys waited.

They hunkered down in the damp musty woods behind facing stone walls on either side of the road. The two younger boys kept watch on one side. Separated by another wall, they stole glances of each other through gaps in the stone. Across from them, an older, taller boy half-squatted and looked back through the mist to the bend in the road that accommodated a large tree. A folded burlap blanket and a length of rope lay on the ground near his feet.

"Sean, do you see him?" one of the younger boys said.

"Quiet, Matt."

"Maybe he's not going to the bank today," the second younger boy said.

"Shut up, will you." Sean glanced up at the bend again. "The fog is beginning to lift, stay down."

A few more minutes passed before the aura of the sun emerged behind the younger boys and a skinny band of muted orange spilled over the top of the hill while the woods on the other side of the road where Sean hid remained black-green and liquid.

"Do you think he's coming, Willie?" Matt said.

"Maybe—we should leave before someone sees us."

"But you want to set them straight, don't yuh?"

"Yeah. But a lot of people take this road—"

"Still he's got it coming, the dirty bastard."

Sean picked up the blanket and rope and jumped the wall. "I don't think we missed him," he said.

Matt joined his brother in the road and they stood there, sharing a cigarette.

"It's just as well," Willie said.

The Cahill brothers walked over to him where he sat on the wall. Sean sucked on the cigarette and blew smoke into Willie's face. "What's wrong with you, Dwyer?"

"Nothing."

"You sound like you just want to forget what the McLeans did to us." He drew within inches of Willie's ear. "Is that what you want to do, just forget about it?"

"No. I just want to know what they're going to do to him."

"That's none of our business—"

They turned to a scuffle of footsteps behind them.

"'Lo boys, early aren't ye?" Bernie McLean walked in the middle of the road not ten feet from them. Watching them and smelling the anger that reeked out of them, he slid away from the crown, drifting towards the shoulder on the opposite side, and passed them.

Sean hesitated, frozen by McLean's sudden appearance. The spontaneity of it cheated him of the excitement of jumping Bernie before he knew what was happening. He glanced at his younger brother and his cousin. Then he said, "What's your rush, tattler?" He dropped the cigarette and started after him. "Wait up, I want to talk to you."

The strap of Bernie's bag slipped to the outside of his shoulder as he lengthened his stride.

Matt pulled Willie by the arm. "Come on!"

The two younger boys reached Sean just as he stepped in front of McLean and blocked his path.

"Out of my way," Bernie said, "I'm late today—"

"Too bad!" Matt said.

"Say, what's going on here?"

"Got a nice suit there, McLean, and a soft hat too," Sean said. "You look like quite the dandy. Doing well for yourself are you?" He stepped up close to Bernie, pulled the bag from his shoulder and grabbed him by the lapel of his jacket. "Since your father stole our pub."

"Hey." Bernie yanked himself free from Sean's grasp and jerked his head back and forth from one brother to the other, the three of them moving in a tight little circle. "I don't know what you're talking about—"

"Your conscience bothering you?" Matt said as he knocked Bernie's soft hat off his head.

"What?"

"Who tattled to the Peelers?" Sean said.

"I don't know—everyone in town knows what happened to your family. That was a—but I didn't have anything to do with it." His head jerked towards Willie. "You know, I wouldn't talk to the barracks about anybody, right Dwyer?"

"You're a bloody liar. We know and so don't our fathers, who are rotting in Kilmainham."

"That's right, McLean," Sean said. "We have spies too."

Bernie rushed Sean and pushed him, enlarging the space between them, and then swung a backhand at Matt, knuckling his face. The younger Cahill fell back a couple of steps, screamed and then ran at Bernie's midsection. He tackled him around the waist and drove him into his brother.

"Help!" Bernie yelled.

Sean hammered him behind the neck with his fist and when Bernie fell over, he dropped the blanket over him and the two brothers kicked and punched him until he was on the ground. "Willie, get the cart," he said. "Matt, grab the rope."

The brothers tied up Bernie in the blanket and sat him in the middle of the road. The burlap squirmed and lifted with anger and then collapsed in fits of sobbing as the two brothers half-squatted over McLean and drove their butts into him each time he moved. "Shut your yap," Sean said, "or I'll give you a good one on the top of your squash."

The minutes dragged on while they struggled to control their captive. "Where's Willie with the cart?" Matt said as he looked up the road and saw a pony turn the bend. "Jesus, someone's coming."

Sean jumped to his feet. "Come on, McLean, get up."

The brothers dragged him to the side of the road near a large flat rock and pushed him down behind it. They sat on the stone and faced the woods, their feet resting on the blanketed McLean who extended beyond the ends of the rock. Sean stomped his heel into the burlap. "Don't you say one word," he hissed.

The pony drawn cart approached them and the boys recognized the driver. "Good morning, Mr. Keegan," they said in unison.

"Ah, the Cahill boys. You young fellas are at it mighty early." He pulled on the straps and stopped the cart in the middle of the road. "Do you need a lift? I'm going to town to drop off a barrel to the cooper."

"Ah—no, our cousin is bringing the cart," Matt said.

"Yeah, don't know what's taking him so long," Sean said.

The old farmer leaned over when he saw the sack beneath their feet. "Are you sure? That's a might large one you're holding there."

"No, but thanks," Sean said. "Just some bricks for the stove."

"Ah, that's it then."

Matt pointed to the bend in the road. "Here he comes now," he said with a rise in his voice. "It was probably the donkey."

"Yeah, it's the damn donkey," Sean said. "He can be stubborn."

"Now, there you go. That's why I keep old Jack here. Donkeys have minds of their own." The old man tapped the reins on the back of the pony. "Well, make it a good one." He nodded and followed the boys' eyes to the sack on the ground.

"Did you see the old fart spying the burlap?" Matt asked after the farmer turned the corner.

"Yeah," Sean said.

"Do you think he'll say anything?"

"Nah, he probably thinks we clipped some turf." Sean slipped off the stone. "And as long as it's not his—"

The brothers watched Willie as he prodded the donkey down the road to where they stood.

TIED BY THE REINS at the opening to one of the stalls, the donkey pawed at the floor and snuffled through the chips, looking for remnants of hay. He snorted and huffed out warm breath and bobbed his head. The wheels of the cart moved a half turn when he took two steps forward. Pigeons cooed in the rafters above him and shards of dingy yellow light entered through the roof in places where the tin had lifted, the sunlight piercing through the dusty air, slanting and spilling into the barn. The warm suffocating air was thick with straw dust and the pungent odor of animal urine.

McLean sat on the dirt floor with his hands tied behind a post. The blanket had been removed from his head and it draped across his body like a sash. Willie and Matt sat on either side of him on bales of hay and guarded him in silence. Willie Dwyer wiped the back of his hand across his mouth and every few minutes glanced at the closed barn doors. The younger Cahill chewed on a piece of straw, sat bent at the waist and flipped an open jackknife over and over in his hands.

"What time is it?" McLean demanded.

Willie stood and tapped Sean on the shoulder and motioned him to the doors.

"You bastards will never get away with this. When the constables get through beating you with their sticks," McLean screamed as they moved away, "you won't be able to shit out of your purple arses. And don't think the rebels will come a-riding into town to save you. They'll be running for their own hides."

The boys walked to the front of the barn and opened one of the double doors.

"And the day they cart you off to the gaol, the drinks will be on the house at Tohers."

A cool spring breeze entered through the opened door moving the stagnant barn air. Bernie lifted his head and let it fall back against the post. The boys looked back at him and then stepped outside.

"How long do we dare keep him here?" Willie said.

"I don't know," Matt said. "I thought they'd be here by now."

"Is that where Sean went, to get them?"

"He went to the cottage and then walked to town to let people see him, you know, and to snoop around and find out if McLean has been reported missing." Matt picked up a stone and flung it across the field.

"What do you think they'll do to him?"

"Sean says that the Brotherhood wants to set an example—what will happen if you talk to the Peelers or if you cause harm to one of its members."

"Like what?"

"He thinks they'll pitchcap him, muck him up a bit. If it makes you feel any better, just remember what he did to our families when he informed. His old man, the banker, sits pretty on our pub, and our fathers are in prison for fifteen years."

Willie let out a breath. "I should go home, Mam will be missing me. She'll need some help with the chores, the others can't do it."

"You can't leave me alone with him," Matt said. "Come on, let's go back inside. It can't be much longer."

EVENING CAME and the heat escaped from inside the barn. The two boys dozed within feet of their prisoner in flat grey light.

"Wake up, Dwyer," McLean whispered. "Wake up."

Willie stirred and when he saw McLean's shoe near, he rolled away and sat up.

"Let me loose, Dwyer, and I'll tell the constables that you helped to free me."

"Why should I do that? We're cooked already."

"Because you and I are chums." McLean twisted and tried to pull himself up straight. "Remember the time when I picked you up in the lorry when you were walking from town with one of your brothers?"

"That was a long time ago—"

"—and we served Mass together."

"We knew each other, but my father isn't the manager of the Bank of Ireland. We live in two different worlds."

"Yeah, but—"

"And I am not an apprentice at the bank. You and your father, with all your manners and all that you have—"

"Sshhh, all right. Let me loose and I won't even mention you were here. Besides, it's really your cousins who have it in for me."

Matt squirmed on the bales and gave out a small moan in his sleep.

"Who are you waiting for Dwyer? Let me go and I'll make it worth your while. My father will pay a ransom."

The dusky light barely lit the inside of the barn now and Willie saw only the shadows of things. The donkey and the cart had disappeared except for the jingle of the harness and the roll of the wheel. And Bernie had disappeared too, except for the murky angles of his reclining body and the grinding of his voice.

THE BARN DOOR RATTLED open and Willie heard deep whispering voices. He could see two men behind a lantern. One man was stout and blunt with sledge-like features and when he bent down to scoop up a handful of dirt, Willie saw the flash of his face, hard and resolved, saw his hand moving like he was panning for gold. He could see Sean, standing in the distance, farther back in the yard and away from the doors. He saw the light penetrate the barn and sweep the area around the entrance. He crawled to his cousin, placed his hand over Matt's mouth and shook him until he stirred.

"Someone's at the door," he whispered.

The boys crawled into a stall and watched from the darkness as the men entered.

The second man had sharp lean features and spoke with an agitated voice, moving into the barn in nervous little darts like a whippet. "Come on, come on, where is he?" he said.

"Who's that?" McLean ordered. "I told you they would find me. I'm back here, tied to the post," he said, his voice cracking.

The boys could hear Bernie's feet and legs scratching at the earthen floor.

"God help you," he said in their direction.

The two men stood at McLean's feet and the barrel-shaped man lowered the lamp until it lit up Bernie's face.

"Untie me," he said and turned his head and eyes away from the glare. "Did my father send you?"

"His head is uncovered," Whippet said. "Why is his fucking head uncovered? Stand up."

The boys could see the long shadow bodies moving on the wall with their arms flailing, could smell the liquor and the sweat, could smell the fear and see the light rising with Bernie's face.

"Get that filthy blanket off my head," McLean said.

"You're guilty of conspiring against the people of Ireland," Sledge said. "Do you want to say a prayer?"

"A prayer? Untie me."

"God have mercy on us all—"

THE BOYS SAW the Whippet jump and the flash of his arm. The shadow of the pistol stretched across the wall just as the flame exploded out of the end of the barrel. Matt screamed out and Willie pushed back like a crab into the corner of the stall. He clamped his mouth to stifle his voice while Matt rocked back and forth and whimpered.

"Get up outta there," Whippet said to them. "Get them up outta there. They have work to do."

The system of discipline seeks to deal with men by hand rather than with machinery; to prove to them that their superiors are guided by common sense and a spirit of fair play, and that, though the interest of the public is always first and the interest of the whole Department is always second, the comfort, the welfare and the ambitions of the individual members of the force are never forgotten.

Stephen O'Meara, Commissioner
City of Boston Police Department
June 1906–December 1918

Chapter One

~

Roxbury, Massachusetts
1 May 1919

The large man with the red bandanna was the face of the mob.

"Put the pistol away, copper, or I'll shove it up your ass." He lunged and grabbed the cylinder of the patrolman's revolver to keep it from turning. "Do you think this pistol is going to stop us? You've got six bullets—there are hundreds of us." He released his grip on the cylinder before winking at the young patrolman. "And some of us also have guns." He held up a long club and shouted, "March on, Comrades," then stepped behind the banner of the Lettish Workmen's Association.

"If I get a chance, I'll shoot that bastard," the patrolman said.

"Easy does it, Albert," said the officer next to him. "The reserves are on their way. Then, you can give him a taste of the club."

"Where the hell are they?"

The two patrolmen stumbled backwards a few steps from the crush of the mob and then moved sideways as additional police took up positions in the hastily formed skirmish line.

"Hold the line, Men," ordered the captain who paced behind Albert Coppenrath and Willie Dwyer. Captain Hugh Lee's face was crimson and clammy and the neck of his high shirt collar was soaking wet with perspiration; he breathed in deep measured breaths. "This is an illegal assembly. You have no permit, Mr. Fraina. I told you last night you would be arrested." Hot acrid bile filled his mouth and he bent over and ejected it into the street.

The red flags of the Bolsheviks hung limp as the protestors and the cops leaned into each other and muscled one another for control. The outnumbered policemen staggered with their batons across their chests, bracing themselves as several hundred demonstrators continued to stack up behind the Letts' banner. Isolated bursts of laughter rose from the rear of the crowd as stragglers ran to catch up to the main body of protestors; well-dressed women scurried forward in ankle-length skirts, who upon reaching the others stopped to adjust hats that had slipped to the backs of their heads. Some of them carried young children or pulled them along in tow. There was a festive air to the civil disobedience of these tag-along Feminists and Parlor Socialists. "To hell with the permit!" they chanted.

Curious bystanders gathered on the sidewalk and taunted the protestors as the last of the Reds funneled out of the Dudley Street Opera House. In a vacant lot across the street, a group of boys halted their game of stickball to watch the demonstrators swell in numbers. One of them took off running.

"Hey, Frank. Where you going?" yelled one of the boys.

"Pile up some hoobies to throw at these bums," Frank Bradley said as he ran across the street. "I'm going to get Joe Dalton and some of the Vets in the tavern."

"But I want to come with you."

"Do what I tell you, Johnny. The cops are going to need some help."

The boys began to gather stones from the lot, filled their pockets with them and then they filled Johnny's wagon.

The large picture window at the entrance to the Dudley Square Tavern was trimmed in red, white and blue. "Hire Veterans" was hand-painted in one of the window's lower corners and "Buy Bonds" was painted in the other. Frank Bradley pushed open the tavern door, held it ajar and squinted to see into the dimly lit barroom. In the corner of the room, Army and Navy Veterans, still dressed in their military uniforms, sat around at tables playing cards.

"Hey, kid. What's going on out there?" the bartender asked.

"I'm looking for Joe Dalton. The cops are trying to hold back hundreds of Reds from marching and parading with their signs and flags."

"Are they?"

"Yeah, and they've got clubs and knives."

"Hey, Joe," the bartender hollered to the back of the room. "You guys might want to see what's going on out here." He reached under the counter and retrieved a club and a couple of lengths of lead-filled rubber hose and placed them on the bar.

At the front of the demonstrators, a slim young brunette, who was taller than many of the men, carried one of the red flags. She moved directly in front of Patrolman Dwyer. "Willie?" she entreated. When he didn't respond, she said, "Isn't that the name your friend called you, Patrolman? You should not be offended by us. Listen to the many different languages being spoken behind me. We all wear red to represent the blood that runs through the veins of all men. She pushed the flag aside and leaned closer to Dwyer. "And you police are workers too, but you are pawns of the cruelest master of all, the Government of the United States."

"Save your speeches, Miss Foley. I know who you are." Willie could hear patrol wagons arriving and setting up in the distance behind him. He recognized the voice of one of his own sergeants from Station 10, shouting orders as the patrolmen dismounted from the wagons.

"Willie, are you going to protect us against the threats of violence at the hands of the hoodlums who stand on the sides of the street and are waiting to pelt us with their bricks and beat us with their clubs?"

Martha Foley continued to make her pitch while Willie could see other armed Letts quietly slipping to the front of the demonstrators. "Those people you call hoodlums are American citizens, Miss Foley, and many of them fought for this country in Europe. And who are you, a Socialist who supports the violent Bolshevik Letts."

"At least dissuade your fellow policemen, Willie, who prepare to mount their assault upon us. Allow us to walk freely the short distance to our hall and celebrate International Labor Day. Remember, you are a worker and we also protest for your right of absolute freedom."

"You're wasting your time, comrade," said the man with the red bandana. "He takes his orders from the fat captain."

"Perhaps he is just misguided, Alex."

"Go back to Russia, Miss Foley," said Dwyer, "and take Alex and your godless revolutionary ideas with you."

"You say that, Willie, while at this very moment our Irish countrymen are fighting the very oppressors that you support. You are being used by the same people who have raped mother Ireland. Did you forget so soon about Trevelyan, Easter Sunday and the poor emaciated Irish who arrived in this city and were left to die on the outer islands, never to set foot on America's soil?"

Willie no longer heard the scurrying of boots or felt the squeeze of additional coppers around and behind him. Instead, he heard the nervous anticipation of shuffling feet, random coughs and large gnarly hands grinding their clubs. He could smell the energy of the additional men and the anticipated fear of the first blow.

Foley moved into his face and said, "Remember, Patrolman, you're just like the rest of us. You might be working for them today, but they don't care anymore about you than the miners that they butchered in Ludlow."

"You heard the captain. You don't have a permit to parade."

"We don't need a permit to fight the just and social war, copper," Alex Sturgis said. "The workers of the world no longer take orders from oppressive and illegal governments, run by imperialists and flunkeys who enforce their laws." He punched his fist into the air and began to move his linked comrades into the police line, plowing the outnumbered cops backward, as women in the rear of the mob sang, "Arise Ye Wretched of the Earth."

Veterans and locals spilled out of the bars along Dudley Street, jeering and swearing at the demonstrators, many of them carrying clubs, ax handles and ice picks, as they moved quickly along the sidewalk to reach the front of the demonstration. "One of my best friends died fighting you bastards in Siberia," shouted Joe Dalton. "There's no room for Bolsheviks in America. Go back to Russia, Italy or wherever you came from before we kick you all the way back to Europe." He arrived at the front of the demonstration and saw the overwhelmed police, backpedaling and swinging their clubs at the surging Reds who began to break through the skirmish line. "Come on. Let's help those guys," he said as he and several other veterans entered the crowd.

The Letts charged through the gaps in the police line and rushed Albert Coppenrath, sealing him off from the other officers, the crowd pushing in on him and choking off his air. Albert's legs quivered as he began to backpedal in anticipation of the wave of humanity that was about to come crashing down on him. He turned his head to avoid the pungent odor of garlic as Alex Sturgis spit, "Kill the police," into his face. In an instant, a frenzy of men and women were all over him, screaming and pushing him backwards. One of his legs buckled beneath him and he stumbled into a protestor who grabbed his baton in midair, punched him and drove his knee into him. He toppled over onto the street where he lay nauseated, snared in a tangled mass of moving legs charging in various directions, some stepping around him and tripping over him, some falling and carrying their bodies down to the ground on top of him, and some making him grimace from blows to his ribs and kidneys. Curled in a fetal position, he saw his helmet lying on its side beyond his reach and heard the slash of wooden sticks whirling through the warm spring air. He rolled up tighter into a ball and reached up with his hands to protect his head as hundreds of pieces of brick and stone rained down on rioters and police. His most vivid sensations were the hysterical screams of women and children, discharging pistols and the distinctive sound of horses' metal shoes striking the cobblestones just before he slipped into unconsciousness.

The fighting, confusion and terror spread from the streets to the doorways and alleys as veterans and other neighborhood residents joined the police in suppressing and beating the marchers and pursuing them when they tried to escape. When the first pistol shots cracked and bullets flew haphazardly, Frank Bradley grabbed his younger brother by the back of his shirt and busted into the first unlocked business he could find as the elderly proprietor nervously fumbled with the bolt. "I'm sorry, mister, but let my brother stay here, will you? I don't want him to get hurt."

"Hurry up—" the storeowner said.

"Stay here, Johnny."

"Where are you going, Frank?"

"I'm going to get my licks in and try to find your wagon. I'll come back and get you when it's over." Frank slipped out the door and disappeared into the mayhem on the street.

Joe Dalton entered the fray when he saw Albert Coppenrath go down under a barrage of clubs, saps and knuckle-dusters and watched as the protestors stormed over him under a solid red flag. He raced to the fallen policeman with several other veterans, punched in the pasty face of a youthful protestor and snatched his flag. He and his friends beat off others with the lead-filled rubber hoses. Two of the veterans lifted Coppenrath under his arms and dragged him to the safety of the Dudley Square Tavern and then reentered the melee.

The sheer number of Letts who squeezed into the valley that was Dudley Street, obliterated the police skirmish line and any immediate effort to control them. They were emboldened by the ease with which they had dispatched the lackeys and they marched confidently to the intersection of Warren Street. The police fought for their own survival, drew their revolvers, shot and were shot at in the close hand-to-hand combat. Willie Dwyer was only arms' lengths away from Albert when the skirmish line collapsed and the demonstrators made their rush. He could no longer see his best friend, but began to move in Coppenrath's direction, slashing his baton through the mob, creating a path and threatening to shoot anyone who attempted to confront him. He made his way the few feet to where he had last seen Albert when he realized that the demonstrators who had already passed him were now retreating and passing him again to escape the charge of a line of galloping horses.

Mounted police wheeled around Walnut Avenue, a block away, and plowed down Warren Street in a tightly formed line, whooping and yelping as they drove their horses into anyone in their path. Those demonstrators who foolishly attempted to engage the horses were bulldozed down or clubbed by their riders. The Reds ran helter-skelter, running over their weaker comrades in their haste to escape the crush of the charging animals that squeezed them onto the sidewalks and flattened them up against the storefronts or pushed them down the alleys between the buildings where they were beaten and stuffed into waiting patrol wagons. Veterans and patriotic locals ducked into doorways, then pursued the fleeing protestors and assisted the police in arresting them. A truck followed the horses with members of the Special Squad flanking it on both sides. Some of the strong-armed members of the Letts managed to elude the horses and began to reassemble in the street when the truck turned broadside and two patrolmen on the back removed a tarp that exposed a mounted machine gun. The police leveled the machine gun and eight shotguns at the Reds as the squad leader commanded the protestors to surrender or be shot.

When the horses made their first sweep, Willie sprinted off the street and climbed the first few steps of a fire escape. From this elevated view, he could see the disruption the horses had caused and watched as the protestors fled for safety. He scanned the street and saw that the police were gaining control. Many of the Letts and their sympathizers surrendered meekly, preferring incarceration to the beatings they were receiving from the hundreds of neighborhood residents who took exception to parading Bolsheviks. He watched a group of Reds flee and enter the elevated railway station. Slipping away with them were Alex Sturgis, another bodyguard, and Louis Fraina. As the horses made their turn for a second pass, Willie jumped down the steps, raced across the street to the train station and found the Letts' banner discarded at the entrance. He jumped the turnstile, vaulted the canopied iron stairs, and reached the platform just as the last car from a departing train squeezed its wheels against the curve of the track, screeching in a high metallic wail before it went out of sight, the three men in the back window staring him down.

WILLIE STOOD on the rear step of the last wagon of prisoners and held on as it turned the corner into the backyard of Station 10, passing a quickly growing crowd that was forming at the front of the building. It came to a halt in a line of other wagons that stood idling as patrolmen removed prisoners and brought them into the police station through the garage.

"Patrolman?" one of the prisoners shouted from inside the van. "I am an American citizen. I was assaulted and demand my rights."

Dwyer shaded his eyes and peered into the darkened interior of the wagon. "Weren't you marching at the front of the parade and carrying a red flag?"

"Yes," the young man said. His boyish face stared out from under a wide-brimmed hat. He was ashen and the flesh under one of his eyes was red-blue and beginning to swell.

"If you are a United States citizen, why didn't you carry the American flag?"

"Because I don't idolize the flag; it is only a symbol just as the red flag I carry is a symbol."

Willie poked the shoulder of a standing prisoner with his baton. "You. Move aside so I can speak to the man on the bench." The prisoner begrudgingly stepped aside and Willie waved to the young man to come to the back of the wagon.

"What's your name?" Willie asked.

"Joseph."

"Do you have a last name, Joseph?"

"Kursh."

"Where do you live?"

"Cambridge."

"Well, Joseph, the difference is that your red flag is a symbol for the Soviet form of government and a Socialist way of life. Am I correct?"

"Yes. I believe that the people who do the work should control the Government and the country's industries. They should have more say—"

Willie grabbed the bar as the patrol wagon rolled forward and jerked to a stop. "And if necessary, you would take control of the country's industries by force?"

"I don't advocate violence, but if necessary to prevent a man or a woman from being treated like an animal, then yes, by force. Even the Declaration of Independence states that the Government derives its power from the People, and it is the Right of the People to alter or abolish it—"

"The Declaration also refers to individual freedoms, Joseph, not mob rule." The wagon backed up to the garage door. "You Parlor Reds want it both ways. You want to destroy the institutions that you believe don't provide 'absolute freedom' and then, when things get rough, you want those same institutions to protect you. I would suggest that you talk to your attorney and the judge about your rights."

"If you're through giving your Civics lesson, Dwyer, I would appreciate some assistance hosing out this moveable water closet before you and I hit the road." A senior patrolman at the station, Fulton Quigley had the reputation of being only slightly short of a stay at the Commonwealth's mental hospital at Mattapan. But he was also the guy you wanted to lead the charge in a barroom fight or be the point man in a crowd-clearing wedge. Underweight for his height, his uniform hung on his six-foot, four-inch frame like a cheap suit on a closet hanger. But his wild maniacal persona packaged with keen instinctive street savvy more than made up for his lack of physical bulk.

He stood on the back step of a patrol wagon that had been emptied of prisoners. "Headquarters is holding the day shift," he said. "And, you won the jackpot, you lucky boy. The sergeant has assigned us to Wagon One to patrol the Hill until the natives wear themselves out or eight o'clock in the morning, whichever comes first."

"Shouldn't I check in upstairs and let them know I'm back from Dudley Street?"

"You can if you want to, but the place is a madhouse of wall-to-wall bloody Bolshies. Tell you the truth, I don't think they'll miss you. Here have a broom."

"Alright, if you say so. Were you at Dudley Street, Fulton?"

"I got called in from time off and they put me on a wagon. But by the time I got there, the fun was just about over." He dipped a sponge into a bucket of soapy water and slapped it against the side of the van. "The boys on the ponies had already broken up the party. So, I was like the guy who follows the parade of elephants, picking up the shit that those enormous arses leave behind."

Willie climbed into the box and began to sweep it out. "Say, did you happen to see Coppenrath? We were standing next to each other on the skirmish line, but when the Reds made their push, he disappeared and I never saw him again."

"I think he was one of the fellas who got kicked around pretty good. He and a couple of other guys were treated by a local doctor and sent packing."

"Is he okay?" Willie jumped down off the wagon.

"He's fine. The Lieutenant sent him home to rest." Quigley played the hose into the inside of the box. "Will you look at the blood coming out of there?"

Fifteen minutes later, Willie Dwyer and Fulton Quigley rode the wagon out of the backyard and up the drive, leaving a watery trail behind them, and slowly navigated through the crowd that now filled the Crossing.

THE CROWD BEGAN to form at the elevated railway on Washington Street, swept through the Dudley Street Opera House, seeking any straggling Reds, and marched toward Mission Hill and Station 10, picking up more and more outraged residents as they stormed down Roxbury Street to the Crossing. They were the unemployed who had worked in the factories, sewing doughboy uniforms and manufacturing munitions with alcohol derived from distilled molasses—some of the nine million Americans who had lost their jobs in a peacetime economy after laboring to 'Keep the World Safe for Democracy.' Creel's Committee on Public Information had given them the will to fight by portraying the Germans as less than human and preached to them about absolute loyalty. So, they canned vegetables, grew their victory gardens, cheered at Wake-Up America parades and purchased Liberty Bonds. The beer makers and livery men who worked at the breweries along Old Stony Brook under a cloud of war-time prohibition, downtown office workers, arriving home on trolleys and trains, and the motormen and Carmen who drove them, off-duty firemen, mill workers and telephone operators who had gone on strike for a living wage, cloth caps and soft hats, all came home to the Hill to drive out the Bolsheviks.

They marched for a nostalgic past and their lost innocence, a simpler and more peaceful time, when nothing of importance appeared in the newspapers and the cost of living was 71% lower. They sang "God Bless America" mindful that they had no jobs or that they couldn't feed their families. With the stars and stripes fluttering in the breeze above them, they were led by soldiers and sailors who had fought in the War of Good versus Evil, veterans like Joe Dalton, who had survived the trenches of Ypres, Marne, Verdun and Gallipoli, had endured poisonous gases and the psychological impact of aerial bombardment, and hurried home with four million others to a life of 'normalcy' that no longer existed. Now as they gathered in front of Station 10, Isolationism surged in their veins and a fog of suspicion draped its invisible cloak around them—to hell with Wilson's League of Nations. Designated by the American Defense Society as the country's gatekeepers, they sought out foreign agitators who dared to spread revolutionary propaganda, those anarchists, beasts, Reds, criminals, Wobblies, Communists and Bolshevists. This wasn't Petrograd. This was Boston, the birthplace of democracy, America's Athens. They would show these slackers that their revolutionary and terrorist activities were not appreciated in the greatest country in the world.

The expanding crowd gathered in the Crossing and stood outside of Station 10 where two patrolmen guarded the door with shotguns. They screamed their threats into the precinct's open windows, chanting calls that described what they would do if the prisoners were released on bail, the discretionary Reds choosing to remain in custody and the safety of the police station. Motorists, locked in traffic, blew their horns to escape the bottled-up intersection, and then, when told of the Dudley Street Riot, joined the irate crowd. Gray-white smoke and chips of incinerated ashes lifted off Columbus Avenue and drifted lazily into the air as captured red flags burned in the street. And when Quigley and Dwyer rode their wagon up the drive, the crowd reached into the cab and clapped the patrolmen on the back.

"We appreciate your support," Quigley said. "Now go on home, fellas. We got it under control." He steered the wagon around the crowd and the agitated edginess that they brought with them. They were a herd of cattle one sharp sound away from a stampede. "Go home, fellas," he repeated, not entirely convinced that they were still in control. A few of the protestors looked down or away, and some reluctantly began to move.

Dwyer pointed out Wesley Ferguson and Parker Ellis, two of the Department's livery boys, who lived and worked at the stables behind the police station, the smaller Ellis sitting on top of Ferguson's shoulders, both arms stretched long in the air, and chanting with the crowd, "The only good Red is dead."

Quigley tapped out a repetitive short warning with the horn as he eased up the wagon beside them.

"Patrolman Quigley, we didn't know it was you in the wagon," said Ferguson. "We'll take care of those Reds for you."

"Why don't you boys go on now? The Bolsheviks are not coming out until they go to court tomorrow."

A soldier climbed onto the hood of a car and held up a Letts banner, stuck it in the middle with a bayonet blade, tore it in half and tossed the pieces into the air. Ferguson and Ellis whistled their approval.

"Judge Hayden will give them what's coming to 'em," Quigley shouted above the noise.

"What's the harm?" Ellis asked. "We just want these bums to know that we ain't going to stand for any more of their stuff."

"I think they got the message," Quigley said. "Come on. You start moving and others will follow."

"Alright, Patrolman." Ellis tapped his friend on the head and Ferguson bent down to allow the small livery boy to jump to the street. "Let's go to the pub," he said and then walked away with some of his friends.

Quigley and Dwyer continued to break up the crowd and convinced the veterans to help them. The more belligerent demonstrators moved to the neighborhood taverns and their places were filled by the less vocal commuters who were more curious than angry, gathering enough juicy descriptive information for the supper table conversation before going home. When just a few stragglers were left, Quigley parked the wagon by the front door to thank the army and navy boys who were now sitting on or standing in front of the station's stairs.

"Say, where do I get a job like yours, Fulton?" Joe Dalton said as he tapped the end of an ax handle on the step.

"You would be continuing the army life, Joe—sixty to one hundred hours a week, sleeping in the stations and never seeing your family—and all of that for a little over $2.00 a day. In there," Quigley nodded to the front door of the station, "we got one bathtub for sixty men."

"Well, at least you got a job."

"Oh, don't get me wrong. I love my job and wouldn't think of doing anything else, long hours and all." He looked across the roof at Dwyer.

"Let's go. I think it's going to be a long night." He shut the door and leaned out the window. "Thanks, again, fellas, for all your assistance today." Then he drove the wagon across the Crossing and turned up Tremont Street.

CARLO VENEZIA OPENED his tailor shop at the corner of Tremont and Terrace Streets at the beginning of the year during the winter's worst snowstorm, exactly six years after arriving in America from Italy. Most new business owners would have put off the opening to a day when the weather was more accommodating and prospective customers were not imprisoned in their homes. But Carlo was not your typical new business owner and when you have a plan—indeed a passion—about your future, little things like a Nor'easter are just an inconvenience, not an insurmountable problem. Besides, it said something to the Mission Hill community about the tenacity and character of the man from Italy.

Like most of the few Italian immigrants who settled in Roxbury, Carlo came from the Romagna Region. They left their small remote towns at the turn of the century, jumped on the immigrant tidal wave from Western Europe and arrived on America's shores full of ambition. Abandoning his rural background, Venezia arrived in New York and settled in a tenement not far from Manhattan's Garment District where twelve-hour days bent over a sewing machine prepared him for a future as a tailor.

He moved his family to Roxbury at the suggestion of some of his fellow Romagnolos where he continued to learn his trade as an apprentice in a small family tailor shop. But unlike his friends, he refused their invitations to become a disciple of the anarchist, Luigi Galleani, and take up the cause of the 'social war.' Instead, he applied for citizenship, studied his new language and registered with the local draft board in compliance with the military conscription act. So, when some of his fellow Italians marched in Dudley Street, Carlo opened his shop and tended to his business.

A fan wobbled on a small table in one corner of the room, moving the hot humid air out a window, a window that also let in the muted patriotic songs, the hard angry laughter and the obnoxious threats that drifted out of O'Neil's Tavern on the other side of the street. A gooseneck lamp hung over the tailor's smallish hands as they guided the cloth material under the needle, his foot pumping the sewing machine peddle while listening to Puccini's *La Boehme*, playing on a tabletop Victrola in the adjoining room.

A third of the length of the cloth that eventually would be a man's suit had cleared the needle when Venezia stopped, noticing the sudden absence of tavern noise, and looked across the street. Yellow light spilled out of the tavern door onto the sidewalk where a group of men stood, staring back. Carlo shut off the lamp and walked across the room like it was the end to an ordinary day, pulled down the shade on the front door half-way and locked it. He slipped into the darkness at the back of the store and watched as some of the men disappeared into the adjoining alley next to the tavern and reemerged, carrying lengths of two-by-fours and tossing stones back and forth in their hands.

The phonograph record had played to its end and the needle scratched back and forth when he looked out and saw them coming. They ran out of the light and into the darkness of the street, led by a man carrying a torch, shouting threats and promising to drive every Red out of the Roxbury neighborhood. The first stones fell harmlessly on the sidewalk in front of the store, but the second and third barrages struck the building and smashed Carlo Venezia's front window. More stones came from shorter distances now, breaking the glass in the front door and the windows to his upstairs apartment. The vigilantes cheered and a few of them took up the chant of the day, "The only good Red is dead."

Carlo could hear his wife running above him to the front window. She screamed his name and then she ran across the floor to the back stairs. "Soggiornare in retro della casa," he yelled to her then ran to his front window with his hands up, shaking them to the crowd. "Per favore, Per favore."

"Speak English, you Wop," one of the men said.

Several others yelled, "Burn him out, the dirty Bolshevik bastard."

He fluttered his hands above his shoulders. "No Bolshevik."

A rock struck Carlo in the shoulder. "No Bolshevik—" And another struck him in the head, opening a half-inch gash in his forehead.

Two of the vigilantes took an eight foot length of four-by-four and rammed it against the door. It gave way, struck the wall behind it and then swung closed again. Carlo jumped away from the window as bricks, stones and bottles rained into the store. He hid behind the counter and held a rag against his forehead. The man with the torch kicked the broken door open and stepped into the shop.

Then Carlo heard the blast of a shotgun.

"The next man that even so much as scratches his arse," Quigley said, "I'll fill him full of Nine-Ball. Put your hands in the air. All of you. Put your fucking hands into the air. You with the torch, get out here. Dwyer, put 'em up against the building."

"What's the problem, Quigley?" one of the men said. "We're giving you coppers a hand, getting these Reds out of the neighborhood."

"Yeah, what's the big deal?" said another. "He's just one of those black Italians who hates America."

Quigley brought the shotgun up to his shoulder and leveled it at them. "How's this? Does this answer your question?" He swept the shotgun down the line of men. "You, bums, found your testicles in O'Neil's tonight and figured that you would scare the bejesus out of this man and his family."

"Listen, Quigley," the man with the torch said.

"Shut up, McKay. It figures that you'd be one of these idiots. Put that fire out."

After the vigilantes were pinned against the building, Fulton asked Carlo to point out the men who threw the rocks and broke his door, but he refused to finger any of them. "Then we'll charge all of them and let them spend the night with the real Reds in our cells."

"No," Carlo said. "I want to live here, in my shop, my home." He faced the vigilantes, held his palms up. "Perchi—" He tapped his chest. "Not Bolshevik, American."

Quigley jammed the butt of the shotgun into his hip. "Take off your helmet, Dwyer." He stepped in front of the vigilantes. "This is what we call instant justice. My friend here is going to walk the line and every one of you will call out your name and address and then empty your pockets into the helmet for the restoration of this man's shop and, if I see one of you not putting something into the helmet, I'll butt stroke you into next week. That is unless you prefer to spend the night at the station and go to court in the morning. So don't try any funny business because I know all of you. Am I correct, McKay?"

"Yeah."

"Good, fill it up." Quigley removed his diary and began to make his entries. When he finished entering the last name, he said, "Now you're going to clean up this mess."

THUNDER RUMBLED in the distance and heat lightning skipped across the sky as the wagon crested Parker Hill Avenue with one lone prisoner aboard who continued to bang his head against the wall behind the cops.

"Shut up in there," Quigley yelled.

"Come on, Quigley, let me outta here," a voice howled back. The wall vibrated again.

"I said to shut up or you'll never get out of that box. You've been carrying on for half an hour. Now take a snooze and sober up and you'll be home before morning."

The wall rumbled with rage as the drunken prisoner punched his fists into the metal.

"Hold on, Dwyer." Quigley suddenly pressed the accelerator and the van jerked down Hillside Street. He turned the wheel sharply and they skidded into the intersection with Calumet; a loud heavy thud sounded in the rear.

Quigley downshifted and let the van roll to a stop. "If you don't settle down back there, Reilly, I'll stick you until you're nothing but ground meat. You think you'll like that?"

"All right, Quigley, you win." A tinny voice said from the other side of the wall.

"That's a good lad, Winslow. We'll stop to get you some coffee in a little while then we'll drop you home."

"Jesus," Willie said. "If you didn't kill him, you'd about to kill me."

"Listen, Dwyer. What choice do I have? I can't bring him into the station. There's no room in the inn. And I can't bring him home, at least not right now because sometimes when he drinks, he uses the old lady as a punching bag." Quigley took two cigarettes from his shirt pocket. "Smoke, Dwyer?" Willie refused with a shake of his head.

"Oh, you're one of those health nuts. Give it time. The job has a way of making you a little bit crazy. Wait awhile, you'll smoke." Fulton pulled away from the curb and drove the van slowly towards Tremont Street.

"It's been a long day." Willie rubbed his face with his hands. "I just want to lie down, even if it is a rack at the station."

"Well, at least you'll get a chance to lie down," Quigley said. "I've got house duties when we get back." Raindrops began to tap a syncopated beat against the metal vehicle; within a few moments, they became a steady drumming. He threw the spent cigarette out the window and let the rain splash over his open palm, cupped his hand and wiped off his face and neck with the water. "There's a box at the corner, why don't you ring in. And after that, you can drive." He jumped down from the wagon and looked into the back and found their prisoner curled up on the bench.

As Willie drove away from the signal box, Quigley retrieved a bag containing a plain brown bottle from under the seat. "Well, what's this?" He opened it and gulped down a mouthful of its contents. "Dwyer?" he said as he offered the bottle.

"One snort of that stuff and I'll be asleep at the wheel."

Quigley closed his eyes. "Suit yourself, but this is good stuff." He repackaged the bag and placed it back under the seat.

"How long have you been a copper?" Willie said.

"Twenty glorious years this August and wouldn't think of doing anything else." The senior patrolman folded his arms and leaned against the door. "Seems like it was only a few months ago when I was a new reserve and paired up with the senior man in the station. I was his last probationary—think I might have burned him out. Say, you must be close to completing your own probation."

"I was appointed a couple of weeks ago."

"I missed it, huh. Where was I at a strike or a parade?" Quigley stretched his arms and legs and contorted his face as he yawned. He thought about his young partner and realized that he didn't know him very well. For that matter, he didn't really know any of the younger patrolmen in Station 10.

The stations had become so busy with all of the extra details that no one had time to get to know these new guys. Usually after a year in a station house, new cops would be tagged with nicknames, like Quickdraw, Stickman or Slick, or labeled with characteristics that, whether justified or not, accurate or not, defined who they were, remaining intrinsically a part of them for their entire careers. But Willie was one of those rare new cops who, other than being typed as quiet and reflective, had not earned a reputation or a nickname. In fact, no one knew a hell of a lot about Willie Dwyer. "So, what's young Willie's story?"

"What do you mean?"

"When did you leave the old country?"

"Ah, I came over on the *Arabic* just before I turned sixteen. Stayed with my aunt. Got my own room now on Iroquois so I can be close to the station. That's about it."

"Didn't want to get stuck on the farm, heh?"

"Yeah, something like that."

"The *Arabic?* Why does that name sound familiar?"

"It was torpedoed by the Huns at the beginning of the war."

"The dirty bastards—So, now you're another Mick who has staked a claim in this great country and become a member of Boston's finest to boot." Quigley fixed his eyes on the wet windshield. "Say, Willie. You know that our Social Club is considering taking a stand against the Mayor and that stiff-necked Yankee Commissioner of ours, don't you?"

"I heard a couple of the fellas talking about it earlier this week." Willie pulled into the alley behind The Switch, the local all-night diner.

"Well, old chum, as the Station's representative, I need to know. Are you with us?"

"Is it true that the Social Club is thinking about applying for a charter with the Federation of Labor?"

"Yes, it's true. It's a shame that Commissioner O'Meara died so suddenly. We trusted him and, even though he was against us joining a union, eventually he would have done right by us. Now, that trust is gone and we need support from the A.F. of L."

Dwyer remained silent.

"You seem a little undecided," Quigley said. "All I need to know is whether you're behind Lynch and the other boys who have been delegated to represent us. We can't let them stand alone." Quigley sat up. "They've got families and they need our support. Otherwise, Curtis and his henchmen captains will ship them to stations away from their homes or assign them to a steady diet of strike duty."

"It's just—"

"Or worse yet, dream up some trumped-up charges and suspend them."

"—I'm new on the job."

"Look Dwyer, we were asked to wait until after the War. Then we were told to be patient and wait for the new budget. We've been waiting since fucking 1913." Quigley's voice climbed. "Meantime, workers from all kinds of industries went on strike and doubled their wages. The "Hello" girls have the right idea. They go out and shut off the telephones and within a few days, they get a $3.00 a week raise. Now, they make more than we do, answering a fucking telephone."

The prisoner turned in his sleep and rolled against the wall. Quigley lowered his voice. "And when Labor goes out, who takes the brunt of their frustrations? Not the guys running the show. We do."

"I'm with the fellas, but—"

"You can't let them hang by themselves, Dwyer. Those political bastards all agree that we're underpaid and our stations are in deplorable condition. We can't wait any longer."

"I can't lose this job. I've been sending what little extra money I have back home. My mother's very ill."

"We all need our jobs, Dwyer, besides most of us have been down that road."

"I heard that the Governor and the Mayor are going to give us and the firemen a yearly increase of $200. Is that true?"

"Big fuckin' deal. That raise is about four years too late. Doesn't even cover the cost of living?"

Willie cracked the door to the van. "I better get a cup of black coffee for our guest so we can drop him off."

Quigley caught Dwyer's sleeve as he leaned out into the rain. "You do that, but just remember this. The Commissioner, the Mayor, the Governor, they're afraid. We got control of the elections twenty-five years ago because of political organization. And because of that organization, we,

Irish, have got boys in the Fire Service, Police Department and other public services. You would have been hard pressed to land a position on the Police Department before that and would still be picking through the rubbish behind some shanty."

"I know—"

"It's all about power, Dwyer, that's why we have to stick together. That's why we need the organization, to stop these bastards now from taking advantage of us any longer." Quigley softened his voice. "We need the union—"

Willie nodded and shut the door and walked into the diner.

The usual cast of characters sat or stood at the counter and filled all six booths in the only place at this end of the precinct where a night crawler could get a cup of coffee or something to eat after 2 a.m. The diner in Brigham Circle glowed with light and hummed with the busy chatter of humans who functioned in a contradictory world from the one that slept in the darkness. It was aptly named The Switch because just outside its doors, railmen operated a gate or switch that gave trolleys traveling to and from Roxbury Crossing access to the Huntington Avenue tracks. Nurses from the local hospitals in starched-white uniforms sat in all but one of the booths, eating sandwiches and drinking coffee while taking their 'lunch' break. Two doctors in the last booth argued whether the Babe deserved the raise in salary he demanded for playing a 'game.' And drivers for several Boston newspapers sat on bar stools bent over the house special of franks and beans, occasionally stopping to support one or the other doctor's argument, while the short order cook pushed out grilled food to the waitress who dealt the plates like cards off the bottom of the deck.

Willie held up three fingers to the waitress and then waited for the sergeant to come on the line. He watched her pour a cup of coffee for a skinny kid in his late teens in a grey undershirt with pasty-white skin and numerous freckles that looked like processed meat. The kid's wild dull red hair jumped electric from his scalp and made him stand out amongst the discipline of medical white as he sat on the last stool at the far end of the diner with his upper body half-turned towards the door and his back jammed up against the wall. Dwyer watched him add a generous amount of cream to his coffee and then count to ten as he held the container of sugar over his mug. Willie saw the waitress say something to the kid in confidence and saw him lift his head with half-drawn eyes that tore into her.

"Sergeant, this is Dwyer, Wagon One, reporting that the Hill is quiet," he said into the receiver.

The waitress walked to his end of the counter after he hung up. "Will that be all, Patrolman Dwyer?" she asked.

He quizzed her face like he had just missed the punch line to a joke. "Yes, just the coffee, Miss."

She gave him the wrinkle of a smile. "I heard you say your name on the telephone." She placed the mugs of coffee into a small cardboard box. "You're new on the Hill, aren't you?"

"Yes, I am."

"Well, I'm sure that we'll be seeing you from time to time. I'm Catherine." She offered her hand, "Catherine Loftus."

"Willie, Willie Dwyer."

She jabbed a pencil under her white cap. "We have an arrangement with our friends in uniform. You can take the coffee with you as long as you return the mugs. You will remember to bring back the mugs, won't you?"

"Sure."

Two dimples on either side of her mouth cut deep into her face each time she smiled. But even with her infectious and light personality, Willie thought that under the sunny disposition lay a profound sadness and a tough winter soul.

"I'm sorry to hear that the captain who was at the riot died during the night," she said.

"How did you know, Miss? The sergeant just told me on the telephone."

"I overheard the newspaper boys talking about him just before you came in. The story about the riot is in all the papers."

"I hadn't worked for him before yesterday, but I know that Captain Lee was respected by all of the men." Willie picked up the box and turned toward the door.

"Don't forget the mugs, Patrolman."

"I won't, Catherine." Willie looked beyond her angular body to the far end of the counter where the red headed kid was cutting him with his eyes.

THE SUN ROSE UP out of the Atlantic, exploded against the Boston waterfront and spilled tongues of red and orange down the parallel streets of the South End and Roxbury until the city glowed like a Chinese lantern. The dull brownstones along Columbus Avenue came to life and the backyards of the bow front chocolate buildings were now busy with young immigrant girls scurrying about, picking up bottles of fresh milk left by back doors and preparing breakfast for downtown financiers before they made their journey along the golden highway to stodgy offices on State Street.

Willie held his left hand over his eyes to avoid the blinding glare that seemed to reflect angrily off every mirrored surface, including the metallic blue patrol wagon, as he steered the van with his free hand into the front yard of the police station. Station 10 sat quiet in the belly of Roxbury Crossing, the place where Tremont Street, Roxbury Street and Columbus Avenue deposited rainwater and a smorgasbord of humanity into a catch basin of variety stores, barber shops, vegetable stands and the Rialto Theater. Ivy hung on the face of the brick building, and above the entry there was a half-moon window with white embossed lettering that read *Boston Police* and under that the number *10.* A dilapidated fence separated the police station from the *Crossing Tavern* where on Saturday nights budding song-and-dance men performed in the back room, drawing larger crowds than the Rialto with a two-bit twofer, a show and a pick from a short menu consisting of baked beans and ham; sliced turkey, mashed potatoes and gravy; and a haddock filet sandwich.

The crowd that had gathered in the Crossing to rid the neighborhood of 'foreign radicals' was gone. The Bradley brothers stood outside the police station with caps on their heads shaven clean to discourage the lice and scabies that thrived in the close confines of their tenement. The Early Edition hung on the insides of their arms, smudged black with printer's ink, the newspapers sticking out from their bodies like wings. The older brother interrupted the early morning hum every few minutes when he shouted the headlines to passing motorists: "*Boston Transcript* and *Boston Globe* here. Read all about it, police battle hundreds of Reds at Dudley Street. Explosives found in New York in May Day conspiracy."

"This is going to be a good day, Johnny. We may need more papers. Did you bring in a couple to the desk?" the older brother said.

"You ask me that every day, Frank. Sure, I did."

"Well, we got to keep the coppers happy or we'll lose the neat spot we got here. That's why I ask you every day."

Johnny passed a bundle of newspapers to Frank. "The big sergeant at the desk asked me again about a license."

"Yeah, and did you tell him that you're not selling, just assisting?"

"Yeah."

"And what did he say?"

"Come back when you have a license."

Frank reloaded his arm and started for the street. "I'll talk to Quigley. Ah, hell, we'll go to City Hall today. We don't want to screw this up."

Fulton Quigley and Willie Dwyer rode the patrol wagon down the circular drive into the station's backyard and parked by the garage doors so the van could be used to transport yesterday's prisoners to court. "Those boys are out there hustling every day. Who are they, Fulton?"

"You mean the Bradley brothers? Frank's the bigger one. I don't know the younger one's name. Their older brother is a problem. Kid's got a mean streak and has been known to beat up their old lady when he's drinking."

"Where's the old man?"

"Dead. The Missus woke up one morning last year and found him next to her, bleeding outta his arse. Rollins and I took him out of there in sheets saturated with blood." Fulton sat in the wagon with the passenger door opened, completing the last of his entries into his pocket diary. "Some kind of hemorrhage problem, ulcers or something. But you know what they say about the apple not falling far from the tree, he was a stiff himself."

"What's the older brother's name in case I ever run into him?"

"Charlie, an emaciated kid with albino skin, red hair, lots of freckles and rotten teeth. And a vicious fucking temper. I broke up a fight between Charlie and two of his friends awhile back and he had a mouthful of their hair lodged in his teeth. I'm sure whatever his brothers earn selling newspapers, he takes a cut." Quigley jumped down off the wagon and twisted his body, stretched his arms over his head and squeezed out a yawn. "Charlie Bradley. I'm sure you'll run into him one of these days. He lives in a tenement not far from the Circle."

"I think I already did," Willie said.

The two patrolmen trudged up the long flight of stairs at the back of the Station and, when they opened the door to the booking room, they found Sergeant McGuiness at a desk, completing the last of the applications for complaints against the Dudley Street prisoners. At one end of the room, two patrolmen were photographing and fingerprinting some prisoners and in two small side offices, detectives were interviewing a couple more.

"I suppose you're going to tell me you had a tough night, Sergeant," Quigley said to McGuiness as he dropped his bag on the floor.

"No, Quigley. Actually, it was a picnic because you were out of the station the entire night. Hope you kept him out of trouble, Dwyer."

"I did my best, Sergeant, but you never can tell with Fulton."

"Ah, it's nice to be appreciated," Quigley said. He opened the cellblock door and peeked into the cells, inhaling the pungent odor of urine, fear and the aftertaste of spent adrenaline and saw the stark expressions of disillusion. "Jesus, they're a sorry looking lot, aren't they? Did you print and photograph all of 'em, Mugs?"

"We're finishing them up now." McGuiness placed his thumbs under the rims of his glasses and pushed them up on top of his bald head. "All part of the battle against the National Conspiracy. The federal agencies are going to be at the court this morning and they asked us to get as much information about them as possible. A couple of these bums are going to be shipped back to Italy and Russia."

"The National Conspiracy, huh," Quigley said. "You mean the 'Red Scare,' the conspiracy created by the politicians and the newspaper boys." He picked up his bag and tipped his hand to McGuiness. "Well, I'd better get a cup of coffee before I take that on." He pushed on one of the swinging doors to the kitchen and disappeared.

"You do that, old boy." McGuiness replaced his glasses onto his nose and began to write again. Without looking up, he said, "Dwyer, give Detective Nolan a hand booking the last of the rioters, will you?"

"Sure thing, Sergeant." Willie walked to one of the small offices where

George Nolan was interviewing the last of yesterday's prisoners. "Long night, sir?"

"A long one, it was." Nolan spoke in the deadpan and bored tone of an interrogator who conducted a night's worth of interviews and heard nothing but bullshit. "Hope your night was more interesting than ours. All we've been getting from these bums is their foolish propaganda about the 'revolution' and how it has to take place in order for the working class to be free of the tyranny of the rich capitalists." Pointing to the cellblock, he said, "There are a few tough ones in there who were carrying weapons, hard line Letts who caused most of the violence. They clammed up and wouldn't tell us shit. We've grouped them together and will turn them over to the G-men. But the majority of the protestors are Parlor Reds and suffragettes, spoiled little rich snots who haven't worked a day in their lives, yet they are going to 'free' the working man. I don't think they are as enthused about their plans for 'revolution' as they were yesterday. Like this twenty-year-old kid here. Father's a doctor, if you can imagine that."

Willie leaned into the office, but couldn't get a good look at the prisoner because a file cabinet partially blocked his view. "You don't say." He stepped back into the larger room, opened his collar and placed his utility bag on a table, his shoulders melting down the sides of his body under the exhaustion of the previous twenty-four hours.

"Supposed to be very smart," Nolan said. "Graduated from Harvard College when he was fifteen or something. I offered him a reduced sentence for information on the Letts and he refused. Too bad he don't use his brains for a better cause."

"Oh, I know who he is," said Dwyer.

"Good. Then I'll give you a chance to get reacquainted." The detective picked up a stack of papers from the desk, handed the cellblock key to Willie and began to walk toward the administrative offices. "Put him back into the first cell while I turn in these arrest forms to the lieutenant."

"Sure." Willie rapped the key on the office door to get the prisoner's attention, but he kept his head down, trance-like, twirling his wide-brimmed hat in his hands. "Okay Joseph, let's go."

Kursh raised his head and cracked his mouth in a little boy's grin, one corner of it caked with dried blood. The eye on the same side of his face was invisible and closed shut, his cheek and eyelid swollen together in an ugly red and blackish-purple bump. Dried blood hung from the end of his nose. He stood gingerly and shuffled to the doorway.

"Joseph," Dwyer said, "you look a lot worse than when I last saw you."

Kursh lifted the tips of his fingers gently to his closed eye. He spoke slowly and without moving his mouth, like a ventriloquist, throwing out his words from the back of his throat. "Bleeding under the surface of the skin," he moved his fingers back and forth above the injured area, "pooled around the eye—hematoma. Much more pronounced today."

"All right, doctor, come on," Willie said as he led the young prisoner by his elbow and directed him back to the cellblock. "Move away," he said to the other prisoners and unlocked the door of the first cell where every space was occupied by a body. Some of the prisoners appeared visibly shaken while others wore their defiance proudly.

"Where did they send the women prisoners?" Kursh hummed.

"They usually house women arrestees at the Suffolk County Jail for the night. Why, are you looking for someone?" Willie rolled the door shut and turned the key in the lock.

"Martha Foley—tall woman, front of our march."

"Do you have some special interest in her, Joseph?"

Kursh ignored Dwyer's remark.

"I noticed that her friend, Alex, beat it when things got rough yesterday." Willie racked the cell door back and forth to ensure that the latch had caught. "He left all of you holding the bag. Now there's a real leader for you."

"Perhaps," Kursh said. "Protecting—the larger interest."

"The larger interest? You mean Louis Fraina, don't you? I saw him with Sturgis. They escaped together and they didn't look like they were too interested in the rest of you."

"Miss Foley—injured?"

"We know about Fraina and his operations on Terrace Street," Willie said. "A big deal in the Socialist Party, I've heard, runs the American propaganda machine for the Lettish Workmen's Association."

Kursh glanced towards the back of the cell. "I don't know—"

"Come on, Joseph. Even I know who he is. An Italian immigrant who scrounged the streets of New York's Hell's Kitchen as a kid. His father died of pneumonia while working in a Manhattan sweat shop, right? Now, he's angry and he wants somebody to pay for that. So, he prints up his Socialist rag, hoping to rally the rest of the downtrodden. What's it called, *Revolutionary Age*? And you and Martha and a small army of believers stand outside of the downtown department stores and the entrances to the elevated, spreading the gospel.

"You know more than I."

"Spreading the gospel is one thing, Joseph, causing a riot, which results in the death of a police captain, is something else. Where do you think he is?"

"I can't say."

Another larger prisoner stepped up from behind Kursh and laid his hand on his shoulder. "I guess you didn't hear him the first time, copper," the big man said. "He don't know nothing."

Kursh moved away from the bars and sat down on the end of the metal cot, placed his elbows on his knees and cradled his head in his hands. Willie left the cellblock, but returned a few minutes later with a piece of ice wrapped in newspaper. He pushed his arm between the metal bars and handed the ice to Kursh. "Keep that on your eye."

"Thank you," Kursh said.

"Martha Foley is incarcerated at the Charles Street Jail," Willie said. "You will most likely see her at your court arraignment."

"Thank you."

Dwyer closed the door to the cellblock and returned the key to the sergeant. Then he collapsed into a chair and stared at the typewriter, just as the station bell began to clang for morning roll call.

In the News

GIGANTIC MURDER PLOT

With the discovery of a nation-wide bomb conspiracy against the lives of many prominent Americans, every agency of the Federal and municipal government was at work today, not only in an attempt to trace the authors of the terrorist plot, but to guard against the "Reds" boast of a countrywide surprise on May Day.

BOSTON EVENING TRANSCRIPT
Thursday, May 1, 1919

SAY BRITISH BOMB IRISH

Irish American Delegates Send New Note to Clemenceau, Ask Investigation

(Paris—Associated Press)

At Versailles, American delegates in the interest of the Irish Independence movement sent a note to Premier Clemenceau charging the British with bombing Irish towns from airplanes and asking for a special investigation.

BOSTON EVENING TRANSCRIPT
Thursday, May 1, 1919

Chapter Two

~

"Where is Father Connolly? He should have been here ten minutes ago." Coppenrath twisted the toe of his shoe into a spent cigarette and leaned into the vestibule of the church.

"Relax, Albert, he'll be here; It's not two o'clock. The bells haven't rung yet." Willie leaned his weight against the jamb of one of the enormous wooden doors.

Albert Coppenrath and Willie Dwyer were about as opposite physically as a roadrunner and a Clydesdale, a disproportionate set of bookends, as they stood on the landing outside the opened doors of Mission Church, silhouettes to the guests in the pews who waited for the priest to arrive to begin the christening. Coppenrath was short, wiry and fidgety and always on his way to or from somewhere while Dwyer had the size and bulk of a large draft horse that plodded slowly but reliably because it knew that tomorrow another field waited to be plowed. Dwyer was quiet and reflective and epitomized the impression that people have about farmers—simple-living folk, hardworking and steady, the salt of the earth. Coppenrath was a Boston street urchin, who was raised in close quarters, from a large family in a neighborhood of large families squeezed into the over-populated tenements of the North End and Fort Hill where quick wits and street savvy were critical to survival.

The Coppenraths had been one of the few remaining Irish families, sharing the little neck of waterfront with the new immigrants, Italians, Russians, Jews and Greeks, who had filled the gap left by the hundred fifty thousand sick and emaciated Famine Irish who had arrived sixty years earlier in coffin ships and were detained on the harbor's outer islands lest they cause an epidemic outbreak in the city, eventually settling into intolerable dens of humanity, disease and crime known by names like Half Moon Place. The impoverished and clannish Irish took the jobs that no one else wanted. They built the docks, laid the rails, dug the tunnels for America's first subway and remained attached to the city's industrial center until they abandoned it for the streetcar neighborhoods after earning a stake in their adopted country while fighting for the Union as conscripted soldiers or 'instead of' wealthy native Bostonians.

While Albert was third generation Irish-American, with a right of entitlement and a connected leg up, Dwyer was one of those first generation, transplanted Irish who toiled quietly in the shadows, bonded to the old customs, the old battles and Ireland's independence. Although polar opposites, Coppenrath and Dwyer had become good friends since Albert landed on the doorstep of Station 10, relieved to be out of '1' and his childhood neighborhood where he had never felt completely comfortable, moving a gang of youths from in front of the same stores that he had terrorized as a boy.

"Whew, that rain shower didn't chase the heat at all." Coppenrath wiped his forehead with the back of his hand.

"You sure this is alright with your brother?" Dwyer said.

"What? Being Elizabeth's godfather?"

"Yeah. You have a large family and I figured—"

"You're my best pal, Willie. And I couldn't think of a better person to take care of her if anything happened to us. Besides, Emily and I plan on having a large family. They'll all get their chance."

Willie flipped his boater onto his index finger and spun it like a pie plate. "How are you feeling?"

"Okay. Most of the bruises are healing to a nice sickly yellow. But I'll have the shoe imprints in my ribs from those Red bastards for the rest of the summer. My father-in-law told me to make sure that I'm one hundred percent before I return to work. He's an old Labor guy. He's knows what he's talking about."

"I hope you will be up to coming to the fights next week," Willie said. "Benny Leonard is fighting a few exhibition rounds as a warm-up for his championship bout with Dundee next month. And there are some good local boxers on the card."

"Oh, I'll be good as new by then." Albert took off his hat and stepped into the church. "Come on. Father Connolly is here."

The priest and an altar boy entered from the sacristy and walked to the Baptismal font at one of the side altars. "Would the godparents bring the infants up please," he said.

"What do we know about this fella that Albert chose to be the baby's godfather," Jim Rankin said in a low whisper in the first pew.

"I've never met him," his wife answered. "But Emily tells me that his name is William Dwyer and that Albert thinks a lot of him. He is assigned to Station 10 with him. I think Albert said that he was made permanent recently."

"Where is he from?"

"What do you mean?"

"You know. Is he born here or is he another one of those shanty Irish that fell off the boat last week?"

"Emily told me that he emigrated about ten years ago from Galway."

"Oh, another dirt farmer from the West still crying that the English treated him poorly? He's been in the country for ten years and this is the best he can do? He's just off probation?"

"For God's sakes, James, keep your voice down. He probably had to wait until he became a citizen." Virginia Rankin stole a look down the length of their bench, surveying the other guests to see if they were eavesdropping. "It wasn't that long ago that your own family stepped off a boat."

"My father was a merchant, Virginia, not a common day laborer who drank what he earned. They were educated people from Wicklow who saw an opportunity in America and took it. My mother, God rest her soul, made linen tablecloths and doilies for the Brahmins and designed the patches for the Massachusetts' Regiments that fought against the South."

"Yes. I know, dear. And your father immediately became involved in politics. I think I've heard the story before."

"We shouldn't forget it. It was the only way we could get some leverage in this town. I saw the most powerful men in Massachusetts walk into that inconspicuous tavern along the waterfront to bargain with old Jeremiah Rankin. Albert and Dwyer have opportunities now that weren't available to us before we organized and used our great numbers to get some say around here."

Virginia's wide-brimmed hat tipped towards her husband. "Well, you certainly have had your say, James," she said in a metallic unattached voice. "Anyway, Mr. Dwyer was sworn in after Albert and that is why he has recently been appointed Patrolman. Besides, Albert says he is honest and hardworking and that's all that should matter."

"Well, we're talking about my granddaughter here. I just want to make sure that whoever is associated with this family is respectable."

"And what about the baby's father? Isn't he the son of a day laborer?"

"Who, Albert? The difference is that I can control things for him and our daughter."

"Well, Mr. Dwyer is a patrolman just like our son-in-law. Shouldn't that be enough?"

"Some of the police are okay, I guess. But there is a danger in being too honest." Rankin studied Willie as he held Albert and Emily's new daughter in his arms while the priest slowly poured holy water onto her forehead. "I wonder who sponsored him."

"Obviously, he wasn't as lucky as Albert to have you." Virginia adjusted her hat so that she could lean against her husband. "We're starting to attract attention. Let's not talk about politics today."

JIM RANKIN'S VICTORIAN HOME on Parker Hill Avenue sat on the highest piece of land on Mission Hill and was visible for a quarter mile in all directions. Considered the political cathedral of Roxbury, politicians and common folk came there to petition the Ward Boss, State Senator and president of Boston's largest labor union. 'Real' business was often conducted in the Rankin kitchen.

In addition to the large extended Rankin family, the guest list for the christening party included most of the Beacon Hill power brokers, several patrolmen who worked with Albert at Stations 1 and 10 and a few ranking police officers who garnered invitations through Rankin's personal assistant. Waiters and waitresses, carrying large silver trays of hors d'oeuvres and glasses of champagne, walked among the guests in the great room where a string quartet played and on to the spacious lawn at the rear of the home.

"Mahatma, how are you? Are they taking good care of you?" Jim asked, extending his hand to the West End Ward Boss.

"Very well, Jim," Martin Lomasney said. "The baby is beautiful. I see she gets her good looks from Virginia's side of the family."

"Well, we certainly don't want her to have her grandfather's elephant ears."

"I'm sorry that I missed the christening at the church, Jim. Did the Cardinal attend?"

"He is recovering from a bout of influenza and didn't want to give it to the baby or spread it among the guests."

"Ah, that's too bad. He's okay though, not that terrible scourge of last year?"

"No, thank God. He wanted to be here to personally thank the police for their aggressive stand against those Red atheists." Rankin stirred his drink with his finger. "Every time I speak to him, he gives me the jab."

"Take care of the poor before the Socialists get their claws into them, right?" the West End Boss said.

"Yes. He's consistent on that one."

Lomasney looked across the lawn. "I notice that a certain prominent Roxbury politician is missing from the party."

"You mean Curley?"

"Yes, James Michael."

"He hasn't forgiven you or me for 'backstabbing' him by supporting Andrew Peters for mayor. I don't think that he realizes that times have changed and that it was time for us to move on. Besides, Peters is harmless enough. He is too busy sailing his boat off of Marblehead to muck things up." Rankin drew slowly on his cigar and exhaled. "Did you ever think of running on the bigger stage yourself, Martin?"

"No. I think that you and I have similar feelings on politics. It begins and ends in the neighborhood. We've been successful because we keep our organizations tight and close to the vest. I might consider a run for the statehouse, but leave Washington to the Fitzgeralds and the Curleys. We'll keep the home fires burning."

Rankin stepped closer to the West End Boss. "Speaking of home issues, in the next few months we are going to have to find work for the boys returning from the war or there are going to be some pissed off soldiers with bellies full of anger to vent. Did you see that their mothers marched in Washington on Sunday, pleading for jobs? It just isn't right."

"Yes, I saw it in the newspapers. Wilson, is too busy trying to save the world instead of tending to our problems here at home. Food prices are the highest in forty years and businesses are closing their doors. The only project in my district is the molasses cleanup. In the meantime, he's running around Europe selling his utopian League of Nations." A couple of the younger Rankin children ran between the two men. "Well, I don't mean to dampen the day's good spirit, Jim. But I wonder, other than the machine-makers, who really benefitted from that war."

On the veranda, Albert and Emily were speaking with several patrolmen and Rankin saw that Dwyer was standing among them. "Let's meet in a few weeks, Martin, and see if we can do something to help these boys. How about dinner downtown? I need to visit a few people at the State House."

He walked away, stopping briefly to speak with a waitress. He slid his hand to the small of her back and lowered his head to her ear. She nodded in reply with the hint of a smile that didn't break the calm flat surface of her face before they separated and she walked into the kitchen.

Emily saw her father approach. "Gentlemen, this is my father, James Rankin."

"Well, if it isn't Boston's finest. Are they taking good care of you, boys?" He lowered his voice. "We have some of the finest whiskey available for you, men. So, drink up because if the teetotalers from the Midwest get their way, the war time prohibition will be the law of the land." When the group laughed, he said, "Obviously, there are no Irishmen in the Midwest."

Rankin drew deeply on his cigar as the group waited for him to speak again. "You know, next to our returning soldiers, I have the deepest respect for the service that you fellas provide to the city. I know it has been a rough go for you with all of the strikes and those damn Reds causing trouble. You have your hands full." He put his arm around Albert's shoulder and pulled him closer. "The dirty bastards are getting too close to home when my own son-in-law is assaulted and kicked and beaten." Rankin looked over at his daughter. "Emily, would you get me a glass of scotch? That's a good girl." When she walked away, he said, "If you get a chance to stick one of those bastards, send him to hell. I know Judge Hayden came down hard on them in court, but we want to make sure they don't come back into our great city." His daughter returned with the drink and handed it to him. "Also, I want to assure you fellas that we are following the Social Club's negotiations with the Commissioner. It's time that we take care of our police. Every other group has received raises in pay and benefits because they have the strike."

Albert raised his glass to the group: "A toast to the man who can get it done." The patrolmen lifted their glasses and saluted Dandy Jim.

Jim waited and then said, "I also understand that you boys are taking up a collection for Captain Lee's family. Well, Albert here will be making a significant contribution on behalf of the Rankin family. To Captain Lee." He raised his glass, pushed it back and looked down the length of it at Willie Dwyer. He emptied it and said, "Albert, aren't you going to introduce me to Elizabeth's godfather?"

"Sure, Jim." Albert put his hand on Willie's shoulder. "This is William Dwyer, a man of high integrity and character."

Dwyer extended his hand, "Willie, sir. It's a pleasure to meet you."

"I hear you are a West Ireland man."

"That's right. Galway, sir."

Rankin let Dwyer's extended hand momentarily hang in the space between them before he extended his own hand and grasped it firmly. "A little softer than I would have expected from a Galway man." He turned his back to the other patrolmen and closed down the circle to Willie, Albert and himself.

"I left Ireland over ten years ago, Mr. Rankin. I guess I have become a little soft in that time."

"Well, that's okay. There's a different kind of toughness needed in Boston, anyway."

"I imagine there is."

"You think so, do you? What will you do when you have to enforce an unpopular law that would prohibit working men from stepping into a pub after a hard day's labor?"

"Well, I—"

"Let me ask you another one. Do you think it is fair to tax the poor for the right to vote?"

"I don't think—"

"You don't think?" Rankin smiled. "Are you going to enforce laws that hold the working man down?"

Willie kicked at the grass. He smirked and looked up. "I enforce the laws, Mr. Rankin, I don't write them. That's up to the politicians." He glanced at Albert. "And I'm not a *politician*."

"Good one, Dwyer. You're a good sport. I was just seeing if you're up to the test." He reached into the inside pocket of his suit coat, retrieved a cigar and handed it to Dwyer.

"Thank you, sir, but I don't smoke."

Rankin took back the cigar and held it. "You're your own man, I can see that. Tell me, Dwyer, have you ever thought of joining the Knights or the Ancient Order? Or are you one of those Socialist leaning Irish like James Connolly or that girl Judge Hayden just sentenced to eighteen months—" He snapped his fingers twice. "Martha Foley?"

"Go on, Jim, Willie is a true American, an Irish-American," Albert said.

"And so he is." Rankin stuffed the cigar into Willie's breast pocket and moved away.

Dwyer watched Rankin warmly greet some of his other guests. "If I had known there was an examination to be Elizabeth's godfather, Albert, I might have thought twice about taking the job. Did I pass?"

"Don't let him rankle you, Willie. You should have heard the interrogation he gave me when Emily and I began to see each other."

"I'm not interested in joining the family, Albert."

"Well, if it is any consolation, I think that you passed with high marks. He values men who speak up for themselves." Coppenrath clapped Dwyer on the shoulder. "Besides, he's not a bad man to have on your side." Albert waved to some cousins who had just arrived and walked away to greet them.

The veranda and the lawn filled with guests as they abandoned the warm interior of the house. Willie could now see the entire inside of the great room and thought that one of the waitresses looked familiar. He entered the room and intercepted her before she could return to the kitchen for another tray of food. "Catherine?" he said. When she turned and faced him, she seemed smaller in this setting and more delicate than the night at the diner, long-limbed and slender. He recalled the waitress whose persona suggested a profound and edgy sadness. "If I had known you were going to be here, I would have brought the mugs," he said.

"Oh, you won't get off that easy. I have you listed on the back of my pad. Willie Dwyer, isn't it, the new patrolman from Station 10?"

"Yeah, you've a good memory. How did you end up here, working for the Rankin family?"

"The man himself stops into the diner from time to time to rub elbows with the common folk. And, I'm always looking for a little extra money to pay the rent and such. I don't get paid a queen's ransom at The Switch as you can imagine. So, between working there, a few days at O'Neil's now and then, and the odd job, well, you know how it goes."

"I think I do."

Catherine heard her name being called by one of the other waitresses. "Sorry, but I have to get back to work. Stop in at the diner when you have a chance."

"Look, I know that we don't know each other very well, but would you consider taking in a picture show sometime."

"A picture show? Ah sure, I'm game if you are." She turned on the balls of her feet and gave a little flip with one of her legs as she darted towards the kitchen. "Maybe afterwards, we could go dancing," she said over her shoulder.

"Dancing?" He watched her skit across the grand room floor until she reached the swinging doors and disappeared. "What the hey," he said.

THE TRAIN from New York City arrived a few minutes behind schedule at South Station. The ever present coastal dampness and the briny ocean air played havoc with the electric switches that controlled most of the rail traffic into Boston's main terminal, forcing the *New York, New*

Haven & Hartford to return to the older but tried and true method of regulating dangerous intersections, the switchman.

The semi-circular granite building sat squat in Dewey Square where trains launched to the South and West. When it was completed at the end of the nineteenth century, it was the largest depot in the world and Boston was an industrial and manufacturing heavyweight. Now the terminal looked tired with a melancholic reminder of an older and grander city. The large murals in the Great Room had dulled and muted, and street mud and small stones, embedded in the shoes of thousands of travelers, had ground and pumiced its once highly polished oaken floor. The salty Atlantic air attacked the mortar that fixed its walls causing hairline cracks in the Ionic columns that supported its roof. And the large clock over its front doors was frozen in time at five minutes past two, like a permanent reminder of the passing of a grander period.

The passengers from Train 125 began to disembark and walk the long open platform to the terminal. A delicate-looking man with a small stern face and sad brown eyes stepped down and walked among the men and women and their excited children who anticipated a day of fun in the city. Impeccably dressed, the young man, partly crippled in one leg, walked with an exaggerated limp. He was an inconspicuous afterthought in the crowd and never suspected of being the architect of the infernal machines that caused cruel destruction to the businesses and homes of America's capitalists. He was the Avenging Angel and had come to Boston to seek retribution against the United States Government for its unprovoked aggression toward the defenders of the working man who only wanted to march in a peaceful May Day parade. He would smite those reactionaries who attacked the meeting houses of the revolutionaries and denied them protection under America's laws because they opposed the War of the Industrialists.

Peter Carlucci was a product of New York's Bowery and lived in the stench of its notorious saloons, dance halls, flophouses and seedy entertainment. He was a stepchild to the streets of the Lower East Side and from the age of nine, he worked them to survive, first as a shoe-shine boy and later as a newsie to feed his family while his father lay ill in their one bedroom walkup. Jacobi Carlucci, an Italian immigrant and a member of the Partito Socialista Italiano, had labored in the cold damp underground, digging the city's East River tunnels, before succumbing to consumption. His widow earned thirteen cents an hour as a seamstress in the Garment District until a night foreman forced himself on her. She punished herself for a mild flirtation, became delirious and spent the remainder of her days in the county sanatorium. Thirteen-year old Peter was left the head of a homeless family and surrogate father to two younger siblings.

A talented writer and poet, his frustration grew as he watched wealthy authors express their infantile ideas to a literary world that accepted them as geniuses. Instead, he channeled his energies to motors and machinery, creating children who were respectful and courteous, and adorned them with just the right clothing before they exploded in hellish fury.

Carlucci walked through the terminal and met Alex Sturgis, who escorted him to a waiting car that was parked at the Summer Street entrance. The aftermath of the May Day riot had quietly moved off the front pages of the newspapers and its stories had been replaced by reports of Labor strikes and the high cost of living. "They are lulled into a false sense of security," he said. "It is time to punish the Boston judges, politicians, the police lackeys and the religious whores who deprive the righteous of their justice and liberty." The two anarchists toasted each other with a flask of vodka and then drove from the city to Roxbury.

AS THE LAST GUESTS were leaving and the large house became quiet again, Albert and his father-in-law sat on the veranda with their feet up on the railing, enjoying Rankin's best scotch. They watched the sun tuck itself down behind the distilleries below them on the Heath Street side of the Hill, their great brick smokestacks standing still and cold in the evening shadows. The two men relished the refreshing Atlantic breeze that drifted up from the waterfront and entered the open windows at the front of the house.

"What kind of progress are Lynch, McInnes and the other boys making with their negotiations with the city?" Rankin said.

"Alright, I guess. But to tell you the truth, I think they are losing their patience with Commissioner Curtis. They have met with the Mayor and he seems supportive."

"He has no weight. He doesn't hold the purse strings. Coolidge is the one whom they have to convince, and the Brahmin Legislature."

Albert swirled the whiskey at the bottom of his glass. "There's talk of joining the A.F. of L."

"Who do the cops think they are, miners or telephone operators, for Chris' sake? That might not be a smart move. Curtis won't stand for it and then it'll be up to Coolidge to make a decision. And you never want to hang your hat on that hook."

Albert could hear Emily and her mother talking in the bedroom above the veranda and he followed their laughter with his eyes to an open window. "Who do you think Coolidge will support?"

"That's a good question," Rankin said. He took his feet down from the railing and leaned forward in the chair. "I worked with him in the senate and found him to be reticent, a slow thinker. But when all is said and done, he usually comes down on the right side of things politically. That's why I supported him in his run for governor." Jim stood and looked out over the lawn. "He seems to be able to read the tea leaves. My guess is he'll support Curtis even though he didn't appoint him. What the hell, they're both Yankee Republicans. And, he just vetoed raises for the Legislature. Tells them, 'service not obligatory boys, but optional.' Speaks volumes, Albert."

Coppenrath stood up next to his father-in-law. "So if the patrolmen insist on joining the A.F. of L, it could cause some serious repercussions?"

"That's correct." Rankin stretched his arms over his head, took a deep breath and let it out slowly. "I love this time of day. You can smell the ocean and dine on its salt." He looked out over the west side of the Hill. "Keep your ear close to the ground and keep me informed. In this city, it pays to know what's going on."

WILLIE STOOD OUTSIDE of the Rankin home and admired the grand view of the Hill. The last of the pink sky reflected in the windows of the buildings below.

"Someday, Patrolman," she said, "someday."

Dwyer glanced at Catherine as she approached him from the side porch door and then looked back at the view. "Beautiful, isn't it? The land, the city. This is the way everyone should see it. Especially the poor souls living on top of one another in those fire traps."

"Listen to the bleeding heart, will you."

"You're a cold one, Miss Loftus."

"I'm a realist." She stood beside him with her apron in her hand and saw what he saw.

"Oh, that's what it is? You see things as they are, not as you would like them to be."

She started down the walk. "Something like that."

Willie stepped off the stairs and followed her to the front gate. "Would the realist consider an escort home or is she too independent for that?"

"Well, you see me dilly-dallying here. Do you need a special invitation?"

"Do you like hot dogs?" he said.

"Sure."

"There's a Joe & Nemo stand— Say, where are we going?"

"*I* am going to my rooming house. It's a stone's throw from the Circle."

"Great, right by the stand. Miss Loftus, may I?" Dwyer lifted his arm and she hooked her hand in the crook of his elbow.

LINED UP like obedient little children, nine decorated packages sat on the kitchen table, each labeled with the name and address of its recipient—politicians in blue, judges, courts and coppers in red, and Catholic churches in green. Peter Carlucci made a perfect four-petal bow, tied off the string on the last of the packages and moved it to its designated place on the table.

He put on his vest and jacket, carried his carpetbag and map, and began to move his children outside.

In the News

NATIONAL DAY OF TERROR
(Boston, New York, Washington D.C., Cleveland,
Pittsburgh, New Jersey, Philadelphia)
Home of Judge Hayden bombed; New York buildings shattered. Attorney General Palmer's house badly damaged; bomb killed watchman; men seen with suitcase; identical red paper circulars found. 'Crime against the people' said Governor Coolidge.
BOSTON EVENING TRANSCRIPT
Tuesday, June 3, 1919

SUFFRAGE GOES TO STATES
(Washington, D.C.)
After forty years of effort, advocates turn attention to state legislatures for ratification.
BOSTON EVENING TRANSCRIPT
Thursday, June 5, 1919

TAX DODGERS FACE JAIL
(Boston)
Five hundred warrants out for delinquents of Poll Tax.
Congressional Committee Gets Wind of Frauds
(Washington D.C.)
Graham Committee is investigating war-time expenditures of the War Department.
BOSTON EVENING TRANSCRIPT
Friday, June 6, 1919

Chapter Three

~

The rat challenged Quigley and stood its ground.

Normally cautious, shy, and nocturnal animals, something had caused this rodent to move about in the light of day and to venture into the confines of the station house. It wasn't surprising to Quigley when he came upon a long-tailed slender roof rat, but the rat that he watched with curious excitement from the top of the stairs was much larger than the ordinary roof rat. And it stood between him and a well-deserved sleep. The rat was the size of one of those yappy dogs that wealthy women from Beacon Hill kept tucked under their arms to substitute for the child they never bore. How a dock rat like that found its way into the attic was not his problem. As far as he was concerned, the devil himself could be convinced to leave the premises with the right kind of persuasion. He squeezed his left eye closed, looked down the six-inch barrel of his .38 caliber and filled the front sight with the largest rodent that he had ever seen. The rat heard the click of the revolver's hammer, looked back and hissed.

In the semi-darkened end of the room, Willie slept with the slow irregular sweep of an electric fan. The clap of the gunshot woke him with a start and he jumped up and took a step towards the stairway on the other side of the room. Disjointed and slightly out of sync, he saw a large distorted man-shape filling the doorway, laughing and looking back at him, the figure becoming clearer and more familiar with its distinctive megaphone voice. Other muffled and more distant voices called up the stairs from the first floor.

"Quigley, what's going on up there?" one of them called.

"What the hell, Fulton?" Willie said.

"And a beautiful June day to you, young Dwyer. You should be thanking me." He stooped down to examine the dead rat. "That's the last time this fella's going to prance around our sleeping quarters."

Sergeant McGuiness charged into the room. "You better have a good reason for discharging a firearm in the station house, Quigley."

"I do, sergeant."

"Well, what is it?"

"An interloper—"

"Jesus, you only see a rat that size in a garbage can at Haymarket." McGuiness walked closer. "It looks like it was shot with a Gatlin gun."

"It's my own special load." Quigley reached into his pocket and took out a .38 caliber bullet with its head missing. "I replaced the ball of lead with smaller pellets. The only thing that's hit is the intended target."

"Well, since you killed him. I'll give you the honor of getting rid of him." McGuiness turned to walk down the stairs. "You will only carry the ammunition that is approved by the Department. Understand, Quigley?"

"Right, sergeant."

"You're lucky I don't put you on report and recommend a court martial. Bring that revolver to me for inspection before you return to patrol." He continued down the stairs. "Roll call in fifteen minutes, Dwyer."

"Yes, sergeant." Willie stooped down to take a closer look at the rodent. "You may have killed more rats than you realize, Fulton."

"What do you mean?"

"Well, either it has been eating awfully well or it's a she. And she's pregnant." Willie looked at the pipe and the enlarged hole in the floor. "That pipe leads to the cellar. She might have a nest down near the coal bins."

"What makes you such an expert on rodents, Dwyer?"

"We had them on the farm. Sometimes, even a water rat like this would come up from the river to the barn. It was hard keeping them away from the feed."

"Sure, it followed the same beaten path as all the other scavengers and vermin that infest this dump."

Willie crossed the room to a row of wall lockers and removed a pair of uniform trousers. Like everything else in his locker, they had the pungent odor of naphthalene from an open box of crystallized moth balls that he kept on the shelf. "You're lucky that it was Sergeant McGuiness on duty and not the lieutenant. It might have been rougher for you."

"I seem to run afoul of anyone above the rank of patrolman," Quigley said. "But, even the lieutenant wouldn't want a rat the size of this fella around the station."

He picked up the dead rodent by its tail and carried it out to the backyard. When he returned to the dormitory he asked: "Have you given any more thought to our discussion about the Union, Dwyer?"

"I'm thinking about it."

Quigley stripped to his underwear and climbed into bed. He stretched the skin above and below his eyes with his thumbs and index fingers and opened them wide. "Jeez, those mothballs are about to clean out my sinuses. You're going to kill every living thing within five miles of this place, including us humans."

"That's the idea, to kill everything that makes me itch."

"And here I was looking forward to bringing home a few small pets to the little woman and the kids." Quigley stretched out in the bed and yawned. "Seriously, old Chap, you're spreading moth balls around this place and I'm killing rats because the politicians are too busy taking care of themselves instead of helping us win a living wage and providing us with better working conditions."

"How come nothing was done when Honey Fitz and Jim Curley were mayors?" Willie said.

"Because Commissioner O'Meara was a Republican. Sometimes, they carry this political party crap too far." Quigley scanned the empty room. "Maybe, there will be a time when we won't have to sleep here, hey Dwyer, and be able to lay our heads on our own pillows in our own homes." He rolled onto his side to face the window and spoke into his pillow, his words muffled and fading. "Nah, that wouldn't work. Home every—"

Willie closed his locker and walked to the stairs. "I don't think the missus would think that was such a good idea. It would probably send shivers down her spine just thinking about you home every night." He looked back at Quigley to see his reaction. "Dead to the world already," he said.

SERGEANT MCGUINESS stepped down from behind the elevated duty desk and walked to the kitchen, the location for the morning's roll call. An understaffed shift of nine patrolmen stood in formation behind one of the long wooden tables while the houseman cleared it of coffee cups.

Other than a couple of senior men, the youngest patrolmen in the Station made up the shift that morning, cops full of piss and vinegar, the kind of cops that gave a Department its good reputation. And the kind that could turn a sergeant's hair prematurely gray or convince him that a transfer to the Records' section was really what he needed. "We're short a few men today because of the pending Fishermen's strike," he said. "And we may have to muster on short notice if things get rough in there. So, I want you to signal in from the boxes on the half hour rather than the usual forty minutes."

"Oops, I feel the jerk of the leash," one of the senior patrolmen whispered.

McGuiness looked up from his notes and then continued. "Station Nine had two burglaries in the last few days in which guns and ammunition were stolen." He placed a list of the stolen weapons on the table. "Check the local gun shops and pawn shops on your patrol. Next, police in New York rounded up about a hundred radicals last week, and during their raids, they found Bolshevik literature demanding the immediate release of all detained anarchists and threatening to shut down the country with a national strike if they aren't released."

"They're always distributing that rubbish, sergeant," the houseman said. "I don't know if anyone takes them seriously."

"The crowd that gathered in front of this building last month took them seriously, Cox. In addition to the literature, the New York cops found detailed plans for making homemade bombs and lists of intended targets. They followed up with a raid on an abandoned warehouse and located fifty devices."

"Did they think any of the devices were coming our way?" one of the patrolmen asked.

"Several were addressed to targets in Boston, but they were held by the Post Office for insufficient postage."

"See, what did I tell you," Cox said. "They aren't smart enough to put the proper postage on their bombs."

"The fact remains that had they been mailed, God knows how many people might have been hurt or killed. And here is what should get your attention—the packages were addressed to the Roxbury Municipal Court and two Boston Police Stations, 9 and 10, our own house." McGuiness leaned on the table. "I don't need to remind you what happened last month. We lost a good man in Captain Lee and several of our boys were wounded in that melee. Since then, those bastards have sent incendiary devices to judges, politicians and business leaders in several cities. It was only by the grace of God that Judge Hayden and his family escaped the explosion at his home."

McGuiness placed photographs of a pipe bomb and a wrapped bundle of dynamite on the table. "These are the devices that these bums have been known to use. They are similar to the devices that were seized in New York. Detective Nolan says that the one used on Judge Hayden's home had a sophisticated timing device and that whoever made it was an expert mechanic. For that reason, Headquarters wants us to inspect every public building in our area for any suspicious packages. Also, introduce yourselves to the owners and managers of every business that attracts large numbers of people and tell them to call in anything suspicious."

"Are the plain clothes dicks looking at anyone in our area?" a patrolman asked.

"The Letts. They've got a few hard core ones who fought in the Russian revolution. Until further notice, the captain wants that building on Terrace Street checked by every shift. And don't forget, we hold warrants for Fraina and Sturgis for the May Day riot. Anytime the Bolsheviks crawl out of their holes, search them, make notes and pass the information along to the detectives. And if they have anything on them or if they do anything suspicious or they're in an unusual place—run 'em in."

The houseman reentered the room and waited for McGuiness to pause. "You have a call at the desk, Sergeant."

"Okay. Lastly, the captain wants us to finish taking the census this week."

"Ah, the really important police work," one of the senior patrolmen said.

"It's all part of the job, Rollins," McGuiness said.

"But, Sarge, you get us all riled up about the Reds and then you finish roll call by telling us to forget all that and take the census."

"What can I say? I do what I'm told." McGuiness stood at the door. "Dwyer, you've got the traffic post at the church. Keep an eye out for those little bastards who have been grabbing the pocketbooks. If you see any of them in the area, collar them and ring up the desk. We've got warrants for most of them. Okay, that's it."

WILLIE HEARD two long blasts of the train's whistle as it raced along the massive one and a half mile granite embankment that the Mission Hill locals called 'Hadrian's Wall.' Like the original that separated Roman Britain from its barbaric neighbors to the North, the wall served as a physical demarcation between the Hill's lace curtain second-generation Irish and their prosperous German neighbors, from the working class Irish who resided in the Crossing, Dudley Street and Eliot Square. The whistle blew again as the train charged towards the bridge in Roxbury Crossing on the early run from New York City to South Station.

Willie sprinted under the bridge and emerged on the other side with a flurry of pigeons, where he resumed his walk up Tremont Street to his traffic post in front of Mission Church. A trolley passed him, filled with the faithful, including the disabled who came to pray at the Wednesday novenas. Easily the largest structure in the Roxbury neighborhood, the church rivaled the Customs House and Holy Cross Cathedral as Boston's tallest building. Officially known as The Church of Our Lady of Perpetual Help, local residents referred to it as the Mission Church, and its surrounding neighborhood of Parker Hill, they called Mission Hill.

A group of worshippers left the trolley and stood with hundreds of others in the plaza near the church's entrance, including two elderly women and a slight young man who walked with a limp. Folded into one another, the women supported each other as they navigated their way through the crowd. The man entered the plaza and shadowed them. He stood an inconspicuous distance from them, his body jacked to one side like a storefront mannequin, his distinctive black cap standing out amid a sea of straw hats, derbies and pastel bonnets.

While not excessively tall, he was easy to follow, like a hawk sailing among sparrows and pigeons. The strap for a large carpetbag hung diagonally across his chest, the bag riding heavy in cadence with his right thigh as he started across the plaza.

The bells in the Gothic Spires began to peal and the crowd stirred. The man closed the distance to the women and came within a long stride of them as they shuffled arm-in-arm in the ebb and flow of movement towards the church entrance. His eyes darted around the plaza. When the crowd jerked to a stop, he fell into the women from behind, breaking their hold on one another. The smaller of the two stumbled and, in the collision, her pocketbook fell onto the stone square and opened.

"*Scusa*," he said. He bent down and gathered the woman's belongings and replaced them in her pocketbook. "*Scusa*," he repeated and offered the bag to her. The stunned woman grabbed at the strap and the young man turned and slipped away into the crowd.

Willie had just taken up his traffic post in the street when he saw the collision. He responded to the shaken woman who was sitting on the steps of the church, clutching her bag. "Are you alright?" he asked.

"Millie, are you okay?" her companion asked. "I'll tell you one thing, officer. These foreigners just don't have any respect for other people."

"It probably was my own fault, Alice, for not looking where I was going," Millie said. Her hand fluttered as she raised it and held it against her forehead.

"He could have stayed to make sure you were alright," Alice said.

"You said he was a foreigner," Willie said.

"I think he was one of those Italians," Alice said.

"What makes you think that?" Dwyer searched the crowd for the black cap.

"Because of his accent," Alice said. "Everything they say—" She began to wind her hand in the air in small circles. "Sounds like they have mush in their mouths."

Millie looked inside her pocketbook and moved the contents. "Alice, hold these things, will you?" After placing several items into her friend's hands, she said, "My purse is gone!"

"Are you sure? Here, let me look," said Alice.

"I looked. It's not in there."

Dwyer stepped onto the landing and searched the crowd for the man. "Where do you live, Millie?"

"Huh?" She continued to rifle through her bag, emptying most its contents into her friend's hands. "Columbus Avenue—"

"Mildred Healey, 1245 Columbus Avenue," Alice said. "That man who knocked you down must have taken it."

"Are you sure you had it with you?" Dwyer continued to look over the remaining crowd that pressed to the entrance of the church.

"She had it," Alice said. "I saw her take a coin out of it to pay for the trolley."

"Now, I'm not so sure," said Millie. Her eyes darted from one face to another with the expression of a lost child.

"But I thought I saw it in your bag," her friend said.

"There," Dwyer said aloud to himself when he thought he saw a man emerge from the end of the crowd of worshippers and move with a distinctive gimp to an empty trolley that was bogged down in traffic. "I'll stop by your home at the end of the shift. Are you going to be alright, Millie?"

"I'll take care of her, officer," Alice said. "Do you see him?"

"Maybe—"

Willie ran into the street and raced down the middle of the two lanes of stalled traffic with his helmet in his hand, blowing his whistle, the high shrill pitch reverberating off the storefronts. The man looked back and hopped down from the trolley when it came to a stop at the intersection with St. Alphonsus Street. He hobbled around the corner with the bag pulled up close on his right side, and disappeared. Dwyer sprinted to the corner, turned and stopped. He scanned the hill for his suspect, but he was nowhere in sight.

An open wagon loaded down with bundles of newspapers, discarded clothing and housewares passed him as it slowly climbed the hill. An old grizzled man sat up on the driver's seat and encouraged his horse to climb the long grade.

"Where did he go?" Willie yelled.

"Come on, Rosie," the old man said. "Rags!" He turned in his seat and looked back at Dwyer. "It's too hot for that kind of exertion." He watched Willie continue to scan the street and then he shook his head. "Come on and catch up if you want to talk. I ain't going to stop the horse in this weather. She might decide to take the rest of the day off." He stepped down gingerly into the street and walked with the reins in his hand. Willie jogged to the wagon and walked beside him, "Well, did you see where he went or not?"

"Why are you chasing him?"

"Never mind that, Jaysus. He knocked down an old lady in front of the church and stole her purse. For God's sake, Man, which way did he go?"

"You're new around here, aren't you? I work on the Hill every day and a guy can buy himself a lot of trouble by fingering someone to the cops."

"Never mind the baloney. Did you recognize him or not?"

"No. I never saw him before today." The ragman pointed across the street at the rear entrance to the closed Coleman Quarry. "He entered the ledges right there. I would say that the way he was limping, he didn't get very far."

"Thanks," Dwyer said and jogged to the entrance.

"You're welcome, yourself. Be careful in there! You can get lost if you're not familiar with the maze of trails."

"Thanks again."

THE SWITCH was in its late morning lull between the early bird commuters and the afternoon luncheon crowd. The diner was empty except for a night shift regular who began the first leg of his day's sleep in the last booth at the back of the diner, the short order cook who was cleaning the grill, and Catherine, who was wiping tables and filling the salt and pepper shakers. Jim Rankin entered, dressed in an expensive suit, a black bowler and the ever present red carnation in his lapel.

He sat in the exact middle of the counter, directly opposite the swinging doors that led to the kitchen. "I'll have coffee, Catherine." The cook's back was in view and he could see that he was occupied with the grill. "Who's in the back?"

She poured Rankin's coffee, then looked back towards the kitchen as if she hadn't worked the entire night and wasn't sure who was working with her. "Oh, that's Stan."

Rankin looked down at the man in the last booth and turned back to the counter. He slid his hand on top of Catherine's. "How would you like to get away for a day?"

"Oh, I don't know," she said. "I've been busy taking some extra work at O'Neil's to keep up with the bills."

Rankin picked up her hand, ran his fingers across her knuckles, and slipped them under her palm, probing the lines in her moist pink flesh. "I have to go to Rhode Island on business tomorrow. How about joining me for the ride?"

Catherine glanced behind her into the kitchen and then at the sleeping customer in the booth. "I'm supposed to work here tomorrow."

"Don't worry about the pay you will lose here. You'll make it up in spades."

"I don't know, Jim—"

"Mr. Rankin. In here, it's always Mr. Rankin."

"Mr. Rankin."

"What do you mean, you don't know? You want to experience a different life than here, don't you?"

Catherine leaned back slightly. "I should put the coffeepot back." She felt his short stubby fingers and thumb enclosing and stroking her hand, and hesitated. She withdrew, turned and placed the pot onto the stove, then rinsed a bar rag in the sink and began to wipe the countertop.

"What's say that I pick you up out back about nine after the early shift?" he said. "That way you won't get into trouble with the boss." The sleeping patron stirred in the last booth. He coughed, turned his head towards the wall and became quiet again. "Besides, you'll keep your job as long as I say you'll keep it. That is, if the diner wants to keep its license." Rankin approached her with the smug crimp of a smile and ran his hand around the curve of her hip. She topped his hand and removed it from her bottom.

Cocking his derby to the side of his head, he tapped it and said, "We both have need of something, Catherine, a fair exchange of sorts." Rankin leaned to one side to get a view into the kitchen and then stood straight. "So, will I see you at nine?"

She nodded without making further eye contact with him. "I guess so."

"Good." He began to walk to the door. He turned and smiled broadly. "Maybe we'll finish the day at Newport and you can look for one of those New York dresses that I know you like."

WILLIE CHECKED his pocketwatch and glanced at Box 14 that was located at the quarry entrance, and thought that he could explain the reason later why he didn't signal the Station as ordered. He squeezed between two large slabs of stone that blocked the entrance, the abrasive brown quartz snagging his uniform, and stumbled into a forest of rock where a vein of puddingstone divided the land in two from there to Brigham Circle a quarter mile away. Rock walls, scarred with striations, rose up from the floor more than sixty feet in some places. Tribal slogans and crude pictures were painted near the tops that gave an archaeological snapshot of the people who had lived and fought on the Hill. *Sinn Fein* was one of the newer painted slogans. High up on the ledges, tree limbs grew out of the rock in several places and tiny rivulets of water ran down the stone in time-worn fissures, leaving the sand moist and damp at the base. Scattered patches of grass and weeds grew in the sandy floor and small clusters of dandelions flowered in the dampness.

Sunlight bombarded the quarry and glinted off the mixture of sandstone and veins of jasper quartz, creating continuous glare. Willie tipped the brim of his helmet forward, using it as a visor, and probed his way a short distance before coming upon an eight foot wall of boulders used to discourage further entry. He heard a sound from the other side of the obstruction and scrambled to the top. In the distance, he saw a large pit that was open to the sky, accessed by three well-traveled sandy trails, and fed by smaller paths only wide enough to accommodate a man.

"There it is again." He followed the sound, shading his eyes to avoid the sun's glare and saw the thief only twenty feet away, limping badly and looking back, one of his hands digging inside of his carpetbag. "Stop," Willie commanded. But the thief continued to flee and ducked into one of the smaller passageways and disappeared from view. Dwyer jumped down from the pile of boulders, landed in a squat and ran to the place where he last saw the man.

He turned into the passageway and stopped—fascinated by the orange flame that flashed before his eyes, hanging suspended in a world of brown and gray, deeply aware of his own vulnerability. He stood frozen in the confusion that was thin white smoke which collapsed in front of him like a moth-eaten bridal veil that once removed revealed a man, haloed and darkly silhouetted by the sun, pointing at him with one arm. Willie saw the black cap, shoulder strap, cloth bag—and pistol.

Then a yip, like the bark of an old dog, and a sharp explosion in the hollow stone place, clapping his ears and burrowing deep inside him. The zip of the bullet, ripping a crooked line into the rock behind him.

He lay stunned in the dirt and the gravel, expecting a second and final shot, but the quarry became quiet. Disoriented and dazed, he scrambled in the dust, flopping and crawling on his knees and belly until he reached a large rock wall. He fumbled his revolver out of its holster, the one the Department had issued him when he came off probation, the one he would bring to training in a few weeks. The one he had never fired. He poked his head up and wildly discharged the Smith & Wesson twice, firing the gun like he was snapping a whip, the sound of the shots rolling through the quarry like a wave.

Dwyer waited, and then for reasons that he couldn't later explain, he crawled to his helmet and placed it on top of a large boulder for safety. The bullet had left a pencil-sized hole in the front just above his identification number and a larger exit hole in the back near the crown. "Two inches more," he said. His ears cleared and he could hear automobile horns and trolley bells in the traffic on Tremont Street, suddenly cognizant of his limited existence and the thin frail thread between life and death. And he thought about Bernie McLean.

"HAVE WE HEARD from everyone, Cox?" Sergeant McGuiness asked as he returned to the front desk.

"Everyone but Dwyer," the houseman said.

McGuiness checked the roll call notes. "He has the traffic in front of the church." He replaced the notes on the desk and shook his head as if to settle the question in his mind. "There could have been an extra-large crowd for the Novena or the priests are feeding him in the kitchen. Give him another couple of minutes and if you don't hear from him, call the rectory and ask them where he is."

"Will do."

"And when you locate him, tell him I want to speak with him."

AT THE TOP of the ledges, the backs of the houses on Calumet Street were visible. The traffic noise grew louder and Dwyer wondered if he was coming to the end of the quarry. He pressed his back against the puddingstone, grunted and charged into the next clearing with his revolver at arm's length in front of him. He dropped down, looked at the sand beneath him. "Lots of footprints," he said. "Kids? Could use one of them to lead me out of this goddam place." He wiped his forehead with his sleeve and listened.

"What's that?" He stood and began to jog to the sound. It grew louder as he got closer and he realized that someone was moving and dropping large stones. He followed the noise, laying his shoulder against the stone wall, and slid around the corner. He was back on the main trail near the front gate that was large enough to accommodate a wagon and its horses or a motorized truck. Chunks of blasted puddingstone filled the steel frame and sealed off the closed quarry. At the top of the barrier, the thief sat, furiously lifting boulders off the pile and dropping them to the ground. Willie jogged to a large pyramid of sand near the entrance and pointed the pistol. "Stop—or I'll shoot you off that pile of rock."

"You won't shoot anyone, copper—"

Willie jerked off a round at the thief and the man shot at the same time. Dwyer heard his round ricochet off the steel entrance. He dropped down behind the sand and made himself small and then jacked straight up and fired again as the man cringed and returned his own shot, the bullets buzzing in the dusty air and skipping off the stone, the pop-pop-zing drifting into the surrounding neighborhood. He stooped down behind the sand and shouted again. "Give up—"

The thief grabbed his bag and held it against his chest, wiggling like a crab on his back through the space that he had created at the top of the pile. He drove one of his heels into the blasted rock and slipped his head under the doorframe.

"For the last time, stop!" Willie shouted.

He ignored Dwyer's command and continued to crawl on his back and shoulders from side to side, crabbing free of the improvised barrier, grabbed onto the top of the doorframe and pulled himself up. "Goodbye, copper."

Willie cocked the hammer back and looked through the pistol's rear site and down the length of the barrel, aiming the gun at the man's chest and the bag that he held against it. And pulled the trigger.

THE STATION TELEPHONE rang several times before the captain heard it in his office at the back of the building. "Where is everybody?" he said. He walked to his office door. "Sergeant?" When he didn't receive a response, he hollered at the top of his voice. "Cox? Do you hear the telephone?"

McGuiness opened the door from the rear stairwell and ran to the desk. "I'll answer it, captain. I went upstairs for a moment and Cox is washing one of the wagons in the garage." He stopped and composed himself. "Boston Police, Station 10."

He listened intently with a pencil in his hand and then dropped it on the desk. "You found your purse? Ah, that's good. No, we don't want to be arresting innocent men," he said, "even if they are foreigners who don't speak the King's English." McGuiness pulled one of his suspenders up and let it snap onto his shoulder. "Yes, I'll be sure to tell Patrolman Dwyer. I'm sure that he has it all straight now."

He picked up the pencil again. "Mildred Healey. Okay, I've got it."

He placed the telephone back in its cradle and it rang again. "What is it this time? Station 10. A what?" He began to write. "Where?" He looked up at the clock on the wall and noted the time. "Okay, we'll have police there as quickly as we can. Yes, and the Fire Department."

McGuiness ran to the back stairwell and yelled, "Cox, come upstairs." Then he relayed the report of gunshots and an explosion to the captain as the telephone rang again.

THE BLAST THAT BLEW the stone barrier back into the closed quarry and left a three-foot crater in the ground where the steel framed doorway had stood started with a moan. Then a knife blade of whole and pulverized stone rocketed one hundred feet into the air and was immediately followed by a shorter but broader wave of mineral chips, silt, sand and dust. Like a prairie windstorm, a ball of sand and dirt rolled out of the blast and violently tumbled into the yard all the way to the main pit, growing monstrously larger and uglier as it collected loose debris in its path, the ball slapping and gouging the walls and painting them gray-yellow. An enormous cloud of smoke, dust and microscopic dirt then rose above the quarry, collapsed and rained down a thick blanket of gray soot on the homes and shops in the area. The force of the explosion cracked chimneys and foundations and blew out glass windows in houses and storefronts on Tremont Street. In the houses that stood high on the ledges, furniture shook and trembled before falling over and opened doors blew shut. The bark on several old chestnut trees split and scored as if the rough gnarly skin was struck by lightning.

Willie later said that he was hunkered down behind the sand with his arms out straight and his hands rock steady against the pile when he fired. And in the instant between the time he pulled the trigger and the monstrous roar of the explosion, there was dead eerie quiet, like a vacuum where nothing happens, and then a brilliant white flash lit up the quarry and blinded his eyes like the coming of Jesus. The earth lurched and wrenched under him, and the air was torn from his lungs like he was struck in the chest by a massive fist and then turned inside out. He remembered nothing else except being in the blackest room, completely devoid of light, and feeling the apprehension of being alone and abandoned. When the firemen woke him, he felt bewildered and slightly deaf, and he still heard the explosion as if he was being held under water.

It was a minor miracle that the firemen arrived so quickly after the explosion and an even greater miracle that they immediately found Willie partially buried under a mound of sand. His shoeless foot was the only part of his body that was completely visible and, at first appearance, seemed to be just another piece of the jigsaw puzzle that once was Peter Carlucci.

WHILE DOCTORS AND NURSES probed and poked Willie Dwyer at the Peter Bent Brigham and the evening editions of the Boston newspapers broke the story of the hero patrolman who nearly lost his life in a *fight-to-the-death* finish, battling a fanatical terrorist in a scene right out of a dime novel, detectives raided a house above the ledges at 66 Calumet Street. They arrested two other men suspected in the recent bombings, after learning that the man carrying the cloth satchel holding twelve sticks of dynamite wrapped in electrical tape and attached to a fuse and a blasting cap was Peter Carlucci, a machine expert who had recently arrived in Boston to participate in the *National Day of Terror*. At the home, stacks of newsletters entitled "*Plain Words,*" and flyers threatening that *We Will Do Anything*, were confiscated. A manual, entitled *La Salute e in voi*, describing the steps for making bombs, was found in a bedroom. A source told Detective Nolan that the Mission Church was on a short list of targets because the pastor had been an outspoken critic of the Reds. Nolan was impressed that Joseph Kursh had come forward on his own after hearing about the explosion and was more impressed that Willie Dwyer's act of kindness after the May Day riot had made the home-grown Parlor Red and would-be revolutionary a valuable source of information. Carlucci, Kursh told Nolan, had visited the church several times and learned that the dynamite would have its greatest effect when placed inside one of the confessionals along the outside wall on Wednesday afternoons during Novena services while fifteen hundred worshippers sat in the pews.

Chapter Four

~

The sultry July day continued the pattern of tropical weather that had settled into the region since May, bringing more heat, high humidity and electrically charged thunderstorms. The latest dumped an inch of rainwater in twenty minutes and left the city damp and clammy. Water ran off Bulfinch's dome onto the Romanesque roof of the Massachusetts State House and leaked into the Great Hall, leaving the marble stairs looking hard and glossy. It pooled on the front balcony, where John Quincy Adams had once stood and received a rousing sendoff before leaving for Washington. And it ran down Beacon Hill past bow-front Federalist homes built by wealthy Brahmins with unobstructed views of Boston Common.

Steam rose off the downtown streets as budget-conscious Bostonians hurried past storefronts, briefly peering in to look for a bargain. Climbing up and out of America's first subway system, clerks from the Washington Street department stores, secretaries and legal researchers from the State Street law firms and brokers from the Boston Stock Exchange emerged at the corner of Park and Tremont Streets and hurried past members of the Elevated Railway Workers' Union who advised them of the possibility of yet another Labor strike.

Edwin Upton Curtis struggled up Beacon Hill from Charles Street and labored in the tropical air. He passed the golden dome and involuntarily jogged down the opposite side of the Hill as he made his way to police headquarters. When he arrived at the entrance, he paused to catch his breath. Perspiration beaded his forehead and he patted his face with a handkerchief. The Police Commissioner looked down at Scollay Square and its sleazy bars and burlesque clubs below him. "Dens of wickedness," he said.

Elected the youngest mayor of Boston in 1895, Curtis was a bright star on the Republican Party's horizon. But in a heartbeat, his career fizzled when the neighborhood Ward Bosses, led by Martin Lomasney, turned their political machine against him in his bid for re-election and supported Josiah Quincy instead. Resigned to the elephant graveyard of obscure political appointments, he was never considered seriously by his party until the previous December when Commissioner Stephen O'Meara died unexpectedly; Governor McCall came calling and Edwin Upton Curtis became relevant again.

He entered his office and looked for the pitcher of water that he expected to be on his desk. "Miss Harris, where is my water?"

His secretary scurried into the office, carrying a tray with a pitcher and two glasses, and placed it on a sideboard that stood against the wall. "I'm sorry, Commissioner. I was busy collecting the station reports and completely forgot about it."

He dismissed her with a wave of his hand and filled his glass. "Irony of ironies, the very race of people who sabotaged my life now surrounds me. Boston will never be a decent city again until it rids itself of these uncouth barbarians."

A stack of reports and the day's correspondence lay on top of his tidy oaken desk, ordinarily vacant except for a legal dictionary and the King James' Bible. He fell into his chair with mild exhaustion, allowing himself a brief momentary respite, and then straightened himself tall and began to sift through the reports submitted by the station captains. A personal letter, sandwiched between two of the reports, caught his eye and when he saw the return address of C. Tucker Appleton, he pulled it out of the pile. "Miss Harris, please note my calendar that I am to meet with Mr. Appleton at The Bank a week from today for a Downtown Club Association meeting."

"Yes, Commissioner," she said from her desk just outside his office door. "I already noted it in your calendar."

"Have the captains arrived yet?"

"They have, sir, and are waiting for you in the conference room."

"Call Superintendent Crowley and ask him to come up for the meeting."

"Yes, Commissioner."

The telephone rang as it did about the same time each morning since he had been sworn into office. He cleared his throat and answered it with an exaggerated tone of command. "This is Commissioner Curtis."

He listened to the voice on the other end of the line. "Yes, I heard you," he said. "So you believe that they will affiliate with the A.F. of L.? That is very unfortunate. Thank you." Curtis hung up the telephone, sat back in his chair and began to rock slightly. "What did they think I would do? Be a good sport and just go along?"

He removed a manila folder from his desk, labeled *General Orders, Stephen O'Meara, Commissioner*, and placed it next to his writing pad. "I offered them a ten percent raise, which was better than the Mayor's piecemeal, a few dollars now and the rest later, and they refused it." He opened the folder and removed a two-page document, dated June 28, 1918 and entitled, *On the Subject of Police Unionization.* "This is still O'Meara's Department." He dipped his pen into the inkwell. "Maybe it's time to change that."

He began to draft a General Order articulating his opposition to any movement by the patrolmen to affiliate with the American Federation of Labor referencing the former Commissioner's Order and opposition. He ended his draft with the warning that every member of the force should weigh each of his words carefully. Then he wrote out a list of officer's names for disciplinary action, eleven for discharge and the others for transfer.

"Miss Harris, tell the captains that I must postpone the meeting and will meet with them in two hours."

"Yes, Commissioner."

He finished the list, slumped back into his chair and looked out to the harbor and the outer islands. He sat there for several minutes and then pulled himself straight, replacing the pen in its holder.

"Miss Harris, please extend my apologies to the superintendent and the captains."

"I will, Commissioner." She stood just as Curtis rushed out of his office past her.

"I will be at the State House, meeting with the Governor's secretary," he said. "In the meantime, I want you to prepare eleven Orders of

Dismissal. The names are on my desk. Have them ready for my meeting with the captains."

"Yes, Commissioner."

CATHERINE HEARD the car horn from her second floor room and looked down at the street from her window. She took a deep breath and a last look in the mirror before walking to the landing. A wisp of a young woman with only the suggestion of breasts, she was prepubescently thin, permanently suspended in an androgynous state and tall, but not so tall that she appeared gangly. Asked to guess her age when she wore no makeup, an unsuspecting person might estimate her to be fourteen or fifteen, but rarely her actual twenty, and dressed in knickers, shirt and a scaly cap, she could easily pass herself off as an adolescent boy. Only her thin light voice might give her away. She wore her veneer of innocence easily.

The loose floating dress hung on her like air, slipping over the subtle changes in her landscape as she moved, and hinted at the delicate sensuousness in the small curve of her hips, the slope of her athletic shoulders and her long shapely legs. She walked to the top of the stairs and paused. She listened to her stomach rumble and swallowed to rid her mouth of its metallic taste. She straightened her dress, stood tall and took her first step, concentrating on maintaining a smile. When she reached the bottom step, she leaned to one side to see past the colored glass in the front door and searched the interior of the automobile for its occupant. Jim Rankin sat behind the wheel, reading his newspaper.

"I want a cut," a voice said from behind her.

Catherine flinched and turned around. Charlie Bradley stooped out from the dimly lit crawl space under the stairs.

"A cut of what, Charlie?"

"You know what I'm talking about. Rankin must be paying you a handsome bit of change for a taste—" He went into a coughing spell and stopped after he spit phlegm and blood onto the hallway floor and rubbed it into the wood with his shoe.

"I don't know—"

"Sure you do," he said with a wheeze. He bent over, his face dripping in front of hers, and smiled with a deteriorated expression that reminded her of rotting food in a damp cellar. "This little business has been going on for what, a couple of weeks now. So I figure you owe me."

"Say, who do you think you are? I got this one on my own."

"And a good one it is," he said. "You certainly took a step up." He grabbed her wrist, squeezed it and pulled her off the bottom step so that they were standing face-to-face. "But our little business relationship doesn't end because you decide to freelance. I remember when you were in my position and who saved your life."

Catherine pulled away, overwhelmed by the foul smell from his mouth, and then heard the blade of his knife click into place. "Listen, Charlie," she stammered. "Our business relationship only involved me fencing a few things at O'Neil's for you because I was a little short on cash. That was a long—"

"And who got you connected to O'Neil's, hmm?"

"You might have got me the connection, but the rest I did myself."

"And do they know about this little tryst or are you really freelancing?"

"I wouldn't keep this from them. But I'm looking for better days—"

"Shut up. We all want better days." He pulled her closer and pushed the point of the switchblade into her ribs. "Your business is my business."

"Alright, Charlie, alright. But I only agreed to accompany him a few times to Rhode Island. There's no funny business going on—" The automobile's horn sounded again and she gently pushed her arm against his chest. "He buys me gifts, that's all. But I'll give you a cut. You know I'm good for it. Besides, I'm getting tired of the grand man."

"You're good for nothing. Get out there before he drives off." He partially released his grip on her. "Remember this. I get my share whether its gifts, cash or whatever." He tapped the tip of the knife on her breastbone and then raised it under her chin. "Do you understand?"

"Yes, I understand." Catherine pulled free of his grip and walked to the door. She wiped the corner of one eye and primped her hair.

"Good." Charlie stared at her with a mad alcoholic glaze and then backed away into the dark space under the stairs.

Catherine's hands fluttered around her, smoothing the wrinkles from her dress. She took a small bottle of perfume from her bag and applied the liquid to all the places where Bradley had touched her. Lastly, she tipped the bottle again, lifted her dress away from her collar and brushed her fingers across her breastbone. She put the bottle in her bag and opened the door.

"Don't forget," Bradley said. "I know what you're doing all the time."

She heard him cough and she felt his eyes staining her.

ALBERT BOARDED the elevated train at Dudley Street, grabbed a strap, leaned back and peered through the crowded car, down to its very end. He saw patrolmen from '9' grouped together, some in uniform and some in civilian attire, looked through the door window to the next car and recognized a few more from the Dudley Street Station and realized that the third general meeting in the last two and half weeks was going to be standing room only. His father-in-law had asked him how the men were holding up and he had answered that the cops were pissed and felt like chumps.

The train jerked and coasted into the Dover Street station and he stepped off with a hundred other cops, fell in with the others and walked the two blocks to Intercolonial Hall, a run-down place that was dry as a timber box with long church windows that shook in a stiff wind. Patrolmen from across the city sat at the tables along the wall playing cards; some stood at the bar and sipped on Near beer while others milled on the open floor in small clusters and cliques. He concluded that there were more than a few understaffed stations across the city by the number of cops in the hall, about one thousand, he guessed. A short distance away, he heard Fulton Quigley's high pitched horse laugh, turned and recognized a group of senior men from the Roxbury Crossing Station and moved over to them.

A patrolman at the podium banged his gavel and attempted to call the meeting to order. "For those of you who don't know me, my name is John McInnes. I see that we have no problem establishing a quorum." He moved out from behind the microphone and walked to the edge of the stage with the unmistakable carriage of a military man. A distinguished cavalry officer in the last campaigns with the Indians, an infantryman during the Spanish-American War and an intelligence officer during the World War, he was well respected by his peers and recognized as the man who opened the original dialogue with Stephen O'Meara about their grievances. And when negotiations came to a standstill with the present commissioner, he took their battle to Beacon Hill and lobbied members of the Legislature.

"In order to save a little time," he said, "John Caulfield and Terrence O'Boyle are on the floor, passing out flyers with a list of our grievances. These are the ones that have been formally presented to the Commissioner as our argument for a higher salary. Now, I don't need to stand here and go through each one of them because they are all familiar to us. You work with these unacceptable conditions every day and are being paid salaries that are close to the poverty level." He glanced over his shoulder. "The four officers standing behind me comprise the committee that is responsible for negotiations. Michael, are you ready?"

Michael Lynch stepped up to the microphone. "I'll get right to the heart of the matter. I assume that most of you have read the Commissioner's General Order and know that eleven officers were dismissed and several others were transferred arbitrarily to different stations." He paused, looked over at McInnes and nodded to a whispered instruction. "Let me address the dismissals first. The committee is presently in discussions with the Commissioner's office to reverse those discharges. At this time, I would rather not discuss the negotiations any further than to say that there are discussions."

A patrolman from the back of the hall shouted out. "Speak up a little?"

"Sure, I can do that," Lynch said in a stronger and more assertive voice. "I also want to ensure each of you that all courtesies have been extended to Commissioner Curtis, including inviting him to tonight's meeting to address you. However, he declined because he had another engagement."

Quigley cupped his hands over his mouth and hollered to the front of the room. "If he thinks that he's busy now, wait until we bring in the A.F. of L."

An awkward response of laughter and a few calls for Curtis' dismissal rose up in the hall. Another member from Quigley's group yelled, "To hell with him. I'm one of those eleven so-called malcontents who were sacked. I can't pay my rent and I'm already on the tab to the grocer."

McInnes stepped to the podium and slammed the gavel down twice. "Let's have some order, please."

Lynch continued, "We prefer to try and work with the Commissioner and anyone else to make this process as painless as possible. We believe that if we act in a courteous and professional way to achieve our end, we will have the support of the legislature and the people of Boston."

Other members of the Bargaining Committee joined him at the podium. "Like you, we have different opinions on how to carry on this campaign," he said. "Some of us are more aggressive than others. But for the time being, we have agreed to remain objective and take into consideration that we are negotiating during a difficult economy and high unemployment."

Before Lynch could resume talking, Quigley raised his arm. "Patrolman Fulton Quigley, Station 10 representative. So, what do we do about Curtis' General Order? And I thought we were here tonight to vote on whether to join the A.F. of L."

"We have had lengthy discussions among ourselves about this and are recommending not taking any action with regards to the Commissioner's Order." Lynch held up the Order. "Personally, I can't say that I disagree with this language. We did take an oath and our job is unlike any other job. The last thing we want is to let anything or anyone compromise our ability to enforce the Commonwealth's laws. I believe we have nothing to gain by taking exception to this language, and as far as the Commissioner's directive not to affiliate with an outside organization, we should just ignore it. So, the Board recommends, at this time, we should table any further discussion and move on with the business at hand."

McInnes walked to the microphone and raised his arm. "Can I have a show of hands in support of the Committee's recommendation to table any further discussion about the Commissioner's General Order, Number 102?"

He looked out over the overwhelming numbers of raised hands. "Secretary Riley," he said. "Would you note that the majority of those in attendance have voted to table any further discussion about General Order, Number 102."

Coppenrath raised his hand. "Albert Coppenrath, Station 10, Roxbury Crossing."

"The chair recognizes Patrolman Coppenrath."

"In February, we authorized our Board to conduct research and make inquiries about joining the A.F. of L., but I think many officers in this room have the same reservations that I have and are somewhat apprehensive about aligning ourselves with a national Labor union. I, for one, don't want to see a gang of Socialists from New York parading our streets representing us."

One of the committee members stepped to the podium. "Let me answer this one. The American Federation of Labor is a legitimate organization, founded by a patriotic American, Samuel Gompers, who, by the way, recently called for stronger immigration laws to curtail those eastern European bums from entering the country. Bill Haywood and his Wobblies are not affiliated with the A. F. of L. and, the way the federal agencies are pursuing these radicals, they won't be around much longer. However, that doesn't mean that a bunch of nutcakes won't try to take advantage of a situation.

"In the last year, one million workers around the country joined the A.F. of L., including police in other cities. And there are several Departments in eastern Massachusetts who have advised us that they are waiting to see what happens with our efforts before they pursue their own affiliation."

"So, what are we waiting for?" someone called from the back of the hall.

John McInnes stepped to the microphone again. "The A.F. of L. vote is the reason we are here tonight. Are there any objections to taking the vote?"

He scanned the one thousand men who sat and stood in the hall, understanding that they were about to step into unchartered territory, and looked into their faces, many of them young patrolmen just beginning their careers who should have been learning the techniques of their trade instead of organizing themselves into another undisciplined group of rabble rousers. They didn't understand nor could they appreciate what the senior men had endured, the closed cliques that greeted the first Irish boys appointed to the force; the one who battled a hooligan alone as an older Protestant cop hid in the shadows because he hated the new Catholic recruits. It wasn't until these earlier Irish cops waded into their own neighborhoods and demonstrated that they could police their own that they were given grudging respect. He thought that some of these young coppers didn't understand that they would never be financially comfortable, that they would always be one step away from the pawn shop, and that they would always be paid only enough to make them come back for another day. And yet, he wondered how many of them were being bullied into making a decision that they wouldn't have ordinarily made.

McInnes also saw the older craggy faces who'd set the bar high and deserved their reputation as 'Boston's Finest.' He wondered if they were being swept along with this out-of-control rush. Many of them had been military men like him and understood that the police force was about as close to a military organization as you could find in civilian life. Did they really want to align themselves with trades that had absolutely nothing in common with being a policeman? Should they unionize because Departments from other states and Canada had affiliated?

To John McInnes, the only important principle was the responsibility, no, the duty, to ensure the integrity of the city, the idea that when the fragile veil of society begins to tear because of selfish motivation, the police officer is the final guardian of that integrity. He looked down from the top of the podium and rapped the gavel twice on the block.

"Our Department was established in 1625," he said. "Everyone else follows us. Now, those who want to take the vote, whether to affiliate with the American Federation of Labor, raise your hand in the air."

DANDY JIM HUNG on her like a bag of wet rags, drooling into the whiteness of her breast, grunting and breathing like each breath was his last. The tip of Catherine's tongue reached out and slid around the ring of her mouth, searching for the bittersweet taste of black licorice. The 'Green Fairy' raced through her veins to the extremes of her fingers and toes and left her in an exaggerated state of weightlessness. She folded herself down over the shorter politician, resting her head on the top of his as they slow-danced in the cool pale shadows of the room's ambient light, her arms and legs lazy and slow, as if she were treading in deep water.

The Ward Boss was soft and gooey without his suit of armor and his face was moist and red. She felt the press of his emancipated flesh and giggled in his ear at the thought of his absurd and stunted shape. He turned with the press of her hip and she steered him to the bed, him slipping towards the pillow and clinging to her neck. “Let go, let go,” she said before he fell back asleep.

She covered him and tiptoed to the bathroom with his briefcase and closed the door.

In the News

MONAHAN'S SALOON DEFIES PROHIBITION
(Boston)
All night celebration in city riotous; drunkenness rife, arrests few; Rhode Island dry; few Connecticut saloons open. Mayor Peters speaks with President Wilson to reconsider enforcement of wartime prohibition law; Representative John F. Fitzgerald states that open bars in Bangor Maine example of disregard of law. Expected to be lifted by January 1, 1920
BOSTON EVENING TRANSCRIPT
Tuesday, July 1, 1919

TEN CENT FARE ON ELEVATED
(Boston)
Public trustees announce; needed to pay expenses of operation
BOSTON EVENING TRANSCRIPT
Tuesday, July 1, 1919

TREATY OF VERSAILLES SIGNED
(Paris, France)
List of those wanted for trial made public
BOSTON EVENING TRANSCRIPT
Monday, July 7, 1919

DOWN WITH SINN FEIN
(Dublin, Ireland)
British take drastic measures in Tipperary; suppress certain organizations as unlawful. Two constables of Royal Irish Constabulary murdered
BOSTON EVENING TRANSCRIPT
Tuesday, July 8, 1919

Chapter Five

~

The color guard wheeled around in the middle of the street and the four Massachusetts Guardsmen pinned their shoulders against each other and made their turn uniform and tight. They half-stepped until the outside rifle bearer came on-line with the others and the soldier carrying the American flag, ordered, "Forward march." Four left legs reached out in unison, their heels digging into the uneven cobblestoned street, and the 26th Yankee Division began its march to Boston Common. Behind them, the Guard's band played "Stars and Stripes Forever."

Dwyer and Coppenrath stood about fifteen feet apart; each kept one eye on the crowd in front of them and one on the soldiers as rank after rank half-turned out of the armory and stepped out down Commonwealth Avenue. The large Independence Day crowd called out the names of brothers and husbands, blew horns and whistles, and enthusiastically cheered the doughboys from Boston who, as far as Bostonians were concerned, had won the greatest of wars single-handedly.

As the last of the soldiers turned out of the armory, the parade backed up and the soldiers marked time in the street behind the two patrolmen. "Albert," Willie called, "look who is at the rear of the troops."

"Where?"

Dwyer took a couple of steps towards Coppenrath and pointed. "There, isn't that Joe Dalton, the guy that helped you during the Dudley Street riot?"

"Yeah, it is. Those poor bastards, Joe and the others, have nothing better to do than march in parades."

"Did you ever thank him?"

"I found out where he lives and went to his home. He's in a tenement with his mother and younger sister over a grocery store on Hampden Street, down by St. Pat's."

"I'll bet he was glad to see you."

"Well, to tell you the truth, it was kind of sad. I brought over a bottle of scotch, you know the real stuff, and his mother became a little hysterical."

"How come she was upset with you?"

"Cause it was the middle of the morning and Joe already had a toot on. I mean, don't get me wrong. I was in uniform and on my way to work and I'm not sure if she knew why I was there, but when I told her who I was and that I was there to thank him, she settled down."

"Gee, that's too bad."

Albert walked over to Willie's post. "He was lit up pretty good for that time of day. They were both upset about the War and everything. He kept saying, 'What the hell good was it?' I guess a lot of his friends got killed over there or died from influenza."

"Then they come home and find there are no jobs for them. And no money to buy food."

"It ain't right, Willie?"

"Joe's got a beef. It's never fair for the families who do the fighting in someone else's war."

A few spectators remained and milled around after the parade ended. They talked on the sidewalk for a while and then they began to stroll to the Charles River to see the German U-boat. The two patrolmen stood in the street and watched in the distance as the backs and the rifles of the soldiers in the last rank disappeared over the hill and the Twenty-sixth Division rolled on in to Kenmore Square.

"Let's go," Albert said. "We're done here."

ON THE CHARLES, other Bostonians celebrated the July 4th holiday. "Good morning, Mr. Mayor. This is a fortunate occasion when we can get you off your boat to come down from Marblehead to one of our events."

"Hello Brad, old fellow. I wouldn't miss this for anything. Our boys deserve a day like this when they can march down the streets of Boston and receive the adulation they rightly deserve from the people. I was sitting in the reviewing stands with the Governor and a few other dignitaries and we all agreed that our Massachusetts boys made us pretty darn proud." A waiter passed the two men, carrying a tray of hors d'oeuvres. Peters stopped him and took a cracker with a smear of salmon on it. "It really is a good day to be a Massachusetts citizen, a great day for democracy, wouldn't you say? Besides, it's not every day that you get a chance to see a German submarine trolling the Charles."

"I agree. That alone should inspire people to support the Victory Liberty Loan drive." Bradford Henshaw took a sip of his champagne and waited for a few other guests to walk out of ear shot. "Are you going to attend the reception tonight at Lock-Ober, Andrew?"

"We are planning on it. My niece is staying at the house for a few days and playing nanny for the children. I hope she is willing to organize a baseball game, otherwise the boys will nag her to death."

"That's terrific, Andrew, I'm glad you came. I'm sure that you need to get away once in a while from the demands of city government."

"Well, it is that time of year to get away. The Governor told me that he has been vacationing in the Berkshires, but made the trip into the city especially to pay his respects to the soldiers."

"Speaking of the Governor," Henshaw put a hand on Peters' shoulder, "I have to say that I'm lined up with him on his laissez faire opposition to price-fixing and letting business operate unfettered by government regulation."

Peters struck a boxer's stance. "Ah, I knew I could expect a little sparring from you, Bradford. A little government intrusion keeps everyone honest, like controlling raw materials during the war. And it can create jobs for our veterans."

"The soldiers are one thing, but I think you've gone a little too far to the side of Labor since the Ward Bosses supported your Democratic candidacy."

"But I never forget my roots, Bradford, always checking my bearings."

"Well said, Andrew. So, will you return to Marblehead after the festivities?"

"Yes, there really are few issues that require my attention that can't wait until September. But when the City Council returns in the fall, we are going to have to pull in our belts and find new sources of revenue to meet the new pay increases."

Henshaw and Peters stood on the balcony of the Weld Boathouse and watched a canoe and a mahogany Chris Craft compete for the last viewing space on the Boston side of the Charles where their occupants hoped to acquire an unobstructed view of U-111. Functions at the historic boathouse ordinarily were happy affairs, usually when one of Harvard's crews had won another national championship. This event had a more reflective mood—thousands of Bostonians stood or sat on every bridge, grassy knoll and structure along the river to view the miniature German submarine that had terrorized the North Atlantic during the war, sinking unprotected merchant ships and boats carrying innocent passengers. The diminutive *Unterseeboot* navigated the serpentine waterway easily with a limp American flag hanging from its bridge. Spectators gawked with a kind of morbid fascination at the symbol of the mechanistic European war. The parade had lifted their spirits; the submarine reminded them of their vulnerability.

The two Harvard graduates watched the slender steel stern disappear around the river's bend with the same reserved introspection and sensed the intellectual sophistication of killing in future conflicts. They turned away from the water and leaned against the railing, facing the interior of the boathouse where some of the guests had gathered around a piano to listen to a rendition of Irving Berlin songs.

"If the devil has a mascot, then that was it," Peters said.

"Yes, it was." Henshaw saw his son enter the front door. "There's Max, right on time."

"That can't be Max," Peters said. "My word, he's all grown up. I remember him as a little boy."

Maximilian Henshaw was half a head taller than his father and thirty pounds of muscle heavier. He wore an open-collared white dress shirt, creased cotton slacks and spats and moved with swagger through the room, approaching his father and the Mayor with an easy good-natured smile. "Hello Father," he said.

"Max, you remember the Mayor, don't you?"

The younger Henshaw shook Peters' hand. "I do. Pleased to see you again, sir."

"I would have never recognized you, Max. You're all grown up." Peters looked at the younger man's ruddy face with the open cut on the bridge of his nose. "Your dad tells me that you're the captain of our football team. How do we measure up this year?"

"Very well, sir. I think we will hold our own if we can avoid some of the injuries that slowed us down last season. But so far, so good. The practices are spirited and the team is quickly picking up where we left off." Max lifted himself onto his toes to look into the room and then rocked back to the floor. "We are fortunate to have only lost six players to graduation."

"Well, good luck," Peters said. "I'll be sure to take in a few games and you can bet your life that I'll be at the stadium for the Yale game."

The younger Henshaw recognized a young woman who was standing with her parents. He excused himself and walked into the boathouse, stopping briefly to greet other guests, as he made his way to the other side of the room.

"You should be proud, Brad," Peters said as he watched Max greet the girl and her parents. "What does he plan to do upon graduation?"

"He has decided to attend law school and follow his grandfather into the family trade. We can use another good attorney on State Street."

"How come you never became an attorney like your father?"

"I like being in the game, Andrew. I've made and lost a lot of money in investments, but I wouldn't change a thing. There's nothing like the smell of the arena." Henshaw turned back to the river, leaned his elbows onto the railing and looked out over the water. "I have been hearing some scuttlebutt about the police and the A.F. of L. Is there any truth to that?"

Peters moved closer to Henshaw to ensure privacy in their conversation. "The Social Club, their association, has threatened to seek a charter with the A.F. of L. as a means of garnering support for their demands of a pay raise and improved working conditions. How did you hear about that? Up until now, the negotiations have been civil and quietly discussed behind closed doors."

"You can't keep a secret like that long in this town," Henshaw said. "Besides, how much of a secret can it be when a thousand policemen meet to vote on whether they should unionize?"

Peters stood stiff and sipped the champagne.

"Andrew, didn't you know about that?"

"Well—"

"I would think that at least someone from your office—"

"I have been on vacation and out of the city. But I can assure you that I have been following these negotiations closely." He placed his glass on the railing and put his hands together as if in prayer. "Here's the problem. The police have a legitimate argument. They are being paid substantially less than the present cost-of-living for doing a dangerous job. And they work long hours away from their families."

"I think most people would concur with that assessment, Andrew, but no one coerced them to join the police force. They knew what they were getting into before they took an oath."

"True enough. But Boston is fortunate to have a dedicated and disciplined bunch of men who have earned high marks for professionalism and, until now, have been very patient with the city. Nationally, the Boston Police Department is a model for professional policing."

"We can thank O'Meara for that."

"And that brings us to the crux of the matter. If O'Meara were still alive, we wouldn't be having this conversation."

"I know the history between Curtis and the Irish, but in this instance, the Commissioner is right. We can't have our police answering to two masters. I know some other cities have allowed police unionization—but it will never happen in Boston."

"What are you getting at, Bradford?"

"The business community, and that includes the Chamber, feels that this trend toward unionism is getting out of hand. There have been three hundred sixty strikes in the country this month alone. Five thousand New England fishermen are out right now. Streetcars and the elevated railway were shut down for four days earlier this month. And on and on it goes. Now, a thousand cops are voting to join the A.F. of L." Henshaw slapped his hand on the railing. "When is it going to end?"

Peters turned his hands out and hunched his shoulders. "I agree with you, but what can we do?"

"We need to—Business cannot weather many more strikes, Andrew. Tomorrow, there is a meeting of the Downtown Club Association. Tucker Appleton has invited Curtis to get his assessment of the police situation and to give him our concerns. This can't get out of control. It could cost the city's merchants and, ultimately, the banks millions of dollars if people feel uncomfortable about investing in Boston businesses or customers don't feel safe in the city. With the flagging economy, this problem with the police could hamper our chances of recovery and more companies will close their doors."

"I think cooler heads will prevail," Peters said. "The police are a proud bunch and Curtis is—Well, neither the police nor Curtis want this to get out of hand."

"I hope you're right, Andrew," Henshaw said.

Ballinasloe Ireland

The wooden shaft stopped short in Kevin Farrell's hands as he drove the sharp head of the slane into the bank. He stood in the bottom of the bog hole and made his horizontal cut into the thick black layer of peat, the best quality of turf to heat his cottage. He pulled on the shaft and the waterlogged earth reluctantly gave back his blade, releasing it with a wet sucking sound. The soles of his rubber boots slipped and skidded on the muddy bottom as he freed his spade from the compressed hard layer and drove it into the peat again.

"All right, Colum." Farrell stood up stiffly and rubbed his arms and shoulders that ached from a lifetime of farming and harvesting the fuel for his home.

His youngest son stood on the top of the bank and methodically sliced into the bog, cutting it down layer by layer, while his father nicked out the bricks and heaved them onto the top of the uncut bog to dry. The team worked with a hypnotic rhythm, horizontally separating and vertically cutting, cutting and moving, and moving and cutting.

Farrell stopped and removed a packet of Woodbine Cigarettes from his waistcoat and lit one. He leaned against the slope of the uncut bog while his son continued to work. "I'm getting too old for this," he said.

"Ha, you told my brothers the same old story," Colum said. "And look at you, still out here working in the earth. You'll never leave. They'll bury you out here."

"Well, I hope not too soon." The father pushed himself away from the slope. "It's getting dark, leave it for tomorrow."

"Go on," Colum said. "I'll strip the top scraw and start the next cut myself."

Farrell climbed out of the hole, slung his tool over his shoulder and began to walk to his farm. He had reached the edge of the bog when he heard his son scream. It rose up from the depths of the bog and struck him at his core. He dropped the slane and ran toward the sound.

He found Colum staring into the hole at the partially uncovered face of a dead boy, not much older than his son.

"OKAY, LIFT HIM UP now and be sure not to jostle the body," the constable said. Graves O'Brien supported the head and shoulders while Kevin and Colum Farrell stood on either side and another inspector took hold of the feet. They picked up the remains which they carefully placed onto the surface of the bog. "There, that's a good job."

"I've heard tales about these bog bodies," Kevin said. "But I never thought I would come upon one after all the years I've been digging out here."

Graves stooped down next to the body and avoided the temptation to start tearing into the peat that mummified it. "I can tell you one thing. This fella hasn't been here very long."

"What makes you say that, Inspector?" the other constable said.

"First of all, the boy found him at a depth of less than one meter. The ancient bodies usually are discovered at three meters or more. We'll know more when we clean him up, but from what I can see, his clothing is modern, definitely not from the Iron Age. Also, things were often buried with those ancient bodies." O'Brien looked up at Kevin. "Would you bring me the gunny, Mr. Farrell?"

"What do you mean by things buried with the bodies?" Colum asked.

"Religious relics and jewelry are often found with important persons or members of a ruling family. If the dead person had broken a community law, you might find a rope around their neck or they could be bound." Graves laid the burlap out on the ground. "Did you find anything near the body, Mr. Farrell?"

"No, nothing at all, inspector."

With the help of the others, Graves wrapped the cadaver and placed it into the wheelbarrow. He negotiated the uneven surface of the bog until he reached the road and a truck that he borrowed from a local merchant to transport the body back to the barracks. "I have a feeling that our friend is a casualty of the unpleasantness caused by separatists."

"Why do you say that?" the other constable asked.

The Ancients buried their dead with ceremony, often laying out the deceased formally. From the position of this body, it looks like it was dumped into a hastily prepared grave."

"Do you have any idea who it could be?" the elder Farrell asked.

"If he is a local man, I can venture a guess."

Chapter Six

~

To most proper Bostonians, the building at the corner of State and Congress Streets was simply known as 'The Bank.' It was an imposing structure of cement, steel and granite that towered over its more traditional five and six story neighbors; it often drew attention from city visitors even if they didn't know that it was owned and operated by some of the more quiet Massachusetts money. One had to travel to New York to find a structure that could surpass it in size and find an institution, within that structure, that traded in a greater volume of capital. It was the home of the Boston Stock Exchange where old money was made with even older inherited money through investments in the railroads, mills, canals, real estate and utilities.

The building's other occupant was the First National Bank of Boston. Recognized as the city's chief repository, The Bank had for its clients, wealthy old line families, Jordan Marsh, Gilchrist's and Filene's department stores, the diamond merchants in the Jewelers Building, the eight Boston dailies, and the small curio shops located along the back alleys of the downtown shopping district.

And since its inception, this institution was the venue for the Downtown Club Association. The 'Club' was formed at the turn of the century by community leaders in Business, Law and Education to promote reform and efficiency in local government by supporting political candidates who possessed proper breeding, education and integrity. The founders of the Club were old guard Yankees, appalled at the new wave of rough and tumble Irish politicians who were more interested in creating jobs, assisting the common folk and helping newly arrived immigrants settle in a new land, while more importantly, creating lifetime careers for themselves. The progress-minded members of the Downtown Club promoted candidates who represented the city at large and not just a select few.

Cassius Tucker Appleton was the second member of his family to become president of The Bank and the first to be elected Chairman of the Board of the Downtown Club Association. After preparing his notes for the monthly meeting, he checked the time and looked outside, scanning the sidewalk for Commissioner Curtis. Secretaries and clerks from the financial district sat on benches or the grass outside of the Old State House and ate their lunches. Messengers on bicycles passed one another on Court Street, as they ran documents back and forth between the State Street law firms and the Superior Court.

About half way up the street, Appleton found the tardy Commissioner and watched with amusement as he waddled from side to side while navigating the uneven cobblestones, tails flying behind him in the gutter as he avoided the pedestrian rush to hasten his trip from Pemberton Square. When Curtis arrived at the intersection of Congress Street, Appleton gathered his papers and walked into the adjoining conference room to greet the other Board members.

He distributed the meeting's agenda and poured a glass of water which he placed on the table in front of the seat that he had designated for his old friend. "The Commissioner will be joining us momentarily," he said. "He has been kind enough to come and give us some sense of the city's incidence of crime for the first six months of the year. Although, I must say that even without a statistical breakdown, it seems pretty clear that the police have been very busy with the numerous strikes, parades and other demonstrations in addition to their regular duties."

Flushed and sweating profusely, Curtis arrived at the bank and was greeted by Appleton's secretary who escorted him to the conference room.

Appleton opened the meeting. "Gentlemen, I am going to forego our other agenda matters until later." He broke off his opening remarks when Curtis began to cough and allowed him additional time to compose himself. When Curtis indicated that he was ready to speak, the chairman said, "Commissioner, would you care to make some introductory remarks on the status of the Police Department? We can then follow with a few questions."

Curtis followed the script well by innocuously listing the various duties of a patrolman. He then mechanically recited the number of arrests to date, broken down by types of crime. Lastly, he gave his opinion of the public's perception of the "Red Scare." ("It is a much larger problem for New York than it is for Boston.") He concluded with the assessment that, while his patrolmen had had extended duty, the Department was following a typical summer routine.

"May I ask a question related to the terrorist activities, Commissioner?" one of the members said. "How is the patrolman who was almost blown to bits by that bomber in Roxbury? And wouldn't you characterize that as a serious problem?"

"The patrolman is fine and back to work," Curtis said. "The man was killed by his own explosives, a New York radical who came to Boston to assist a local cell of Bolsheviks. And thanks to the vigilant efforts of that patrolman and other officers from Station 10, the anarchist and his collaborators were stopped before they could cause any deaths or additional property damage."

"That's comforting to hear—"

"We communicate with the New York Police and the Federal Authorities regularly and share intelligence."

When there were no additional questions about the "Red Scare," Appleton said, "Thank you for that brief and concise report, Commissioner. Now, I know the members would like to ask a few questions about another matter. Mr. Henshaw, would you like to go first?"

"Thank you, Mr. Chairman. Commissioner, is it true that the police association—What is it called?"

"The Boston Social Club."

"Yes, I'm sorry, the Boston Social Club. Is it true that the Boston Social Club has made overtures about acquiring a charter from the American Federation of Labor?"

"Yes, I have been advised that a general membership meeting took place for the purposes of voting on whether they should seek a charter with the A.F. of L."

"I didn't think Gompers offered charters to the police," another member said.

"The A.F. of L. changed its policy in June, Harry," Appleton said. "Go on, Commissioner."

"I want to state that my relationship with the Boston Social Club has been professional and cordial. And there is continuing open dialogue between my office and the membership, mostly through a Grievance Committee, which I created for just that purpose."

"A commendable and progressive move, Commissioner," Appleton said.

Henshaw leaned forward and folded his hands on the table. "Can you tell us, if you know, what was the result of the police vote?"

"I do know. Other than a handful of votes in abstention, it was unanimous in favor of unionization."

"I see."

"Do we know the number of patrolmen who voted for the charter, Edwin?" Appleton said.

"The number that was reported to me was nine hundred and forty."

"That's a majority of the police force," Henshaw said. "That is unacceptable. We have enough problems in this city without the police unionizing."

"The officers of the Social Club are veteran patrolmen," Curtis said. "In the end, I believe that their leadership will control the more radical members."

"Let's hope so."

Curtis prepared to leave. "Before his sudden death, the former Commissioner set the Boston Police on a course to make it the top Department in the country. And in the process of attaining that goal, he made some difficult administrative decisions. I will continue to make those decisions that will put the Department at the top of its profession. Recently, I issued a General Order and had it posted in every station, referring to Mr. O'Meara's opposition to unionization and my support for his opposition."

"Thank you, Commissioner," Appleton said. "I want you to know that you have our full support. And, I would like to personally thank the Commissioner for taking time out of his busy schedule to address the committee."

"You should have told me, Tucker, that I was stepping into the lion's den," Curtis said as Appleton walked him to the door.

"Don't worry about Henshaw, Edwin. He's tweaked because he lost a substantial sum of money in munitions when the war ended. Then the molasses tank gave way and, all of a sudden, he not only doesn't have the demand for ammunition, but the lawyers are beginning to circle with wrongful death complaints."

"I didn't know he had ownership in that tank."

"He didn't, but he was heavily invested in U.S. Industrial Alcohol and he leased them the land on which the tank stood. You know the lawyers, always looking for the deep pockets."

"Well, he doesn't have a reason for concern. These Irish cops still have to feed those large families of theirs. They'll only push so far."

"Off the record, Edwin, the merchants are a nervous group on the best of days, and I don't have to tell you that they have real concerns with the present economy. So, anything, like the city's Police Department considering unionization, could cause panic. I mean, they would consider that bold move tantamount to anarchy." Appleton opened the lobby door. "Other cities have had terrible violence and disruption during this battle between Labor and Management. Just look at Lawrence." He shook Curtis' hand. "Keep me informed, would you?"

"I will, Tucker. As I said in there, the police are being led by mature and reasonable men."

"That's all well and good, but be prepared."

"I am."

BRADFORD HENSHAW WAITED for Appleton to come on the line.

"So, what do you think?" Appleton asked.

"I think we could have a serious problem on our hands, Tucker," Henshaw said. "I am not as confident as Curtis that he has the situation in hand. Think of the ramifications if those Irish cops become affiliated with a national Labor union. We could lose control of this city all together."

"And what about Peters? You said that you spoke with him."

"He wasn't even aware that a thousand cops met to seek a charter with the A.F. of L."

"Sounds like he is distracted."

"He's distracted alright, a long distance distraction."

"I've known Edwin a long time," Appleton said, "and have genuine affection for him, but—"

"But what?" Henshaw said.

"But I also know that he has an axe to grind when it comes to the Irish."

"So—"

"It may influence his thinking."

Henshaw sat down at his desk. "Do you know that fellow that I told you about?"

"The investigator?"

"Yes, his name is Brodsky. He comes highly recommended and can handle just about anything."

Appleton paused before he responded. "What are you proposing?"

"A preliminary background investigation, you know, some snooping around. Dig up some dirt that might give us leverage." Henshaw could hear Appleton release a long slow breath into the receiver.

"Us?" Appleton said.

"Curtis, the city, us." Henshaw opened his desk drawer and began to fish around in it. "We need to stay one step ahead, Tucker."

"Okay, under one condition. It has to be done quietly and discreetly and," Appleton paused for effect, "it absolutely cannot be traced backed to us."

"Okay. I'll need some money up front to pay for his services."

"Call me after you've spoken with him and let me know what the costs are."

Henshaw hung up the telephone and continued to search until he found the business card that he had placed in the drawer out of view. "No wonder this guy is successful," he said as he read the name on the card. "His parents must have hated him or purposely saddled him with a name that would make him one tough son of a bitch."

Brodsky was born to Russian immigrants in one of the run-down tenements on the lower East Side of New York. His mother had planned and prayed for a beautiful baby daughter, but instead she was rewarded with a boy who resembled an emaciated plucked chicken when he was laid across her abdomen. His chest pulsated with rapid little breaths like a dime store wind-up toy. She stared at the five pounds of transparent and wrinkled yellow skin with the oversized head and thick red curls that popped off his crown like coiled sofa springs, and wept. Her midwife in an attempt to console her asked her what she planned to name her baby boy. Brodsky's mother looked up at the woman and said, "Pearl."

At six years old, Pearlie Brodsky lived on the streets and was familiar with every bookie and crook within a five-block radius. He ran numbers, clipped fresh fruit and vegetables and sold them to the poor for a tenth of their value; he scavenged the docks for anything left down accidently or otherwise. By the time he was sixteen, he was known as the 'Procurer' because he had a knack for locating and acquiring anything that a client required.

At eighteen, he opened an investigative agency that catered to the business community. Using techniques that skirted local and federal laws, he built himself a reputation for stemming business losses. And when American workers organized and challenged every major public and private industry in America, he recruited an army of some of the most nefarious criminals and gangsters and became Management's answer to Labor's disruption. By the time he turned twenty-one, Pearlie was the most effective strikebreaker and head banger on the East Coast, using strong-arm techniques and savage beatings to convince the harried worker that he should return to his job.

"Mr. Brodsky, please."

"Speaking," the voice on the other end said.

"Mr. Brodsky, your business card was given to me by someone who is familiar with your work in the New York Transit strike a couple of years ago." Henshaw leaned back in his chair and put his feet up on the desk. "I need your services to conduct an investigation into the background of some of our police who are leading a campaign to unionize. Can you handle that?

"Yes, I can," was the reply.

"Good, good," Henshaw said. "I also want to check on some of our local Labor leaders who may support them. What's that? I know that you are busy, sir, but I represent a business consortium that could open up future opportunities for you in the New England area." He listened as Brodsky quoted his rates. "I am sure those costs can be justified when one considers the alternatives."

Eamon de Valera speaks at Fenway Park

Chapter Seven

~

Boston opens its arms to you. The birthplace of liberty welcomes you." Andrew Peters looked out from home plate and waited for the whistles and applause to subside. They stood now, all fifty thousand rising to a frenetic level, as the great man sat on the stage behind the Mayor. Peters had decided that this was a cause to embrace— families fragmented by famine and British indifference, emigration and a fight for independence. A Nation and a culture buried alive by colonization. And because the Mayor was the rarest of Boston politicians, a Yankee Democrat, there was that repayment to the Irish Ward Bosses and their constituents who ensured the electoral edge in the neighborhoods.

"This land," he said, "is a refuge for the disenfranchised, the disillusioned and the oppressed. Ever the guardian of freedom, America stands alongside you and demands justice for Ireland's sons and daughters." The crowd interrupted again with even more boisterous roars of approval, and behind and under the acclamation, a distant chant of "Sinn Fein" started in the grandstand, expanded and grew until it rolled over the larger polite applause.

Willie and Albert stood in the gangway just behind the stage and waited for the introductions to end. Dressed in suits and ties and wearing straw hats, they easily melded with the rest of the crowd, but for purposes of identification, wore their badges over their breast pockets while they screened V.I.P.'s.

Peters continued. "We have witnessed some great events here at Fenway Park. Last summer, our Red Sox became world champions. But speaking as mayor for the people of Boston," he looked back to face his guest, "a gathering in the cause of freedom will always be remembered as this stadium's greatest day." He extended his hand and said, "I welcome the courageous leader of a free Ireland, Eamon de Valera."

When he stood to walk to the podium, the bespectacled president of the Dáil Éireann appeared more bookish country schoolteacher than a larger-than-life revolutionary. Thin wire-framed glasses sat on his large and prodigious nose; his long neck exaggerated further by the tilting slope of his shoulders. He stood patiently at the podium and respectfully waited while the immigrant citizens of Boston broke into another thunderous applause before the clapping gave way to a rousing rendition of "A Nation Once Again."

He removed his speech from his jacket, unfolded it and ran his hand across the pages to flatten them out. The collective voice of the fifty thousand moved him and he stood there with his hands resting on the podium and his eyes closed. When they had finished singing, the crowd settled into their seats and except for a few isolated whistles, a hum settled over the baseball park. He looked up and scanned the crowd from the left field stands to the seats along the first base line and, for the first time, broke the thin line of his lips with a smile and said—

> *Gaels and friends of Gaels. They told us during the war that we had lost the sympathy of our own blood in America. I did not mince my words, but told them they lied. I knew that the people of the land that showed the world the way to true liberty, the land in which I had the honor to be born, was not going to misunderstand the struggles of a people fighting against a tyrant far greater than Germany.*

Dwyer and Coppenrath moved closer to the scaffolding that supported the stage and were confronted by two members of de Valera's executive security who advised them to keep their distance.

"We're Boston patrolmen, assigned to protect the Mayor, Mr. de Valera and the other dignitaries," Albert said.

The taller of the two men slid his jacket back and placed his hands on his hips. "Are you now. Well, Peter, we have only one person to guard. I guess that makes these two Yanks pretty tough blokes."

"Take it easy," Willie said as he stepped forward. "There's no reason to cause a stir."

The shorter bodyguard was older and built like a barrel. His hands, which hung on his lapels, looked like knotted rope, brown-stained hands built strong from hard physical labor. "Now there's an accent I've been waiting to hear since we landed in Boston," he said. "A Galway man. I've heard that the city is full of them."

"That's right. And I'm guessing that you have dug your share of turf," Willie said, nodding to Peter's hands. "It takes a Galway man to know a Galway man."

"Don't mind Fahey," the bodyguard said. "He's a little jumpy. You probably read in the newspapers that Mr. de Valera has not been welcomed in other American cities as he has in Boston and that an English bounty is on his head since his escape from Lincoln Jail."

Dwyer extended his hand. "Willie Dwyer from Ballinasloe."

"Peter Quinn from Kilconnel— I visited Ballinasloe from time to time, especially during the October horse fair."

Albert stepped up beside Dwyer and put out his hand. "Albert Coppenrath, Boston, born and raised. My parents were from Cork."

"And the best to you."

"How long are you fellas here for?" Willie asked.

"For as long as the president wants." Quinn stooped and picked up a small handful of gravel from a trench that bordered the gangway and served as a French drain. He shook his hand like he was rolling dice, rattling the gravel and sifting the sand, until all that remained were larger pieces of stone.

Albert laughed. "Or until de Valera has squeezed every last dollar out of the Boston Irish."

Fahey turned away from the stage. "That's easy for you to say, Yank."

Quinn rubbed his hands together, rolling the stones from the tips of his fingers to the heels of his palms. When he completed his ritual, he looked up at Willie from his stooped position with the stoic look of a man who had made up his mind with no consideration for the consequences. "That money will support our fight for independence from the Brits. With it, we win in my lifetime, without it, we win in my grandchildren's lifetimes." He stood and faced Coppenrath. "Unlike those who chose to leave, we live to fight until there are none left to fight."

"And that is why the Irish in this city and other American cities freely give their hard earned money to the cause," Willie said. "How about a drink after the rally?"

"What do you say, Aiden?" Quinn said.

"Sure, why not."

"Agreed." Willie pointed to left field. "If we get separated, meet us on Lansdowne Street on the other side of that wooden wall.

"You know, you look a little familiar, Dwyer." Quinn tilted his head to get a better view of Willie.

"I was thinking the same thing myself. Maybe, we met somewhere."

"Maybe—"

A roar went up from the crowd as the fiery Irish patriot called for American support in Ireland's fight—

> *"I do not fear for a moment that the people of America will make a shuttlecock of our cause, to pass it from party to party. I know they will not do this. I believe that Americans can differ as to politics about America, but they are united in the cause of liberty."*

As Dwyer and Coppenrath returned to their posts, Willie glanced back at the two bodyguards. "There's something familiar about it," he said.

"What did you say, Willie?" Albert said.

"Something familiar about him."

"Who?"

"Huh, oh nothing."

Willie had seen Quinn's ritual before. How did the old ditty go? Stooped down for a handful of earth, shaking and sifting 'til only stone—eliminate the living, and save the bones.

A HALF-FILLED BOTTLE of Jameson Whiskey sat in the middle of the table in the corner of the ancient little cellar bar that was tucked between the Kenmore Hotel and the Boston and Maine Railroad tracks. A Pickwick Ale poster hung on the back of the tavern door, the place where men had met over a drink since the eighteenth century to build a nation or plan a robbery. The owner served as his own bartender and waiter and he wiped the tables like it was a Friday night and the place was open for business. Every once in a while, he would look out the window to see if any of the passing legs stopped at the top of the stairs.

Coppenrath sat between Peter Quinn and Aiden Fahey while Dwyer sat in a chair pushed up on its rear legs with his back against the wall.

"How did you get away from guarding Mr. de Valera?" Willie said.

"He's dining with some of your politicians and we passed the detail on to other men," Quinn said.

"How many of you travel with him?" Albert asked.

"You ask a lot of bloody questions," Fahey said.

Quinn poured a small one and set the bottle back in the middle of the table. "We have thousands of brothers and a few women too who would give their right nut or right tit for the man. So, we never run out of guards." He rubbed his hands together as if warming them by a fire. "But, we're always looking for new volunteers."

"I didn't mean anything by it." Albert reached inside his jacket and removed a box of cigarettes, took one for himself and threw the rest on the table.

"You can still get the Jameson's, Willie, even with your Prohibition law?" Quinn asked.

"I never took the pledge." Dwyer put his hand in the air to catch the bartender's attention. "Can we have four draws of beer, Mr. McDonough? And the good stuff, if you please."

"Could you imagine if they tried to pass such a law at home, Aiden?"

"Yeah, it's the one thing that we can agree on with the British. We both like a taste now and then."

"It just runs counter to the nature of man," Albert said. "Cavemen had to have a snootful before they went out on a hunt."

Aiden Fahey's mouth turned up in a smirk. He stared at Albert and fingered his chin like he was in deep contemplation.

The bartender placed four mugs of beer in the center of the table. "Here you are, the real stuff."

"Thanks," Willie said. He pushed the mugs in front of the other three and lifted his in salute. "Slainte."

Quinn put his mug down, "The stadium, your Fenway Park, do they play any other athletic contests there besides baseball?"

"No, that's it," Willie said.

"Seems a waste, a beautiful place. A tiresome sport though, baseball. Don't think I could ever sit there that long with nothing happening."

"That's the one thing I miss about home, Ireland's contests," Willie said. "They seemed to mean more."

"Now that's the truth," Fahey said.

Quinn looked into the bowl of his pipe. "Albert here mentioning cavemen got me to thinking about something. You know how your mind wanders. Well, when he said 'cavemen,' I thought about archaeologists and how they are always digging up old bones to discover how ancient civilizations lived. Then, for some reason, I thought about Ballinasloe, probably because you and I were talking about the town, Willie." He rapped his pipe against the sole of his shoe and crushed the still burning tobacco into the plank floor. "Like burnt rope." He removed a knife and a plug of tobacco from his jacket, cut off a piece and jammed it into the pipe with his thumb. "Anyway, it got me to thinking about a story I heard recently about this Mclean family from Ballinasloe. Do you remember them, Willie?"

"No, I can't say that I do."

"I heard they were pretty prominent in the town—"

"Nah, been gone close to eleven years now, doesn't sound familiar."

Quinn tamped the tobacco in the pipe with the butt end of his knife.

"I seem to draw a blank for the old place." Willie rocked his chair off the wall and sat with his arms on the table.

"Well, the story goes that the McLeans had a son and years ago he went missing. At first, everyone thought that he had left the country to follow a girl—" Quinn lit the pipe and exhaled the smoke over his head. "You remember Tohers, don't ye, Willie?"

Dwyer nodded. "Right, Dunlo Street."

"Owned by two Catholic families—can't remember their names," Quinn said. "Not a lot of Catholic business in Ballinasloe back then."

Willie turned and faced the bar. "Mr. McDonough, can we have another round, please?"

"Sure thing," the bartender said.

"So what happened to this McLean?" Albert said.

"Do you need a hand, Mr. McDonough?" Willie said.

"No, I'm fine."

Quinn glanced at Dwyer. "Well, Tohers had a reputation of being a meeting place for separatists, diehards from the old I.R.B. on the verge of reorganizing—"

"Who?" Albert said.

"The Irish Republican Brotherhood."

"Okay?"

"Irish freedom fighters," Fahey said. "You know—Fenians, secret organization with sworn oaths. Here in America, they're called Clan na Gael."

"Oh—sure."

"Didn't hear much about the I.R.B. back then, but they were still around. Anyways, they started up a campaign against the R.I.C." Fahey saw another quizzical look on Coppenrath's face. "The Police—"

"Now I get it," Albert said.

Quinn said, "They planned a rising—like the fight at home today—hit and run to eliminate constables and their barracks."

"Sounds like the Reds, here."

"Not quite the same thing," Quinn said. "Anyway, the R.I.C. put an informant into Tohers, someone who could walk in and not be taken for a Peeler."

"McLean?"

"Right," Quinn said. "They raided the pub and they hit the jackpot, guns, ammunition, dynamite—the whole arsenal."

"Must have happened after I left for America," Willie said, "would've remembered that." He walked to the stand-up closet at the end of the bar.

"They shut the pub down and the original owners lost it to the bank," Quinn said.

Fahey poured out three small glasses of whiskey. "The barracks was popular with the town at the time, Albert, and the I.R.B. was not trusted. People were suspicious."

"That's right," Quinn said. "They had seen it all before and what did it get them."

The bartender placed four more full mugs on the table.

"So, how did the I.R.B. discover who squealed?" Albert said.

"Every group has its talker," Quinn said. "The Brotherhood waited and listened. I would imagine that the Constabulary thought that that was the end of it."

Fahey watched Willie come out of the water closet. "Everyone has his price."

"So they found out it was McLean," Albert said, "and he was killed?"

"Executed," Quinn said, "justice served."

Willie returned to the table and reached for the bottle of whiskey. He poured himself one and slumped back into his chair. "Peter, you said that you remembered something about this McLean fella. What would that be?"

"Excuse me, Gents." Albert stood and left the table.

"When your friend mentioned cavemen," Quinn said, "I thought about scientists digging up their bones. A few weeks ago, men were digging peat at the Poolboy Bog and they lifted up McLean."

"So, he was killed."

"Yeah."

"And how sure are they that it's him?"

"I guess the body was preserved pretty well by the bog and the investigators believe it's him."

"And how did you fellas find out?"

"It's important that the Chief stays in touch with what's going on back home.

"Ah."

Albert rejoined the other three at the table and finished his beer. "I have to call it a night, gentlemen. I have a wife and a baby daughter at home and I don't need to wake them up in the middle of the night. I'll have a hard enough time walking home as it is. Peter, you never told us how the cavemen reminded you of McLean."

Willie stood and placed his arm around his friend's shoulder. "I'll tell you the rest of the story on the way home. That is if we can find our way home."

"So, you never heard of McLean or his story, hey Willie?" Fahey asked. "I mean being from Ballinasloe and everything."

"No, the family aren't writers."

"Well, we need to be up early in the morning ourselves for the trip to Springfield," Quinn said. "What do you say, Aiden?"

"You're the boss," the younger man said. "Thanks for the company and the hospitality." Fahey and Coppenrath walked outside.

Willie walked round the table and shook Quinn's hand. "I'm glad that we were able to extend you a warm welcome. Do you have a place to stay?"

"The Chief takes good care of us."

"Ah, well then—"

They stepped out into the alley where the other two were waiting. "Good Luck," Willie said to the two guards. "Let's go, Albert. Let's see if we can find our way through the Fens."

Chapter Eight

~

Congress promises prompt action. It says so right here." The orderly held up the newspaper so his friend could read the headline.

"Prompt action, my eye. Let me see that." The second one pulled the newspaper away. "'No threats, Wilson warns Labor Unions.' What a lot of baloney. If you ask me, he's too busy trying to run the world. Maybe if he spent a little less time in Paris, we could get our own country in order."

"Here you go, boys. Two hot turkey dinners right off the stove." Catherine dropped the meals in front of the orderlies and walked to the back of the diner to an empty table. She placed one knee onto one of the benches, leaned forward so she could see out the window and searched Huntington Avenue for the night waitress. Her straight shift dress rode up the back of her leg to the top of her calf and one of the orderlies leaned out into the aisle to get a better look.

After a couple of minutes, she walked down the aisle to return to the counter. "Seen enough?" she asked the orderly as she passed his table.

"I'm just admiring the new fashion," he said. "You usually wear one of those cardboard uniforms. You don't see a dress like that around here."

"Well, Buster, maybe I don't plan on being around here forever."

"Oh yeah, where are you going?"

"None of *your* business," she said.

"Ah, go on. In twenty years, me and Bobby will still be sitting right here and you'll still be slinging the eggs."

Catherine pulled a cook's apron over her head and sat on a counter stool. "You and Bobby might still be sitting here, Mack, but I'll be living the high life."

The night waitress opened the diner door and entered. "Sorry I'm late, Honey. I had to walk because the streetcar never showed up after I waited for half an hour."

"That's all right, Valerie. Mr. Dwyer, the policeman should be here any moment," Catherine said while looking at the orderlies. "He probably had to walk also. Half the time those streetcars don't show up, and when they do, they're late."

"This is the third or fourth time you've seen him, isn't it?" Valerie said in a subdued tone the orderlies couldn't hear. "You must be serious about this feller."

"Third, if you count the time he walked me home from the christening party."

"Is he taking you anyplace special?"

"We're going dancing at the Totem Pole Ballroom." Catherine jiggled her foot nervously and glanced out the diner's window. "That's if he ever gets here."

Valerie tied on her apron. "By the way, is that creep still hanging around here at night? Any guy who talks to you, he looks at them like he would cut their throats."

"Who, Charlie? I can handle him."

"Yeah, well if that bum ever bothers you, just call Mr. Dwyer," Valerie said, nodding to the entrance.

Catherine slipped off the stool. "Yes, that's just what I'll do." She blocked the door as Willie opened it. "I suppose you're going to tell me that the streetcar didn't come." She hooked her arm into his and steered him back out the door. "Anything exciting happen today, Mr. Dwyer?"

"Nah, nothing you'd be interested in. Say, that's a nice dress you're wearing. I like the color too."

"You like it? A friend bought it for me. It's called virgin linen."

WILLIE OPENED his tie and the top button of his collar. He pushed back his hair and wiped the perspiration from his forehead. He and Catherine sat on the edge of the miniature bridge with their legs dangling over the brook. An orchestra played in the hall behind them and she swung her legs in time with the music.

"Are you having a swell time?" he said.

"Why shouldn't I? I'm free as the wind, drifting along with the music, with not a care in the world. And I'm in the company of one of Boston's most handsome patrolmen."

"Oh, I wouldn't go that far."

"And why not? Some girls might even say you're a regular guy."

"Yeah, but once they got to know me—"

Catherine looked at Dwyer's flushed face. She decided that it was a handsome face even if it had a broken nose with a left Pisa lean. He had a nice build and she guessed that he had labored with his hands at one time or exercised regularly. When he danced, his footsteps, while not adept to the new styles, were light and smooth. Perhaps, he had been a prize fighter, she thought. The flecks of premature gray in his black hair suggested an older man or one who had endured some inordinate tension. She found him attractively shy, with his intense face and dark green eyes and suspected he harbored many secrets. While his suit was not new, it was pressed and fit him well and, in the light from the dance-hall, the toes of his shoes shone brilliantly. Mr. Dwyer was meticulous and neat, she concluded, and someone who strived for order, setting things straight. And maybe a wee bit scrupulous.

He was a complex man, she could tell. This was someone who had lived a life, probably with its share of bumps and treacherous turns. Not unlike herself. And not like the sports with daddy's money who played their roles of pretend, but always had the safety net of the family to fall back on. No, he was like a large slab of raw granite, a collection of deposits with the hardness of diamond and a razor sharp edge. He was solid alright, but with an underlying edginess that suggested his patience could suddenly wear thin. Sure, Boston had its share of men like him, but many succumbed to the reality of their existence when they realized that what they were is what they were. But William Dwyer, she sensed a kind of kinship with him.

"What are you staring at?" he said.

"Why, you silly."

"There's not much to see."

"Sure there is. Lots of girls would like to have you on their arm."

"You're embarrassing me now. You know, you're not so bad yourself, but—"

"But what?"

"I get the feeling that you'll never be happy, Catherine."

"Why's that?"

"Like a lot of women, you want all the glitter. And I know that I could never give it to you. Not on fourteen hundred a year."

"Getting a little ahead of yourself, aren't you? Do you think I'm that simple to figure out?"

"No, no—"

"Then let's take it slow."

Her words came easy without pretension, with brutal honesty. Excitement lurked in her voice, expressions were rides down a steep hill. She made him believe that each day, each minute existed for her inquisitive mind, something to be experienced, something to be learned. She challenged life, and Willie sensed her stirring deep within him.

"But that doesn't mean we can't be friends," she said.

"Ah, that's it now, just friends."

"Don't be sore."

"Sore? There are a hundred reasons why I'm not sore, Catherine."

"Good, then let's have a grand old time."

"Sure, we can do that. Tell me something." He looked up to find her eyes watching him. "What's your story?"

"My story? It's the same old one. Family shipped me over here at fourteen, one less mouth to feed, one less daughter to worry about. And here I am in this enormous country, pretty much on my own."

"So what happened?"

"I got picked up for being a truant and a vagrant and the judge gave me the choice, girls' reformatory or the Mary Magdalene Home." She checked him for his reaction. When she didn't see one, she continued. "So, I made the first right decision in my life. I chose the home."

"And the nuns treated you alright?"

"Yeah." She pulled up the hem of her dress and removed a cigarette from her rolled down hose. "Got a light?"

"Don't smoke."

"I should give them up too." She replaced the cigarette back into her hose. "The nuns get a bad rap sometimes, but they were good for me. Put order into my life, made me stand on my own two feet." She folded her hands into her lap and looked up at the night. "But you've got to swear that you'll never tell anybody about that."

"If that's what you want."

"Yeah, that's what I want. Mary Magdalene has the reputation of being a home for wayward women and once people know you're from there, well, they either ignore you like you don't exist or they try and take advantage."

"I won't say anything. Besides, it's none of their business."

"You're alright, Mr. William Dwyer. Say, why did you join the police force?"

He flinched his shoulders. "Steady job, and I like working with people. Felt like I was doing something for someone, if you know what I mean."

"Sure, I do. I work the diner and O'Neil's for the same reason. I mean I like the money." She glanced up at his eyes. "But a lot of interesting people pass through that diner, doctors, nurses, newspaper reporters—"

"And O'Neil's?"

"Same reason. Although at the tavern, you can sit at the bar with an insurance man on your right, a burglar on the left and two Fenians huddled in a booth behind you. I know the Church would rather I be a good Bridget and slave for some wealthy family on Beacon Hill as a maid and learn good manners. But I'd rather be in the mix with my sleeves rolled up, better than walking around with one of those starched uniforms and wiping some rich kid's snotty nose."

Willie warmed to her feisty attitude and looked at her with a Cheshire cat grin.

"What are you grinning about?" she asked.

"You mean you wouldn't want to be a Suffragette?"

"Are you daft, man? Not on your life, those snooty Protestants and their Temperance Movement."

"Did you get that chip on your shoulder in the old country? What county?"

"Wexford, from a little hamlet named Newtownbarry," she said with a trace of agitation. "What is this, the third degree, copper? Okay, no more questions."

"Agreed." Rain began to fall and they watched the first few drops plunge into the little stream. Willie nodded towards the dance hall. "Let's go in. You can teach me some new steps."

THE SHOWERS had stopped for the moment and Huntington Avenue glistened. Wrapped into each other, Willie and Catherine stumbled up the five wooden stairs to the landing with Catherine hanging on like an inexperienced ice skater. A nearly empty streetcar rattled past them. "Sshhh— Come on," she whispered as she pulled on Willie's arm and tried the outside door to the boarding house. "I hope I'm not locked out." She pushed on it and fell across the threshold. "Take off your shoes," she giggled and tripped when she tried to remove one of her own. "Oops, I think I've had a little too much to drink."

Willie caught her before she fell. He held her in the crook of his arm and placed his finger over her lips. "Hush yourself. You're going to wake everyone in the building." He lifted her onto his shoulders like he was carrying a sack of coal and tiptoed through the foyer and gingerly navigated the stairs to the second floor landing. "Where is your key?"

"You'll have to put me down," she said. "I'll never be able to get it from here."

Willie stood her up against the wall and she bent over like a rag doll and began to fumble with the bottom of her dress, picking at the hem unsuccessfully without being able to control it with her fingers. "Oh, the blood is rushing to my head." Catherine fell sideways and crumbled into the wall, erupting into a fit of full blown laughter.

"Sshhh, I'll have to remember next time to shut you off earlier." He placed his hand over her mouth. "You're going to wake the dead."

The door in the middle of the landing opened and an old woman's face pressed out of the shadows. She looked at the two of them in disgust and pouted her lips, slipped back into her apartment and slammed the door.

"Where is it?" Willie said.

"I think I'm going to be ill." Catherine scratched at her leg and attempted to lift her dress. "It's in here." She poked her thigh with her finger.

"Jaysus, Catherine." He checked the closed doors on the landing and leaned over the railing to look up to the third floor. The only noise that he could hear was someone coughing in a first floor room. "Okay." He leaned her against the wall and lifted her dress to mid-thigh. The key was rolled into her silk stocking just above her knee. He backed out the stocking, took the key and opened the door.

"Up you go," he said. He cradled her with his arms and carried her into the room and laid her on the bed. "Are you going to be okay?"

Catherine lay there motionless, quiet and still. In her unconscious state, her face had fallen into itself, her vivacious youth disappearing into the cavities between her bones. He walked to the bed, bent over and kissed her lips. "Good night, Gray Angel, take care."

Willie glanced around the room and saw another key for the door in a dish on her bureau. The scalloped edges of the glass dish were thick and intricately cut with minute details and shaped into flower petals. Willie weighed the dish in his hand and turned it over. The gold seal on the bottom read—Designed by the Federal Glass Co. especially for the Cliff Walk Hotel, Newport, R.I. He returned it to the bureau, locked the door and walked out to the first light of day.

THE LETTER with the forwarding address could have been a land mine, planted on the floor just inside the door to his room. Willie recognized the stamp immediately and felt the anxious anticipation of a person who associates correspondence with bad news. "What happened?" he said as if he was standing again in the tiny kitchen of the old farmhouse. His family wasn't in the habit of writing often and he knew that a letter delivered news from home like a sledgehammer drives a stake; something of importance had taken place.

Willie recognized his younger brother's penmanship on the envelope.

He unfolded the letter and began to read. Mim detailed their mother's illness and untimely death. He sat on the edge of his bed, empty and ten-years distant, unable to express emotion and tried, without success, to conjure up an image of the woman who owned his soul. If only he had heard her voice, something, anything to breathe life into the shapeless cloud of memory that drifted behind his eyes. He tried to remember the mother who bore him and nine other children, who tirelessly cared for them and the high inhuman scream of her keening when another of her babies succumbed to cold damp Ireland, the blue lifeless child buried against her bosom as she bargained her soul for one of God's miracles.

Grief and sadness consumed him more than if he had been at home, finally recognizing that his American years were a life sentence. He rested his elbows on his knees and looked around the modest, but neat room. "Mam," he said, "you made order out of chaos." Willie lay back on the bed and closed his eyes.

He pictured himself standing, once again, in the three-room cottage that his mother ran with business-like efficiency. The simple and gentle woman's back was turned to him and he watched her sweep out the corners of the room. And he realized that this was his lasting image of her, standing with her back to him on the docks at Queenstown, purchasing a one-way ticket to America. And when the ship's horn blew, she turned, but never looked up at him and led him by the arm to the gangway. "No turning back," she said. "You have to do what you have to do."

He boarded the ship with a nauseous turning in his stomach, heard the engine room bells and felt the boat rock as it moved away from the shore. No parting wake the night before could he treasure in his memory, his departure was quiet and without fanfare, like he had evaporated with the morning dew or fallen into an uncovered well. He watched her standing there on the dock, small and tired, the horn, blowing a melancholy warning, the boat shaking itself free. From the railing at the waterline deck, he waited for his mother to return his wave. But she just stared.

The *Arabic* pulled away and he vaulted the rope barrier and raced to the second deck. The steamer turned its bow to the Atlantic, cutting through the channel's water, roughing the glassy surface. Just before it cleared the quay, he found her again, standing alongside the station house, one open palm held up just above her shoulder, her face taut and resolute, a mourning face. He jumped onto the rail so she could see him, but when he looked back to shore, she was gone.

Chapter Nine

~

The door rattled each time the knuckles struck it. Willie woke to the noise with a head the size of Worcester after an evening of dancing, too much alcohol and a night of tossing and turning in fretful sleep. His mouth tasted like it was filled with sand and his head felt like it had been split down the middle with an axe. The odor of stale cigarette smoke hung in the room.

"Mr. Dwyer?" Mrs. Gerhard said outside his door. "Sorry to bother you, but you have a telephone call in the parlor and, being that it is two o'clock in the afternoon, I thought you might want to take it. Mr. Dwyer?"

Willie opened the door a couple of inches to his landlady. "Yes?"

"Oh, I'm sorry Mr. Dwyer, I didn't realize that you were still sleeping. Wasn't even sure that you hadn't gone out."

"That's okay, Mrs.—"

"I have a telephone call for you in the parlor. It's a young woman. I thought you might want to take it."

"Please tell her I'll be right there."

Dwyer splashed handfuls of water into his face and hurried downstairs to the parlor. "Hello."

"I just wanted to make sure that you made it to your room in one piece," Catherine said.

"You sound pretty chipper compared to the last time I saw you."

"I'm a quick healer. You have to be in this town."

"I don't have to report to the station until six, so I've got a couple of hours to take that walk in the Fens we talked about last night."

"Oh, I'd love to, but I have something else planned."

"Oh sure."

"I've got to, ah, work at the diner. Maybe, another time."

"Okay, if I get the Circle's patrol, I'll stop by."

"I'll be gone, silly. I'm on the early shift today."

"Oh, I see, playing hard to get?"

"No, of course not. Well, I just called to say hello," Catherine said. "Gotta run."

"Sure, thanks for calling."

"Willie?"

"Yeah."

"I had a nice time."

"That's swell, me too."

Willie opened the door to his room and saw his brother's letter, sitting open on the bureau. He sat on the bed and reread it, hoping that the message might have changed during the night. When he reached the end, he realized that it continued on the backside in a postscript—*You may have heard that the constables found Bernie McLean. At any rate, Graves O'Brien has been by, asking questions. Love, Mim.*

SERGEANT MCGUINESS completed the roll call for the evening shift, leaned against the table that was behind him and glanced around the room. "I have never taken a stand on the question whether you, patrolmen, should unionize, at least publically. I believe that each of us must do what our conscience tells us to do. And I still feel that the decision for each of us is to be made without harassment or retribution. Ultimately we must be guided by our own moral compass."

The Desk Officer poked his head in the door. "Sergeant, there is a report of an automobile accident in Brigham Circle, several cars and they're blocking the streets."

"It never fails," McGuiness said. "Dwyer, Coppenrath, that's your patrol. I'm not one for grand speeches anyway. I would just ask that all of you make your decisions wisely when voting for a charter with the A.F. of L. because it appears from the Commissioner's response that you may be going down a road of no return."

Willie and Albert remained in formation, looking at McGuiness for direction.

"Go ahead," he said to them. "Just read the Commissioner's changes to Rule Thirty-five. They're posted on the bulletin board."

"Did you read them?" Albert asked Willie as they turned out of the yard. "Crank the siren."

"No. What do they say?"

"Basically, it says that we can't join any organization that would fight to get us a living wage."

Willie yelled over the siren. "What does it really say?"

"I forget exactly," Albert yelled back. "But it keeps us from joining any outside organization—other than the military. Curtis feels that if we join up with the A.F. of L., we will no longer enforce the laws objectively."

"As if that never happened."

"The Dry Law—" Albert drove around a truck that was double-parked near the Mission Church. "—the boys in South Boston aren't going to be told they can't have a stiff drink once in a while."

"Ah, I think it's just a conspiracy to put the Germans out of business, anyways," Willie said.

"You may have something there."

Willie pointed to three damaged automobiles that blocked part of Huntington Avenue and the streetcar tracks. Stopped traffic plugged up all the streets entering Brigham Circle, and two streetcars filled with commuters sat idling in the afternoon heat.

They pulled up to the damaged vehicles, checked the occupants for injuries and pushed two of the cars to the side of the street with the cruiser. Fifteen minutes later the intersection was open and the traffic was moving again.

Albert turned into the intersection where Dwyer was directing traffic. "Come on, I'll buy you a cup of coffee."

Willie leaned on the vehicle and looked through the passenger's window toward the Switch. "I better stay here for a while until things clear themselves out."

"Is she there?" Albert said.

"What? No." He turned his attention back to Coppenrath. "I mean I don't see her."

"Boy, someone's got it bad. What's her name again?"

"Catherine. I never said that—"

"Right, Catherine."

Willie stepped away from the driver's door window and started to walk away. "She's a lot of fun, but right now I'm not rich enough for her tastes. But you never know, if we ever get our raise."

"Our raise? That's money in the bank. You can pick out a ring if that's what you really want to do, because by hook or by crook—"

"Why are you so confident?" The cruiser began to creep forward and Dwyer walked along with it.

"I've heard some things, you know. It's a question of getting certain powerful people behind us. And from what I've heard, all the big unions and the important politicians up at the State House are supporting us."

"And what else did your father-in-law tell you?"

"Jim? Oh, I've got other sources than Jim Rankin. Besides, I haven't seen much of him lately. He's been going back and forth to Rhode Island, attending meetings about getting the economy going again." Albert stopped the car from rolling. "If we play our cards right, Curtis will have so much pressure on him that he'll have no choice but to accept the fact that his police are union boys now." He put his hand to his ear. "What's that? Can that be the sound of our money riding into town?"

"Who have you been hearing that from? Guys like Quigley?"

"Not just Quigley, the older patrolmen have been around and they believe that now's the time."

"And you?"

Coppenrath tapped the bill of his helmet and saluted Dwyer with two fingers. "You can bet on it. I'll meet you at the Switch at seven o'clock for supper." He started to roll forward again, but then he stopped. "You are going to Fay Hall tomorrow night to vote for the Union charter, aren't you?"

"Yeah, I'll be there."

"Good, I'll meet you at your rooming house and we can take the elevated together." Coppenrath turned the automobile up Tremont Street and entered the flow of traffic.

WITH THE EXCEPTION of a brushstroke of yellowish pink that tinted the waters of the Charles, the sky behind the cold granite police headquarters and the Suffolk Superior Court beside it remained a melancholy slate gray.

"Miss Harris, what is today's date?"

"The fourteenth of August, sir." She left her desk and walked to the Commissioner's office and stood at his doorway.

"Thank you. I have the draft ready for you. Have you advised the printing department that I want the notices for discharge and suspension tonight?"

"Yes, sir. They will call when they are ready."

"Fine."

"Sir, with all respect—"

"We are talking about insubordination, Miss Harris," he said without lifting his head to her. He rolled his pen back and forth between the tips of his fingers while he read the language of the notice again. When he finished, he stood and faced the window. "For God's sake, John McInnes is an exemplary military man and the patrolmen respect him, and Michael Lynch, a gentleman." He blew air from his mouth. "But, be what it may." He turned and faced his secretary and handed the draft to her. "Let me see it before you bring it to the printers."

"Yes, Commissioner."

"Tell them we need two thousand copies."

"Yes, sir."

"Hopefully, Miss Harris, I'm not going to need them."

"Hopefully."

"COME ON, DWYER. Let's get something to eat. I'm starved."

"I can't remember a time when you weren't starving. For a runt, Albert, you can put away more food than a gorilla."

"It's a quarter past ten for Criss' sakes. Maybe, if I ate when I was supposed to, my appetite would be like everyone else's."

Willie jumped up onto the running board and rode from his foot patrol on Huntington Avenue to the box across the street from the Switch. "I'll signal in. Why don't you order me one of their specials?"

“What if it’s something you don’t like?”

“Are you kidding? At this time of night, it’s always something I like.”

Dwyer made his call and opened the door to the diner as Valerie came out of the kitchen with two meals. “Here you go, boys, two blue plate specials. The cook says, ‘On the house.’ Although, Patrolman Dwyer, I may have to charge you for the extra time you’ve been hanging around here bothering my waitress.”

“Aw, I haven’t been that bad, have I?”

“He’s hooked,” Albert said, “and he doesn’t even know it.”

Willie looked away and glanced around the diner.

Valerie poured him a cup of coffee. “She worked early, changed shifts—”

“I knew that,” Dwyer said.

The waitress disappeared into the back and returned with a pan of hot soapy water and a rag. “I’m going to clean this place up before the next wave hits. Take your time, don’t let me rush you.”

Albert slid out from the seat. “Do you mind if I ring up the wife at home.”

“Go ahead, knock yourself out,” she said and then took Albert’s seat at the table. “How are things, Willie?”

“That sounds like a loaded question.”

“Did you and Catherine have fun last night?”

“Yeah, why? Say, is there something I should know?” He took two sugar cubes from the bowl and dropped them into his cup.

“You ask that like you expect me to know the answer.”

“Aw, forget it. It’s not important.”

“You’re a nice guy, Willie. A girl would be lucky to catch a guy like you.”

“Yeah, sure.”

“No, I mean it. If I was a few years younger—”

“What are you getting at, Valerie?” He stirred his coffee methodically.

She looked over Dwyer’s shoulder to where Coppenrath was standing. “Look, don’t get sore, okay. But she told me to tell you that if I saw you tonight she’s going to be tied up for a while.”

“Other plans, heh?” Willie said. “You mean she’s seeing someone else.”

"I don't know." Valerie looked down at her hands.

"She must really be busy, so busy that she couldn't tell me herself."

"I'm sorry."

"Don't worry about it. I knew from the beginning that she had big plans. Ah, maybe I was getting ahead of myself. Who's she seeing?" Willie tapped his spoon on the lip of the cup. "Nah, forget it. That's none of my business."

"I don't know. She's been quiet about whatever she's doing. Sometimes, she gets going, you know. She lives hard, full steam ahead. Been that way since I've known her." She watched Albert hang up the phone. "Only tells me what she wants me to know."

"Do you think she needs money?"

"I usually know when she's short on cash; she'll ask for more hours. Hope it doesn't have anything to do with Charlie Bradley?"

"What would she have to do with Bradley?"

"They had something going on at one time before she showed up here, something to do with O'Neil's."

"I remember seeing him in here the night I met her."

Valerie started to slide out of the seat as Albert approached the table. "He didn't look as bad as he does now. All I know is that the guy makes her nervous and gives me the creeps." She stood up and picked up the pan of water. "There you go, Officer Coppenrath, all warmed up for you."

"Thanks, toots." Albert slid into the booth and waited until she walked to the other end of the diner. "Who was she talking about? "

"Huh, nobody. Just some guy who comes in once in a while and is a nuisance. She gets a little spooked when she works late and there is no one in here."

After they left the diner, the two patrolmen stood by the police car in the deserted street.

"You didn't eat much," Albert said.

"Wasn't hungry after all," Willie said.

"Well, while it's quiet, I'm going into the station to file a report. Do you want a lift?"

"Thanks, no. I'm going to take a stroll in the opposite direction and check Huntington Avenue to the town line," Willie said. "I haven't been down there yet."

"Suit yourself." Albert cranked the patrol car, climbed in and drove up Tremont Street.

Willie walked the abandoned avenue of closed businesses and dark apartment houses. He appreciated these quiet times, free from the noise and the posturing of daylight, and relished the reverence of the nocturnal emptiness, when the rest of the world slept in a slow-motion turn and black mystical silence. He was sensitive to the sights and sounds that lost their presence during the day–a shaft of wind rattling the leaves in the trees; the dripping of water from the edge of a roof; or a door that closed a block away. He moved under a streetlamp, made an entry in his diary and then walked the block to Catherine's boarding house. The building, like all the other buildings on the street, sat quiet and undisturbed. The drapes in her window hung open and the room behind them was dark and still.

It was at these times in the vacuum of the night when he heard the gunshot again and felt the clap in his ears, saw the body collapse like a sack of grain. Constable O'Brien must know, he thought, that the rumors and the whispers of the past ten years are true. Bernie McLean, the tattler, has risen to tell his story again.

He walked another block and rattled the doorknob to a variety store and was jolted by obscenities and the scramble of bodies that violated the night's spiritual silence. High pitched screams and wails echoed in the street. He heard the desperate voices of a woman and a child and saw several people struggling at the entrance to a tenement. One man had his back to the street, his arms extended out from his sides and jammed against the doorframe. He released one arm at a time to swipe at the others with his hand.

The fight tumbled back and forth in the foyer as the door swung open and closed while one combatant tried to push it open and the other tried to shut it. Willie heard his own voice echo through the neighborhood when he ordered them to stop. "Bradley," he shouted.

He recognized Charlie as the man in the doorway. He ran to the building and saw that the other people were his younger brothers, and he guessed that the small frail woman in the nightdress with the iron gray hair was his mother. Frank wrestled with his older brother and tried to drive him through the doorway while the diminutive woman pried at Charlie's fingers to free them from the jamb.

She screamed at her oldest son with desperation. "You're not staying here tonight," she said. "Not in that condition, you're not."

"I'm not going anywhere, assholes," he said. "Get out of my way so I can go to bed."

"You're leaving, Charlie." Frank lifted him off his feet, but his older brother grabbed the doorframe in a different position and held on.

Out of the violence of the struggle, Willie heard the sobs of ten-year old Johnny, pleading with his older brothers to quit fighting. Dwyer removed his billy and brought it down on Bradley's arm, immediately releasing it from the doorframe. He wrapped Charlie into a headlock, dragged him down the stairs and slapped him up against the building, brought the club down across his back and dropped him in a lump on the sidewalk, Charlie's head hanging like it was attached to his body by a string. Bradley began to cough in a fit of tubercular rattling. Blood ran out of his nose. He gagged, cleared his throat and spit on Dwyer's shoes. Willie raised the billy.

"Go on, pig, finish it," Bradley screamed.

"Shut up."

"Put me out of my misery, you fucking bastard."

"Stop," his mother pleaded. "You'll kill him." She took hold of Dwyer's sleeve with both hands. "Please, I just want him out of the house. We need one night without fighting, without his ranting and raving and crazy threats. Just one night of peaceful sleep. Please." She turned to her younger sons. "Frank, take Johnny into the house."

Dwyer saw the two younger brothers in the doorway, Johnny sniffling and Frank looking down at his older brother, sitting on the sidewalk like a pile of discarded bones. He turned to their mother and patted her hands. "I'll take him to Fenwood Road. They'll dry him out. Come on, Bradley, get up. What have you been drinking?"

"He's all right when he just takes the beer," his mother said, "but when he gets on the wild stuff, he's a changed person." She went to her son, knelt down next to him and wiped his nose with a tissue.

Willie lifted Bradley under his arms and stood him on his feet. Charlie stumbled and Dwyer caught him before he could fall. He stared at his mother defiantly, his head jerking in convulsive little movements. "Thanks, Ma. Turn me into the cops?"

"I'll come and visit you," she said.

"Don't bother."

Dwyer put an arm around his waist, but Bradley stumbled away. "I can walk, copper—"

"We all need a little help, Bradley."

The two men struggled for the two blocks to the mental health clinic, moving in a three-legged way and repelling off each other every few steps. Bradley's legs gave way as they approached the entrance and he collapsed on the lawn.

"We're almost there," Willie said. "Come on, stand up. They'll be able to help you."

"Maybe I don't want to be helped." Charlie sat by the edge of the brick walk. "Got all the answers— He coughed up strings of blood and spit onto the grass. "Phenobarbital or paraldehyde, what's on the menu tonight?" He stuck out his tongue and grimaced. "Nightmares, straps? I'd rather be dead."

Willie knelt down next to him. "If you get past the nightmares—"

Charlie twisted his head and turned his face long. He grinned. "I know about your little girlfriend. Seen you standing outside her door."

"Don't know what you're talking about, Bradley. Come on—"

"Saint Catherine? Seen you at her building, Mr. Policeman—"

Willie reached over and pulled Bradley close to him. "You bother her anymore, you'll answer to me." He let go and Charlie fell back onto the grass.

"Don't worry—" he giggled. "We're old friends from O'Neil's." He put his hand on Dwyer's trouser leg and patted it, laughed in spasms, like an engine trying to start. "She's doing just fine—"

"Enough of your gibberish." Willie pulled him up. "Come on, let's go. Before I lose my patience again."

"Watch her—"

"Come on, Bradley."

Charlie began to sob.

"Come on—"

Bradley stopped, turned his head up and looked at Willie with the eyes of the dead. "Saint Catherine—"

Willie lifted him up and carried him in the front door.

Chapter Ten

~

Dublin Ireland

Constable Graves O'Brien leaned back in the seat and closed his eyes. He was reasonably sure that Bernie McLean, or rather the remains of Bernie McLean, lay in the next car, wrapped in burlap and bagged like first class delivery post. They were an odd couple, he concluded, intrinsically paired by events that took place ten years earlier and now their destinies took them to Trinity College where scientists would pore over the latest discovery out of the bogs of West Ireland—a dangerous place for unsuspecting travelers who ventured too far across the living earth and disappeared into one of its pools; a sleeping place for Celtic Iron Age mothers who died in childbirth; or a Limbo place for young virgins and members of powerful families safe from the beast who roamed the netherworld.

And some, O'Brien knew, were imprisoned in the spongy sarcophagus after being murdered and buried there. But a few of them, like Bernie McLean, would rise unexpectedly after a brief stay in purgatory when an unsuspecting farmer dug them up while harvesting peat to burn in his stove.

The constable stepped down from the train at Kingsbridge Station and secured a carriage to bring the body to the entrance. Mary McKeigue met him there with a car and drove him the short distance to the college.

"So, Inspector, what makes you think that our friend back there is this McLean fella?" McKeigue said.

"Well, Doctor. It is Doctor, isn't it?"

"Yes, but why don't you call me Mary."

"Right, Mary. I have had cases over the years when I not only didn't know the identity of a bog body, but didn't even know whether the victim was from our era or from the time of the Roman Empire."

"So, why are you so sure that you know the identity of this man?"

"Because I have the best kind of supporting evidence."

McKeigue drove through the college gate and stopped outside the building that housed the University's laboratory. "I have worked with enough of you investigators, to know that when you say you have the best kind of evidence you mean that you have a witness or an informant. Which is it?"

"Both," O'Brien said. "Since the body was found, I have had the extreme good fortune of having a suspect provide information about an unsolved murder."

"And this person is reliable?"

He shrugged his shoulders. "Is any informant reliable, Doctor, I mean Mary?"

"I would assume that their reliability is based on your capacity to corroborate their information."

"Exactly, and that is why your examination is important."

She unlocked the laboratory door and entered a room with a large skylight. "Bring Mr. McLean in here."

"In this case," O'Brien said, "the informant was a member of a group, which I believe was responsible for this man's death."

Dr. McKeigue cut the outside packaging and removed the dry ice that was placed with it to keep the body in its original state. She then removed the burlap. "Did you take photographs of the place where you found the body?"

"Yes, the next day." Graves opened an envelope and removed several black & white pictures and arranged them on the table. "It's freezing in here."

"Now—" She pulled on rubber gloves and walked around the table to view the specimen from all sides. "These bodies remain preserved because of the bog's highly acidic environment, a lack of oxygen, and the cool temperatures of the air and water. We believe that most of them were likely placed in the bog during the winter or early spring when the water temperature is less than 4°C, which allows the acids to saturate the tissues before decay and that initiates a sort of embalming process that takes place as the peat grows around the cadaver." She looked through a magnifying glass at the head. "This unusual environment is also responsible for tanning the skin. By maintaining the cool temperatures during examination, we can reduce the chances of decomposition."

"Is that why you instructed me to immediately pack the body in dry ice?"

"Correct." The pathologist opened a cabinet and retrieved a camera. She took several photographs of the body from different viewpoints, including a close-up shot of his head. "Because the victim was in the bog a relatively short time, his condition is remarkable." She made several entries into her notebook and placed it on the end of the examining table. Then she handed the investigator a pair of rubber gloves. "I'll need your assistance in removing the clothes." She lifted the victim's coat on the left side. "Do you have any idea what happened here?"

"I see that," O'Brien said. "I believe that was caused when the farmer's son sliced into the peat with his shovel."

Graves and the doctor removed the clothing and placed it aside. McKeigue rinsed the body with water and began a close examination, beginning at the head. "Sometimes the sheer weight of the bog can crush bones and confuse the investigators as to the cause of certain injuries. But this body is in good condition. Show me the picture of the place where the victim was exhumed."

O'Brien handed two of the photographs to the doctor.

"I'm glad that you took this longer view of the site because it shows the approximate depth where the body lay."

"We were lucky on that one because the track way is still intact and accessible. It hasn't sunk below the surface."

The doctor pushed back the hair off the cadaver's forehead. "Hmm, an entry hole about an inch below the hairline. I guess you could say that is a clue." She opened the cadaver's mouth. "Oh, my. The tongue is gone."

"Well, it wasn't missing the first couple of years after the victim's disappearance," Graves said.

"What do you mean, constable?" She reached into the cadaver's mouth with a pair of tweezers and picked out a piece of lint.

"Shortly after ole' Bernie disappeared, a tongue was found nailed to the front door of Tohers, a pub in Ballinasloe. We think that it was removed with a sharp knife or a razor because the end where it was attached to his throat had a clean even edge."

"Obviously, there's a message in that act of brutality."

"There is. Don't talk to the Peelers. This man was labeled a tattler because he cooperated with the constabulary, specifically me. And why this particular investigation has gnawed at me for all of these years. The I.R.B. hadn't obtained a claw-hold in the community yet—

"Wait, inspector. What year was this?"

"1909."

"I thought the Brotherhood was dormant at that time."

"Right. Constitutional nationalism held the day, but there always remained cells of hard line Republicans who would settle for nothing less than a fully independent Ireland, established by force, if necessary. We were able to stay one step ahead of these separatists with our informants. Without them, we would be out of business."

"Hmm—" The doctor turned the cadaver's head and examined the ears.

"It can be a messy business," he said. "So I try to take care of my informants."

"What happened to the tongue?"

"It was taken down by the family and brought to the barracks where it was kept in our evidence room, ah, actually more like a storage room."

"Do you still have it?"

O'Brien cleared his throat. "It's a long story. Suffice to say, it dried up and became like leather." The inspector averted McKeigue's eyes. "And then, one of the boys thought it would make a good chip and he entered the town's annual contest with it. And well, that was that."

"And now it's gone?"

"Yes, Ma'am. Years passed and no one ever heard anything about McLean."

"Believe it or not, constable, I've heard those kinds of stories before when it comes to the protection of physical evidence." McKeigue stopped and made additional notes in her book. "Tell me what you know about McLean's death."

O'Brien opened his case book. "He was reported missing on 9 March 1909. This was a few months after he had provided valuable information to me about the goings on at a pub in the town."

"Tohers?"

"Right. We believed, at the time, that a resurgent I.R.B. was using the pub to plan an attack on a barracks in a neighboring town. Two families, in particular, were active in that area of Galway, the Cahills and the Dwyers, co-owners of Tohers." Graves wrote a note to himself. "It's amusing to see some of yesterday's young guerillas, now older and wiser, campaigning for passive resistance and social justice, supporting land acquisition and the Labor movement."

"Yes, but they're often replaced by another generation of younger more violent radicals. What else makes you reasonably sure that this is Bernie McLean?"

"After your examination, I will let the family have a look. But he resembles Bernie, a good-looking lad with trimmed hair and no beard or mustache. Smooth hands and fingernails always cut back, similar to our friend here." Graves picked up the remnants of the cadaver's clothing. "And this man is wearing a business suit, similar to what I recorded in my notes ten years ago. This is not the clothing of a farmer, but a merchant, or I should say a banker. He worked as an apprentice for his father."

Dr. McKeigue pulled a high stool over to the table and sat down. "How did McLean get tied up in this?"

"He knew that I was trying to develop a case to bring before the magistrate against the Cahills and Dwyers because I had been reviewing the bank's records for the pub, hoping to show some connection between Toher's and the Brotherhood."

"And did you?"

"No. But those two families didn't have the funds, and had to have support from someone. At any rate, one day Bernie takes me aside and tells me that he can prove that the pub is being used as a meeting place for separatists."

"And he gave you information to conduct an assault on the pub."

"Under the pretense of being favorable to the I.R.B., he attended their meetings and garnered enough information so that we conducted a raid on the pub and found a hidden storage vault that contained guns and explosives. Sean Cahill and his cousin, Thomas Dwyer, were arrested and sentenced to Kilmainham."

O'Brien leaned on the table and looked down at the corpse. "It was shortly after they went to jail that Bernie disappeared."

"Why do you think he came forward, constable?"

"At first, I thought that it was the act of a good citizen because the Brotherhood, at the time, had little support. But about a year after he disappeared, his mother stopped me in the street. She looked terrible. Was very bitter against her husband and me. The family had been shunned by some of the townspeople and when she confronted a couple of women one day, they told her that her husband had conspired against the Cahills and Dwyers and that her son had paid the price."

"Did he?"

"I can't say with certainty, but the bank seized the pub when the two families defaulted on the loan. Later, rumors swirled that McLean's father ended up as the backroom owner."

"Make a note, constable. There are indentations on both wrists that indicate they were tied." She removed a small fragment of rope with the tweezers and held it up. "And here's the proof." She placed the fragment into a glass jar.

"Well, that matches what the informant told me." Graves entered the information into his book.

"Now, let's roll him up on one side so I can see his back." McKeigue stooped down so that she was at eye level with the table. "So, how did our man here get fingered?"

"One of our own, a separatist sympathizer."

"And Bernie McLean was marked as a tattler."

"Yes. At any rate, McLean was kidnapped off the road on his way to the bank and brought to an old barn." O'Brien retrieved a box of cigarettes from his jacket pocket. "Can I smoke in here?"

"Outside."

"Right. The boys, who kidnapped him, held onto him until the I.R.B. showed up."

"Did they know that he would be murdered?"

"They thought something should be done, just not sure what." McKeigue and O'Brien rolled the body down on its back.

"The condition of the body supports that he wasn't abused," the doctor said as she examined the inside of his legs and genitals.

"Things changed when the two battalion leaders arrived late from Spiddal, hard-core Republicans and belligerent when it came to establishing the Brotherhood."

"There is nothing extraordinary about the body, other than the missing tongue and a bullet hole in the forehead," the doctor said. "Do we know how he ended up in the bogs?"

"The two I.R.B. members took the body to the bogs where they made the boys dig out a grave."

"Dirty the boys with the killing, tsk." The pathologist placed a sheet at the bottom of the table. "The history of the West is different than the East, isn't it? Whole families lost during the Great Hunger to starvation and disease and those who survived exiled in Canada and America. A healthy amount of bitterness towards the British government, isn't there?"

"That's right," O'Brien said. "And still deep splits in allegiance, those who support the Crown and those who support an independent Ireland. So, we still have our informants and freelance spies who look upon the Brotherhood as spoiled goods."

The constable and the doctor took opposite corners of the sheet and pulled it over the body. They left the laboratory and stood on the outside landing. Graves removed two hard sweets from his pocket and offered one to Mary.

"Thank you, no. Well constable, I know how you fellas work. What kind of situation has the informant gotten himself into that makes you believe him?"

"Obviously, I'm not going to identify him as if I didn't learn from my earlier experience. Suffice to say, he has been charged with being an accessory to the murder of a British Auxiliary who was supporting the R.I.C. in rousting out the Republicans."

"The Auxiliary—?"

"Yes."

"Some of their tactics are every bit as heinous as those who conduct ambushes for the Republicans."

"I suppose some are of the mind that the Auxiliary's death is a justifiable killing during war. But seeing that Ireland has not won its independence from the United Kingdom, the local magistrate views this act as unlawful homicide." O'Brien removed the wrapper from the sweet and placed the candy in his mouth. "However, the court may be receptive to a reduction in sentence in exchange for witness cooperation. He will serve reduced time and be incarcerated in the county prison rather than that dungeon in Dublin."

McKeigue pushed her hands into the pockets of her lab coat. "And how many of these men are still around?"

"Of the boys who kidnapped McLean, one of them is dead. Sean Cahill, the son, died in a shootout with the British Army just six weeks ago and his younger brother, Matt, is already in Kilmainham, but may be moved to a local prison. The third boy was one of the Dwyers and he hasn't been seen in years. It seems that he disappeared about the time that Bernie went missing. You know, it's odd, in a close town like Ballinasloe, eventually someone will say something or hear something, but never a word about Willie Dwyer."

"Maybe he's dead and buried in the bogs with McLean," Dr. McKeigue said.

"You never know. I do know that his mother died recently and he never made an appearance at the funeral."

"So, if your informant is not one of the three boys then he has to be one of the two men who killed McLean. Wait a minute, who are you going after? The separatists were responsible here."

O'Brien placed his cap on his head and turned to the doctor. He extended his hand. "Let's just say that one of the I.R.B. men is out of the country and considered off limits and the other one will be going to the county gaol."

"So, your target is—"

"My target is anyone who hasn't been brought before His Majesty's court."

"That leaves the Dwyer boy. It's always the way it goes, isn't it, constable? The real criminal goes free while the misguided and the unfortunate pay the price."

"I have a responsibility to the McLean family and the law-biding citizens of Ballinasloe." Graves looked out over the manicured campus. Two runners turned the corner on the track, sprinted past O'Brien and the doctor, and raced to a finish at the opposite end of the campus green. "I never said the rules were fair, but if he is still alive, and I believe he is—"

"But whose rules?" She turned toward the door and looked back. "I'll forward a report when I finish my examination."

Roxbury Crossing

"READ ALL ABOUT IT, Police vote for A.F. of L," Johnny Bradley said in a lazy soprano voice from the fence in front of Station 10.

Frank picked up a small bundle of leftover newspapers. "Come on, it's nine o'clock."

A desk sergeant sat on the raised platform and looked over the railing that separated the public from police operations as the brothers entered the station. "Howdy, boys. Do you have a few papers for us?"

"Yes, sir," Frank said.

"How come it's so quiet in here today?" Johnny asked.

The sergeant stepped down from behind the desk and took the papers from Frank. "We are a few patrolmen short on the shift."

Johnny pushed the cap off his forehead. "Was that because you coppers, were celebrating?"

"Celebrating?" The sergeant stood and rested his fists on his hips.

The small boy backed away, slipping behind his older brother.

"I think my brother was talking about the headlines," Frank said. "You know, about you guys signing up with the A.F. of L."

"We didn't all sign up."

"Oh," Frank said. "Well, we just came in to give you the papers." He put his hand on Johnny's back and gave him a nudge towards the door.

Johnny stepped towards the exit and then turned back. "And we wanted to talk with Mr. Dwyer—"

"If that's okay," Frank interjected.

The sergeant returned to the platform with one of the newspapers. "Dwyer is not here right now." He pointed to a patrolman who had entered the room. "But you can talk to him, he'll be working with him later tonight." He took a coin and flipped it into the air. Frank snatched it and stuck it in his pocket. "Nice catch, young fella. Red Sox could use you."

The brothers caught the patrolman just before he entered the kitchen. "Mr. Quigley?" Johnny said.

"Ah, the Bradley boys. How are you fellas getting along? And how's that older brother of yours? Staying out of trouble, I hope."

"That's why we wanted to talk with you," Frank said. "The sergeant told us that we can leave a message for Patrolman Dwyer."

"I'll see him tonight."

"He took care of Charlie for us the other night and my mother wanted to thank him."

"And us too," Johnny said. "Been nice and peaceful."

Quigley knelt down on one knee in front of the small boy. "I'm glad that he was able to help you gentlemen. I'll be sure and tell him for you." Fulton stood and shook their hands.

"Thanks," the boys said in unison as they turned to the door.

"Where did Patrolman Dwyer take him?" Quigley asked.

"Fenwood Road."

"Good place for him."

Another patrolman joined Quigley as he said goodbye to the boys. "What did they want?"

"Coffee?" Fulton said as he filled a mug. "They left a message for Willie. He helped them out with their older brother."

"Speaking of Dwyer, was he at Fay Hall for the vote last night?"

Quigley poured a second mug of coffee. "Yeah, he was there and voted the right way too. I was a little worried about him."

"Fulton, did you hear about the private dick who tried to get into the hall?"

"Yeah, one of the guys at the door threw him out. It just goes to show you how low Curtis will sink to stop us from organizing and getting what's coming to us."

"What makes you think it was him?"

"Who else would try to sneak a private dick into our meeting?" Quigley said. "He didn't need to come into the hall. All he had to do was stand outside, watch and listen to the noise, the hooting and hollering, the whistles." He sat down at one of the long tables. "That dick will work to our benefit. When he reports how many cops were at Fay Hall and voted for the Union, Curtis will realize that it's over."

The other patrolman joined him at the table. "Yeah, you're right, Fulton. But he didn't need a private dick to come snooping around. I'm sure one of his finks reported back to him."

In the News

RACE RIOTS HIT CHICAGO
(Chicago)
State troops in full control of the Black Belt of Chicago; Rioting pronounced at an end; Thirty-four men now dead as result of riots, fifteen hundred injured; Large packing companies paid off one thousand of their Negro employees at a Y.M.C.A. and a Negro bank in the Black Belt; Negroes return to their jobs in the stockyards
BOSTON EVENING TRANSCRIPT
Friday, August 1, 1919

BIG POLICE STRIKE FAILS
(London)
English authorities assert only small percentage of men quit; Labor organization says 65,000 are out; Threat to march to Premier's home; Edward Short, Home Secretary, reports to the House of Commons that the strike has been a failure
BOSTON EVENING TRANSCRIPT
Friday, August 1, 1919

STRIKE MANIA RAMPANT
(Boston)
Strike spirit spreads; Situation in Massachusetts today unprecedented; In Boston, no less than forty strikes in last three months; Few industries not hit in past three months; Fall River school boys and girls walk off jobs as dinner carriers; Building trades upset; Victory of the Telephone Girls; Cigarmakers in determined mood; Fishermen out more than a month; Truck drivers win shorter haul; Plant shoe factory closed three months; Trouble along waterfront; Marine workers compromised
BOSTON EVENING TRANSCRIPT
Saturday, August 9, 1919

Chapter Eleven

~

It all came back to him so easily. Jim Rankin stood at the microphone and saw admiration on the faces of the audience that only comes from possessing real power, the kind that determines whether a man works or not, clothes his children, pays his bills, or for that matter, whether he eats or not. He slipped into character instinctively because he had been doing it all his life, making a career out of convincing people that he knew more about how to live the American dream than they did and that only with his help and direction could they hope to attain it. He had convinced them that their collective power was only formidable when harnessed by his enlightened leadership, and that it was proportionate to his singular but relentless battle against the captains of industry and the Massachusetts Republicans. He was the "working man's working man," Dandy James Rankin, your state senator, Roxbury Ward Boss and president of the Boston Central Labor Union.

He stood at the podium and rolled up his sleeves. He was one of them again. No dickey, expensive double-breasted suits or fedora for the man who led the charge against the gluttonous rich tycoons, who wallowed in the troughs of luxury and ate off the backs of the workers. They had saved him for last because he was that special kind of Boston firebrand who could recite in detail the many injustices that the immigrant and the sons and daughters of the immigrant endured while laboring for pennies at jobs that robbed them of their health and their lives. He had been the Ward Boss who met them at the end of the gangway, found them a cellar to stay in until they got on their feet, and won them a job that provided an opportunity and gave them dignity. And when the Union replaced the Ward Boss on the front lines in the Labor Movement, it was fiery Jim Rankin they chose again to lead the fight for workers' rights. They hadn't heard one of his sermons in a while, it wasn't necessary, they believed. They had seen what the power of the many could accomplish, tackling the giants of industry and confronting the despots in government, to garner a living wage, to work in a safe environment and to be free from retaliation—dress makers and telephone operators, trolley men and railroad men, coal miners and ship builders, actors and lumbermen, steel men and firemen, all had embraced the Union Movement as the means of obtaining a living wage, securing rights and moving towards that American dream.

But he had mixed emotions about campaigning for this particular group of laborers and supporting their fight. Granted, the police worked in terrible conditions for longer hours and less pay than a girl working the line in the Garment Industry. And it was a dangerous job these men did, these gatekeepers of the city who held at bay the criminals, the anarchists, the malcontents and the general riff raff. But he cringed when he recalled how the boys in blue chose the side of Business in other Labor disputes, charging into a picket line as strikebreakers with raised clubs and beating into submission a working stiff whose only crime was demanding a living wage. It was ironic that the police, many of whom were Irish like him, now were in the same fix as the rest. He had hesitated. But he had come to the realization that supporting the policeman was for the greater good—a unionized cop might consider the cause of the man who stood with a sign at the gates. He had thought about his daughter and Albert and what they would think if he didn't support them and concluded that when a government lackey tells his employees, even the police, they can't organize, it was a direct assault on Labor, and if left unchecked, would cause an onslaught of further attacks on the working man.

Rankin started in easy. He pushed his straw hat off his forehead and gripped either side of the podium. He spoke in a soft voice, thanking Frank McCarthy, the national representative of the American Federation of Labor, for welcoming the Boston Police, Number 16,807, to the ranks of organized Labor and for speaking about the dilemma that faced the brand new Local. And he thanked McCarthy for introducing a resolution that described Commissioner Curtis' amendment to Rule 35 as 'a tyrannical assumption of autocratic authority and an attempt not only to undermine the principle of collective bargaining, but to attack the American Federation of Labor itself.' Finally, Jim thanked him for his pledge of 'every atom of support that Labor can bring to bear.' The members broke into thunderous applause, whistles and shouts and then they slowly quieted down and waited for their president to begin.

"Imagine," Jim began softly as he took his hands off the podium and stepped back, hooking his thumbs behind his suspenders. "Imagine," he repeated more forcefully, so that his voice now penetrated the microphone four feet away and demanded a response from his audience. He knew that he had them once again, all the way to the back of the hall, every face turned his way. He didn't hurry, but waited as if on cue, and then stepped back to the microphone, leaning into the podium with one hand. "Imagine," he said for the third time with deliberate and controlled tremor, "being one of three hundred city laborers who were given the axe on Christmas Eve." He let that piece of information settle into the audience of husbands and fathers and burrow deep into their consciousness. Low undertone remarks buzzed around the hall, like electricity. He had struck a chord.

"It was the esteemed Mayor Edwin Curtis who was responsible for that unconscionable decision," Rankin said. "The same man who has never had to worry where his next paycheck was coming from because he has been on the Government dole his entire life—a Collector of Customs for the port of Boston and an appointed member of the Metropolitan Park Commission. And he has been the City Clerk."

He shook his finger over his head. "This is an old guard Republican who is out of touch with the working class, who has never had to scrounge for a job or labored at one that has beaten him up, stealing his youth and making him an old man well before his term." Rankin leaned on the podium and wagged a finger at the crowd. "He is the same man who sponsored an amendment at the Massachusetts Constitutional Convention that prohibited public funds from being used to assist any private religious institution, school or hospital. A slap-in-the-face if there ever was one," he thundered, "and so egregious that even the Cardinal remarked that it was an insult to Catholics."

A few patrolmen stood at the back of the hall. They began to chant, "To hell with Curtis."

He waited for a return to quiet and then said, "We come here today to discuss whether to support our newest union brothers against this same man in his latest political endeavor as the Boston police commissioner. Let me assure you, my friends, that the villain in this piece is Edwin Upton Curtis, the same man who fired those three hundred laborers on Christmas Eve.

"Now, I know that in the past our brothers in blue have stood on the opposite side of the line from you. And there are a few of you who wonder whether we should support them. So let me address that issue and put you at ease. First of all, they are sworn to keep the peace regardless of the identities of the contesting parties. Sometimes, we have been unsympathetic to that difficult role. And conversely, they may be more sympathetic to your cause, now that they are unionized."

His last remark brought the representatives to their feet, applauding and whistling. Rankin waited for them to quiet down and then continued. "Until now, I have told you that the Commissioner has forbidden them from unionizing, an arrogant abuse of power that is an attack on Labor itself. I have told you that the patrolmen of the Boston Police, one of the truly professional Police Departments in the country, are paid less than an unskilled factory seamstress. But what you don't know are the terrible conditions that they are forced to endure. Imagine, working seventy or more hours per week and being required to sleep in the same bed as numerous other patrolmen. One gets up and reports for duty and another lays down—in the same bed."

He rolled down his sleeves and buttoned his collar. "The station houses are falling down around them because the Commissioner and the Republican politicians don't think it necessary to invest any funds to repair them. Many of our patrolmen are in debt. And if it wasn't for the generosity of our local merchants, they wouldn't be able to feed their families." He straightened his collar and adjusted his bow tie. "And if that is not enough to persuade you, how would you like to have your clothing infested with vermin and carry them home to your families?

"How do I know these things?" The president of the BCLU was assisted in pulling on his suit coat. He tugged at his lapels and straightened his jacket. "Because my son-in-law is a distinguished patrolman of the Boston Police and even if you were to vote 'No' to support them, I must." He placed his straw hat on his head, cocked to one side, and Dandy Jim stepped out from behind the podium, walked to the front of the stage and threw his voice to the back of the room. "Because family is the core of Boston society, it is what makes this city great. And when I helped you in the past, it was because you were members of my family." There was a slight hesitation in the crowd's reaction, like a fifteen foot ocean wave momentarily stalled at its apex, an instant of harnessed explosive energy. "Will you stand the line with me?" he said.

The deafening roar of the crowd and its thunderous ovation lasted a full four minutes. Jim Rankin received a unanimous vote to fully support Local 16,807, with a resolution—to walk, to strike and to shut down the City of Boston, if necessary, to support their brothers in blue.

CATHERINE CLASPED her hands between her knees and gazed at the ivory silk dress that lay on the bed. She stood and held up her present, felt the silk against her fingers, slid her hands through the holes and let it tumble down her arms, falling past her breasts and over her hips with the softness of water, the hem stopping just below her calf. She traced the shape of her mouth with lipstick, touched the end of it to her face on either side with enough pressure to leave a tiny smudge of red on both cheeks and circled the tips of her fingers into the lipstick until the highlights on her face glowed warm and young. She supported her weight on the edge of the bureau and leaned closer to the mirror. "What a way to spend my twenty-first birthday, sneaking around with a married guy to hide-a-way places? And then put on the shelf for another day."

The telephone rang and Catherine listened as the hotel clerk passed a message to meet Mr. Rankin by the front door. She half turned in the mirror to see how the dress hung in the back. "Aw, hell, Mr. Ziegfeld would love me," she said. "I can act and dance with the best of them." She lifted herself tall. "At least for a little while longer."

"Catherine, let's celebrate," Rankin said when she slid into the seat beside him.

"What are we celebrating, James?"

"I just gave the speech of my life. So, we are celebrating Life, Catherine."

"Why not?" she said. "Life is grand."

The next morning, the sounds and smells of summer drifted on easy into the Buick as Jim and Catherine arrived back on Huntington Avenue. The car slid side to side on the trolley tracks and another automobile blew its horn at them for coming into its lane. Rankin never looked about, but continued to drive straight ahead with the limp profile of self-importance. They slowed at Fenwood Road and Catherine glanced down the street and saw the Bradley brothers sitting outside the clinic. She asked Jim to turn down the street so she could check on something. As they passed the entrance, she caught Charlie coming out of the door, being helped by a nurse and feeling for that first unsure step like he was slipping off the edge of the world, his face pale as wallpaper paste. Satisfied by what she saw, Catherine told Jim she was mistaken, had picked the wrong street and he sped off.

JOHNNY BRADLEY looked expectantly up the brick walk to the front door while Frank stared into his shoes, oblivious to the traffic and the good-natured shouts of the butcher at the corner who joked with his truck driver before he left for their supplier in Haymarket Square in the downtown section of the city. An automobile turned the corner from the avenue, slowed to a roll, jerked as it shifted gears and sped past the front of the clinic.

Frank looked up, watched it rumble down the street and dragged on a cigarette until it glowed orange in his mouth. He screwed up his face and blew the smoke out through a crack at the corner of his lips. "Did you give Mountain the rest of the papers?" he asked.

"Yeah," Johnny said. "Say, what's eating you?"

"Nothin.'"

"I told you twice that I gave him the extras." Johnny turned to the squeak of the screen door hinge. "Here comes Charlie."

Frank turned around and saw a ghost of his brother holding the door with apprehensive indecisiveness while determining whether to step out and reenter the world. The morning light painted Charlie's face colorless except for the black rings around his eyes. He sampled the morning air like he was sucking on a straw, the surly defiance gone, and held onto the door with desperation. He turned his head away and shielded his face from the glare, peeked out from behind his hand and smiled weakly at Johnny who stood in a frozen and hesitant step. Charlie waved as a nurse behind him guided him over the threshold. "Can you give me a hand, Frank?" he asked.

Frank stood, threw his cigarette into the street and walked up the sidewalk where he relieved the nurse of his brother. He took him under the arm but avoided Charlie's eyes. "Let's go," he said. "Ma's waiting for us. She's making something for you to eat."

"I don't know how much I can eat. My stomach feels like it's been turned inside out, still got the shakes." Charlie looked into his brother's face who still avoided making eye contact with him. "I'm going to change."

"Yeah, I've heard it before," Frank said. "Do you remember anything about how you got in here?"

"No, but this time I mean it."

"Like I said, I've heard it before."

They reached the end of the walk. Johnny slipped under Charlie's other arm and supported him like a crutch. "Ma's waiting for us, Charlie."

"That's great, Johnny." He looked down at Frank. "I don't deserve a chance, but I'll show you this time."

"Sure you will, Charlie," Frank said. "Sure you will."

A SHAFT OF angulated light spilled across the wooden floor as Commissioner Curtis sat at his desk and made the last corrections to his Special Order, summoning to headquarters the eight patrolmen responsible for the Social Club's affiliation with the American Federation of Labor and the creation of the Boston Police Union. Eight names that were reported to him within an hour of the breakup of the meeting at Fay Hall, names with which he was familiar, names of good men who had stepped over the line. Men who had to be disciplined to prevent anarchy. He carried the draft to his secretary's desk where he leaned over and drew a pencil line through the first item on his 'To Do' list. He left a note for Miss Harris to type the Order first thing and to distribute it to the appropriate captains.

It was clear to him now that his battle with the patrolmen would not be an easy one, but it seemed to him that allegiances were evenly divided between support for him and support for the police. And even if he had fewer supporters, he believed that he had the right kind of support, the kind with real influence. The Governor supported him, albeit quietly and without enthusiasm, and Tucker Appleton promised that the Downtown Club, the Chamber and the Business community would stand behind him. But the unions were another matter and they worried him. "If the BCLU backs the patrolmen and all those unions vote to strike," he hesitated in mid-thought and grimaced with an all too familiar discomfort, "and the citizens are faced with a locked down city, my name will forever be remembered among the worst scoundrels in Massachusetts history."

Anxiety squeezed down on him suddenly, his throat became constricted, and a stinging pin-pricking pain traveled from his left shoulder into the side of his neck. He began to sweat and became cognizant of something that was more important than his battle with the police. He stumbled back to his desk and collapsed into his chair, instinctively massaging and holding the left side of his chest. A terrible metallic taste filled his mouth and he belched and began to pant in short shallow breaths. He closed his eyes and concentrated on managing his breathing and relaxing the muscles in his face, tried to forget his public and private battles and listened to the sounds of his body, turning his concentration away from the frustrations of the outside world. He lifted his legs and placed his feet against the bottom drawer of the desk and waited for the pain to completely subside, opened his collar and unbuttoned his vest and sat there removed from it all, the job, the police, his political enemies, thinking about Lincoln's loneliness and the betrayal of Jesus. He opened his bible and read from the Book of Psalms—"But, as for me, I almost lost my balance; my feet all but slipped, because I was envious of the arrogant when I saw them prosper though they were wicked." He let the book sink into his lap and he surrendered to an overriding temptation to sleep.

THE LAUGHTER and good-natured banter of two patrolmen, standing just below his window, woke him and separated him from his brief hiatus from his troubles. The pain was gone and his breathing had returned to normal. He looked at his watch and noted that it was twenty-three minutes past six o'clock. His deepest sleep in the previous three days had lasted eleven minutes. He lifted the telephone receiver from its cradle. It was going to be a long day.

THE DEVIL HIMSELF felt comfortable in the presence of the Superintendent of the Boston Police. The rural charm and hospitality of West Ireland embodied his personality. Squarely built with the gentle hardness of a farmer, Michael Crowley greeted cops and citizens alike with unpretentious good humor and a soft handshake. In his mind, every human being deserved his respect.

Cops trusted him, and although he was their superior, they admired and respected him because he was fair. Those who had gone to the woodshed with Crowley often said that he made the trip enjoyable. Veterans who patrolled the streets with him in his earlier years recalled an intelligent and instinctive investigator who fit the policeman's description of a 'good cop.' His reputation was earned by actually doing the job. Where the Commissioner was an appointed politician, Crowley was a promoted field warrior.

"Good morning, Commissioner," he said after knocking first on Curtis' door.

"Ha, good morning, superintendent," Curtis said. "I'm sorry we had to cut your vacation short." He rearranged several papers on his desk so they were interleafed in the order of a plan of action. "Have you had time to speak with former Superintendent Pierce about raising a volunteer force?" He picked his head up and saw Crowley standing at the door. "Come in and sit down," he said directing Crowley to a chair.

Crowley sat and leaned his head to one side to see past the lamp on

Curtis' desk. "Excuse me for saying, Commissioner, but you're looking very pale right now. Are you okay?"

"Fine," Curtis said, "fine. But thank you for asking."

Crowley waited for Curtis to finish making a notation on his pad before responding to his question. When he looked up, the superintendent said, "I spoke with Bill Pierce by telephone last night. He has contacted and acquired the services of thirteen retired officers."

"That's it, thirteen?"

"Yes, sir. Many of them support the Union charter and a couple of them told me that, if they were still on the job, they would be in favor of it. They also don't want to be remembered as scabs. And the older retirees feel that time has passed them by."

"What about the newspaper advertisement?"

"Volunteer Police advertisements will run in all the papers over the weekend and Pierce has ordered five hundred badges."

"Good, there are plenty of able-bodied veterans out there who can't find a job."

"You're right, Commissioner." Crowley paused to pick his words carefully. "But the men who lead this unionization movement are good patrolmen and have served this city with distinction. I hope—"

Curtis snapped his hand up flat in a "stop" gesture and snorted through his nose. "They were good men when they performed their duties in a professional manner, but they voluntarily took an oath to serve the city and the commonwealth. And I will not be questioned." His face became flush and he jerked himself side to side in the seat before he rested his elbows on the desk. "I'm sorry, superintendent, I know that you have a good relationship with them but they are public officials and it is my opinion that their membership in a Labor organization is not compatible with their duties to the people of the city. John McInnes is a military man. He should understand that."

Crowley pressed his lips together and waited for the Commissioner to speak again.

"I am a little concerned, superintendent," Curtis said, "that you will be able to carry out your interviews objectively and without prejudice."

"My allegiance has always been to the Boston Police Department. I respect these men but I will perform my duty and conduct the interviews appropriately."

"Good, I want—" Curtis hesitated. "Give them the respect that they deserve, but we need to document three things—their length of service, their understanding of the meaning of Rule 35, and their participation in acquiring a charter with the A.F. of L."

Crowley wrote down the instructions. "Is that all, Commissioner?"

"One other thing, cancel all time off for sergeants and commissioned officers."

"Will do."

"That's all. Thank you, superintendent." As Crowley stood and turned toward the door, Curtis added, "And one more thing, I want them in here and interviewed this morning."

"Yes, sir."

BRADFORD HENSHAW could still smell the repugnantly sweet syrupy aroma of molasses that had permeated the neighborhood eight months ago and seeped into the wooden buildings, sewer system and the psyches of the people who resided and worked in the North End. He shut the office window to rid himself of the odor and the reminder of the long litigious future that lay ahead.

"Yeah, I can see how that odor can get to you if you have to breathe it in every day, Mr. Henshaw." Pearlie Brodsky reached into the inside pocket of his suit coat to retrieve a folded sheet of paper and the stub of a pencil. "So what can I do for you?"

Henshaw walked away from the window and sat down on the edge of the sofa next to him. "Well, as I mentioned in our telephone conversation, the city is a heartbeat away from chaos. As you know there is a wave of discontent that is sweeping the country and, if left unchecked, will destroy the very fabric of this great nation. We're in the throes of a terrible post war economy, the cost of living is through the roof and millions are out of work. For God's sake, our veterans can't even find a job. And in the middle of all this, we have these slackers, abandoning their jobs and shutting down America's engine at a time when industrialists are attempting to retool and modify their operations so that America can continue to be the world's greatest producer of innovative goods. Businesses, by the way, that provide means for them to feed and clothe their families."

"You'll not get an argument from me on that point," Pearlie said.

"And then we have an even more sinister group about to jeopardize the safety and security of this great city," Henshaw said. "Our public servants are about to abandon their posts in pursuit of gluttonous wages, thus leaving society to the whim of robbers and murderers?"

"The police—"

"Yes, the police—and the firemen, the transit operators, the telephone operators. What's next, doctors and nurses? It is out of control and our elected officials don't seem to be able to stop it." Henshaw paused and gathered himself. "I'm sorry. I get a little carried away when I hear our government officers tell me that everything is fine when I know it is not."

"Mr. Henshaw, I am a business owner myself and I know exactly what you are talking about." Brodsky curled his lips up at one corner of his mouth and broke into a sneer. "I have been all over this country the last few years. I've broken strikes for the City of New York. Why, I can walk from one end of Broadway and have a thousand men before I reach the other end." He paused. "My experience tells me that behind many of these walkouts are anarchists whose only purpose is the destruction of our free enterprise system."

"We need to drive those bomb-tossing bastards out of this country and tighten up our immigration laws," Henshaw said. "I believe they are attempting to infiltrate every facet of American life in order to poison it with their Bolshevist philosophy, to sabotage this nation, with their damned world-wide proletarian revolution."

"You can well imagine what the people would think if they thought that their police were affiliated with the Reds," Brodsky said.

"Hmm, you may be onto something there," Henshaw said. "Tell me what I can expect from you."

"We're an all-American enterprise that provides assurances to businessmen that the machinery of this great country will continue to run even when men abandon their jobs." Brodsky shifted the paper and pencil to one hand and stuck his little finger into his ear. He twisted it a couple of times before removing and inspecting his fingertip. "We can help you in a variety of ways." He pointed his thumb up and began to count off his list of services. "First, very discreet investigations can be conducted to discover any dirty little secrets that will give you leverage when conducting negotiations with the strikers. This may include placing a spotter spy, a mole if you will, among the targeted workers so they can gather evidence needed to obtain said leverage. Or it could be something as simple as finding an open door or a busted door lock when no one's home. Another way is to pick through rubbish. It's like having a person tell you their life's story. Or it could be reading their mail, very enlightening." He raised his index finger. "Second, inducements can be an effective means of coercing key individuals in the organization into making decisions that are favorable to your side. And third, we can provide manpower to protect property and continue public services. During the New York transit strike, my boys operated streetcars to keep the public transportation system running so people could get to work."

"As I told you, the potential strikers are the city's police. Are your men armed?"

"We have every kind of fire power that could possibly be needed, pistols, rifles, shotguns, machine guns. And a tank."

"Good God, a tank?"

"One of those modern French tanks, Mr. Henshaw. The war's ending and that's when enterprising businessmen can find bargains in the purchase of all kinds of surplus materials."

"You don't say. So what have you found so far?"

Brodsky snapped open the folded piece of paper. "I conducted some preliminary background research on the names that you provided on the phone. Actually, the police are a pretty subdued bunch. There are a few of them that owe money to local merchants and a few that like to swill down the booze, but otherwise no skeletons in the closet, and that includes the Union's officers."

Henshaw stood up and walked to the window. "That's it, huh. We need some kind of leverage to break their solidarity." He looked out at the vacant lot where the tank of molasses had stood before it collapsed.

"There is one thing that might be of interest," Brodsky said.

"What's that?"

"You asked me to look at some of the other supporting union heads and I learned that the president of the Boston Central Labor Union might have an appetite for young women."

"Are you talking about Rankin?"

"That's the one."

"Go on."

"We did some cursory surveillance, you know hit-or-miss stuff, on the top police union officials, the heads of the major local unions and the head of the Central Labor Union."

"And—"

"One of my agents followed Mr. Rankin to an apartment on the lower end of Huntington Avenue in Roxbury, near the Brookline town line. You can't lose this guy because of the snappy little automobile he drives. Is he in government?"

"Yes, he's a state senator in addition to being the president of the BCLU."

"That fits, then. Well anyways, my agent follows him to this apartment and a young girl comes bounding down the steps and jumps in next to him. And, my agent tells me that the way she jumped into the car she couldn't have been his daughter because she snuggles up real close and he starts to mug her up."

"Do you know who she is?"

"We're still working on that. My man tells me that we know one thing for sure."

"What's that?" Henshaw said.

"It sure isn't Mrs. Rankin. I sent another man, actually a woman so she wouldn't draw attention, to keep an eye on his home and we have positively identified her. She's, ah, excuse the expression, a frumpish dour old bitch about fifty."

"Virginia Rankin. Her family is quite wealthy, that's where he gets his real power. He gives everyone the bullshit that he worked his way up. He married into his money."

"Do you know Rankin and his wife?" the investigator asked.

"This is a small town, Mr. Brodsky; it's hard to keep a secret." Henshaw stood and walked to his desk. "This is very good news. What's next?"

"Next, Mr. Henshaw? You give me a bank check for twenty-five thousand dollars as a retainer for my services."

"And what can we expect to pay when this is all done?"

"At a minimum, operations like this, if nothing goes wrong, fifty, sixty grand."

"Can I give you the retainer next time we meet? I have some other associates—"

"I'm afraid it doesn't work that way. When we spoke on the phone, I told you that I would have several agents working this assignment. And they had to travel with me and set up camp. If I want to keep good men, I have to pay them. You should also know that if the police go on strike and you retain me for some muscle work, it is going to get a lot more expensive because I'm going to have to bring in additional men. Think of us as an army, a strike-breaking army."

Henshaw removed a checkbook from his desk. "Alright, I'll make the down payment, but I'll have to get approval for the rest." He saw Brodsky screw up his face. "These funds are good. I have an open line of credit with the Bank of Boston." As he began to write, he said, "How did you get into this line of work?"

"I'm an entrepreneur. Started my first business when I was a kid, selling second-hand goods. But this one, this one is my baby. Similar to yourself, Mr. Henshaw, I saw a niche and filled it."

Brodsky took the check and blew on it to dry the ink. "Since Labor got aggressive, we have been very busy. There are other agencies out there that do this kind of work, but you won't get better or more professional service. This is money well spent." He turned to the door and opened it. "We'll get right on this. Let me know how things are going or if you will need us to step in sooner than we had planned."

"I'll do that. Oh, one other thing. You mentioned a spotter spy? How could you ever use someone like that with the police?"

"The mole doesn't necessarily have to be planted with the police themselves."

"I see." Henshaw waited for the investigator to leave his office and then looked out his window. "I wouldn't want that man coming after me." Brodsky drove out of view and Henshaw picked up the telephone. "Hello, it's all set."

He looked out the window again as if to assure himself that Brodsky had really left the area. "How much? Twenty-five thousand for the retainer, but it has already produced a valuable bit of information."

Henshaw picked up his driving gloves as he listened on the telephone. "We need some support from the newspaper boys. The Red Scare, yes, that's it."

The North End was congested with pedestrians, pushcarts and bicycles. He wondered how many radicals were squeezed into that tiny band box neighborhood.

Chapter Twelve

~

Ballinasloe Ireland

Graves O'Brien entered the Post for the third time in a week, hoping to speak with J.J. Connarty. The constable had been assigned to the Ballinasloe garrison over twenty years and knew almost every person in the town. He had an especially good relationship with the postmaster and the fact that Connarty was absent each time he stopped by was unusual at best. The postmaster was one of his favorite sources of information, along with the local pharmacist and the town's telephone operator, and, over the years, O'Brien had acquired a significant amount of intelligence from them because he always made his visits discreet and found creative ways of presenting their information in his affidavits and before the magistrate.

He suspected that Connarty was avoiding him so he waited for the weekly street fair and made his entrance through the front door in the middle of the day when the town center was busy with sellers and buyers.

The clerk greeted him in a slightly pretentious and cheery voice before Graves had even closed the outside door. "Inspector O'Brien, how are you today?"

He stepped back outside without responding and ran around the building. There, Connarty, still wearing his postal coat, had one foot up on the running board of his motor car. "Been giving me the slip, J.J.?"

"No, No, nothing like that Graves, just about to run an errand."

"You look like a desperate man. Why don't I go along with you and we can talk."

Connarty stepped down from the car. "That's alright, we can talk here."

"Afraid that we might be seen together?" O'Brien sat down on the running board. "You know me J.J., I've never received a bit of information from you that has ever gone any further. What you tell me stays with me. What has got you so upset?"

"I know what you're going to ask me about, Graves, and I'd rather not be a part of it." Before O'Brien could respond, Connarty said, "Things are different today. Years ago, the Republicans were a sorry lot with few supporters in the town, but ever since Easter Sunday, the I.R.B. and its volunteers have grown significantly. They are well financed and they have eyes and ears everywhere. I don't have to tell you, that the only thing that the Brits have accomplished is shifting the people's sympathies to the Republicans. So, I don't need to get on the wrong side of that."

"How do you know what I am going to ask you?"

"Go on," Connarty said. "Ballinasloe was a sleepy farming town when that horrible bit of business between the McLeans and the Cahills and Dwyers occurred, the shunning and everything. So, it became part of its folklore. You know that better than I." He removed the blue postal coat. "The whole town is talking about the body in the bog and they know that you are conducting the investigation. The stories have been resurrected along with poor old Bernie."

O'Brien pulled up a cigarette from the package and offered it to the postmaster.

"Thanks, no. Those two families, the Cahills and the Dwyers, they know everyone, and sooner or later, they'll find out that I fingered one of them."

"J.J., I'm not looking for you to finger anyone. I'm just seeking the whereabouts of someone."

"Jesus Graves, you're looking for Willie Dwyer. It really isn't that difficult to figure out. He and McLean disappeared at the same time, and we know where Bernie has been." Connarty turned away from O'Brien and rested his upper body across the hood of the car. "Let it go, for Criss' sake—"

"I'll make it easy for you—tell me if the Dwyer family is receiving any letters from outside the country?" O'Brien watched the muscle in Connarty's face tighten. "When young McLean disappeared this town knew what happened and no one came forward. So, I don't give two flying fucks for what they think."

"Well, I do—"

"These small minded pissants took it upon themselves to act as judge and jury. It has taken me years to track down McLean's murderers and you think when I'm down to my last suspect that I'm going to just quit?"

Connarty turned his ear up and listened to O'Brien's words echo in the little boxed-in yard. "They're not letter writers." He looked around the yard. "Around the time their mother died, Mim, Willie's younger brother, sent off a letter to Boston. I probably wouldn't have known about it, except that he asked the clerk how much postage he needed."

"Hah." Graves slammed his fist into his palm. "Thanks, I'll keep that bit of information to myself."

"You'd better or Ballinasloe may need a new postmaster." Connarty turned and faced the constable. "He was just a boy when that happened, Graves. Why do you need to bring that back into his life, into your own life? For God's sake, the town's life. Nobody needs it. It's not going to bring young McLean back."

"Catching him closes the case."

"Catch him? Is the R.I.C. going to send you to Boston to arrest him?"

"There is special interest in Dwyer, J.J. Even I don't know what it is." O'Brien lowered his voice. "But you placing him in Boston just bolstered that interest."

Connarty rested his fist on his hip. "I've known you a long time, Graves, and this has the air of vigilantism. Everyone knows who killed Bernie. What does young Dwyer's arrest solve?"

"It's my own little message to the Republicans—who knows where this country is going? But it must be civilized and there should never be the casual acceptance of homicide. Willie Dwyer was an accessory, a participant, in the kidnapping and murder of Bernie McLean." Graves stepped away. "The day that I went to the bog, I promised him that I would get every last one of them. Thanks for your help."

Hotel in Rhode Island

"ARE YOU READY, Catherine?" Jim Rankin tried to turn the doorknob to her bedroom, but it was locked. "I've got to leave early today."

She opened the door with one arm in her robe. Her nightgown clung to her like cellophane, rested on the nubs of her breasts and folded into the 'Y' of her body. Rankin pressed against her and moved her back towards the bed, burying his head into her neck and inhaling her. His hands slid around her breasts and down her sides.

"Whoa, big boy," she said. "Easy does it."

"Come on, Catherine."

She pressed her hands against his shoulders to put separation between them. "I'm not ready to surrender, James, not yet anyways."

He took a half step back, his hands resting on her hips. "What's the deal here, Catherine? I thought we had an arrangement."

She lifted his hands up and held them under her chin. "We have an arrangement, but I control my end of it."

"What are you talking about?"

"I mean that I control the when and the where."

"Listen here, Miss Loftus, I've paid for these little excursions. And I'm getting tired of your putting me off."

Catherine dropped his hands and moved back, placed her other arm into the robe, walked to the bureau, and picked up her hairbrush. "What did you think I was doing when I agreed to accompany you, Jim? Whoring myself for a silk dress or putting out for a pair of stockings?"

"Now, you wait a minute—"

"No, you wait a minute. You don't own me, Jim Rankin." She sat down on a stool and began to brush her hair in the mirror.

"I just assumed."

A giggle of laughter escaped her lips. "Well, you assumed wrong." She stood and walked behind a changing screen. "You wanted companionship on these trips—" She tossed her robe over the top of the screen. "And that's what you got."

"Who do you think you're talking to?" Rankin walked out of the room to the parlor.

The hotel cart sat by the door, its top shelf filled with the night's used dinner dishes and utensils, covered by two soiled napkins. Two half empty bottles, one gin and one vermouth, sat on the far end of the bureau. He picked off a glass from the cart and threw it against the wall. Catherine left her bedroom and saw him leaning against a chest and staring into the mirror above it. He combed back his neatly trimmed black hair that sat like a skull cap over a laurel wreath of gray, slipped on his suit jacket, discarding the wilted carnation, and picked up his bag.

"Let's not argue, James," she said. "It's a beautiful day out there and a reason to enjoy it." She knelt on the couch, pushed herself up onto her knees and touched his elbow. "Let's ride out to the ocean. We can stop at the clam shop there and get some chowder. Call who you need to call and tell them that you are ill and can't make it today."

Rankin pulled his arm away. "I'm leaving in ten minutes with or without you," he said. "It's a long walk back to Huntington Avenue."

"Come on, tell me what's eating you."

He turned away from the mirror. "Catherine, you're probably the most beautiful girl I ever met, but let's be honest with each other. We're from two different worlds."

"I hate it when you talk that way. In case you've forgotten, you're a married man and it takes a girl some time—" She bent over and tied her shoes, sat prim on the sofa with her hands on her knees.

"Let's go." He opened the door.

"I have to get my things together—"

"If you're not outside in five minutes, I'm leaving without you."

Jim passed through the lobby of the hotel and the clerk called him. "Mr. Rankin, I have an envelope for you."

He stood at the counter and looked at the handwritten scribbling on the outside. "Who gave you this?"

"A short stocky fellow, about thirty-five year's old, brown hair—"

"Is he a guest here?"

"No, sir. But he knew you were staying here, even your room number." The hotel clerk pointed to the scribbling. "Your name's on the outside of it."

Jim tapped the envelope against his hand and looked toward the elevators.

"Told me you were old business associates and that he would be in touch with you."

"Hmm," Rankin said. "Did he leave a business card?"

"No, sir. I assumed that the envelope contained a note."

"What did he—never mind." Rankin walked to his automobile and threw his bag on the back seat. He opened the envelope and found inside a handwritten note on stationery from the Cliff Walk Hotel—*Your woman companion left this item at the hotel. Thought she might be needing it.* Jim shook the envelope and out dropped an earring that he had given to Catherine as a gift.

ALBERT PAUSED on the side porch before he opened the door. Both floors of the house were quiet, which meant that either Emily was alone and the baby was taking her morning nap or that his wife and mother-in-law had taken the baby for a stroll. He hoped for the former. He and Emily had abstained for the entire one hundred days (one hundred, four days, nine hours and forty-three minutes to be exact) to allow her body to heal and return to its prior girlish figure.

He stepped inside, climbed the stairs to the second floor and looked down the long hallway that divided their apartment in two. "Hello, Emily?" he called. "Are you home?" He walked towards the kitchen at the back of the house, glancing into the baby's bedroom and bathroom as he passed them. "Shit, they're gone."

He entered the kitchen, removed his helmet, and began to unbutton his tunic when he detected the sweet scent of jasmine. There were petals of the white flower in the doorway to his right that separated the kitchen from the dining room and a serpentine trail of the delicate plant meandered aimlessly in and around the table and ended at the threshold of his bedroom.

"Ah, the last time the scent of jasmine awakened my Celtic loins, I was on my honeymoon." Albert began to collect the petals and followed their path to the bedroom. "But I can't remember the name of that delicious girl who brought me to that special exotic place. Let me see, was it Theresa? No, that wasn't it. Abigail? No, that wasn't it either." He continued to pick up the flowers until he reached the door of the bedroom. "Alice, that's it, Alice."

"Well, if it's Alice," Emily said, "Then, you're in the wrong bedroom, Pal."

"Alice, Emily, who can keep them straight?" He picked up the last petal, inhaled the sweet aroma and placed them at the foot of the bed. He began to remove his shirt, then stopped and admired his wife. She had spent many days in her robe with her hair piled up into a rat's nest, running the first-time mother's exhaustive race of trial and error. But baby Margaret had survived with a little help from Emily's mother and the three of them had settled in as a family.

Emily lay in the bed, wearing a carefully arranged silver nightgown. Her toes were manicured and painted red and they stood out in erotic contrast to the alabaster sheet and silver gown. He stared at her toes. Then, he followed her hand with his eyes as she stroked her leg up into her hip.

She invited him in with a pat on the sheet. "What took you so long," she asked. "My mother is a wise old lady. When she knew that you would be home this morning, she offered to take the baby for a walk. I think she winked when she left."

"You're a wicked young wench, Mrs. Coppenrath." Albert lay down beside her and traced each little pore and dimple with the tips of his fingers.

She stroked his hair and led his hand to those places where she wanted him to go. "It's good to be wicked again," she said.

THE BOTTOM of the curtain fluttered away from the window, collapsed against the sill and then lifted again, gently like a sail under a westerly breeze. The lace flew higher on the small current of air, floated to the bottom of the window frame and began the cycle all over. They lay there wrapped into each other mesmerized by the repetitive lifting, rolling and settling down.

"I could stay here the entire day," Emily said.

"I know." Albert began to stir and separate himself from his wife. "But I'd rather not be in this position, like a couple of kewpie dolls, when your mother comes back with Elizabeth."

"It's just that we have so little time together. You see more of Willie Dwyer than you do me."

"Oh, jeez. I forgot all about him."

"What are you talking about?"

"Willie, I invited him over for a late breakfast after our shift."

"Great, now you tell me."

Albert rolled over, kissed her on the lips and patted her exposed thigh. "Poor Willie, he needs to have something like this to loosen him up." He jumped out of bed and ran into the bathroom. "Hurry up, he'll be here any minute."

When Dwyer rang the doorbell on the side porch, Albert and Emily were dressed and she was making poached eggs. Albert bounded down the stairs and opened the door.

"What took you so long?"

"McGuiness grabbed me on the way out for a report that I owed. With all the talk about the showdown with Curtis, I think the sergeant is afraid he'll be stuck writing all the overdue reports."

They climbed the stairs and walked to the kitchen. "Come in, Willie, and see how a married man is treated." He gave Emily a love tap on her bottom. "Of course, there are high stakes that must be paid for this kind of treatment."

"Some high stakes," she said. "Himself lives in my parents' home and is responsible only for putting out his own trash." She placed a serving of egg in front of Willie. "Good morning, Willie."

"Thank you, Emily, and a good morning to you."

"Would you listen to this, Dwyer? She doesn't appreciate the stress on my body each time I have to drag the trash all the way to the sidewalk, probably taking years off my life."

Willie cut the egg and toast in quarters and scooped up one of the pieces with his fork. "Oh, I meant to tell you. After you left, the sergeant collected all nightsticks. I heard that if we go out on strike, they'll reissue them to a volunteer force."

Emily turned away from the stove and glanced at the two men. "That doesn't sound good."

"No, it doesn't," Albert said. "It sounds like the brass doesn't believe our chances for a negotiated settlement are very good."

"You've been attending the meetings," Willie said. "What do you think?"

"McInnes and the Board don't want to strike, but Curtis doesn't appear to be interested in negotiating any longer." Albert turned in his chair to partially face Emily. "He is holding a hearing tomorrow, charging the eight officers of the union for violation of Rule 35 and, if he suspends them— we may have reached the point of no return." He watched her mouth turn down and the bloom disappear from her face.

The back door at the bottom of the stairs opened and they heard Virginia Rankin enter. "I should go down and see if grandma needs help," Emily said. "You boys finish your coffee."

Willie and Albert retreated to the porch. Dwyer stood looking over the hill while Coppenrath sat on the glider and lit a cigarette.

"It's worse than I let on in there," Albert said.

"What do you mean?"

"Curtis intends to bring up charges against eleven more guys who were involved in acquiring the A.F. of L. charter. If he suspends all nineteen, we're going out."

"Do we have the support of the other unions?"

"Yeah, they're lined up good. What I said in there about our Union not wanting to strike is true. McInnes, Lynch, even that A.F. of L. representative, Frank McCarthy, emphasized the need for cooler heads. But Curtis and Parker, his lawyer, seem to be hell-bent on going to war."

They heard the back door open and shut again and the distinctive voice of Emily's father. His words and Virginia's responses were indistinguishable, but the tone was unmistakable to Albert and Willie. There was more than the usual tension between Mr. and Mrs. Rankin. Dwyer looked at Albert and he shrugged his shoulders. Then they heard Jim say, "I'm going upstairs to see the boys."

"There you are," Rankin said as he entered the back porch. He looked noticeably disheveled for Dandy Jim's usual impeccable appearance, and he needed a shave. The confidence and clean hard demeanor of the political infighter were missing. He sat down on the glider beside Albert.

"Don't ever get married, Dwyer. They never give you a day's rest even when you're slaving for them twenty-four hours a day."

"Have no fears, sir," Willie said. "Women aren't knocking—"

"Don't let him fool you, Jim," Albert said. "There's a lady in waiting."

"Be careful, Dwyer," Rankin said. "What's her name? A good Irish girl, I hope?"

"There are no plans—"

"Catherine," Albert said. "She works at the Switch."

"Catherine?" Rankin said. "Hmm, nice name—"

"We're just friends."

"You're blushing, Dwyer," Albert said.

Rankin ran his hand over the stubble on his chin and gazed at Willie. "So, what are we talking about?"

"What else?" his son-in-law said. "I was just saying that Curtis is determined to make an example of our Union officers and fire or suspend them."

"You might as well face it. You and your fellow police are in a class war." Rankin saw the two mugs of coffee. "Get me a cup of coffee would you, Albert? It's been a rough day already."

"Sure," Albert crushed the butt of the cigarette on the bottom of his shoe and walked into the kitchen.

"So, how long have you known this, ah, Catherine?" Jim asked.

"I met her here at Elizabeth's christening."

"Well, you're smart to keep it on a friendly basis," Rankin said. "Besides, always think of moving up, Dwyer. A waitress is alright—"

"What did you mean by a class war, Jim?"

"You're still new to the politics of this city and don't have an appreciation for the battle that the Irish had to fight to get a stake in it. Your fight with Curtis isn't about raises in pay and better working conditions. Not anymore, it isn't. Not when you have the Chamber of Commerce offering their building as a recruiting station for a voluntary strike-breaking police force."

Albert returned to the porch and handed a mug to his father-in-law. "Here you go, Jim."

Rankin drank a little of the coffee. "Ever since eighty-five when Hugh O'Brien took office as mayor, the Yankees have conspired to keep the

Irish at bay. That's why the cute bastards in the State House moved the authority for appointing the police commissioner from the mayor to the governor. They must have been shitting themselves when they considered the political power of the Irish neighborhoods." He put his mug down and loosened his tie. "You guys are like General Custer; you're surrounded by Indians—Curtis, Coolidge, Peters, they're all Yankees. And we can't forget Curtis' lawyerly hatchet man, Herbert Parker, that self-righteous bastard. It's a stacked deck."

"Didn't you support Coolidge and Peters, Jim?" Albert said.

"Yes, I did. I thought they were the best choice for the neighborhoods and the city, but right now I'm wondering if it was a good idea. Although Coolidge is up for re-election in two months, so he'll not want to piss us off too much."

Rankin yawned and covered his mouth. He swiped his eyes. "By-the-by, you know who they are planning on using for replacements in case there is a strike? The Harvard football team. Now, if that doesn't play into a conspiracy theory, I don't know what does.

"Well, if those sons of bitches up in the State House want a fight, then a fight they'll get. If one policeman is discharged, every organized man and woman—" He stopped in midsentence and wiped the corners of his mouth. "Look, you tell the boys running this thing that we're behind them. But they should try and settle it without a strike, Boston doesn't need it." He took a mouthful of coffee, then stood. "I should go and see Virginia," he said and started downstairs.

Emily passed him as she entered the porch with the baby. "Dad, do you want some more coffee?"

"No, thank you, Dear." He rounded the turn in the stairs and disappeared.

"That was odd," Albert said.

"Don't try and figure him out," Emily said. "You'll go daffy. Here, take Elizabeth for a minute while I get her a blanket."

Coppenrath held the baby's head against his chest and stroked her back. "I've got it pretty good, Willie. We live here, pay no rent or utilities, but I don't know how some of the fellas with the big families are going to do if we go out."

"I don't know either. I'm lucky, I just have myself to worry about." Willie picked up his cup and carried it to the kitchen. "I'd better be going. Why don't we plan on bowling at St. Alphonsus Hall our next night off?"

"I'll have to embarrass you again, you big lug."

"We'll see," Dwyer said.

THE BELL AT the top of Memorial Hall rang out over the yard as one hundred and twenty-five members of Harvard's football team trudged like buffalo, steam rising off their great rounded backs in the coolness of the late summer evening, as they made their way to Seaver Hall for an unplanned meeting that was sprung on them at the end of practice. Coach Bob Fisher stood at the door as they entered and instructed them to remove their cleats. The players moved slowly and deliberately to the auditorium seats. Once inside, they were surprised to see University president A. Lawrence Lowell, several serious-looking men in suits, and a uniformed Boston Police officer waiting for them on the stage.

Lowell waited for all the players to be seated and then said, "Please close that door and let no one else in until we have completed our task here."

The athletes turned in one direction and another, trying to read their companions' faces, but they all wore the same expressions of confusion and anxiety, responding to questions from other team members with shrugs. Maxwell Henshaw had the distinct advantage of knowing the reason why they were herded into a secured auditorium. He sat in the first row like a kid on his birthday aware of the contents of a surprise gift and could hardly contain his excitement. When asked if he knew what was going on, he said, "You'll see. This is going to be more interesting than a lecture by Professor Houghton."

"You men represent the finest qualities of dedication, diligence and true character," Lowell began. "You are the best examples of what it means to be a Harvard Man. And to our distinguished guests, please excuse an obviously biased and solicitous appraisal, but these men are the best football team in the country." A controlled and polite enthusiasm rippled through the hall in response to the president's remarks.

"Before I begin, let me introduce the other men on the stage. To my left in uniform is Captain Malachi Hackett of the Boston Police. And on my right and dressed in civilian attire are retired Police Superintendent William Pierce, Lieutenant Stephen Morse and Sergeant Paul Reynolds.

"You are probably aware that the Boston Police patrolmen are in negotiations with the City for increases in salary and improved working conditions. The discussions have bogged down for various reasons, including difficulties in procuring funds for their raises during this depressed economy. Unfortunately, discussions came to an impasse when the patrolmen obtained a charter with the American Federation of Labor, a direct violation of the Department's Rule 35. Commissioner Curtis has taken steps to punish those officers who were responsible for the violation and, as a result, there are strong indications that the patrolmen may strike en masse, leaving the city and its citizens unprotected."

Lowell paused before he continued. "It is in times like these that America stands alone and demonstrates to the rest of the world that it can survive and maintain its democratic principles even when the guardians of those principles abandon their posts. Europe may succumb to the violence of the rabble, America will not, Boston will not.

"Today, I have released the following statement to the Press, setting out the University's position in the event of a strike— In accordance with the traditions of public service, the University desires in times of crisis to help in any way it can to maintain order and support the laws of the Commonwealth. I therefore urge all students, who can do so, to prepare themselves for such service as the governor of the Commonwealth may call upon them to render."

He removed his prepared statement from the podium and said, "I have chosen to direct my remarks to you because our other students have not arrived on campus for the fall semester and, as a group of young men, you are better conditioned and experienced in physical engagement than most."

He turned and invited Captain Hackett and retired Superintendent Pierce to the podium. Then he redirected his attention to the football team. "Men, you are about to enter the examination period of your education here at Harvard. It is a difficult examination, one that will test every theory that you have learned in the classroom, but one that I am confident you will pass with flying colors.

"Superintendent Pierce, who is in charge of volunteers, will walk you through the Voluntary Police recruitment process. You will be registered and fingerprinted as part of the enlistment."

Lowell turned away from the podium to leave when he recalled something he wanted to say. "Oh, one last thing I need to make very clear. You are not offering your services as strike breakers, but rather as protectors of life and property."

In the News

NO SOLUTION YET IN POLICE FIGHT
(Boston)
Chairman James J. Storrow with James J. Phelan and George E. Brock of the executive committee of Mayor Peters' Citizens Committee finished their conferences with officers of the Boston Policemen's Union

SIX BOSTON THEATERS CLOSED BY STRIKE OF ACTOR'S ASSOCIATION
Stage Hands and Musicians Quit as Soon as First Member of Casts Leave
(Boston)
Managers declare majority of actors are opposed to strike; Houses closed indefinitely; One firm of producers plans suits against strikers; Writs served at Tremont

MANY EX-SOLDIERS AMONG UNION MARCHERS
(Boston)
In ostentatious array, upwards of 8000 workers, with the men of the metal trades from arsenal and shipyards predominating, marched yesterday in Boston's Labor Day parade, the formal observance of Labor's 37th National holiday

RUTH HITS 24th HOMER AS RED SOX WIN TWICE
(Boston)
Nearly 30,000 fans go wild when swat wins second game; Washington beaten 2 to 1 and 4 to 1 in holiday battles; White Sox add to lead
BOSTON DAILY GLOBE
Tuesday, September 2, 1919

Chapter Thirteen

Andrew James Peters was the antithesis of John Calvin Coolidge, like the masks of Comedy and Drama in Greek theater—the Mayor simple, sensitive, liberal and affable, the Governor shrewd, cerebral, frugal and puritanical, one excitable, the other introspective, one frenzied, the other unhurried. Coolidge epitomized the mannerisms of the New England farmer, accomplishing tasks with persistence and limiting his words to necessary conversation. He was raised with the classic democratic principles found in small-town government and believed that the least government was the best government.

While Coolidge was country quiet, Peters was urban excitement. The energetic Mayor sought distinction through political fame. Eager to please, he lacked the dedication to learn his craft. He had a high-pitched voice with bright friendly eyes and politically quivered between the Boston Brahmins and the two-fisted Irish. He was elected with the support of the Downtown Club in collusion with the neighborhood ward bosses. Consequently, he focused his energies on pleasing the majority and was always aware of present public sentiment.

When Peters arrived back in Boston on the Friday before Labor Day, he immediately reacted to the stalemate between the commissioner and the police with passionate knee-jerk reaction. And while the Mayor buzzed around the city, attempting to appease the antagonists, and appointed a committee led by the exemplary James J. Storrow to study and make recommendations to defuse the situation, the glacial Governor sat back and watched the younger man chase his tail like a three-month old puppy until he completely exhausted himself.

On Labor Day, the two politicians sat side-by-side on the temporary reviewing stand that was constructed on the Beacon Street side of the

State House, the Governor, lean and angular and dressed in a square-cut business suit, sitting impassively quiet in confident stillness while the exuberant Mayor, pink and fleshy and decked out in long tails and topped in a high hat, vibrated like an idling motor car.

Peters stood up, walked to the edge of the stand and leaned over to shake the hands of several passing union Carmen. "What a beautiful day after all the heat and humidity of the summer," he said to the Governor and the world in general when he returned to his seat.

"Yes, it is." Coolidge gave a reserved wave to a block of Teamsters as they passed.

"Will you be available for a brief discussion after the parade or sometime over the weekend?" the Mayor asked.

"And what is the subject of this proposed discussion?"

"I think that we need to take a more assertive position with regards to this matter between the police and their commissioner."

The State Guard color detail, carrying the United States and Massachusetts flags, approached and Coolidge and Peters stood and removed their hats.

"That 'matter,' as you call it, has nothing to do with me or, for that matter, you. I have no responsibility for the conduct of the police."

Back in their chairs, Peters tilted his head to the Governor, leaning back to ensure privacy. But the Mayor's effort to draw Coolidge into an intimate discussion was countered with cool indifference. Coolidge retained his lack of expression and his attention remained directed towards the street.

"I have a responsibility to the people of Boston," the Mayor said with a slight edge of anxiety and a calculated rise in his voice. "I'm afraid that the police and the commissioner are reaching an impasse and that the police may go on strike."

Coolidge finally obliged Peters. "We all have our responsibilities, Mr. Mayor, but I think what is called for here is calmness."

"Would you at least consider publically endorsing The Storrow Committee's proposals when they submit their report? They are developing a plan that will provide a compromise for both parties."

"I have no more jurisdiction over Commissioner Curtis than I do the police. So there is no legal advantage to commenting one way or another on the recommendations of this committee."

"Won't you at least consider the committee's compromise?"

"Commissioner Curtis has my full support. We all recognize the validity of the police grievances, but we all must work, Mr. Mayor, and in that work, there should be no interruption."

"If the nineteen police union leaders are suspended from duty, hundreds of policemen may strike. As the Mayor of Boston, it will be an outrageous dereliction of duty on my part, if I don't try to do something to prevent it and its obvious consequences."

The last group of laborers at the end of the parade marched out of view as Coolidge turned to Peters and extended a soft hand. "Do what you need to do then, but I will maintain my position. However, you may keep me informed of the Storrow Committee's progress. Now, I have to leave to give a Labor Day speech in Plymouth. It is good to see you again, Mr. Mayor."

Peters stood there with his top hat in his hand, perplexed by the Governor's lack of emotion; he watched him enter a car just beyond the reviewing stand and drive off.

BRADFORD HENSHAW didn't like Herbert Parker. He thought the commissioner's attorney was cocky, pompous, and wound tighter than a pocketwatch. And, being summoned by the arrogant little bastard to his Beacon Hill apartment as if he was one of his flunkeys only caused Henshaw's blood to bubble to a boil. It galled him that everyone identified the former Attorney General as one of Harvard's brightest, when he, in the long tradition of the Henshaw family, graduated near the top of their class. He believed that he was often underestimated and dismissed by the uninformed because he ran his business out of an odd nondescript building near the North End.

But Henshaw did begrudgingly note Parker's sense for Massachusetts' politics and acknowledged his uncanny ability to always be on target—the calculating attorney had correctly read Coolidge's position on police unionization and even the Governor's unconditional, but insufferably reticent support of his police commissioner.

Henshaw did share some common ground with Parker, which was

why he sat across the room from him. Both ultra-conservative, anti-union Republicans, they believed that all Labor unions were an unjustifiable restraint on trade. And membership in a police union, by God, was a crime punishable in the courts of the Commonwealth. More importantly, the former college rivals agreed that the best opportunity in years for regaining control of the city's politics and eliminating worker militancy presented itself in the police's attempt to unionize. They agreed—the cops could be the sacrificial lambs.

In his no-nonsense inimitable style, Parker drew a desk chair up close to Henshaw, pulled up his tails and sat down. "So, what do we have?"

"Always a direct thrust, Herbert, never a prod." Henshaw said.

"Let's get to the point. What did our investigators find out?"

"Brodsky—"

"No names. I don't want any details about who they are or what they are doing. Results, that's all I want."

Henshaw ignored the remark. "They are applying their talents on three fronts. First, the police—"

Parker raised his hand. "Stop. Only discuss results, not methods."

Henshaw felt the heat rising in his face. He stood, walked to the sideboard and poured a glass of water—slowly. He could feel Parker's arrogant eyes burning a hole into his back and so he continued to pour the water deliberately. When finished, he turned and faced the attorney. "So far, the agents have found nothing that can be used against the police. Between the hours that the cops spend performing their responsibilities to the Department and their activities with the Union, they don't have time for anything else. McInnes, their president, has an especially impeccable reputation."

Parker combed his moustache with his fingers. "What else?"

"Our investigator has his agents conducting background inquiries and keeping an eye on the heads of the other local unions. They'll be the ones who will make or break a strike."

"And this won't be traced back to us?"

"No," Henshaw said.

"And no problems during these activities?"

Henshaw hesitated: "Two of the investigators were confronted by a group of toughs at a local union hall who guessed that they weren't members."

"We can't afford to have these men talk and tie their activities to us." The attorney folded his arms and squeezed his shoulders narrow. "What happened?"

"They were hand-picked by the investigator. Both of these guys are unemployed steel workers, so they know a thing or two about Labor lingo. They were able to talk themselves out of a beating by telling the union thugs that they were sacked in Pittsburgh after some scabs took their jobs and that they'd come to Boston looking for work."

"Alright, so what did they learn?"

"What they learned can be very valuable. Not all of the local unions are unanimous in support of the police and may, I emphasize 'may,' not strike if the police go out."

"Old wounds are slow to heal." Parker drummed his fingers on his knee. "Tell your investigator to stay close on that one. Go on, what else?"

"And along those lines, we are working on what could be the best piece of all." Henshaw hesitated, attempting not to disclose his glee. "There are strong indications that Jim Rankin is dallying his wares in—ah, virgin territory."

"Hmm, that fits. He never could keep it in his trousers. Do we know the identity of the young lady?"

"'Young' is the operative word. We are working on that."

Parker shook his head. "Talk about reckless, a state senator and president of the B.C.L.U."

"Yes, wonderful, isn't it?"

"I want photographs and any other evidence, documents, receipts, anything, and quickly." He stopped and placed his index finger in the air. "I will be the person to decide what details, if any, are to be passed on to the commissioner."

"They are working on it as we speak." Henshaw dry washed his hands and then brought them together in front of his chest. "I may not be a lawyer like yourself, Mr. Parker, but understand that I too will not be a party to anything that is going to embarrass me in this community. This is my home and generations of my family have contributed to its great reputation. And don't worry, I'll make sure that your hands don't get dirty."

"Point taken." Parker stood. "I'll see you out."

The apartment door closed and an inner door opened and Edwin Curtis entered the room.

"How are you holding up, commissioner?" Parker asked.

"I'm fine other than a little indigestion." Curtis folded into the sofa like he was deflating. "Are we making progress?"

"Yes."

"And they are staying within the boundaries of the Law?"

"Yes."

"Good, let's work on that press release.

ON LABOR DAY, the evening shift at Station 10 walked out of roll call in quiet clusters, passing Sergeant McGuiness without comment. Things had changed. The good-natured give and take between McGuiness and his shift had dried up like water on a boiler room floor, jokes at his expense replaced by guarded anticipation, his boys anxious and focused. None of them stopped for that half a cup before starting patrol. The men needed to escape, to let go of the breath that they held from the time they entered the building, the ever present tensions between themselves and Management, the ever present reminder that they stood defiant in the face of every tradition that had built the reputation of the Boston Police, the closest organization to a military operation bivouacked in the middle of an undisciplined, anarchistic civilian world.

He watched them file out as he stood at the duty desk and wondered if he would have had the balls to do what they were doing. Their fight was his fight, for God's sake; they fought for all of them, patrolmen to captain. No one need explain to him about the shitty working conditions, he lived them. The salaries were an insult. He knew that if they were successful, every one of them, regardless of rank, would benefit.

But he felt the foreboding chill of disaster deep in his bones and in the darkest recesses of his soul. McGuiness had been around this world a little longer than most of them and he knew exactly who would be the Christ and who would play Pilate. He knew the identity of the villains—the power brokers and the politicians, Democrats and Republicans alike. In their minds, the police were a calculated risk, a necessary force to keep the riff-raff at bay while they conducted their own filthy business, some bodies to shovel the human excrement so they didn't soil their own shoes. McGuiness recalled hundreds of strikes when his boys stood tall and sacrificed themselves to maintain order and protect the integrity of America's industries, when workers vented their frustrations and anger at the keepers of the peace, and then returned to their jobs. And on this Labor Day, he watched his boys file out and longed for the yesterdays when police, his police, weren't workers. Just cops.

The afternoon sun slanted across deserted Roxbury Crossing and telephone poles and streetlamps cast long gray shadows down Columbus Avenue. Willie and Albert stood like Mutt and Jeff on thc landing, Coppenrath jabbering away as usual while Dwyer stood like the Sphinx, cool and silent, the smaller man flailing his hands like he was shaping each word in a new kind of sign language, the larger man stooped towards his friend with his hands stuffed into his trouser pockets.

"We're going to be okay, Willie, you'll see," Albert said. "Just got to believe."

"I hope you're right." Willie started down the stairs, paused and looked back. "I'm going to check Terrace Street and see if any of those Red assholes are hanging around, being that it is Labor Day. I'll meet you later for supper."

"I thought they abandoned that old building."

"I haven't seen anyone around it in weeks, but that's what the sergeant wants."

"Okay, see you later then."

Willie turned onto Terrace Street and walked the two hundred yards to the boxy red brick building that housed the Lettish Workmen's Association. He tried the front door, but found it locked. He pushed on the door with his shoulder and it hardly moved, making Dwyer believe that it was bolted from the inside. He started to walk away when he heard the repetitious clickety-clack of a machine. Halfway down the side of the building, a window was partially opened. He bent down and looked into a small bathroom, and could hear the rhythmic noise coming from a room behind it.

At the rear of the building, Dwyer found a bicycle and the outside door ajar. He pushed it open, walked inside and followed the sound down a hall where he discovered an unattended running offset printing press. At the end of the machine, he caught the front page of the Socialist newsletter, *The New England Worker*, and read the headline.

BOSTON POLICE STRIKE FOR FAIR WAGES

Three articles dominated the front page—

Call for General Strike—rallied the city's local unions to support the police and walk away from their jobs;

Boston Press: Lackeys for the Wealthy—accused the newspaper publishers of blatant jingoism.

Boston Police Join the People's Movement—reported that the newly formed American Communist Party supported the striking police.

Something heavy landed on the floor in the next room and Willie quickly moved to the side of a closed door and took out his billy. The door opened and a cardboard box slid into the room, pushed by someone's shoe. He punched the shoulder of the man as he entered the room, pinning him against a table with the club. "Hold it there."

The terrified smaller man dropped a box of paper and cowered. "Don't hit me."

"Kursh? What are you doing here? I thought the Reds moved out of here a while ago."

"They did. I'm glad it is you, Officer Dwyer, and not one of the other men in blue."

"You can bet they wouldn't have been happy with this." Willie held up the front page of the newsletter. "We don't need this kind of support. Where did you get an idea like this anyway? Who's giving the orders? Fraina? Who?"

"Fraina is in New York, left two months ago. He knows the police have an arrest warrant for him."

"Who's behind this?"

"A new wing of the New York Party."

"What new wing and what interest would they have here in Boston?"

Kursh ignored the question and bent down to pick up the paper from the floor. "You know that I aided your detectives when you encountered Peter Carlucci and his bomb in the quarry."

"Yes, Detective Nolan told me, but that doesn't give you a pass." Dwyer held the newsletter in front of the younger man. "Why do this, Joseph?"

"I abhor violence. The war was the reason that I joined the Socialist movement. And I would rather promote change through education and reasoning—" He removed his glasses and wiped them with his handkerchief. "But sometimes change is disruptive."

"So a little bit of violence is okay, huh?" Dwyer said. "Selective violence, is that it then, the just war?"

Kursh knelt down again and gathered the sheets of paper into a pile. "When Detective Nolan spoke with me, he showed me Carlucci's bloodstained shoe and told me that shoe could have been yours. It made me sick. So I took a stand against unessential violence even if it meant informing on the Letts."

"So, the Letts are planning on taking advantage of the situation if we go on strike."

"Yes, it will give the movement new life. This is good news for them."

"Give me the names of the people who ordered the printing."

"I don't know who they are," Kursh said. "I have only met one man, the man who ordered the newsletters."

"With Fraina's blessing? This is his press, right?"

"Yes."

"Did you write these articles?"

"No, Fraina did. I know his style."

"Jesus, this will play right into the newspapers' trash about a national revolutionary scheme."

"That's nonsense—the Communists are too fragmented. There are thirty different groups, each with its own agenda. They're too busy fighting among themselves."

"So, someone working with the Letts wants to associate the cops with the Reds. Who would benefit from that?"

Joseph put the rest of the sheets on the table. Willie reached over and grabbed him by the collar. "You're supposed to be a pacifist?" Dwyer held up the newsletter in his other hand. "And yet you're printing this inflammatory bullshit that may be the cause of hundreds being hurt or killed? Do you want to talk about violence?"

Joseph was standing on his toes and he gurgled as Willie twisted his collar like a tourniquet. "I assisted Detective Nolan with Peter Carlucci—" He began to cough in spasms and choke on his tears. He pulled at his collar with his fingers. "Wait—"

"Who ordered these newsletters?"

Kursh's hands fluttered around his face and tears streamed down his cheeks. When he tried to speak, he wheezed.

Dwyer released him and guided him to a chair. "Sit down. You need to understand something. There are twelve hundred men who may put their careers on the line in the next few days and there will be wives, mothers and children who may lose the cops' meager salary, the only thing that allows them to eat and live in a dry room. I don't care who doesn't get along with whom with you Reds. All I want from you is to tell me who ordered these fucking things. Give me a name!"

Kursh opened his collar and felt the front of his neck. "I can't—" he gasped. He wiped his nose with his handkerchief. "The man who paid for these newsletters— He's as big as you are, and from the looks of his hands and face, he can be just as dangerous." He leaned forward in the chair. "Can I have a glass of water?"

"Go ahead."

Kursh swallowed the water like it had sharp edges. "He knows who I am—"

"So how did this guy get in touch with you?"

"I met him here. Fraina had my name and telephone number from a master list, and, because I was the only one who could operate the press, he told me to meet this man. That's all I know. I don't think Fraina knows him."

"Or cares, right? Just as long as someone is interested in screwing things up?

"He gave me the impression that this person was an outside supporter of the cause or, at the least, from a different group."

"Give me the name of the guy who ordered the newsletters. Come on, Joseph."

Kursh stooped down to an empty box. He tore off the paper that was attached to it. "This is the only information I have."

"Salvatore Rossini, an Italian." Dwyer removed his pocket notebook and transcribed the name. "There's no address. And probably a phony name. How are you supposed to get in touch with him when the job is completed?"

"He's coming here, Wednesday."

"What does he look like?"

"He has thick black hair that stands straight up, with a receded hairline, late twenties, maybe thirty. Strange and shifty, kept looking around, with one eye half closed, staring like he had just escaped from a nut house." Kursh looked around like he expected the madman to leap out of the shadows. "He scared the devil out of me."

"All right, Joseph. I hope I didn't rough you up too much, but tying us with the Reds? That's not going to make you a lot of friends."

"He can't find out that I fingered him."

"The only person I'll talk with is Detective Nolan."

"What should I do with these newsletters?"

"Finish the order, but don't let them out of your sight. And don't deliver them, until I give you the word. Call the station and leave a message for me when you know exactly when this guy, Rossini, will be picking them up."

"Okay," Kursh said. "I don't want any trouble with this man. I think he'd kill me in a minute."

"When's Fraina coming back?

"This week." Kursh picked up a stack of the newsletters.

"Give me one of them," Dwyer said. "And lock that back door. You never know who might come knocking."

WILLIE STEPPED onto the second floor of the station house, followed the chatter of voices to the detective's office at the end of the hall and stood outside the open door.

George Nolan leaned back in his chair and held his hands close to his chest. He sipped in a breath, bent the tips of the cards over and examined them. "I'm loaded. You guys might as well give up while you got a chance."

One of the dicks from '9' scoffed and threw out a bid. "Three hearts, how's that for tossing in the white towel."

"Yeah, well my partner's got my back," Nolan said, "and here's what I got to say about that, four clubs."

Harry Tingle, the other detective from Station 9, waved his hand as if swatting away an annoying insect. "Pass."

Myles Boyle took a second look at his cards and looked over at Nolan. "You're finessing or you're the luckiest shit on the planet. It's all yours."

"Hah, a complimentary hand if I ever heard one." Nolan threw his opening card onto the table when he saw Willie standing at the door. "Come in, Dwyer, don't stand out in the cold. We're celebrating Labor Day, the day when the world rests. And for once, we get to discuss intelligence with our brethren from '9' without the fucking world coming to an end. It's like Christmas."

"Detective, can I have a minute?" Willie asked.

"A lot quieter than prior Labor Days, that's for sure—What did you say?"

"When you have a moment, can I speak with you about something?"

"Sure, kid. Let me play this hand and we can step outside. Jack of spades, oh you bastard, Harry. You dirty sandbagger."

Willie slipped out of the room and started for the stairwell.

"Take that," said Nolan as his partner laid down a card.

"An ace of spades, Boyle?" said Tingle. "Whose arse did you pull that one outta?"

Downstairs in the Roll Call room, Willie looked at the organizational chart for the Reds-Bolshevik Movement that was created by the detectives from Stations 9 and 10 to assist officers in gathering information when out on patrol. There were photographs, many of which were taken the day of the May Day riot, identifying suspected members of the organization and indicating an approximate chain-of-command, if there really was one. Across the top of the chart were names that were vaguely familiar to him—Luigi Galleani, Mario Buda, Louis Fraina, Emilio Coda and Carlo Valdinoci. And below them, other names with whom he was even less familiar. It all seemed dark, alien and mysterious. Halfway up from the bottom, a mug shot of Joseph Kursh stared back at him. He wondered who had conspired to associate the police union business with their radical revolutionary cause.

"There you are. Do you have it memorized yet?" Nolan entered the room and went straight to the coffeepot.

"It's confusing. I think if I studied that chart for a week, I still couldn't figure out who belongs to whom."

"Don't feel like you're the class dunce. The bums on that board don't have it straight either." Nolan sipped the coffee from his cup, screwed up his face like he had swallowed a mouthful of vinegar. "The country has got the jitters and consequently any group that advocates change or is proposing something that they don't understand must be Bolshevist."

"What do you mean?"

Nolan topped the coffee off with hot water. "It used to be if someone sent a bomb through the mail, then they were identified as a radical anarchist. Now, if you're a member of I.W.W., the Socialist Party, a Labor union, or anyone who doesn't agree with the majority, then you're a slacker and a Red. A German, Russian or Italian immigrant? The same, you're a radical. Pretty soon we'll all be up on that chart."

"What about these guys on top?"

"Oh, those guys. They fit the mold of what an Italian radical is—a peasant who grew up on a farm and at an early age was sent to the city to work long hours in a factory. Pissed off, they escape to America and guess what they end up doing—working long hours in a factory."

"A lot of immigrants work in factories," Willie said.

"That's right, but here's the difference. The Italians don't speak the King's English and have little interest in learning it. They tend to stay with their own. They refuse to become citizens, they don't buy Liberty Bonds and they refused to fight in the War. And they bring their suspicions about Government with them when they emigrate. You add that all up and people assume that they are conspiring to overthrow the American Government."

"So are they?"

"I interviewed a couple of guys that were associated with Galleani and friends and they told me that most of them, including Galleani, are good family men. They work in factories during the day and they come home for supper like other people. Then they congregate with other Italians at their neighborhood clubs, and on weekends they organize community picnics. Sound familiar?"

"Yeah."

"The difference is that when they are at their clubs or attending picnics, besides gathering with friends, they get themselves all lathered up and start grinding out inflammatory journals and leaflets on their makeshift presses. And occasionally when they really get excited, they make a bomb and blow off a finger."

"Ah, they're a hot-headed race anyway."

"Hold on there, Sport. We Irish, have our own revolutionaries, James Larkin, the late James Connolly and the lovely Martha Foley to name a few, who run around mouthing the same. Hey, in some circles, even Eamon de Valera is considered a militant Socialist." Nolan found some saltine crackers in the breadbox and sat down at the table. "Now, don't get me wrong. I'm not sympathetic to the bomb tossers, but if you stuff all that rhetoric into a meat grinder, what comes out the other end is basically the same—everyone wants their own piece of the pie, just like us coppers." Nolan held out his hand in invitation to Dwyer to sit across from him at the table.

"All respect, detective, sounds like you sympathize with them."

"Who, me? Nah, I just like to wax philosophical once in a while." Nolan folded his hands on the table. 'So, you wanted to talk with me?"

"I have something to show you." Willie reached inside his tunic and retrieved *The New England Worker* and laid it out on the table.

The detective picked up the paper in his hands and whistled as he read the headline. "This isn't good."

"Read the title of the article at the bottom of the page," Dwyer said.

"Boston Police Join the People's Movement—Where did you get this?"

"I was rattling doorknobs over on Terrace Street. And I checked the Letts building and found the rear door opened and a press running. Hundreds of these things were being printed."

"Who was there?"

"Joseph Kursh."

"That little bastard. Does he think he has a free ride because he gave us a little information?"

"He told me that he's afraid that the guy who ordered them will kill him."

"If I get my hands on him, I'll kill him. His free ride just ended." Nolan jumped up with nervous energy and walked to the chart with Kursh's picture and poked it with his finger. "His rich daddy won't be happy to see this on the front page of the Boston Herald."

"I know you have a lot more experience than me, detective, but I believe him when he says that he is printing the newsletters for someone on the fringe of the Letts."

"What did he tell you?"

"He said that Fraina called him from New York. Oh, by the way, he's coming back to Boston."

"Good, I can't wait to lock his arse up."

"Anyways, Fraina told him that a guy by the name of Rossini would meet him at their headquarters with articles to print in the newsletters. Kursh didn't think that Fraina knew Rossini very well."

"Where are the rest of the newsletters?"

"I told him to lock them up in the building and not to take them from there. Rossini's picking them up on Wednesday."

Nolan returned to the table, sat down and lowered his voice. "That's good, we need to find out about this Rossini, if that's his real name, and put him out of business before those asshole Bolsheviks are linked to us."

"What if the Bolsheviks are not behind this?" Willie said.

"What?" Nolan's knee vibrated against the underside of the table.

"Who else would benefit from tying us to the Reds? Of course, they have to be behind this." He clapped his hands together. "Ha, well nothing we can do until we know who Rossini is. Get hold of me as soon as you know about the pickup."

"Okay." Willie started to the door.

"And, Willie, for the time being, keep this to yourself."

Chapter Fourteen

~

Ballinasloe Ireland

Michael Dwyer walked cautiously across the tin roof, carrying a bucket of tools, and sat down at the last section that needed to be repaired. Beneath the lifted tin, he could see the cows in the barn shifting and swishing their tails to swipe away the flies, shaking their large comical heads and occasionally stepping broadside into the sides of their stalls. He took an apple from his overalls and bit into it, closed his eyes and turned his face to the sun.

"Now, you're seeing it, Mim," the voice from the ground said.

"Darren, how's the day for you?" Michael said.

"If I can continue to make my rounds on days like this, then I've already died and gone to heaven."

"Ah, there you go. Leave the mail on the porch, would you?"

"I'll do that, Mim." The postman rested his satchel on the ground. "Em, can I have a word?"

Michael flung his apple core from the roof into the pig's trough. "I'll be right down." When he reached the bottom of the ladder, he invited the postman into the house for tea.

Darren walked to the stove in the corner of the Spartan stone room and rubbed his hands together. "There's nothing more comforting than a peat fire. It's like elixir for the bones."

"To tell you the truth, if I stay too long in front of it, the day becomes mysteriously short." Michael placed the tea on the table. "So, what great news do you have for me today?"

"Unfortunately, Mim, it's news that I would rather not have to bring to you." Darren stirred a spoonful of honey into his tea.

"Well, let's have it."

"Graves came by the Post several times, looking for Connarty, and finally cornered him a few weeks ago. I didn't know what he wanted, but I had my suspicions because of his investigation into Bernie McLean's death."

"Go on."

"Now, I have to tell you, Mim that J.J. put O'Brien off until the constable caught him sneaking out the back door."

"Has this got to do with my brother?"

"Yes, I'm afraid it does." Darren pushed his cup toward the center of the table. "Graves knows that Willie is living in Boston. He has a warrant for your brother's arrest for being an accomplice in Bernie's death."

"Jaysus." Michael turned to the small window over the table and began to drum his boot on the stone floor. "Why do I have the feeling there is more."

"I'm sorry, Mim. I found out this morning while nosing around that Graves sailed for the States last Friday or Saturday."

"The R.I.C., the fucking Peelers, paid his ticket all the way to America?"

"Yeah, they're making a statement."

"That's Graves, the self-righteous bastard. If I was there, I'd kill him myself."

"I'm sorry for your troubles." Darren picked up his satchel. "I'd best be finishing my route." They walked outside to his bicycle and he slung his bag across his back. "Mim, you've known me a long time. I didn't want to bring this kind of news to you, but I thought you should know."

"I'm not grateful for the news, Darren, but I'm thankful that you brought it." Michael put his hand on the postman's shoulder. "I hold no animosity towards J.J. either. I know how O'Brien can be, he's relentless. So tell him he need have no fear of me."

"Thanks again, Mim. I know that he'll be glad to hear that."

THE CABLEGRAM was sent to their aunt's apartment on Leroy Street as per arrangements made over ten years ago when Willie left for America and Aunt Delia was still alive. Michael Dwyer forwarded his message with Fenian assistance from the Valentia Cable Station and hoped it would arrive in time to warn his brother.

The youngest Dwyer remembered the day Willie left as if it were yesterday. He had risen to find the cottage unusually quiet, his brother Tom, already preparing his garden for the coming season, his older sisters gone to school, the home hollow and empty of sound. And when he called 'Mam,' his voice fell flat without resonance and disappeared into the wood. He ran through the rooms, listened to the vacant house and sat down in the middle of the floor. Tom came in when he heard him calling and joined him. Michael felt the comfort of his brother's dirt-stained calloused hand, running through his hair, and the safety of his arms, his head rising and falling against his older brother's chest.

Later, the Dwyers gathered as a family and he was told that Willie had left on a ship and was 'buried' in America, that his oldest brother had 'died.' Only years later, Michael learned that his brother had 'risen' to live again.

Brigham Circle Roxbury

Valerie splashed the floor with a spaghetti mop, swishing it back and forth like a sailor swabbing a deck. She was pushing the mop in and around the bar stools when the diner door opened. "We're closed until four," she said without looking up.

"Hi, Val." Catherine shut the door behind her.

Valerie let up on the mop, leaned on the handle and turned around. "Well, look who's come limping home. How's yourself, Kid?"

"Okay, I got no complaints." Catherine plunked down into the first booth. "Can I get a cup of coffee?"

"Sure, you know where it is. Help yourself." Valerie went back to mopping the floor. "You look like you're doing pretty well. Nice duds you're wearing."

Catherine returned to the booth with the coffee and lit a cigarette. "I was wondering—"

"Yeah."

Catherine looked up at the chalkboard with the evening's specials written on it. "I could use some hours."

"Who, you? Thought you were all through with this." She wrung out the mop and then leaned it against the counter. "I don't know—"

"Yeah, I deserve that. But I'll take whatever you got, nights, weekends. I know you always have trouble filling those shifts."

"We do, especially when girls don't show up when they're supposed to."

"That ain't going to happen again. I'll be here when I'm supposed to be here."

"Well, that's nice of you to say." Valerie opened the door, walked outside with the bucket of dirty water and dumped it into the gutter. She came back inside and sat on the first stool while the floor dried. "I'll speak to Stan, but I ain't promising you anything."

"I know." Catherine dropped the cigarette into her cup and slid out from behind the table and sat on the end of the cushion with her legs splayed out in the aisle.

The two women were sitting close to one another now, and Valerie saw Catherine clearly in the light. She looked like life had sucked her face gray. The older woman guessed that Mr. Wonderful wasn't so wonderful and that Catherine now fought the battle of redemption, and requesting her job back was the first step. She picked up Catherine's cup and saucer. "You'll be a little wiser next time around, Kid." She put out her hand. "You can start your old shift tomorrow night."

"What about Stan?"

"Stan? Hey don't you know who wears the pants around here?"

"Thanks, Val."

"You look a little worn out. Homemade soup's on the stove."

"Thanks, anyways."

"So," the older woman said. "Was it worth it?"

"Every experience is worth it, Val, as long as you survive." Catherine stretched her arms over her head and yawned.

"I know it's none of my business, but—" Valerie slid to the edge of the stool and lowered her voice. "I hope you're using contraceptives."

"What do you think, I'm stupid?" Catherine broke into a giggle. "So far, I haven't needed them. He gets going on the hooch and all I have to do is wait him out."

"And here I am worrying about you."

"Tell you the truth, all that running around took a little of the spark out of me. I need to keep things calm for a while, if I can." Catherine stared at the tile floor. "Has Willie been around?"

"Yeah, he comes in from time to time, usually on the late shift. Now, that's what you need, a little stability."

Catherine's eggshell face broke into a tiny sad smile. "If he stops by, tell him I said hello, would you?"

Valerie walked with her to the door. "You can tell him yourself the next time you see him in here."

Chapter Fifteen

Kursh called the station on Thursday, not Wednesday as he had said, but he did call. Dwyer and Nolan squatted in the brush where they had an unobstructed view of the back door of the Letts headquarters, and waited for Mr. Rossini. Willie put his fist to his mouth to stifle a yawn. On the second day of his current tour, following a patrol from 1 AM to 8 AM, he was operating on two hours sleep. And now he was on his first surveillance. A fleck of sunlight from the windshield of a car jarred him as it drove into the back yard. He turned his head in Nolan's direction and saw that the detective had been trying to get his attention.

Kursh had described Rossini well, but Willie expected him to be more ape-like and sinister in appearance. His eyes were definitely shifty and he had a nervous twitch, but he appeared more like a successful boxer, rough in demeanor, but impeccably dressed in a pin stripe suit and an expensive silk shirt and tie. He removed his hat and placed it on the hood of the car, then stood there with the arrogance of a man who had had his share of battles and always walked away the winner. He placed a cigar between his teeth, opened his suit coat and pulled up on the waistband of his trousers before moving to the back door of the building.

Willie shifted in his crouched position and Rossini stopped, took the cigar from his mouth and turned around, squinting with his chin down, tilted at an angle, not looking with his eyes, but his ears. Both men froze and listened. Willie held his breath, felt suddenly sluggish, his legs unhinged like someone had cut his hamstrings. The humid September air closed in on him and, even at that late hour of the morning, the pungent odor of the damp underbrush and rotting mulch hung in his nose and throat like death. He remained motionless below the brush line, stooped in a curl close to the ground, the .38 Special pinned between his knees. He blew a soundless whistle and had to restrain an impulse to leap at Rossini's throat if for no other reason than to quit the agonizing balled-up position. Rossini glanced at the thicket with a squinted sneer and then ground his shoes into the gravel and entered the building.

"Willie," Nolan whispered. "Willie," he said a little stronger. "Get the car's plate number."

"Okay." Dwyer said. "I thought for a minute he saw us."

"Nah, the sun was shining right into his eyes, but I think he thought he heard something. So be careful, he's liable to get cute. I'll meet you halfway. Make it over here without standing up."

When he reached Nolan, Dwyer said, "When I finally stand, I don't think that I'm going to be able to walk."

"It goes with the job, kid. You'll get used to it eventually. This work can be tiresome and boring, but if you do it right, the satisfaction of seeing one of these cute pricks with that 'what the fuck happened' expression on his kisser is worth all the trouble."

"So, what's next? Do we take him?"

"No. What's next is going to take a little luck. When he came here, he drove in from Tremont Street. I'm not sure, but I'm guessing that he came from one of the downtown hell holes, probably in the North End." The older cop twisted his torso. "You think you've got aches and pains. Wait 'til you're my age."

"Should we move back so we can stand?"

"No, stay right here. Just in case something goes wrong—if he gets wind of us and tries to make a run for it, I want to be in the best position to grab him."

"Okay."

"When he starts to load the newsletters, I'm going to slip out through the brush and get to the car. You stay with him until he drives out of the yard. Then run like a track star to meet me. If all goes well, he'll come out of Terrace and turn right on Tremont and head for the Crossing. I'll meet you at the bottom of the embankment."

Willie looked up. "I thought I heard something."

"He's probably getting ready to leave. Okay, now listen, if he turns left when he comes out of the yard and goes in the opposite direction, run to the front of the building and I'll meet you there. I'm in a good position to see which way he goes."

"Look, there he is."

"Easy. He's loading his car with the boxes. As soon as he goes back into the building, I'm going to slip out."

Rossini opened his back door and put a box onto the seat. He seemed more comfortable and didn't take the precautions that he had earlier. There was a change in his demeanor, casualness in his movements, even whistling as he went back into the building. Nolan slipped away and left for his car.

Kursh carried the last box and Rossini loaded it into the car. He drove to the front of the building and turned right onto Terrace Street. Willie crashed through the brush, leaped down the railroad embankment and slid on the sand and stone to the bottom where Nolan was waiting for him.

"Get in. He's in the traffic ahead." Nolan made a U-turn in the Crossing and stayed a few car lengths behind as they traveled down Columbus Avenue towards downtown. "Nice car for a Communist. I thought they wanted to share everything." He drove around a car that stopped and double parked. "I guess we're all going to get one of those when the Reds take over."

"I saw Kursh. He looked nervous, but Rossini didn't seem to notice."

"Probably thinks the little professor is harmless. Okay, let's see where this bum is taking us."

Nolan followed the other car into downtown and stayed several automobile lengths behind it as it drove through the Garment District and Chinatown, then turned towards South Station.

"Ha, what did I tell you, Willie, he's going to the North End. Do I know these assholes or what?"

"Should we notify '1' that we're working a case in their area?"

"We're still in the city of Boston, aren't we? Some of the dicks are friends of mine. I'll tell them about it when—hey, he's not going to the North End. Where the hell is he going?"

Rossini turned right at South Station and Nolan followed him over the Fort Point Channel and the Summer Street Bridge.

"You don't think he spotted us, do you?"

"I don't think so—"

Rossini slowed down and when the traffic on the opposite side of the road cleared, he suddenly made a U-turn and reversed his direction.

"Shit," Nolan said. "He's a cute bastard, this one. Watch which way he goes Willie." Nolan parked on the side of the road.

"I think he stopped at a shop just before the bridge on the other side of the street."

"There's a cigar store right about there. Wasn't he smoking a cigar when he arrived to pick up the newsletters?"

"Yeah, that's right."

A few minutes later, Rossini got back into his car, made another u-turn and was headed in their direction again.

"Here he comes," Nolan said. "Duck down until he goes by. I'm still not sure if he's on to us."

The detective let a couple of cars pass and then pulled out, only to travel less than a block when Rossini turned, drove parallel with the Fort Point Channel and pulled into the back yard of one of the open loft buildings that was used for the light manufacturing of confectionary products.

"What the hell is he doing?" Nolan said. "He's either on to us or he's getting into the candy business."

"Maybe, he's lost"

"Maybe—" Nolan drove past the front of the building. "356 . . . 356 Necco. Put that address in your diary with a description of the building, what's next to it and across the street."

"Okay."

He circled the block, returned to Necco Street and parked behind a building on the channel across from 356.

"What are we doing?" Dwyer said.

"Come on." Nolan jumped out of the car and walked into the building with Willie running to catch up. "Say, how are you doing, Toots," Nolan said as he briefly held up his badge to the woman who sat behind the desk "Boston Police, who's in charge here?"

"Mr. Chipman, Stewart Chipman, he's on the floor, but he can't be bothered—"

"Oh sure, Stewart. We go way back."

"He's directing the boys who are off-loading—"

"We're not going to take up much of his time. Just a few minutes to conduct an inspection." Nolan and Dwyer walked past her and opened the door to the warehouse floor.

"Inspection? What inspection?"

"Ah, geez, they didn't call you, huh. Well, don't worry about it. I'll take it up with Mr. Chipman." Nolan scanned the floor and looked for someone who acted like the universe rotated around him. "That's got to be him," he said to Willie, pointing to a portly middle-aged man, wearing a suit and fedora on the back of his head. He was directing about twenty dock-wallopers who were moving dollies loaded with bags of sugar and flour. "Say, Mr. Chipman," he said as they crossed the floor. "How you doing? I'm Detective Nolan and this is Investigator Dwyer. You've got an interesting place here, right on the water, huh."

"How did you get in here?"

"There's no problem, Mr. Chipman. We just need to do a walkthrough for the captain. We're inspecting every warehouse on the street for illegal booze."

"We don't have any illegal liquor here."

"Yeah, I know it's an asshole law, but the wartime prohibition is still on the books and it includes the manufacturing and transporting of liquor, which is what most of these businesses do down here, right. I mean manufacturing and transporting. And if we don't do our inspection, I'll be out on one of the islands doing my next patrol. And I can tell by looking around that you don't have anything illegal, right?

"You're damn right—"

"So, you don't mind if we check upstairs?"

One of the dock-wallopers dropped a bag from his dolly and its contents dumped on the floor. "Hey," Chipman screamed. "If you want to be out on the street, drop another one of those sacks." He looked at the two cops as if he just remembered that they were standing there. "Yeah, go ahead. You'll find nothing up there."

Nolan and Dwyer stepped onto the second floor and found a large open area that was partially filled with seventy-five pound bags. They walked to the end of the floor and looked out the window that faced 356. "Jaysus, a busy little beehive isn't it?" Nolan said.

"I've counted eight guys already going in and out of that warehouse," Willie said.

"Notice anything funny about them?"

"Yeah, none of them are wearing laborer's clothes, all suits."

"All chiefs and no Indians," Nolan said. "We need to get a closer look. Come on, let's go. We'll come back later tonight."

"You're all set sir, no problems," Nolan said when they returned to the first floor. And you don't have to worry, we won't be back for another week or so."

"That's good to hear—In another week?" Chipman said. "Why so soon?"

"I'm sure you've got nothing to worry about," Nolan said. "Say, maybe you can save us some leg work. Any of these warehouses empty down here on the pier? No use banging on empty doors."

Chipman turned away from his laborers. "No, most of them are up and running. Can't help you there."

"That's too bad. Well, we'll see you in a week, or sooner."

"Oh, wait a minute, the operation at the one across the street slowed up when the war ended and it closed down when the molasses tank collapsed. I think they shipped ammunition from there." Chipman snapped his fingers. "That's right, had crews running twenty-four hours a day at one time."

"But pretty quiet now, huh?" Nolan said. "Well, there's one that we can forget about, Willie."

Chipman looked at the two cops. "Ah—" He glanced at his laborers at the shipping door. "You know there's been some activity around that place for the last week or so." He turned in the direction of his laborers again and saw that they were busy. "A lot of guys coming and going, off-loading trucks. Looked like they were unloading army cots and tables and benches. I think I even saw big cooking pots."

"You don't say. Army cots, huh? Maybe it's the militia. Well, thanks, Mr. Chipman. We probably won't need to come back for at least a couple of weeks."

"Wait. Look, I got to tell you. They're a tough looking bunch. So, keep me out of it, okay?"

"We'll do the best we can, Mr. Chipman. You have a nice day."

Nolan drove off the channel and turned down Summer Street. "Let's see what we can find out about old 356 before the government buildings close."

"You didn't let Chipman off the hook, did you?" Willie asked.

"He's a lying sack of shit. If we had looked close enough, we would have found something illegal from stolen goods to undocumented immigrants. And another thing, those bums know everything that goes on in this tight-ass little world of theirs. He knows that something fishy is going on there, but he wasn't interested in sharing it until he thought we might be back at any time."

DWYER STEPPED sideways into the aisle between two stacks of bound volumes of the Suffolk County real estate records and searched the sequential numbers on the spines of the books for the number provided by the research clerk.

"Volume 5791. Yeah, that's it." Willie pulled the book out of the stacks and handed it to George.

"Let's see," Nolan said, "page 75." He flipped through the pages until he came to the right document. "It says, 'A certain parcel of land with the buildings thereon, situated on the northerly and westerly sides of Necco Street in Boston, Suffolk County. For consideration paid Three Thousand Five Hundred Dollars. Grant to the Patriot Realty Corporation of 85 Commercial Street, Boston, Massachusetts.'"

He pushed the book towards Willie. "I should have known. These cute bastards hide behind corporations, trusts and any other legal-schmeagal tricks their attorneys can think up. Here, put this information into your notes while I go see the clerk. Maybe she's got some ideas about finding the true owner."

As Willie shelved the book on the stacks, Nolan returned and grabbed his cap from the table. "Let's go."

"What did she tell you?"

"85 Commercial Street is close to where the molasses tank stood before it collapsed. She also told me that Patriot Realty owns a lot of property along the docks."

"So how do we find out who's hiding behind Patriot Realty?"

"Secretary of State's Office."

"What's there?"

"Hopefully, the answer to your question."

THE CLERK at the Secretary of State's office brought an index card to the counter and handed it to Nolan. "I think this is the one you want," she said. "There are several corporations with similar names. But didn't you tell me that your Patriot Realty is located on Commercial Street?"

"That's right, Miss, 85 Commercial."

"Okay, this is the business listed for that address. But that doesn't necessarily mean the address is the actual place where business is conducted. Sometimes, the listed address is an attorney's office and sometimes it is the location of the main administrative office."

"I don't know too many attorneys who hang their shingles out along Commercial Street," Nolan said. He turned the card around so she could read it. "Who are these people?"

"Those are the corporate officers—the President and Treasurer is Bradford Henshaw and the Clerk is Richard L. Ogden, Esquire. That's your attorney." She leaned over the counter and Nolan picked up the scent of her perfume. "If you like, I can bring out the application for Patriot Realty, which describes the company's operations."

"Yeah, that would be nice."

The clerk left for the files and within a few minutes returned to the counter. "Patriot Realty, as the name implies, purchases and sells real estate and they also act as a management company, probably for their real estate holdings."

"Can you help out an old cop, Miss? You deal with these records every day. For how long?"

"Say, you're not so old, detective." The clerk slid her hip and thigh onto the desk just below the counter where the cops were standing. "I've been working here six years."

"Six years, Willie. I'll bet Miss— I'm sorry, what was your name?

"I didn't give it. But it's Margaret."

"I'll bet Margaret can tell us things about this corporation that we would never know because she works with these records every day." Nolan handed the index card back to her. "If you were to interpret this particular record, what would it say to you?"

"Well, the business was incorporated about forty years ago and the president and the treasurer are the same person. That tells me that it is a smaller company, probably an old family business run with old money. And they incorporated to protect themselves personally."

"Probably an old Yankee family, you mean," Nolan said.

"Probably—if the principal address is on Commercial Street, my guess is that it is the main office and that it owns property near the North End and along the waterfront."

"What did I tell you, Willie," Nolan said. "We're going to end up in the North End after all." He stopped writing and pushed his cap to the back of his head. "Anything else?"

"One other thing. Patriot Realty probably owns warehouses and buildings and leases its space to other companies. And I wouldn't be surprised if they own some of the tenements in the North End and the Fort Point area."

"But at any rate, Patriot Realty owns 356 Necco. And Bradford Henshaw is the man to see."

"That's where I would start, detective."

"Thanks much, Margaret. You've been very helpful."

She slipped her hip off the desk as Nolan and Dwyer moved away from the counter. "Are you fellas going out on strike like the papers are saying?"

"Ah, don't worry about that," Willie said.

"Most of that stuff in the newspapers is rubbish anyways," Nolan said.

DAMPNESS AND FOG greeted the two cops later that night as they drove along the docks where Haymarket pushcarts were stacked in rows like barricades. Boston was a different place when Willie Dwyer and George Nolan returned. The money men and their attorneys from the financial companies, insurance houses and law firms that occupied the business district along State, Milk and Devonshire Streets were gone, as were the clerks and the judges from the courthouses and government buildings on School Street, Commercial Street and Post Office Square. Willie crossed over the channel at the Summer Street Bridge and parked a short distance away from it.

He took a kerosene lantern from the back of the car and lit it. "How are we getting in without a key?"

"What do you call these?" Nolan pulled a ring of keys out from under his seat. "Tools of the trade, Willie, a locksmith's best friends. And we're locksmiths, so to speak."

They walked the short distance to the channel and found the back door to Chipman's building. Nolan tried a couple of the keys and within a few minutes they were inside. "Kill the light," the detective said. They climbed to the second floor and looked out with a pair of binoculars to the building across the street.

Muted yellow light bled from behind newspaper that covered the building's windows. A couple of guys opened the front door, stepped outside and the loud boisterous sound of men followed them, men in the company of other men who spoke with swagger and in expletives.

"Did you hear that, Willie? It sounds like that building is full of those bums. It's like standing close to a beehive. And that asshole, Chipman, says, 'Oh, by the by, I seen a little activity at that building that I thought was empty.' For Chris' sake, if he didn't notice what was going on there, he should have his pulse taken to see if he's still alive. Let me have the binoculars." Nolan scanned the building from one end to the other. "Hmm, I wonder how many little bees are in there?"

"And where in the hell did they all come from?" Willie asked.

"And here's an even more important question—what the hell are they up to? We're going to have to find a way to get in there." The detective passed the binoculars back to Dwyer. "Here, your eyes are younger than mine. See if you can see anything."

"We know one thing. One of them looks like he could be a psychopath."

"Yeah, that's right. But there's something larger going on here. Something that I think we need to discover before we charge in there."

"Charge in there? There's a lot more of them than you and me."

"Well, maybe not literally. Let's watch them for a while until we figure out what the hell they're up to." Nolan took off his jacket and cap and laid them on the floor. "Did you give Rossini's automobile plate number to Boyle?"

"Yeah, he said that he was going to call the New York Motor Vehicle Division and see if they can come up with an owner's name." Willie swung the glasses to both sides of the building. "It looks like they're bedding down for the night. Those guys went back inside and they just killed some of the lights." Dwyer looked up to the end of the street. "I see some movement. Yeah, there it is. There are a couple of guys walking in the direction of the building."

"I see them," said Nolan. "They look like they're new to the area, the way they're looking around. Geez! They're both carrying baseball bats."

The two men looked up and down the street and then one pointed to the numbers '356' on the building.

"Kind of late to be selling bats door-to-door don't you think," Nolan said. "Open that window easy. I want to hear if these guys have anything to say."

Willie slid the window up a few inches and Nolan put his ear to the open space. He watched the two men knock on the door and someone inside open it a couple of inches. One of the men touched his chest and then pointed with his thumb to his companion. "Introductions," the detective said. "The guy inside mustn't know them."

"A car just turned the corner," Willie said.

"Open that window a little more."

Dwyer raised the window and they both stooped down to listen. The driver of the car got out and approached the two men with the baseball bats. "Hey," Willie whispered. "That's our friend."

"This is Joey Ventresca," the cops heard Rossini say to the guy at the door. He gestured to the other guy. "And this is Carlo Ricci. Oh, you met them. Why the fuck didn't you say so, you big prick?" Rossini stepped in front of Ventresca and Ricci, pushed the door open and walked inside. "Come on, you guys. Pick out a cot and make yourself comfortable." The voices from inside became subdued like Rossini's presence was significant. Just before the door closed, the cops heard him say, "I got them over at Salem Street."

"Salem Street? That's the North End again." Nolan said. "You know I'm getting an uneasy feeling about this. We need to find out how many of those assholes are in there." He closed the window and sat on the floor with his back against the wall. "Let's wait until it gets really quiet. We'll copy the plate numbers off any cars or trucks out back." He turned back towards the window and looked outside. "And somehow, we're going to get a peek inside." He sat there in the dark and mulled over the events of the last twelve hours. "Salem Street?"

CATHERINE SAT in the last booth at the back of the diner with her legs stretched out in front of her, her head dropping each time she dozed off, one of her hands still wrapped around a damp dishcloth. It was the lull in the wee hours of the morning and she had succumbed to the hypnotic hum of the empty diner. In the kitchen, the cook was asleep across two chairs.

The bell over the door rang weakly and two men slipped into the diner. One of them closed the door so that the latch snapped into place without notice. The other one, the larger of the two, walked behind the counter and poured two mugs of coffee. The smaller man hung his hat on the hook at the end of Catherine's booth and sat down on the stool closest to her. After he had fixed the coffees, the big man gave one to his associate and slipped into Catherine's booth on the opposite side of her.

"She sure is a beauty, Jack," said the man on the counter stool.

"Just the way I like 'em, Hump. And Beef Stew, what do you think he would say if he was here."

"Yeah, he'd be impressed. It's too bad he got jammed up with that broad in Middletown. We could'a used him on this job."

Catherine stirred with the sound of their voices, lazily opened her eyes and then jumped into a seating position. "Oh, I didn't know that anyone had come in," she said. "What can I get for you guys?"

"The coffee will do, Miss," said Hump.

Jack broke into a stupid smile. "Yeah, the coffee will do."

"Oh, well if you change your minds."

She slid over and started to stand when Jack reached across the table and put his hand up to stop her. "Ah, before you go, Doll Face, we need to conduct a little business."

"What kind of business?" Catherine asked.

"Geez, Jack, you probably scared this little girl half to death. Where are your manners?" Hump said. "And we don't want to wake our sleeping friend in the kitchen. First, an introduction. My name is Reginald Schultz, but I'm better known as Hump. And my large friend is Jack McCarthy. I'm sorry if he frightened you, Catherine."

"How do you know my name?"

"We know a lot of things about you. How do you think we knew you'd be here? But you needn't worry, we're here to offer you a proposition."

"I want a cigarette," she said. "They're behind the counter."

"I'll get 'em." Hump walked behind the counter and found the box of cigarettes and flipped them on the table. "Here you go."

Catherine removed a cigarette and wrapped her fingers around it, trying to keep her hand from shaking. She placed it in her mouth and before she could light a match, Jack lit one for her and held it up, leering at her from behind the flame.

She blew out the smoke. "So, what's this all about?"

"We understand that you're friends with a Mr. Rankin, James Rankin," Hump said.

"I don't know what you're talking about." She began to slide out of her seat again.

"Now, where do you think you're going?" McCarthy leaned his large head over the table and held her at bay with one hand. "A spirited little bitch, aren't you? Maybe I should ask the questions."

"Let's not be hasty," Hump said. "Show her the item."

Jack removed an earring from his pocket, placed it on the table and slid it across the table. "Look familiar?"

"Maybe. And maybe not." She pushed away from the table and braced her back against the seat. "There are lots of earrings like that."

"Look, we're trying not to get rough here, Miss," Hump said. "But that's not a piece of junk you're holding there. It's got a thick gold band with a diamond chip."

Catherine picked up the earring. "It sure is nice." She stared at it vacantly for a few minutes and then put it back on the table. "Where did you get this?"

"We have some very, what should I say, talented people who work with us. I believe that it was clipped along with its companion from a room at the Cliff Walk Hotel in Rhode Island." Hump reached over and turned the piece of jewelry over. "CL" stands for Catherine Loftus, doesn't it?"

"What if it does? What do you want from me?"

"It didn't end on a good note, did it? You and Mr. Rankin, I mean. Nasty display in the parking lot." He nodded to McCarthy and directed him to check on the cook in the back room. Hump took his seat in the booth. "I like your style, kid, and I know you ain't living high on the hog. So, why shouldn't you get a chance to make a little scratch and maybe have the last laugh?"

"What makes you think I'm interested? I don't even know you guys." Catherine put out her cigarette and chewed on her cuticle.

Hump reached into his wallet and placed a hundred dollar bill on the table. "That's for nothing," he said as he pushed it across to her. "You already marked yourself with Dandy Jim, that's what he's called, right. I could see it in your eyes. So, the hundred is yours to keep."

She held the bill up to the light.

"You don't have to worry, it's real."

She put it into her apron pocket. "So what else are you driving at?"

"See? I told Jack that you was one smart broad." Hump twisted the ashtray around with his finger. "We need a photograph of you and our Mr. Rankin." He smiled like the odd uncle. "A personal and interesting photograph."

"Doing what?"

Jack began to snicker at the door to the kitchen.

Hump gave him the high sign. "Get in there, you dope, and keep an eye on the cook." He waited for McCarthy to leave and then said, "There are nine more of them hundred dollar bills to go along with the one you already have in your apron."

"Nine? Jeez, that's a grand for doing what, sticking up a bank?" She sat up rigid and traced a line with her eyes from Hump to Jack and back to Hump. "Say, I ain't doin' nothing that's gonna get me in trouble with the law."

"You got no worry, there, kid. In the meantime, see if you can fix your problem with Mr. Rankin."

"I'll think about it. Besides, that's not goin' to be easy. I don't know if he wants to see me again."

"Don't take too long." Hump slid out of the booth and stood. "I'm sure you'll think of something."

He and McCarthy walked to the door and opened it.

"Wait," Catherine said. "How am I supposed to get in touch with you?"

"Don't worry, we'll get in touch with you."

When they left, Catherine walked to the hook where she hung her coat and put the hundred dollar bill into the pocket. She sat back down in the booth and picked up the earring and turned it in her hand. "A grand," she said.

"WILLIE, WAKE UP." Nolan kicked the sole of Dwyer's shoe. "It's time to go to work."

Dwyer was still sitting on the floor beside the window with his back to the wall. "What time is it?" He ran his tongue around his mouth and raked his hand through his hair. "My mouth tastes like a cow shit in it. How long have I been asleep?"

"It's just after three. You've been out long enough for you to have a dream or, I should say, a nightmare." Nolan put his suit coat back on and checked his pockets for his notebook and pencil and picked up a can of gasoline he found in the building.

"A nightmare? Why, was I shouting or something?"

"Not really shouting, but I heard you huffing the name Bernie."

"Bernie?" Dwyer shook his head like he was trying to clear it. "What are we doing?"

"Come on. Those bums have been quiet for a while now. And there is a nice low-lying fog out there. It's time we found out who they are." George walked to the window and peered out. "When we get out on the street, stay out of the sight of their windows. Newspaper or no newspaper, they probably have a sentry on duty."

They made their way across the street and past the high arched windows to the lot out back. There were three cars and a truck parked there; two of the cars had New York registrations, the third car and the truck had Massachusetts plates on them.

"Have you got them?" Nolan whispered.

"Yeah."

"Good, and now for the crème da la crème. Where are those papers and rags from Chipman's building?"

"Right here. What are you going to do with them?"

"The chances of us getting into that building and looking around without being seen are slim to none. So, we need to smoke 'em out. There's a burn barrel near the back entrance. Come on. Grab leaves, grass, anything that will make a nice smoky fire."

They placed the barrel next to the door on the platform, left a rag wick hanging out of it and lit it. Then the detective lit several other rag wicks he had soaked in gasoline and stuffed under the shingles of a small toolshed located next to the building.

As a parting shot, Nolan dropped an old inner tube into the barrel. "That should give it just the right consistency. Come on, let's get back to our perch. The bees are going to be pretty pissed off when they come out of there."

Inside Chipman's warehouse, Nolan made an anonymous call to the Fire Department and reported a blaze on Necco Street, said you could see it from the other side of the channel. He and Dwyer watched the black acrid smoke rise from the barrel and crawl under the belly of the fog, groping its way towards them and the channel like it was trying to find a way out. Thin grey smoke followed it, strands of it escaping towards the water and some of it floating back towards the warehouse. Voices began to scream inside the building. The front door blew open and the street filled with half-dressed and excitable men, their angry voices echoing into the night and across the water. Armed with pistols and shotguns, they raced from the building and ran in a disoriented helter-skelter way until Rossini began shouting angry instructions at them, until the first gongs could be heard from the fire trucks that were crossing over the Summer Street Bridge. Until a team of horses thundered out of the fog and raced down Necco Street with the pumper barely touching the cobblestones.

"They're an excitable bunch of little bees when they're rousted from their sleep, aren't they?" Nolan said.

He and Dwyer stayed in the dark of the room and continued to watch the firemen as they extinguished the blaze. Fifty or more men, dressed in street clothes and carrying various sorts of firearms, milled around the building. Some of them pulled up the collars to their suit coats and buttoned the top buttons. They stood with scaly caps and felt hats on, stood back-to-back with their guns at the ready.

"You seeing what I'm seeing, Willie? There's more of these boys than all the cops on the streets of Boston tonight and they ain't the local chapter of the Red Cross, that's for goddam sure. I wonder what they told the firemen about being there?" The detective took out his notebook and began to write. "Start writing everything you see."

"Like what?" Dwyer said.

"Everything. Descriptions, ages, nationalities—you name it. You take the bums to the right of the front door and I'll take the left. When we call New York, I want as much information as I can give 'em. Maybe there will be something about this group that will ring a bell with them."

"Who do you think they are?"

"Like I told you, I'm not sure, but I know they're a tough looking bunch, like ex-cons." Nolan closed his notebook. "We need to find out who they are, but then we need to answer the more important question—who's fronting the money to bring these assholes to Boston? You want to know why something happens, Willie, or how something happens, follow the money."

He stood in the window and saw the firemen leave, followed the fire trucks with his eyes and as they passed the men in the street, found himself looking directly into the gaze of Salvatore Rossini. He was separated from the others and turned towards Chipman's building, holding a match up with cupped hands, lighting a cigar and looking directly up at the window, staring with the eyes of the dead. He lit the cigar and broke into a thin crooked sneer, walked to a small circle of armed men and leaned into it, said something in confidence and then entered the building.

"Let's get the fuck outta here." Nolan ran across the floor.

"What's the matter?"

"Rossini knows we're here and I think he and a bunch of his goons are about to pay us a visit." He jumped down the stairs in two giant leaps with Willie right behind him. "Out the dock side and take off your jacket." Nolan ran to the back door and opened it. They heard threats and angry foul curses reverberate in the street and between the buildings, and a shotgun, discharging and shattering glass at the front entrance to Chipman's building. The cops sprinted to the wall that ran along the channel. "Hurry up! Take your jacket off and make a sack, put your gun and your diary into it."

"They're coming around the side of the building." Willie twisted his jacket into a sack. "But hey, Detective, why aren't we just telling those fellas who we are?"

"If you want to stand here and show your badge, go right ahead. But these guys don't give a fuck about badges. They'll fill your belly full of lead." The cops stood staring at the water. "There's only one way out of here," said Nolan. "I hope you can swim—"

"A little—" Dwyer watched the detective leap out into the fog, suspended in air for an instant, wrapped in the mist like a Christmas spirit, and then he was gone. "Oh, shit." Willie heard the footsteps behind him, getting louder and larger. And then he jumped, eyes closed in a leap of faith, into the mist and darkness. He plunged into the black water, the impact opening his eyelids, and was sucked down into the channel that was deeper, darker and colder than he had expected. He kicked continuously until he broke the surface in a gasp for air, bobbing above the waterline like an unanchored buoy. He heard multiple rounds being fired into Chipman's warehouse, shotgun blasts, pistol pops and bullets pinging and zinging off of wood and metal, and sing-song voices calling, "Come on out. We won't hurt you."

"Willie," Nolan whispered. "Willie, where are you?"

"George? Over here."

"I think I see you." Nolan paddled easily in the fog to Dwyer. "Try to relax. Let the current take you. Don't fight it and don't talk until we're out of the water." George slipped into the mist with only his voice still visible. "Damn, I'm getting too old for this bullshit."

They floated down the channel making their way to the far side of the bridge. The barrage of gunfire had petered out to a few random pistol shots fired into the blackness when a voice called out, "Come back here, you pricks, and we'll kill you."

"Round one goes to them." Nolan choked on some water and laughed in hiccups. They waited for a few minutes under the trestle and then climbed out. "Oops, there's the bell for round two, Willie. That fucker has not heard the last from us."

"REMIND ME to get a couple of bottles for those guys at Engine Company 38," Nolan said as he and Dwyer parked behind the Roxbury Crossing station. "The dry clothes and the whiskey shots finally stopped the shakes."

Willie picked up the damp pages to his diary off the back seat. "I heard you talking to the lieutenant about how we ended up in the water, but didn't hear what you said."

"I told him that we fell in the water when filling buckets to put out the fire."

"Did he believe you?"

George scoffed. "Nah, but he didn't ask any more questions either."

"What do you make of the alibi that Rossini gave the firemen for camping out at the warehouse?" Willie said.

"Industrial guard service? My eye! They might be here because the merchants want some protection in case we strike, but there is something else going on with those bums. First of all, no one is going to pay them to sit around unless someone is pretty convinced that there is going to be a strike." Nolan stepped out of the car in a pair of trousers and a borrowed shirt. "You work enough strike duty and you get to know some of the private dicks because they're like a traveling sideshow, going from one strike to the next. Did you see those guys? I didn't recognize any of them. They look like goons from murderers' row."

Dwyer took his wet clothes from the back of the cruiser and tied them up in a ball. "Maybe they're just guessing and figuring that if we do go out, they'll be ready."

"Just guessing, huh. I've been around too long, Willie, to buy that. The odds say otherwise. Someone has to be paying for their food, ammo—whatever. " Nolan piled his wet clothes in his arms and bumped the car door shut with his hip. "Maybe this is the start of the revolution that the Bolsheviks have been talking about since Petrograd. Who knows? Judgment Day may be just around the corner."

"You really think so, George?"

"I'm kidding, Willie. Jesus, don't take everything I say literally."

Nolan and Dwyer avoided the questions and stares as they walked through the station. The detective was deep into a running conversation with himself. "What do we have here anyways? Fraina tells Kursh to run a bunch of newsletters for Rossini, a guy he doesn't know, with headlines reporting the Boston Police are on strike. How the hell can they predict a strike when we don't even know what's going to happen? I mean there's a chance of it, but—"

They dragged themselves up to the second floor and settled into the detectives' office. The ceiling snapped with the hard heels of shoes above them as the day shift pulled itself out of the rack and readied itself for roll call. They could hear the cops on the third floor and it sounded like any other day in the station, guys full of piss and vinegar, breaking each other's balls and bitching and moaning about the job, saying what they would do when they were no longer cops, saying nothing that hadn't been said by cops ever since there were cops. They could hear Quigley's voice riding over the general buzz of conversation like a ball peen hammer striking the end of a steel drum.

"Listen to those guys," Nolan said. "That's what I love about this job. It's the fellas that we work with that make it the best fucking job in the world. Not another one like it on the planet. And the stories that only cops can appreciate. You'll have a good one to tell over a couple of tall ones after last night, Dwyer. Between that and the bomber in the ledges, you're set for life."

"Is it too early to call New York about Rossini and the others?" Willie asked.

Nolan stretched his arms over his head and yawned. "We've been going all night, and I don't know about you, but I need to catch a few winks. There should be a couple of open beds now that the day shift's gone." He struggled to his feet, took his cap and placed it on the radiator. "What do you say? It's going to be a long day when we come back."

"You go on," Willie said. "I'm going to wring my .38 out and put some oil on it. Then I'll crash."

In the News

POLICE UNION DECISION NOT BEFORE MONDAY
Mayor Peters Asks For Postponement
(Boston)
The crisis in the police situation in Boston will not come until next Monday, at the earliest. Statement released by Commissioner Curtis after a conference with his adviser, ex-Attorney General Herbert Parker, attorneys James H. Vahey and John F. Feeney, counsel for the Policemen's Union, and seven officers of the union.
BOSTON EVENING GLOBE
Thursday, September 4, 1919

KEEP FAITH WITH THE WORLD, WILSON'S APPEAL TO AMERICA
League of Nations Alone Will Carry Out the Pledge of Peace
"Don't Let Them Pull It Down" He Pleads
(Columbus, Ohio)
"The only people that I owe any report to are you and the other citizens of the United States, and it has become increasingly necessary, apparently, that I should report to you. After all the various angles at which you heard the treaty held up, perhaps you would like to know what is in the treaty."
THE BOSTON DAILY GLOBE
Friday, September 5, 1919

WILL AMERICAN NEGROES BE DRIVEN INTO AN UPRISING
After three lynchings in a week in Louisiana, Tennessee and Georgia
THE REPUBLIC
Saturday, September 6, 1919

Chapter Sixteen

Dwyer grabbed a cup of coffee on his way through the kitchen, climbed the stairs to the detective's office and plopped into a chair.

"Ah, bright eyes, ready to go to work?" Nolan bounded into the room, sheets of paper rolled into his fist. "I got some very interesting information from New York." He jumped into his seat and spun it in Willie's direction, jabbing his index finger into the papers. "Here's a list of names that are most likely some of the bums that gave us the bath in the channel. And I'm betting that every one of these assholes has a record and an outstanding arrest warrant just waiting to be served."

"Say, did you sleep at all?" Willie asked.

"I nodded on and off for a couple of hours, but I felt like I had just stuck my finger into an electric box. So I got up and got a few things done. Here, take some of these names and check on them."

"Who are they?"

"They're members of a strikebreaking gang run by a whacko named Pearlie Brodsky, a collection of certifiable odd balls. He digs them outta poolrooms, saloons and dives on the East Coast." Nolan pointed to several names on the list. "Start with these. The New York dicks think he even recruits them from the funny farm because he's got arsonists, rapists and murderers among his band of outlaws."

"All those guys at Necco Street are nut jobs?"

"Not all. He'll beef them up with local guys on the down-and-down who'll take anything that'll put a few bucks in their pockets."

"How's he keep them in line?"

"With an iron fist. And the more men hanging around, the larger the pool of cannon fodder he has to recruit from. Supposedly, he doesn't have any problems hiring Negroes or Italians either. If the strikers are white, then he hires black; if they're Irish, then Italians fill the gap. All comes down to who wants to eat the most."

"Is that why he's recruiting in the North End, cheap labor?"

"Right. Remember our boy, Rossini?"

"Yeah."

"Brodsky's chief slugger and recruiter, real name Isaac Jacobs, aka, Tommy Stillman, a real pip. He's already served two terms in the state pen in Elmira for larceny, extortion and manslaughter. And wait until you hear this. During the elevated operators' strike in New York City, he killed another one of Brodsky's goons while driving a streetcar."

"Who the hell would hire these bums?"

"Big money, Willie—from the owners of coal mines and department stores to steamship lines and even cities like New York and Chicago. If there's a Labor dispute, one of these so-called detective agencies can't be far behind." He lit a cigarette. "Some of them are legit and professional and some, like Brodsky, play by their own rules, busting heads and shooting up picket lines." Nolan snapped his fingers and jumped up, the butt dangling from his lips. He opened his cabinet, rummaging through the drawer until he pulled out a file. "I knew I heard that name before. Brodsky busted a strike in Norwood a couple of years ago."

"What are they here for—us?" Willie asked.

"What else can it be? Boston will be a fucking Coney Island for these guys. No cops on the streets? Are you kidding me? I've got the names of the places where they've been. You know there's got to be a trail of paper. So, let's get on it."

"Wait, why would they want the Reds' newsletters?"

"That's a good question, Willie. Haven't figured that one out yet." Nolan crushed the half-spent cigarette into an ashtray. "The New York cops told me that Brodsky thinks of himself as an All American hero and we know that the Commie Socialists' objective is to dismantle America. Doesn't fit. I think we'll find out the answer when we learn who brought these shit bums into our city. We've got to talk to the captain about notifying the other stations and then we'll get cozy with this Bradford Henshaw."

THE CAPTAIN LISTENED to their story without comment, but his body language spoke volumes. His eyes never strayed from the speaker, which most of the time was George Nolan, fixed like open windows that allowed the world a view of the man inside. As the details of the investigation rolled out of his detective's mouth like a bad case of heartburn, Keveney fidgeted and changed his sitting position several times. Dwyer read the captain's reaction as thoughtful and concerned; Nolan, with many more years on the job and knowledge of the man who sat across from him, read the captain as annoyed and calculating, as in, how does this bullshit affect me.

George W. Keveney was the second member of a large West Roxbury family to rise to a commissioned officers rank. Upon his promotion, he had lobbied for assignment to the relatively new station on Centre Street where he could be close to home and free from the bump and grind of the older, poorer and more populated precincts. But his godfather politician convinced him that a tour of duty at one of the larger and busier stations would be beneficial to his career so he landed in Roxbury Crossing, never quite comfortable with the grit of the Mission Hill experience, and just tried to survive the 'Field' requirement for his resume.

"So that's it, Captain," Nolan said. "It looks like we're going to have to muster a large detail to hit the warehouse. Do you want to call South Boston or shall I give them a call?"

Keveney pursed his lips and then squeezed down the ample flesh around his eyes, squinting like the pungent odor of the detective's story had just reached his olfactory gland. He turned from Nolan and glanced at Dwyer, then directed an authoritative stare back at his detective. "Do you know who Bradford Henshaw is?"

"Right now, sir, all I know is that he might be the owner of a warehouse where more than sixty armed felons are holed up."

"He is a member of an old and highly respected Boston family and," the captain lifted his index finger to make a point, "he is a member of the Downtown Club Association, a prestigious civic organization whose members include some of the city's most influential businessmen who are politically enabled and who have sponsored and endorsed many of our elected officials, including our current mayor."

"I'm not saying that Mr. Henshaw is even aware of the thugs that are using his property as an armed camp, Captain, but if he is a highly respected citizen, I'm sure that he would want to cooperate in removing this group of criminals from his property and the city limits."

"If this turns out badly, detective, the repercussions will be great. I will probably lose my command and you will earn yourself an assignment transporting drunks to Deer Island."

"Sir, we have confirmed arrest warrants for twenty-two individuals who we either positively identified or are known regulars in Brodsky's army. With enough cops, this could be handled without incident."

"Without incident?" Keveney barked. "You tell me that these thugs shoot up an innocent man's property so that he can't conduct his business because you were conducting an unauthorized surveillance from it, which happens to be in another station's area. Is that what you mean by 'without incident,' detective? The way I see it, this is a Station 6 investigation and they should handle it. If they want our support, I will be glad to provide it."

"But Captain, what about the assault on us?"

"When they conduct their round-up, you can serve your warrant for Rossini and anyone else you can identify."

Nolan glanced at Dwyer with a 'do you believe this asshole' expression. "Yes sir." He held up his notebook. "What about the information we've developed? I'd like to pass it on to '6.'"

"I'll call Captain Richardson and tell him that you will be contacting his detectives."

Nolan and Dwyer stood. "Is that all, sir?"

"I know how you feel, Nolan, but your Labor Union has put us and the city in a very precarious position. If the Union strikes, Boston may actually need private investigators like Brodsky to keep the mob from destroying it."

"Right, sir. I'll type up a short report to brief the South Boston detectives. Can I keep Dwyer while we transfer our information to them?"

"He can stay with you, if Station 6 requests our assistance."

"Thank you, sir."

AS DWYER PASSED the duty desk, the sergeant handed him a note.

"Your landlady called, Willie, something about a cablegram from Ireland. I think she said that it's marked 'urgent.' I would have broken in, but I could hear the captain's voice and didn't think he would appreciate the interruption."

"Thanks," Willie said. He caught up to Nolan and followed him into the detectives' office. "I need to stop by my rooming house."

Nolan fired his notebook against the wall. "That fucking ball bag, he's worried more about—"

"Do you think I can get an hour off to go home?"

"This could be the biggest thing that this Department has ever been involved with." Nolan collapsed into a chair, seething and mumbling under his breath. "It's all a racket—everyone's protecting their own arse."

Willie stood in front of Nolan's desk like he was vibrating. "Did you hear what I said?"

The detective looked up. "What?"

"I need to stop home—family problem."

"Sure, go ahead. Hope everything is okay. Go on, get out of here and take care of business." Nolan picked up his notebook from the floor. "Give me your diary and I'll type up something quick for South Boston."

Willie started for the door.

"When you're finished, call me here. I'm thinking that '6' is going to request our help, if I phrase it the right way. I'll pick you up at your room."

"Imagine what the captain would have said if he knew about the fire and the swim across the channel," Willie said.

Nolan chuckled. "Yeah. Some things are better left unsaid."

WILLIE SAT on his bed, opened the cablegram and dislodged the memories of people and places that he hadn't thought about in a while, the distinctive sounds and smells of the small family farm, the three-room cottage, and the living scents of his younger brothers and sisters. He unfolded the cable and read.

William Dwyer
45 Leroy Street
Boston, Massachusetts

USA
Dear Willie [stop] Da not well [stop]
Dublin accommodations killing him [stop]
Graves O'Brien arriving there next week [stop]
May try and contact you [stop]
Doesn't know where you work [stop]
If you see him, show him the sights and
tell him we said hello [stop]
Mim

"So Constable O'Brien is coming for me, all the way across the Atlantic." Willie began to drum his fingers. "He's not tagging me with Bernie's murder when I was a bystander trapped in that barn. Not going back—" He slammed his fist into the bed. "The Sledge! That's who Quinn is, the I.R.B. man in the barn that night. Now de Valera's bodyguard—Peter Quinn. No wonder he looked so familiar."

In the News

VOLUNTEER POLICE

Able Bodied Men willing to give their services in case of necessity for part of day or night for protection of persons and property in the City of Boston. Apply to me at room B, Third Floor, Chamber of Commerce Building, Boston, daily except Sundays.

WILLIAM H. PIERCE
Supt. of Police (Retired)
BOSTON EVENING GLOBE
Thursday, September 4, 1919

Chapter Seventeen

~

On many days, Edwin Upton Curtis would sit at one end of the expansive screened porch at the back of his summer home in Nahant where it faced the bay, always maintaining the stiff reserve and self-imposed restraint of the Curtis family, which aspired for recognition from older founding families. But today, he surrendered to the ravages of his heart, struggled with the removal of his long double-breasted coat and collapsed into the overstuffed chair next to the fieldstone fireplace. Protracted discussions with the police union and its attorneys had taken their toll. He had stood his ground in defense of social order and had made it clear that the police were not workers, but guardians of that social order. Now, at the waterfront property, he rested and attempted to regain his strength, absent from the annoyance and exasperation of Boston politics. The only person permitted to intrude into his time-out sat reading at the opposite side of the fireplace.

Herbert Parker finished the last line of text and closed the document entitled, *Report of the Executive Committee to Mayor Peters,* placed it inside his briefcase and closed the latch. "So, what do you think?" the attorney said.

"It has no bearing on my decision," the commissioner said. "I absolutely refuse to consider any proposed solution that might be interpreted as a pardon to men on trial. Come Monday, I will suspend the nineteen patrolmen for violation of Rule 35." He grimaced and rubbed his hand back and forth across his chest. "By what right or authority do Peters and Storrow think they can interfere?"

"Are you alright?"

"I'm fine."

"You don't look fine. Frankly, Edwin, I'm concerned about your health."

"I'll be better when I can finally relieve myself of the stress of dealing with this police union matter. What will help is the knowledge that I am standing on solid legal ground in prohibiting the patrolmen from affiliating with the A.F. of L. That is the only issue here."

"I assure you as your counsel that you stand on the high ground. A police officer cannot belong to a labor union and consistently perform his sworn duty. It's as clear a case of conflict of interest as I can think of. The idea that patrolmen would attempt to intimidate the citizens of the Commonwealth by threatening to strike—because you might suspend nineteen of their members for disobeying a *direct order* not to affiliate with a national union—is thuggery at its best and cannot be tolerated. It is high time that someone in this city stood up to these Irish hoodlums."

The clock in the foyer began to sound the hourly refrain; there was a pause and then it struck four times. Curtis appreciated the warmth of the fire, rested his head against the chair and closed his eyes. "Why did you change your mind and agree to the Mayor's request for a postponement?" "There were several reasons for allowing a continuance. But the most important consideration was for time, time to do things right."

The attendant entered the parlor, carrying two glasses of warm cider, left them for the two men and exited the room.

Parker took a glass from the tray. "How this all plays out will affect future Labor negotiations in the city, the state, and, I dare say, the country. This is not the first attempt by a Police Department to unionize and it will not be the last. How we handle this will be critiqued by municipalities all over America. So far, we have received high marks." Parker sampled the cider and put his glass down. "Americans do not like the idea of striking police, Edwin, and they are genuinely fearful that this kind of radical behavior is being championed by a certain element within the Police Department that is affiliated with the Bolshevik movement."

"Do you really believe that?"

"It's not important whether I believe it or not. The letters that you've received from concerned citizens are all the evidence you need. Don't be afraid to use that fear to your advantage."

Parker continued. "Postponing the announcement on punishment places you in the best position for success. Besides, what harm does it do? You have the support of that cunning fox, Coolidge, albeit lukewarm support, but remember, he is the only person who can remove you. You will remain the commissioner as long as it does not reflect poorly on him. Granting the Mayor and his committee a continuance makes you look magnanimous. You've been around Boston politics long enough to understand that you can do almost anything as long as the people believe you are fair and have their interests at heart."

The attendant reentered the room. "Excuse me Commissioner, shall I have another place set for dinner?"

Parker gestured with his hand to Curtis. "Thank you, but no. I have another engagement and I think you could use the rest." He turned to the attendant. "Would you get my umbrella, please?

"Don't get up," Parker said as Curtis began to stand. The attorney waited for the attendant to leave. "There is also a pragmatic reason for granting the postponement. I need not bother you with the details, but suffice to say, in politics, it is important to know the answers to questions even before they are asked."

"Questions, Herbert?"

"Questions like—will the other unions, particularly the BCLU, strike on behalf of the police?"

"I think that's a moot point," Curtis said. "From what I am being told by the superior officers, most of the patrolmen will not strike."

"I guess I am an old pessimist. But I would rather see us plan for the worst and hope for the best. I'll prepare a response to the Mayor regarding the Storrow Committee report. In the meantime, get some rest and breathe in this clean ocean air. I'll speak with you tomorrow."

After the attendant escorted Parker to the door, he brought in a carriage blanket, covered Curtis and placed a couple of logs on the fire. The Commissioner put his feet up on the ottoman and closed his eyes. He thought about the turbulent months since his appointment and reflected on an old Puritan prayer. *My trials have been fewer than my sins.* He pulled the blanket close around him and soon dozed off.

MAX HENSHAW spun a football in his hands and after every couple of turns, flipped it into the air and caught it. "Coach Fisher is really pleased with the team and its execution. He says it's better than last year."

"Great," his father said. "By the way, how many footballers signed up for the Volunteer Police force?"

"About a hundred."

"I'll tell you something, Max. You'll learn more about this city in a couple of days on the street than you will in a year in the classroom."

"I know from talking to the other fellers that everyone is looking forward to the season, but I don't think any of us would pass up that kind of an opportunity if it happens."

"You'll have your season, but when there is a call for civic duty, you have to answer." His son threw him the football and he caught it against his chest. He tossed it back to Max and then walked him to the door. "Be a good sport and stop by Hanover Street and pick up the rents."

"Okay, but—"

"But what?"

"I feel like Simon Legree when I go over there."

"We need the revenue from those buildings, Max. With the end of the war and that damn molasses tank disaster, our commercial properties are costing us a fortune. It's the residential properties that are keeping us afloat." He opened the office door and put his arm across his son's shoulders. "Sometimes, it's an unpleasant business we're in, but if we didn't do it, someone else would. Okay?

"Okay—"

"Tell your mother I will be a few minutes late for dinner because of some pressing business."

Henshaw watched his son leave the alley between the buildings and disappear as the telephone began to ring. He glanced at his watch and saw that it was precisely six o'clock, the time that he had asked Pearl Brodsky to call.

"Yes? Hello, Mr. Brodsky. Fine, yes I'm fine. So, how are we coming?"

Henshaw dipped his pen into the ink. "What about the girl? Will she cooperate? I see. Well, stay on that. It's very important." He wrote himself a short note.

"Are your men making any progress with the Italians? And these men are some of your moles? What? Well, the newspapers are reporting that the Union leaders will be suspended on Monday and that the rest of them will strike on Tuesday. I'll know better later today. But, in a few days, we may need fifty to seventy-five guards to protect certain earmarked businesses. Will you have enough men? Good."

"A problem?" Henshaw asked. "What kind of a—at my building? Do you know who it was? Not sure if it was cops? That won't do at all. Move your men out of there immediately. I can't afford to have—" He was distracted by a car pulling into his driveway. "I have another place for them to stay, much more secure and off the beaten path. What? Oh, it definitely will keep them out of sight. In the meantime, tell them to start packing."

Henshaw lifted his head to a knock at the door. He looked up and saw the silhouette of a man through the frosted glass. "Okay, Mr. Brodsky. That's good work. But remember, move those men immediately. Yes, good night."

"Come in, counselor," Henshaw said as he replaced the telephone in its cradle.

NOLAN AND DWYER pulled into the Boston Coal yard, parked the cruiser behind the building and out of sight, and walked the two-block distance down Commercial Street, carrying lunch pails, like a couple of mopes dragging themselves home after work. They made their way to the waterfront where Nolan pried open the door of a small shed across the street from Henshaw's office. "If we have to sit on this guy, we might as well keep dry," Nolan said. "Feels like it's going to pour any minute."

Dwyer ran across the street, confirmed the name on Henshaw's building and the location of the entrances. "That's it," he said. "'Patriot Realty' is on the door."

"How many entrances?"

"Two. We're looking directly at one and there is another in the alley by the fire escape." Willie stepped away from the window. "I think there are a couple of guys in the office."

Nolan sat in a chair with a view of Henshaw's front door and the driveway. "You don't think you were seen, do you?"

"No, they were busy talking to each other."

The detective pulled his pocketwatch out of his trousers. "Hmm, almost six o'clock on a Saturday, an unusual day and time to be conducting business, don't you think? Look at the street, not another soul on it."

Dwyer moved another chair close to the window. "So, should I ask how we remained on the case?"

"Assisting, Willie. The operative word is 'assisting.' All the stations are in the same fix as we are with the possibility of a strike."

"The Station 1 detectives seem like good fellas."

"Mulvey and Byrne? They're the best. You can trust those guys with your life. If they say they'll check Necco Street in the morning, you can count on it."

"How come South Boston isn't going to check it?" Willie said. "It's their area."

"They're sending a uniform for backup." Nolan leaned to one side for a better view. He pointed to the window. "Is that someone leaving?"

Willie jumped up to take a closer look and nodded. "Yeah, looks like a young guy, athletic build, maybe early twenties. He's walking towards the Italian section, but he's dressed too well to live there." Willie started for the door.

"Where're you going?"

"To tail him."

"Just sit tight. A young guy like that, well dressed, I'm guessing he's a numbers man for the business and needs the weekend to crunch the books. Could even be a relative." Nolan shifted in his chair one way and then the other as he tried to get a better look. "Maybe that's why someone is in there on a Saturday. They're cooking the books. At any rate, I don't think he's the person that's calling the shots. Let's wait."

The first few drops of rain began to beat a rhythmic patter on the roof.

"Oh shit," Nolan said. "This may change our plans."

Willie stood closer to the window. "Hey, there's a car slowing down. It's driving into the alley between the buildings."

"If it's Rossini, Jacobs or whatever the fuck's his name, let's grab him."

"The car stopped in the alley near the front entrance," Dwyer said. "A little fella got out, ram-rod kind of guy. He's dressed in tails and a top hat right out of Jolly Old England."

Nolan poked his head up. "Well, well, well. I know who that is. Keveney would have a heart attack if he saw this guy."

"Who is it?"

"Willie, you have just seen the most interesting development since we got caught up in this little drama. That man who just entered Henshaw's office is none other than former Massachusetts Attorney General, Herbert Parker. This case gets more interesting by the minute."

"Isn't he the Commissioner's advisor?"

"Yeah, I met him one time with some other cops when he was in office. He wasn't very warm, like he just tolerated us." Nolan slipped to the back of the shed and picked up his scaly. "Come on. It's time to get wet again."

They made their way along the dock to avoid being seen, crossed the street and walked back to the alley. Willie tucked himself under the fire escape and listened by the back door of 'Patriot Realty.' Nolan duck-walked to the passenger door of the attorney's car, squeezed the door handle and pulled on it when Henshaw appeared in the window. He froze as the businessman casually glanced out and pulled the drapes closed.

He opened the door and found the attorney's briefcase under the front seat and fumbled with the latch before he was able to open it. Inside, there were several legal documents containing Parker's signature and a rubber stamp engraved with his name and a Worcester business address. Nolan pulled back his jacket and shirt and stamped his forearm. He glanced up at the office window, lifted the documents in the briefcase and found the Storrow Committee's report, read the first few lines—

> *The Boston Policemen's Union should not affiliate or be connected with any Labor organization but should retain its independence and maintain its organization for the purpose of assisting its members concerning all questions relating to hours and wages and physical conditions of work . . .*

The two cops made their way along the sea wall until they returned to the coal company and their cruiser. During their ride back to Roxbury,

Willie told Nolan that he only heard two men talking and that one of them seemed to be reporting to the other. "At least, one person did most of the talking."

"That's got to be Henshaw because Parker doesn't report to anyone," Nolan said. "Were you able to see anything?"

"No. And I only heard little bits and pieces."

"What did he say?"

"Something about everything's in place."

"That's it, huh?"

"Yeah. Oh and he said 'she.'"

"She?"

"I'm not sure," Willie said. "I thought he said something about 'she' and the BCLU, but—"

"Some dame and the BCLU? I wonder what that's about? 'Everything is in place.'" Nolan covered his face with his hands and let out a sigh. "You know this pisses me off. Our guys are doing everything on the up 'n up and these sons of bitches are conspiring against them. They don't want to negotiate. Did you hear them say anything about the Commissioner?

"The one that wasn't talking much?"

"Parker."

"Yeah, I think he said that Curtis is sick."

"That's got to be Parker. He's the only one close enough to Curtis to make that kind of observation. When we get back to the station, I'll call the boys at 1 and Station 6 and tell them that we have to hit Rossini and friends early tomorrow morning, round them up and see what they have to say. Then we've got to talk with our Union boys. Thank God tomorrow's Sunday and we have another day before Curtis brings down the axe on the Union." Nolan crossed his legs at the ankles, his top foot jiggling in quick little jerks. "And thank God we don't have to answer to Keveney for another day. If he knew we were watching Parker—"

HENSHAW PULLED BACK the drape and watched Parker's automobile start up and roll across the cinder drive. "You pompous little jerk," he said after the attorney's car drove out of sight. He opened the drawer of his desk, removed a bottle of scotch, and poured a tumbler full. He heard a noise and jumped, startled to see a man standing in his doorway. The tall natty stranger entered without emotion, staring with a hard face, bottomless eyes and a smile that was more of a sneer.

"Can I help you?" Henshaw asked.

"No, Mr. Henshaw," he said, "but I think I can be helpful to you. Sit, please." He opened his suit coat, exposing his vest, high collared white shirt, silk tie and gun. He sat down on the couch and crossed his legs with his bowler on his knee. "My name is Salvatore Rossini and I am the Number One noble for Pearlie Brodsky."

"Ah, Mr. Rossini, you gave me a start." Henshaw tipped the bottle to him. "Would you like a glass?" He pulled open the desk drawer again and Rossini flinched, quick and smooth, slipping his hand inside his coat. And when Henshaw produced another glass, the hand slid out just as easily back to his knee. Henshaw poured a second tumbler of whiskey, walked it to the couch and offered it to Pearlie's man. "Mr. Brodsky mentioned your name and spoke about you in glowing terms. He says he can trust you. That's an important asset today."

"You earn trust, Mr. Henshaw, it's not an entitlement." Rossini toasted his host with his glass and drank down the scotch. "A few minutes ago, you met with a young man, your son?"

"Yes, my son, Max."

"And then you met with an older gentleman who was dressed in tails and a top hat."

"Yes—a business associate."

Rossini's face screwed up with a crooked smile and he cocked his head to one side with an expression of friendly contempt. "Did you and your 'business associate' discuss anything that you prefer to keep private?"

Henshaw's brow knitted and narrowed. "Why?"

He pointed towards the window. "Because I have been sitting in that building next door, watching your office and driveway."

"But why?"

"Shortly after the man with the tails and top hat arrived, two men came from the shed across the street. The older of the two with graying temples searched your business associate's car and the younger one listened at your back door."

"Do you have any idea who they are?"

"I believe they are the same two men who were spying on our guards at your building on the channel."

"Police?"

"Possibly, or private investigators working for someone else."

"Working for whom?"

"Other Boston labor unions, federal agents, the A.F. of L, anyone with interest in the outcome of the game. Anyone looking for a leg up, Mr. Henshaw."

Henshaw stepped in front of his desk. "I think it is important that we discourage any further intrusion."

"And how much emphasis do you want us to place on 'discourage'?"

"The level of persuasion should be in proportion to their insistence to interfere. If they are the police, once the strike starts, it will all be moot because they won't be police much longer." Henshaw picked up the bottle of whiskey again. "For the time being, we need to stay out of the traffic. We need your men out of Necco Street."

"They will be out by dawn."

"Good. Would you like a little more scotch, Mr. Rossini?"

NOTICE
Locating a Friend
William Joseph Dwyer
26 years
Ballinasloe, Ireland
LKA: Boston, Mass.
Contact: Mr. Graves O'Brien
United States Hotel
A/O Tuesday, 9 September

Chapter Eighteen

The sea lay calm and flat with a metallic finish, giving the deceptive appearance that little depth existed beneath its surface. The sky above it was a curtain of pale yellow and it rose out of the sea from horizon to horizon and gave the impression that the ship sailed under a dome of vellum. Unable to sleep in the uncomfortably warm cabin, Graves O'Brien made his way along the deck, shielding his eyes from the sky, and groped his way up the stairs to the top of the ship where he entered the Wireless Telegraph room.

It was the constable's third visit to the Wireless office in the last two days. He had sent and received messages from several Boston newspapers regarding instructions on how to place a public notice. This time, he would transmit the notice itself per the instructions of his R.I.C. contact in the States. He passed a handwritten note to the operator and turned to leave.

"Is he a friend of yours, sir?" the operator said.

"Who?" Graves asked.

The operator held up the message that was scribbled on both sides of a Sani-Towel. "Him, 'William J. Dwyer,' the name on your notice."

"Oh, you could say that. I guess I have known him for ten years or more."

"Does he know you're coming?"

"I think it will be a big surprise for him. I haven't seen him since 1909."

"Well, if you wait, I will tap out your message right now."

"Grand," the inspector said.

Chapter Nineteen

~

Rossini moved his strikebreakers, now one hundred and fifty strong, along with cots, tables, camping stoves, pots-pans-utensils and assorted tools of the trade—clubs, tear gas, hand grenades, revolvers, shotguns, rifles and enough ammunition to keep the local militia in business—in less than two hours. The warehouse had been transformed from the holding area of an electrically charged armed camp of thugs, perverts and gangsters to just an abandoned building on Necco Street, a victim of the depressed and collapsing economy. He scoured the joint clean of any evidence of human habitation, took every bit of it, stuffed it into burlap bags, weighted them down with stones, then sank the evidence in the channel before leaving for the North End, and all before the sun rose over the harbor. All before an expectant army of cops descended on the building.

Brodsky's captain looked across the street at Chipman's boarded-up building and then handed one of his bangers a bucket of paint and a four-inch brush. He placed his cigar between his teeth, pulled his collar up and turned to the last two finks as they left Henshaw's warehouse. "Is everything out of there?"

"Yeah, that's it," one of them said.

"Say, where are we going?" the other one asked.

"You're getting a sawbuck a week, ain't ya, for sitting on your ass?" Rossini said. "Shut the fuck up and get moving."

The truck carrying the last of the strikebreakers pulled up to the door of Chipman's building where the gang member had just completed his painting. 'THE END IS HERE' was written in large red letters across the front of the building and under that 'THE AMERICAN ANARCHISTS.'

"That's good, get in," Rossini said.

A different place greeted Detectives Byrne and Mulvey and the Uniform from Station 6 when they showed up at 0545 hours. The brick three-story at 356 Necco Street was quieter than a Catholic Church on Good Friday. A dusty brown haze covered the windows, dirt and windblown trash had settled around the front door, and at the back of the building, the cinder parking lot was undisturbed.

The cops drove down Melcher Street and turned slowly onto Necco, guessing that they would only get one pass. But the closer they got to 356, the more obvious it was that no one had been near the building in some time so they drove into the yard, got out and checked the windows and doors. After satisfying themselves that the place was unoccupied, they started to leave when Byrne noticed a reflection near a small patch of rogue grass at the base of the building's foundation. He combed back the grass with his hand and found a single brass cartridge from a .38 caliber bullet partially embedded in the cinder. He flipped it into the air, caught it and stuck it in his pocket. The three cops made a closer inspection of the property and found other cartridges and spent shotgun casings.

Mulvey and Byrne walked across the street to Chipman's building on the channel, saw the destruction and the painted message, and then left for their meeting with Nolan and Dwyer.

TIMOTHY MULVEY twitched and searched the shadows in the dank cellar for the rats that he knew were there, crouching down behind a pipe or lying at the top of the fieldstone foundation of the Pickwick Tavern. One dimly lit bulb cast just about enough glare to light the improvised table, where the four cops sat on empty kegs, eating scrambled eggs and toast sprinkled with sugar, and washing it down with mugs of contraband Haffenreffer beer.

"If it wasn't you, George, I would have said that someone was trying to screw with our heads," Byrne said.

"That clean, huh?"

"Like there hadn't been anyone there in months. If I hadn't found that first brass cartridge, I would have thought the armed camp was a figment of your imagination."

"Well, luckily I have a witness sitting right next to me who also took a dunk in the channel." Nolan produced a list of arrest warrants for Brodsky's gang. "I've got copies of the warrants being mailed to us so that we can get the court to hold them until the strike is over."

"Do you really think we're going to strike?" Willie asked.

"Sure, it's playing out like a runaway train. Curtis isn't backing down and neither are we. He'll sack our Union leaders and our boys, being pissed off, will walk. And the rest of the political assholes in city hall and the State House will stand around like they're at a cock fight."

Byrne passed the list to Mulvey who ran his finger down the names to see if any of them looked familiar. "How did you confirm the warrants so quickly?" Byrne asked.

"That was easy. Once the New York dicks told me that Brodsky left their city for Philadelphia, I followed the bouncing ball."

"And then the Pennsylvania cops passed you on to the next city."

"That's right," Nolan said. "Everywhere these bums go, they leave a trail of shit behind. They're like carnies, only worse. The warrants pile up quicker than the bugs at our stations." He wiped up his plate with a piece of toast. "We need to take them out."

"We can do that," Byrne said, "but finding them is another story."

"We know they are trying to associate themselves with the Reds because of the newsletters printed at the Letts headquarters," Nolan said. "They set up camp along the waterfront and have recruited on Salem Street. That tells me that their interest is in the North End and the Italian Socialists. So, my suggestion is that we concentrate our efforts there. Willie and I will keep an eye on Terrace Street."

"If Brodsky thinks of himself as an American hero, why would he want to align himself with the Reds?" Mulvey said.

"I don't know. That keeps eating the shit out of me." Nolan started to mush his words while he chewed on his food. "Except, Brodsky's reputation is built on his ability to break strikes, right? And he is paid handsomely for his efforts. So, my guess is, how he gets the job done isn't as important as getting the goddam job done."

"What the hell are you talking about, George?" Byrne asked.

"From what those New York and Philadelphia cops told me, it's all about his payoff."

"So you're telling us—" Mulvey jerked his head towards a noise in the ceiling. "—that someone has hired this guy to break our strike and the way to do it is by tying us up with the Reds?"

"It's a guess, but yeah," Nolan said. "Once they do that, we're done. I mean why else the newsletter."

"Yeah, but who's going to believe that shit?" Byrne said.

"Come on, Malcolm," Nolan said. "Have you seen the newspapers? They're already suggesting that a police strike is the start of the second revolution. You saw the messages left on Chipman's warehouse."

"But the people, our people, won't believe that rubbish."

"George might have something there," Mulvey said. "People are running scared today. There's no certainty about anything. And they're gullible. They'll believe anything because they want to be standing on the winning side."

"If Brodsky and his gang fly around shooting up the city, creating panic with the ordinary Joe and all those nationalist assholes, it could be bad. And who takes the fall?"

"The dumb cops," said Byrne.

"That's the way I see it," Nolan said.

"But who's picking up the tab for these guys and why?" Mulvey said.

"Good question." Nolan washed out his mouth with beer and spit it into the dirt floor. "All I know is we got Parker meeting Henshaw who owns the building where Brodsky's thugs are camped out and they're talking about some dame and the BCLU, our Union's biggest supporter."

"I meant to tell you," Willie said. "I saw Jim Rankin at Coppenrath's about a week ago and he acted a little strange. Even Albert noticed it."

"What do you mean strange?" Nolan said.

"One minute he's saying that every Union man and woman is behind us, ready to walk. Then he tells us to tell our Union to settle without a strike, because a strike is not good for the city."

"It sounds like we got a problem," Mulvey said.

Byrne put his foot up on one of the kegs and tied his shoe. "Okay, we'll check out the North End. But it's a closed world. They're all related and they don't talk to coppers. For Chris' sakes, most of them have no interest in becoming American citizens because their enlightened leaders like Galleani pump out hundreds of articles preaching that militant bullshit about never accepting anything less than a clean sweep of the established order."

"I wonder when the Paesanos are going to wise up to those cute silver-tongued bastards like Galleani." Nolan squeezed lemon juice into his hands and rubbed them together until they were dry. "He comes into the city, riles them up and then runs home forty miles to his little dirt farm in the Wrentham countryside."

"Hey, how easy is it to hide sixty armed bums in a close neighborhood?" Mulvey asked.

"We'll soon find out," Byrne said.

"Sixty or more." Nolan dug into his pocket and fingered the change in his hand. "Watch yourselves, those guys can be dangerous." He pulled out six bits and dropped the coins on the table. "In the meantime, Dwyer and I are going to pay a visit to Mr. Bradford Henshaw."

"WOULD YA LOOK at this dump, Willie?" Nolan drove the car between the brick pillars and followed the long winding drive lined with Alberta spruces. Located off the Boston and Worcester Turnpike in Brookline Village, Bradford Henshaw's home was a stone's throw from Mission Hill and Roxbury, but galaxies away in lifestyle. A rolling green that rivaled the fairways of The Country Club separated the house from the road. Ten foot rhododendrons at the top of the lawn obliterated any casual observations of the entry and protected the identities of guests who visited the estate. They reached the end of the drive and parked near a circle with a fountain and a statue of Venus rising out of the pool of water. Nolan jumped out from behind the wheel, while Willie, stunned by what he saw, remained in the car. "Come on," the detective said, "I'm sure we already have his attention."

"Jeez, who did he have to kill to get this piece of heaven?"

Before they reached the door, Henshaw's man opened it and when Nolan told him that he and Willie were Boston Police officers, the butler asked for identification. "Is this good enough for you, Sport?" Nolan flipped his badge and stuffed it back in his pocket.

"I don't believe you have jurisdiction in the Town of Brookline, detective." Henshaw stepped out from behind the mahogany door. "So, if you have something to say, you can say it quickly and then get off my property before I make a call to your commissioner."

Nolan stepped inside the foyer before the butler or Henshaw could object. "Aren't we a bit feisty. Wot say, William?"

"Aye." Dwyer followed the detective and turned a small pirouette as he admired the home. "Must be the weather."

"What is your name?" Henshaw demanded.

"Nolan, Mr. Henshaw, George Nolan. And this is Patrolman William Dwyer."

"Write those names down, Phillip. And what is—"

"Station 10, Roxbury Crossing."

"I'll give you one question, Nolan, and that is all."

"One, it is, Mr. Henshaw." The investigator folded his arms. "Can you tell me why you would allow your property on the Fort Point Channel, a warehouse at 356 Necco Street, to be used as an armed camp by a gang of thugs, one of whom has served time for manslaughter? And before you answer, let me inform you that we are actively involved in the investigation of several felonies, which allows us to follow with fresh pursuit, even beyond city limits."

"I don't know what you're talking about. I drove to that property this morning as I do with of all of my properties, something that I have done on Sunday mornings for the last ten years." Henshaw stepped from behind his man and closed the distance between himself and the cops. "It was locked up tight and it looked like it has looked since the government decided it didn't need my Lessee's services any longer." He took hold of the inside doorknob and stood with the door partially opened. "You've had your one question. Now, get out of my house, and I *will* be calling Commissioner Curtis as soon as you leave."

"Well, seeing that I have nothing else to lose at this point, let me tell you that we know that between fifty and one hundred armed criminals, many of whom are wanted by other cities for various heinous acts, were housed on your property and you may consider yourself an accessory to their acts and any planned future acts in the city of Boston."

Henshaw's face grew from pink to red and he began to visibly shake.

"Get out," he screamed, his voice echoing off the marble floor and rising into the foyer's domed ceiling. "Get out, now!"

"You know, Mr. Henshaw," Nolan said as he stopped at the door, "I told my young associate that suspects will often lose their phony demeanor as soon as a good interviewer tweaks their balls, just a tiny bit. I'd say you fit that characterization quite well. See you around."

As Nolan and Dwyer stepped outside and before the door slammed shut, Henshaw said, "Get me Commissioner Curtis' number."

"Say, wasn't that fun?" Nolan said as they drove around the circle twice for good measure and made their way back to the roadway. "I just love tweaking an asshole like that and slamming his nuts in the vice."

"Well, if we don't go out on strike, we'll be fired," Willie said in between rifts of coughing and laughter.

"A bum like that isn't going to call Curtis and I'll tell you why. He's up to his ears in it, Willie."

"Do you think Curtis knows what this guy is up to?"

"Nah, even though both would prefer us gone, Curtis is not going to be sucked into this guy's treachery. I could easily see him manipulating people and events to fit his purposes, but a conspiracy where armed thugs are running through the streets? I mean think about it. Why would Curtis try something that borders on the criminal when the deck is already stacked against us? The Storrow report came down on his side and opposes us from affiliating with an outside Labor Union."

Nolan stopped at the end of the drive before taking the turn. "If you deal long enough with these shitheads, you get to know how they think. But more importantly, what do you think? Has Henshaw got something to worry about?" Nolan approached the Riverway Bridge and the Boston town line.

Dwyer placed his hands behind his head. "Well, after objectively weighing all the evidence, I think he's up to his— Look out!" Willie sprung up from his seat and braced his hand against the passenger door as a truck from the opposite side of the road plowed into the cruiser and drove it into the bridge abutment.

Nolan never said a word, never had time, just pulled on the steering wheel, hard right. The detective's head turned towards the oncoming truck, its lights glaring and charging at them like white knives, growing rounder and larger as the truck came closer, until the crush of metal on metal. His body wrenched sideways and backwards and collapsed in half like Raggedy Andy onto the long stick of the gearshift.

In an instant, Willie saw the truck veer across the road at them, heard the screeching and scrunching of metal as the truck's bumper punched into the side of the cruiser just behind Nolan's door. The impact knocked Dwyer's hand and arm free and he felt his shoulder jam against the passenger door, felt the cruiser being pressed against the cement abutment. But when the car came to rest, it was the sound of the voice that Willie continued to hear above the hiss of steam. It was the voice that left the final impression, like he had fallen into a well and the truck driver stood at the top of it, shouting hysterical obscenities at the top of his lungs. And while Willie dug his revolver out of its holster, he thought he recognized the voice. And when he saw the two men standing in the street, and lit up by the truck's lamps, he recognized the face. He knew that the man who was driving the truck, the one in the street holding a bottle, was Salvatore Rossini.

It seemed to Dwyer that everything happened in frames—he and George's laughter at the moment of impact, shards of glass suspended in the air, the violent lurching of George's body, Rossini's maniacal screams of delight, and a momentary silence when everything went slow and dull. Then a taste of fire. He didn't hear the bottle with the dangling rag break after landing on the floor behind them, but he caught the pungent odor of gasoline and saw the backhanded flame race across the seat and flash into the ceiling, didn't think of the possibility of fire, he actually didn't think at all, he just acted on instinct. Willie kicked out the remainder of their windshield with his heels and came out firing, cranking off several rounds with the .38 in the direction of the truck. And when no one returned his fire, he plunged his upper body back into the cruiser, reaching down and grabbing a handful of George's hair, pulling on it until he could take him under the arms, Nolan moaning as Willie lifted. "Help me, George. You've got to help me. Push with your legs, push."

With Nolan's help, Willie cleared him from the cruiser and sat him down on the wet roadway as flames shot out of the car and the truck, climbing into the night until they licked the underside of the bridge. He knelt near the detective and looked for the two men, but they were gone. George reached up and felt his face and stared at his hands, mesmerized by his own blood. Dwyer cradled him against his body and continued to scan the street, listening for the sirens of the responding cruisers and fire trucks.

WILLIE STOOD just outside of Nolan's room at the Peter Bent Brigham Hospital and dialed the telephone. "John, this is Dwyer. George is out of commission. We've been chasing some bums who are trying to sabotage the Union's negotiations with Curtis and George thinks— Oh, you are. Okay, thanks I'll tell him." He dropped the receiver, deflated and numb, and then returned to the detective's bed. "George, the Union attorneys told the Board tonight to accept the conditions of the Storrow Report, including surrendering the charter with the A.F. of L. Looks like the battle is over."

The heaviness of the narcotic sedative left Nolan thick-tongued and pressed down on him like the weight of a small elephant. "I don't trust—" He couldn't string more than a couple of words together. "Who—that?"

"John Whitten, our V.P. You gave me his telephone number."

"Oh—"

"The Board is going to make the recommendation to the general membership tomorrow afternoon," Willie said. "We won't be going out."

"I'm—not—" Nolan closed his eyes and his head sank into the pillow.

"I'll see how you're doing in the morning," Willie said and walked out.

He stood in the doorway of the hospital and looked out into the rain, frozen stupid like he had just limped in from a weekend drunk. He thought about the last couple of days and he remembered Graves O'Brien. "Ah, shi—" He walked across Brigham Circle and saw the light from the diner spilling out onto the street, the passing cars splashing the puddles and scattering the reflections. Catherine filled the window, all angles and curves, wiping down the tables with a dishrag. The adrenaline of the night leaked out of him in a slow drip. Small cuts stung his face and neck and the parts of his body that he had used to batter an escape from the burning car throbbed in one continuous dull ache. He longed to lay with her still and quiet, wrapped in and around her, separated from this life in the deep black vacuum of space. The rain dribbled off the brim of his cap and down the length of his coat. He stood hesitant in the middle of the street and watched her head turn towards the counter, the light glinting off the flecks in her hair and her mouth moving in profile as she spoke to someone in the back of the diner before moving away from the window. Willie remained numb in the street as a passing car skidded by him and blew a long ahh-ooga with its horn. He jerked backwards and stumbled to the sidewalk, walked away from the diner and started the trek towards the Crossing.

Catherine heard the horn, turned back to the window, knelt on the cushion of the booth and looked out into the Circle at an empty street and an empty sidewalk.

UNABLE TO SLEEP, Edwin Curtis got up, tip-toed out of the bedroom and walked down the stairs to the spacious living room, then stepped out onto the porch and looked out towards the bay. Fog shrouded the grounds and the shoreline. The sun wouldn't rise for another three hours, but the day already had an extraordinary feel to it. The Commissioner sensed the heavy warm September day that hung over the Atlantic in the east and he felt it coming, the pressure of it, the inevitability of it, squeezing him small.

A table lamp burned in the corner of the veranda and he sat in his favorite chair with a blanket pulled around him. In his head, he replayed the conversation with Attorney Parker that led to the drafting of a letter of response to Mayor Peters. His attorney had convinced him that they were in the best possible strategic position and that if the patrolmen left their posts to strike, they would lose what little support they had. In careful legalese, Curtis dismissed the Mayor and the Storrow Committee's report and any action that would usurp his authority. "Damned, if I will be swayed. It's too late for abdication of the A.F. of L. charter." Later that morning, he would make his decision public—the nineteen accused patrolmen, members of the Boston Policemen's Union, are guilty of violating Section 19, Chapter 35 of the Rules & Regulations. All are suspended.

Chapter Twenty

Shortly after daybreak, Catherine's head had touched the pillow and three hours later she slept on her side in the same serpentine position, a sheet half pulled up and sliding off the curve of her hip. She lay with her head at the bottom of the bed, close to an open window where a curtain hung motionless and soft muted light bled into the room. Her waitress' uniform and undergarments hung on a chair.

A persistent rapping on her door became part of her dream and then interrupted it. She got up on her elbow and ran her hand through her hair. "Who is it?" No one answered, but the rapping continued. "Who is it?" She slipped out of bed, wrapped her robe around her, got down on her hands and knees and looked through the small space between the bottom of the door and the threshold and saw men's shoes, heard the heavy clumsy shuffling of them on the landing.

She stood and listened with her ear against the door. "Tell me who you are, or I'll scream for the police." She heard the snort of a man and a short hard laugh. She took her chair and jammed it under the doorknob.

"Okay, enough, you dumb jerk," a voice said from the opposite side of the door. "Catherine? Miss Loftus? Mr. Schultz and Mr. McCarthy here. Could you open the door, please?"

She turned the key in the lock and slid the chair back, then opened the door just wide enough so she could see out. She recognized Hump and his disturbing friend. "What do you want?"

Schultz leaned his head towards the door and said in a low tone, "We would like to continue our conversation we began a few days ago. It's hard to talk out here."

"How did you know where—" Catherine looked behind Hump and saw McCarthy leaning against the railing with a clownish grin on his face. Across the hall, an apartment door opened, one of her neighbors peered out and then closed it.

"Wait a minute." Catherine opened the door as wide as the chain would allow. "You can come in, but your friend waits outside."

Hump turned around. "Go on, get in the car."

When McCarthy reached the bottom of the stairs, she removed the chair and unlatched the chain.

"I'll not keep you long." He stepped inside the room. "Have you thought about our proposition?"

"Yeah, I've thought about it."

"And can we do some business?"

"Maybe, but I've got some conditions."

"What are they?" he asked, his mouth drawn tight.

She reached for her cigarettes on the bureau and lit one. "First of all, I don't want that creep anywhere near me. I don't even want him in the same town. If I see him or even think he's anywhere in the vicinity, the deal is off." She fidgeted and held the lit cigarette up with a bent elbow.

"You got a lip on ya, kid. Don't worry, you won't never see him again."

"Next, as soon as the picture is taken, you have a car waiting for me and you'll take me wherever I want to go."

"Done. And I'll personally do the driving."

"And lastly, because I figure—Say, does this have anything to do with that big Labor Union and the cops?"

"Would it make a difference if it did?"

"It might."

"Don't worry about it. Besides, what do you care? You're going to make your money."

"I don't need the cops coming down on me. You got it?"

"You got a pretty big chip on your shoulder for a young broad. The cops ain't in the picture."

"Good. I know someone thinks this photograph is real important."

Hump leaned his shoulder against her door, his expression frozen. "Go on."

She crushed the cigarette into an ashtray and placed it on the bureau. "The price has gone up."

"How much?"

"I figure if you're offering a grand, then it's got to be worth five times that to your customer."

Hump walked to the window, looked outside and nodded. He turned back to Catherine. "You're talking five grand." He walked over to her and extended his hand. "You're a real smart broad. But that's the limit. We'll pay you five grand—"

"Before—"

"Before what?"

"I want the money before the photograph is taken."

"I said you were smart, but don't get too smart. It could be bad for your health." He sat down on the edge of the bed and ran his hand across the still warm sheet. "We need to protect our investment. How do I know you've even made contact with Rankin?"

"Trust me, I have. Tonight, he asked me to go with him to the A.F. of L. conference in Greenfield in the western part of the state where he is going to give a speech. We're leaving here at two. You can call the Greenfield Hotel and they'll confirm it."

"No need. We know about the speech." Hump stood and walked to the door. "It's kind of short notice, but this may work out for everyone. We'll get in touch with you out there to make last minute arrangements."

"I want the money deposited in the Shawmut Bank in Brigham Circle today in an account for Miss Catherine Loftus. Here's the account number." She handed him a small piece of paper. "Before I leave, I will check with the bank and if the money is not in my account, I'll cancel my trip immediately."

"You've covered all your bases, Toots, but for that kind of money, we're going to want as compromising a photograph as we can get."

"You'll get your money's worth," she said to him as she held the door open. "You just make sure you take a good picture."

DETECTIVES TIMOTHY MULVEY and Malcolm Byrne stopped on the corner of Hanover and Parmenter Streets in the North End after they had scoured the neighborhood like frantic fathers looking for one of their lost kids.

"I know every one of these streets, probably better than my own neighborhood," Mulvey said. "And I just don't get it. How the fuck do you lose a hundred raving lunatics in a closed little community like this." He wiped his face and the back of his neck with a handkerchief. "All of a sudden everyone has amnesia, including some of my best squealers."

"What did that kid tell you that you let walk on the larceny beef?" Byrne said.

"A man in a bowler—I guess that's Rossini. Been paying off some neighborhood capos to help him organize a march."

"Maybe they aren't lost, Timothy. These people wouldn't give you 'Irish Mick' the time of day. But bring in a hundred shit bums wearing red bandanas, preaching the gospel of social revolution, and handing out money? Now you got their attention."

"Jeez, they could be anywhere or everywhere," Mulvey said. "For Criss' sakes, a hundred paesano families could have adopted one each."

"Still, someone else should have seen or heard something. Only so many places they can hide in this dollhouse neighborhood."

Mulvey pushed his soft hat back and placed his hands into his back pockets, turned a slow complete circle, scanning the buildings, store fronts and every physical thing. "Jesus Christ, it's right in front of us." He walked across the street and pulled down a letter-sized poster that read—*Contro la Guerra, contro la Pace, per la Rivoluzione.* "They're here."

"Those signs are forever hanging on this street."

"This sign is new, fresh off the press, Malcolm. Look around." Mulvey held his hands out at his sides. "Have you ever seen this place so quiet at this time of day? Where are the little street monkeys who always have a hand in your pocket? They're usually running at or from someone, kicking a ball, or something."

"You're right. Or they're hanging in their doorways or cooling themselves on the roofs. It's like a ghost town."

They watched a small elderly woman dressed in black clothing step out of a closed butcher shop. She never looked over at them, but began to sweep the front of her entrance with a broom. There were shadows on her side of the street that ended like punctuation marks in front of the shop and the woman stepped in and out of the shadows as she swept.

"She sees us without even looking at us," Byrne said. "It's like she can smell the corn beef and cabbage all the way over there."

Mulvey looked up the length of Hanover Street again and saw a small boy run from a tenement on one side of the street to another one on the other side, never looking one way or the other, and disappear. "Nolan's not going to be happy. He wants Rossini so bad that if he was here he would do a door-to-door with a flame thrower."

"It's Judgment Day, Timothy," Byrne said. "Curtis has made his decision and rejected the Storrow report. And all things will cease to be."

"I think you're right, partner. I really would like to help George out, shit, help us all out, but the boys are going to strike, come hell or high water, and some of the more aggressive ones will probably welcome the mob no matter who is leading it, thinking that every bit of destruction will make us more valuable."

"I hope they're right," Byrne said.

They reached the end of the neighborhood and Mulvey stepped out into the middle of the street and shouted, "Now is our time." He was answered with dead empty silence. But as they walked away, the cop could feel all the eyes, picking his bones.

COPPENRATH STOOD at the door of the detectives' office as he put on his tunic. "Are you alright, Willie? I heard about your accident with Nolan."

"It was no accident, Albert."

"Yeah, someone told me." The first call bell sounded for roll call. "What are you fellas working on, anyways?" Before Willie could answer him, Coppenrath said, "Tell me about it at Fay Hall. "

"You think the vote to strike will pass?"

"Yeah. This is it, Willie, the end of the line." Albert finished buttoning his tunic and picked up his helmet. "If he discharges the Union officers, that investigation you're working on will have to wait." He turned to leave when Nolan bumped into him as he limped into the office.

"I don't mean to give you the bum's rush, Coppenrath, but Dwyer and I have some business to conduct."

"Yeah, that's all right. I was just leaving for roll call anyway." He started to walk away, but he hesitated when he saw Nolan's face. "Say, how are you doing?"

"Just fine." Before he reached his desk, he short stepped and turned around. "Say, how's that father-in-law of yours?"

"Who Jim? He's great, right behind us. Told me that the BCLU is ready to give us all the support we need."

"You don't say." Nolan grimaced.

Willie pulled the detective's chair out so he could sit down. "When did they release you?"

Nolan eased himself into the chair. "Don't do too well when sitting. I convinced them that I would be less of a pain in the arse if I was anywhere else but at the hospital. Told me to go straight home to bed." He picked up a stack of incident reports left by the night patrols and started to flip through them.

Coppenrath reached into his pocket and took out a folded piece of newspaper. "Say Willie, I meant to give you this. Do you remember a fella from Ballinasloe by the name of Graves O'Brien?"

Dwyer jerked his head towards the door. "What did you say?"

"I saw this advertisement in the paper and thought he might have been trying to find you."

Willie opened the newspaper and looked at the notice. "Nah, don't know him, Albert. There were several William Dwyers just in my school."

"Well, I thought you might have—"

"No."

The final bell sounded and Coppenrath stepped out into the hall. "I'll see you this afternoon."

"Sure." Dwyer listened for Albert's footsteps as he left. When he heard him on the stairs, he said, "You don't seem to have much use for Coppenrath."

"Oh, he's all right, I guess." Nolan scanned one of the reports. "It's just that some guys spend more time beating their gums and running around stirring the pot than actually doing the job."

"He likes to talk and listen to the rumors, but he's a good fella."

"Seems to think Rankin is still in our corner—" Nolan put down the report. "Look, I might as well tell you. I'll probably end up not being the most popular patrolman in the station if things continue the way they are going. I may not strike, Willie. If all these boys go out, it's going to be bad. Someone needs to know what to do because these volunteers they're recruiting certainly will not. So, if you'd rather go back to uniform—"

"No. I respect your decision."

"Okay—Mulvey left me a message at the Desk. They searched all over the North End. No sign of Rossini or his gang of hoodlums."

"Do you think they left town?"

"I doubt it. Either the goombas are keeping them under wraps or we're looking in the wrong place." He grimaced again. "Ooh—finish up what you're doing there. We're going out."

"Where are we going?"

"Back to Terrace Street. When all else fails, return to the starting line."

ONE OF NOLAN'S eye sockets was a painful black and blue and he breathed through his mouth like he was sipping through a straw, shifting from one hip to the other in the cruiser as it pulled out of the yard.

"Where are we going?" Dwyer asked as he turned right onto Columbus Avenue.

Nolan looked at him. "What's wrong with you?"

"Nothing—"

"Well something's been gnawing at you for a while. Does it have anything to do with that newspaper notice that Coppenrath gave you or that message from your brother in Ireland?"

"I don't want to discuss it right now. Maybe later."

"Suit yourself. But in the meantime, you're going the wrong way for Terrace Street."

An older Dodge coupe was parked at the back of the Letts building when Dwyer and Nolan pulled into the yard. "Do you recognize that car?" Nolan said.

"No."

"Maybe the chickens have come home to roost."

Dwyer went to the front and Nolan stayed at the back and they both banged on the doors simultaneously. "Police, open up," they echoed from either side of the building.

The front door opened just wide enough so that the person standing inside the door could see out. "What do you want?" he said.

"Police, open the door," Dwyer said.

"We don't recognize your authority here, copper. This property is a Communist island in the midst of your capitalist cesspool."

"Yeah, yeah, heard it all before." Willie saw enough of the man that he thought he recognized him from the Dudley Street riot. "Sturgis? Alex Sturgis, open the goddam door."

"Shouldn't you be standing alongside your brothers, ready to take to the streets?" He opened the door wider.

"Stand aside, Sturgis. I have an arrest warrant for you."

"I have fought stronger men than you, copper. If you want to enter, be my guest."

Dwyer heard two shots at the back of the building and when Sturgis flinched, Willie drove his shoulder into the door and crossed the threshold, straight-arming the bigger man with the palm of his hand. When Sturgis countered by grabbing Dwyer's wrist, Willie jammed his .38 into the Russian's face and cocked the hammer. "One fucking move—" He backed Sturgis up. "George," he yelled. When he received no answer, he slapped the Russian on the side of his face with the gun and knocked him down.

Willie reached inside Sturgis' coat, removed a snub nose pistol and opened the cylinder, dumping the bullets onto the floor. He pulled aside a curtain that separated the lobby from the rest of the building and could hear the printing press. "George!"

"I'm down here with the head Red," Nolan said. "We'll be right up."

Dwyer placed a come-along on Sturgis wrists.

"Is this your idea of liberty, copper?"

"Get up." Dwyer pushed Sturgis onto the couch behind him.

Nolan pulled the curtain aside and limped into the old lobby with Louis Fraina in one hand and a copy of *The New England Worker* in the other. "Would you look at this, Willie? Hot off the press, an announcement of the birth of *The American Communist Party.* Listen to this bullshit. 'We support the Boston Police in their just cause of striking for better salaries and working conditions against a government that refuses to consider them as human beings. The Communist Party shall assist the police and participate in their struggle as working men, not only to achieve the immediate purposes of the strike, but for the greater glorious revolution.'" He directed Fraina towards the couch and pushed him down next to Sturgis. "Where is Salvatore Rossini?"

Fraina stared at the wall on the opposite side of the room. "Who?"

Nolan pulled a small chair from behind the counter and sat down easy in it directly in front of the Letts leader. "We're through playing games. As you can see, we have had a couple of bad days. So you can understand why we're not in very good moods. When my friend or I ask you a question, you give us a straight answer. When was the last time you heard or saw Rossini?"

"I don't know anyone by that name."

Dwyer began to move towards the couch, but Nolan put his arm up to fend him off. "One more smart answer and I'll let him go. Try it again—Salvatore Rossini."

"I'm not intimidated by your friend, detective." Fraina moved his eyes from Dwyer to Nolan. "What do we get in return?"

"How about the chance to walk outta here on your own two feet?" Nolan watched Fraina for his reaction and when he saw none, he said, "I'll consider not arresting you for your activities during the May Day riot."

"Do you really want to do that, George?" Willie said.

"What do you say, Fraina?"

Fraina leaned forward and pulled his cuffed hands away from the back of the sofa. "Take these off."

Nolan stood him up, removed the restraints and sat him back down.

"I haven't heard from him in over a week," Fraina said. "I expected him to pick up the last of these newsletters by now."

"How did you meet him?"

"You don't have to answer their questions, Louis," Sturgis said.

"Shut up," Dwyer said.

Fraina glanced at Alex. "Rossini came to a couple of our meetings in New York and introduced himself as a member of a group that recently formed in Brooklyn. Said he wanted to become active in the national campaign and that he had raised significant funds."

"How did he get set up in Boston?

"He said that he has connections in the city, money connections, and that he wanted to contribute to the Boston campaign."

George touched his nose with the back of his hand and blotted a trickle of blood. "I want you to think carefully before you answer the next question. Who is fronting him the money?"

"I don't know. He only said that there were persons in Boston who have an interest in seeing a change in power. So, I sent him ahead with articles that I had written for the newsletter, gave him some names to contact and called one of our members to include the articles in the monthly printing."

"Where is Rossini now?" Nolan said.

"I told you I haven't seen him. He told me on the phone that he has recruiters handing out newsletters in the Italian section. That's everything I know."

"Get up, Sturgis." Nolan handed the Russian off to Dwyer, gesturing to take him outside. He took out his cigarettes and offered one to the Red.

"No," Fraina said. "It was Joseph, wasn't it?"

"What are you talking about?"

"Kursh was the only person who knew about our relationship with Rossini. He is like a younger brother to me."

"Do you think for a moment that we wouldn't continue to check this building, especially when the newspapers are already aligning us with you Reds?"

"That's unfortunate. Joseph has that rare combination of intelligence and charisma. He would have brought American youth to the Communist Party."

"Let's have it. Where's Rossini?"

"I think he's in the North End."

"Yeah, I guessed that. What's the street address?"

Fraina sat staring at the wall.

"Give me a description of the building—when did you last speak with him?"

"It's too late, detective. The wheels are already in motion. If your police strike, we will have the greatest opportunity to change America."

"You're an arrogant son of a bitch, aren't you? You think you have all the answers. We're all being used—you, me, the cops, the workers and even Kursh by the very people you most want to hurt. They are the ones who are behind Rossini. You've been suckered, just like the rest of us."

"As I said, it's too late."

"You're right." Nolan pulled him up and replaced the restraints on his wrists. "Willie," he yelled, "we're coming out."

"Where are you taking us?"

"Jail. I am charging you and Sturgis with causing an affray and inciting to riot for the May Day disturbance, and accessory to manslaughter for the death of Captain Lee. After that I'll call a friend in the federal authorities about your deportation."

"What about our deal?"

"What about it? You told me shit."

"You lied."

"Whoops."

"Do you think by incarcerating me you'll stop the inevitable? The revolution is here and you coppers hand delivered it. It's a new day, detective. You won't get away with unlawful incarceration much longer."

"Maybe I will, and maybe I won't. But you two are going to miss the party. You're going to jail and hopefully it will be your first step out of the country. See, that's one of the drawbacks of not applying for citizenship." Nolan pushed him through the door to the outside. "If I were you, I would be hoping, no praying, that I'm not in one of our five prisoner cells when the mob hits the building. You really should have stayed in New York."

Dwyer stuffed the over-sized Sturgis into the back seat with Fraina and slammed the door. "Time is running out," he said.

"Yeah," Nolan said. "As soon as we finish booking these two at the station, we'll stop over at Fay Hall."

WHEN THE NINETEEN Union officers took to the stage in Fay Hall, a thunderous round of applause, hoots, hollers and sharp ear-splitting whistles greeted them. The Irish 'Elephants,' the cops who kept the city under control with strong doses of muscle and street sensibility and, who historically, performed their duties professionally and with unquestioned loyalty, stirred and shifted. They were pissed off and looking for a fight. Some of the more radical union members, like Fulton Quigley, raged about the arrogant Commissioner and, to the delight of the others, questioned his manhood.

John McInnes stepped out of the line of officers and approached the podium. The Union president listened to his fellow coppers and knew that the inevitable precipice had been reached. He had sat across the table from the Commissioner, had seen the man's eyes and heard his words, listened to the tremor of his voice and perceived his rigid essence. McInnes knew there was no turning back, knew that Curtis would never negotiate, and knew that at the afternoon roll call he and the other Union officers would be separated from the job they loved. He decided to wait for the Commissioner's move and recessed the meeting for an hour. The cops filed out of the hall with an unchecked chip-on-their shoulder and waited for the inevitable other shoe to fall.

Outside, Albert bounced on his toes, shifting his weight from side to side, and tried to burn off the nervous energy that had taken him hostage. He fired up a cigarette and called out to cops he knew from around the city. He convinced himself that all they needed was the support of the ordinary Joe and the other unions to break the Commissioner's back. No politician in his right mind wanted to see the entire city brought to a grinding halt. His father-in-law had assured him of that, hadn't he? Curtis and the city were going to have to get used to police bargaining, right? He tossed his cigarette into the gutter, crossed the street and joined a gang of Roxbury Crossing patrolmen.

In a bathroom behind the stage, John McInnes removed his jacket and rolled up his shirtsleeves. He turned on the cold water and splashed it over his face and neck. He cupped his hands, strained the water with his fingers and ran them through his hair. The electric buzz in the hall still rattled inside his head and he could feel the pulse of his heartbeat throbbing in his temples. He heard it in his ears and heard his stomach gurgle. Only the battlefield skirmishes of the war, he thought, trumped the agony of the last few days. He looked at his reflection and wondered how he would be judged years from now if it all went badly. A soldier's soldier, he always followed orders to the letter and now he was the point man in an insurrection that tested the very principles by which he lived.

An intrusive squeal jacked him upright and, in the mirror, he watched the bathroom door pause at half-open. He snorted and grinned when he saw the reflection of Nolan's face. And then McInnes did something he hadn't done in a week. He laughed.

"You're a sight, George. What happened to you? I told you to stay away from those beer wagons; I knew one day those kegs would run you over."

"What can I say? I like my suds nice and fresh." Nolan extended his hand. "Am I shaking the hand of the sainted Union president or the ordinary man after his trip to the stall?"

McInnes finished drying himself with a towel. "Oh, I washed them." He shook Nolan's hand. "But then I threw up in my mouth and wiped my face with them."

"It's good to see you haven't lost your sense of humor."

"So, what is all this conspiracy business that you spoke to Whitten about?"

Nolan checked the stalls to ensure that they were alone. "We're being set up, John. It's as simple as that."

"How?"

Nolan went through all the events of the past week and gave his reasons why he believed that a group of old line Yankees was trying to regain control of Boston's politics by removing the Irish domination from the present police force. "They want to push back the Celtic influence in the city to before the Civil War. When you think of it, John, where the hell is Coolidge? He's the one person who could settle this and get Curtis to reconsider his stand."

"So, you're telling me that, if we go out on strike, they intend to create so much havoc that the people will turn against us, the other unions will stand clear and Curtis will be able to replace us?"

"That's my theory. The papers are already playing up the Bolshevik connection. Think of it. How many veterans are still without jobs? There are plenty of men waiting to step into our positions."

McInnes put his jacket over his arm. "Curtis refused to even consider the Storrow Committee's recommendations. He's boxed us in, and I don't think I can stop this. Besides, if I call it off, where will we be then? Those boys out there feel betrayed and are looking for someone who will stand up for them." He stopped talking and let the buzz of electricity from the hall fill the bathroom. "Listen to that. Sometimes, I think that with all the negotiations and the wrangling, we have forgotten why we are in this position in the first place. We have served this city with honor and this is the way it treats us. We're still waiting to be welcomed and respected."

Nolan clapped him on the shoulder. "I don't envy you."

Across the street from Fay Hall, Albert Coppenrath watched the patrolmen scatter during the recess. Some of them told him that they were stopping at home, if they lived nearby, others sat outside under trees to escape the heat, a bunch of them found prohibited beer in hideaway holes and filled themselves up while they ranted about the Commissioner and the double-crossing politicians. And a handful of cops quietly slipped away to their undermanned stations, reported for duty and answered a call. Albert saw all of this and walked away to find a telephone where he could talk in private.

In the News

CURTIS FINDS 19 POLICE GUILTY
DISPOSITION OF CASES AT 5:45 P.M.
(Boston)
Commissioner Curtis says he has favored and promoted the formation of the Boston Policemen's Union. His rule against that union's joining the A.F. of L. was issued only after mature reflection and exhaustive consideration of the legal position of policemen as "officers of the law," not mere employees or servants of the state.

FIRST WOMAN MASTER OF A BOSTON MIXED SCHOOL
MISS MARY E. KEYES TAKES CHARGE OF NEW WILLIAM LLOYD GARRISON DISTRICT
(Boston)
The appointment was made from a newly established merit list. Miss Keyes outdistanced the man ranking number one.

WILD WELCOME TO GENERAL PERSHING
A.E.F. COMMANDER GREETED IN NEW YORK CITY
(New York)
Standing on the bridge of the huge Leviathan, itself symbolic of victory over Germany, the commander of the greatest army ever gathered under the Stars and Stripes came slowly up the bay today, world-famed and hailed as a conquering hero should be.
THE BOSTON GLOBE
Monday, September 8, 1919

Chapter Twenty-one

~

Jim Rankin received spare polite applause from the A.F. of L. audience. He was not in his best form and he knew it. And he could see it in the eyes of the regional reps as he shook their hands. The BCLU president broke away and retreated to a bank of telephone booths to take a call that was being held for him. He entered the booth and, for a moment, considered not answering it.

"Calm down, Albert, and just tell me what's going on there."

His excitable son-in-law described in detail the levels of emotion of the Union patrolmen and he reported that McInnes defused their anger by recessing the meeting for an hour. "He wants us to wait until roll call when the Commissioner announces his punishment for the Union officers."

"Well, he's right in waiting. It's all up to Curtis now. The ball is in his court."

"There's a rumor that some fellas left the hall and returned to work," Coppenrath said.

"You're not going to get them all, Albert. I learned that a long time ago. It's a difficult decision and they're going to make their decisions on how it best serves them. Even if Curtis discharges the Union officers, some cops will return to work."

"Well, I know what I'm going to do when the time comes—"

"What you are going to do is keep your emotions close to your vest. Keep your mouth shut and watch and listen! And keep me informed."

"What if some of the fellas ask me about the BCLU?"

"Tell them that the other unions consider the police struggle their own and that we will call for a special meeting either Wednesday or Thursday."

He hung up the telephone and waited. Then he lifted the receiver to his ear and waited for the hotel operator to answer. "Room 333, please." When the person on the other end answered, he responded with a prearranged password. "Hello, Grace calling. I wonder if we can meet this evening." He scheduled the time and left the booth to find a drink.

A half hour later, Dandy Jim stood at a sink in a lobby bathroom and let the water and lemon solution swish back and forth in his mouth before he spit it into the sink. He straightened his tie, put on his vest and suit coat and walked to the agreed upon meeting place, a suite on the third floor of the hotel that was at the end of a long hallway and separated from the conference delegates. He rapped lightly on the door and waited, feeling fuzzy warm as the alcohol took its effect. The door opened, leaving just enough room for Rankin to enter, and closed as soon as he cleared the threshold.

The attendant inside directed him to a small waiting room where he had an unobstructed view of the adjoining parlor and the Governor who sat profiled, watching the flames of a newly started fire stretch themselves into the throat of the chimney. For weeks, Rankin fought with himself about family and cultural loyalty on one hand and the stand of a shrewd politician on the other. In the long run, he decided that they could be compatible. He sat nervous and restless, eager to relieve himself of the burden of his decision. The first few minutes dragged on as the waiting and the anxiety wore out his patience, and for a moment, he considered leaving. But he was drawn to the tick-tick-tick of a grandfather clock in the room and watched the pendulum make its hypnotic back-and-forth swing. Coolidge continued to stare at the fire and gave no signal that he was ready to talk while Rankin became calm and resolute. Another politician might have grown weary of Coolidge's game, but Dandy Jim had been friends with the quirky little man since their days in the state senate and he knew that the Governor was a man of principle and the rarest of politicians, one who granted favors and asked for nothing in return.

It wasn't until the clock rang the half hour that Rankin realized that he had been sitting and watching the Governor for close to twenty minutes. As the last chime sounded, the attendant reappeared and brought him into the parlor. Jim stood beside Coolidge for a few additional moments before the Governor acknowledged him and motioned for him to sit down. The heat from the fire rolled back on him and he remained silent while he waited for Coolidge to open the discussion.

"Sometimes, I do my best thinking while sitting in front of a fire," the Governor finally said.

"It is addictive," Rankin said.

"How are Virginia and your daughter?"

"They're fine."

"And a grandson?"

"Granddaughter, my pride and joy."

Coolidge nodded and allowed himself a small smile. He lapsed back into silence and continued to stare at the fire. The attendant entered, placed several large logs into the fireplace and left. The flames licked at the bottoms and sides of the new logs and Rankin and the Governor watched the first gray worm of smoke escape from the wood. Coolidge said, "I heard your speech, Jim."

"It wasn't one of my better ones."

"No, it wasn't. But your worst is better than most men's best." The Governor turned and faced him. "You appeared troubled and I wondered whether your heart was really supporting your message."

"Governor, I remember several times when we were in the senate and you pulled my, excuse the expression, arse out of the vise." Rankin turned away from Coolidge and leaned forward. He watched the fully engulfed logs burn; one green log sizzled as water escaped from its ends. "The police are out of control—"

Coolidge sat stiff and unmoved.

"They are the city's only defense against the mob," Rankin said. "If they strike, I am going to recommend to the Board of the BCLU that we provide moral support, but that is all." He turned towards the Governor. "You have my word on that. You'll have no problem with us."

Coolidge made a short squawking sound as he cleared his throat. "Is this your decision, Jim, or are others pressuring you?"

"I've agonized over this for days, gotten no sleep—" Rankin ran his hands over the tops of his thighs and held onto his knees. "This is my decision. A police strike is not in Boston's best interests. But their grievances are real, their pay unfair and scandalous." Jim waited for Coolidge to comment, but when he didn't, he said, "You have no intention of stepping between the combatants, do you?"

"The police are the commissioner's responsibility, Jim. I have no duty to speak with him or entertain the Mayor's compromise plan."

"Someone needs to—"

"I hear that the police are meeting as we speak to determine whether to strike. It could start as early as tomorrow."

"These are my people—" Rankin hesitated. They were both seasoned warriors and knew the wisdom of not rushing headlong into politically sensitive territories. "Some of those cops consider themselves exiles, Ireland's exiles. They will strike because they believe they are fighting the old war of English domination once again."

"And where do you stand, Jim?"

"I support Ireland's cause for representation in the British Parliament, not the establishment of an autonomous and independent state that some like Eamon de Valera want. I am an American of Irish descent, America first—Boston first. I can't support the police."

The two men sat there while a bed of hot red coals began to consume the last of the remaining logs. "I would ask one favor of the Commissioner," Rankin said. My son-in-law, Albert Coppenrath. He's young and rambunctious. But he is family."

Coolidge lifted his head and folded his hands in his lap. He stared into the fireplace, and nodded.

Jim stood. "Station 10, Roxbury Crossing." He showed himself out and went directly to the lounge.

ONE SPOT on the wooden floor under the Oriental rug squeaked every time Catherine walked over it. She paced the parlor from the windows at one end to the French doors at the other. She chewed on the cuticle of her finger and worried whether this would go as planned. Ah, yes, the grand scheme, she thought. She wondered what buffoon had thought it up, her part in it—'unlock the door with the key before you retire to bed. Not to worry, though,' Hump had said. 'We have a pass key, just makes it easier.' That and, 'Oh by the way, make sure he has as few clothes on as possible. And signal, for Criss' sakes don't forget the signal.' The only part of the plan she liked was the five thousand dollars that sat in the

Shawmut Bank. She looked out the window for the third time and saw Schultz's car parked in the drive.

"Jesus, how did I get tied up in this?" She sat on the arm of the couch and fingered the upholstery. The big man, himself, had come to her rooming house and made the contact, instead of the other way around. Said he had to see her and make it up to her. Told her he had been under a lot of pressure. She had stood in her apartment window with a sustained smile when he left, her face like white china, waving her hand in a delicate little turn, until Rankin got into his car and drove away. "Ah hell, I didn't have to set the little Napoleon up. He did it himself.

"So, here we are teetering on the trapeze and waiting for the grand finale to begin. Take your seats, ladies and gentlemen—" Catherine pulled her stockings up tight and sat down at the mirror. For a moment she thought that she couldn't go on. *Just tell him the game is over.* She became giddy and gave a queer little hysterical laugh. Her willowy image stared back at her, her face like a pale moon at the end of her long slender neck. "What's that—" She jumped when she heard the key in the door lock. "Show time," she said.

Rankin entered the suite, carrying a bottle of scotch and two tall glasses. The glasses rattled against each other as he reached back with his foot and closed the door. He didn't say anything, but went directly to the bar, picked up a couple of ice cubes, dropped them into his glass and poured himself a large one. He took the bottle and walked with determination to the couch and sat down. In one swallow, he drank a third of the liquor before pouring more scotch into the glass. He kicked off his shoes and extended his legs, slouched back and stared up at the ceiling.

Catherine gave a small, excitable self-conscious laugh and looked about the room. "Am I invited to the party or do I have to sit in the corner by myself?" When he didn't respond, she took the bottle and filled the other glass with ice, slipped in some water and poured a small amount of liquor. She slid up against him on the couch and nuzzled her head against his shoulder. "I thought we could go dancing after you catch your breath."

"Catherine, you don't—"

"Sure, I do. It's been a little while since we've been together and it'll take a little getting used to again." She ran her hand over his forehead and into his hair, then pressed her lips softly into his neck. "It's like riding a bicycle, James—" She put her glass down, hiked up her dress, stepped over his legs and sat down on his lap. "Just straddle the seat and ride."

Jim continued to stare at the ceiling and moved his head only to drink. "Bottoms up." He tipped the glass back until it was empty of liquor. It fell from his hand onto the floor and rolled a short distance where the ice cubes spilled out onto the rug.

She began to kiss his lips and then brushed them against his neck again. "You're so tight, James. Let me help." She opened his vest and unbuttoned his shirt, then let her fingers feather across his chest and his stomach, dragging the blade of her fingernail across his skin. She reached for the buttons on his trousers and unfastened the top one as she felt his hand slide up along the contour of her thigh and stop at her hip. He stroked her there while his other hand cradled and guided her head, leading her lips into his own and probing her mouth without feeling at first, his tongue determined and intense.

He broke away from her lips and laid his head against her breast. "This makes the day almost tolerable."

"This?"

"You, finally giving yourself."

"Wait—" She slid up onto him a little more, reached up and shut off the table lamp that burned in the window behind his head. "Let me take off this dress." Catherine stood and pulled it over her head, dropping it onto the floor. "I'll be right back, don't go anywhere." She slipped into the bathroom and ran the water and waited a few minutes, reentered the parlor and found him in the same position. She pulled on his hand to coax him up, walked him into the bedroom and took off his trousers.

They lay there with his head resting between her breasts. She felt her leg twitch. Her hands shook with a slight tremor and she massaged them deep into his back to regain her control. With each disturbing moment, she felt the urge to jump up and run. Then, there was a noise at the bedroom door—a man stood with a camera mounted on legs and another man held a dish on a pole. The photographer called out

"Rankin," and then the flash. Dandy Jim froze to the sound of his name and was blinded by the powder explosion. Catherine turned away.

"Christ—" Rankin buried his head in the pillow while a small cloud of acrid metallic smoke hung in the air.

Catherine ran into the parlor and wrapped her long coat around her. She fumbled with her shoes. Muted voices shouted to each other in the drive and she heard a car start up. She ran to the window and saw Hump Schultz and the two men drive away. "Oh wait," she said. When she turned to run out of the suite, Rankin was blocking the door.

"Did they leave you in the lurch?"

"If you touch me, I'll scream so loud they'll hear me all the way to Albany."

"Bravo," he said. "What a fool I was to underestimate you." He spoke in a flat unemotional monotone. "Who are you working for, Burns, Pinkerton?"

"Listen, Jim. I have no animosity towards you."

"Nor do I for you. As a matter of fact, I applaud your treachery. If it wasn't you, it would have been someone else. You are to be commended, you performed with great skill." He placed his arm into his robe. "Smoke or a parting glass for old time's sake?"

"No, I just want to go."

"I hope you were paid handsomely for your little stunt because you certainly gave them what they wanted." He walked to the bar and poured two drinks. "Let's see, how does this all play out? Blackmail, the second oldest game in the history of man." He turned and faced her. "And we both know the oldest game, don't we?" He walked towards her and made an exaggerated bow and offered her one of the drinks.

"No."

"I'm not going to give you the song and dance about my wife not understanding. Because as a matter of fact, she does understand, in a cosmopolitan way as long as my indiscretions are discreet."

"I feel sorry for her."

"Don't." He sipped his drink "If it hadn't been you, it would have been someone else. You were—what's the word—convenient." He stirred his drink with his finger. "My wife doesn't like it, but she tolerates it because she doesn't want to give up the power, the prestige. She likes being treated nicely by people, especially the Brahmins, even if their respect is given begrudgingly."

"I'm leaving."

"You know, it's ironic. I think your friends are going to try and coerce me into doing something I have already done."

"What are you talking about?"

"The cops, that's what this is all about, isn't it?"

"What—No? I don't know. They told me—"

"Well, I'm not up for reelection. And my bases are all covered in the senate and the BCLU." He swirled the ice in the glass and took another long drink. "Whose side are you on?"

"What did you do?"

"I've survived all these years because I have an instinctive weather vane spinning inside me. It tells me when the political winds are beginning to shift. And, my little tart, they are a-shifting." He reached into a box of cigars and removed one. "I'm not going to get high and mighty like their commissioner, but the coppers are the bridge between order and anarchy. Striking cops serve no one."

"But what about those men?"

"Life's not fair, Catherine." Rankin sat down on the couch and cut the end of the cigar. "The police have great power. They can take away another man's freedom, but unfortunately, they always have to play by the rules, even when the rules are not fair." He turned his hands out to her. "Besides, why such compassion for the cops. Or is it one particular copper?"

"You're a hypocrite."

Rankin lit the cigar and exhaled a cloud of smoke. "No one really cares. As long as they get theirs."

"And you get yours." She picked up the rest of her clothes and stood in front of him. "The mighty Jim Rankin."

He saluted her with the cigar still between his fingers and gave a hard little laugh. "And most of all, that too." He stared at her over the rim of the glass as she walked into the bedroom. She returned dressed with her bag. Rankin opened the suite door. "Good luck,

Catherine. Be careful of your new friends. If they learn that I beat them to the punch—"

She walked out into an empty hallway as the door shut behind her. The elevator stopped at her floor, but she didn't recognize the operator. He wasn't in uniform and kept looking at her from the bottom of his eyes. Catherine jerked away from the door and ran down the hall. She poked her head into a broom closet, and then opened the door to the stairwell. She could hear heavy footsteps coming up the stairs below her, and men speaking in hoarse whispers.

"Dirty double-crossers—" She found another closet with soiled linens piled into a laundry basket, climbed into the basket, pulled the used towels and sheets over her and waited. A half hour later, she heard the closet door open and heavy breathing. The soiled laundry began to move on top of her and she held her breath. The basket began to roll and more linens were piled on top. She heard a man humming and then the clanging of large metal doors and more movement. It stopped in a room with loud voices and machinery. She listened and heard someone whistling, and then the voices trailed off. She pulled off the dirty linens, jumped out and saw two workers loading washing machines. For a moment she and the workers stood frozen staring at each other until Catherine ran. She found the door to the loading dock, slipped out and sprinted to the woods and waited again until she saw Jack McCarthy open the same door and step outside. A car stopped and picked him up, and when it was out of sight, she began to walk.

"SO, THIS IS AMERICA." Constable Graves O'Brien paused at the top of the gangway and took in the first sounds and smells of Boston. Men struggled beneath him while wheeling pushcarts stacked with trunks and baggage, weaving in and out of pedestrians along the quay. The salty Atlantic water lay almost motionless in the harbor and it lightly brushed against the seawall while the air hung in layers thick as blankets. The ship's smokestack was a beacon of color amidst the browns and grays of the waterfront and the buildings that climbed the hill. "Like Dublin," he said, "and the same pungent odors."

His R.I.C. contact told him that he wouldn't be long in Boston.

Nothing else, just stay put until he called him at his room. On the dock, he stopped at the ticket window for the Cunard Steamship Company and inquired about directions to the United States Hotel. The agent was hidden behind a newspaper, reading an article and murmuring to himself, when O'Brien interrupted him. He put the newspaper down briefly and told him how to get to the hotel and which streetcar to take and then returned to his reading. O'Brien heard several hammers and a saw ripping wood, leaned away from the ticket window and watched as carpenters covered windows in the buildings near the dock. "Are you expecting severe weather?" he asked. The clerk never looked up, but continued to read his paper.

O'Brien looked through the window bars, glanced down at the agent's newspaper and read disjointed words from the headlines—19 Police Guilty—Disposition at—Boston Globe. There was a photograph of some policemen on the front page. "What is happening with the police?" he said.

The agent looked up from the newspaper. "Did you just get off the boat?"

"As a matter of fact, I did."

"Ha, that's right, sorry. The police and their commissioner are at war with each other over the coppers' right to join the A.F. of L."

"The what?"

"A national labor union. Anyway, the Commissioner found nineteen of their Union officers guilty of something and the coppers are meeting as we speak to decide whether they will strike."

"Strike?"

"You know, walk out, leave their jobs."

"Yeah, I know what the word means. Will they close the garrisons?"

"Garrisons?"

"Yeah, garrisons."

"Oh, you're talking about the police stations. No, they won't close down, but they will be severely undermanned."

"When did you say this might happen?"

"Hold on, now. Let's not get too far ahead of ourselves, here. I just said that they are meeting. No one has called a strike yet. Although, it doesn't look good." He snapped the newspaper straight and then folded it small.

"It all depends on the politicians and whether they want to stop it. And right now, they don't seem to have any interest in it."

"By the looks of the buildings, it appears that someone believes there will be problems."

The clerk looked out his side window. "You know what they say, 'It pays to be prepared.'"

O'Brien picked up his bag. "Fuck that Special Agent. This city could be in rubbles any time the way they're talking."

"What did you say?" the ticket agent said.

He ignored him and started up the hill.

"People," that was his first impression, so many people coming and going and brusquely bumping up against him as they passed. No one seemed to have time to stop and lend assistance. He already missed the rural pace of Ireland and its hometown friendliness. "These Bostonians are a queer lot," he thought after he attempted to ask a woman if he was walking in the right direction and she passed him by without an answer. "They seem so serious and occupied with their own thoughts. The faster I can get back on a ship, the better." Climbing up the hill in the sultry air, he sensed a foreboding in the city that hung heavy on it like a woolen overcoat.

His trousers clung to his legs and his shirt lay wet on his chest and back as he trudged with his bag to the Common and the Park Street underground. He looked around and saw no police and wondered if the strike had already begun.

AT FAY HALL, the evening shift voted, reported to their stations and then the day shift took their turn. They were energized by their collective stand against Curtis and had convinced themselves that they were right. Nolan emerged from the hall and walked to the car to wait for Dwyer. He had voted his conscience, but he felt squeamish and dirty. McInnes told him that the vote was overwhelmingly leaning to strike and, as a matter of fact, thought that his vote might stand alone. He was on the outside, looking in at his friends and his brothers with the weight and the stink of betrayal hanging on him. Nolan couldn't even tell them why he voted against the strike. He had no wife, nor kids or sickly parents waiting for him when he came home. It was just instinct, that gnawing in the pit of his stomach that convinced him that it was the correct thing to do. He took the good-natured kidding, the whispers behind his back and the more aggressive insults as tiny ripples in a puddle of dirty rain water. He would make his stand in the streets rather than strike and he was going to take the battle to the persons who were really responsible for this tragedy. "And better an old fossil like myself than the young Turks," he said. "They will have their own battles someday."

He watched Willie as he approached the car and noticed that he failed to make eye contact with the other cops who stood in front of the hall and turned away when any of them indicated that they might want to talk. "I hope you did the right thing in there," he said when Willie closed the door.

"Yeah, sure I did."

"So, if the boys strike at tomorrow's roll call like they say they will, then we have less than a day to solve the world's problems?" When Willie didn't answer but just stared into his lap, George rested his hands on the steering wheel and looked over at his protégé. "What's eating you, kid?"

"I should have stayed and fought."

"What are you talking about?"

"Ireland, ten years ago, I should have stayed and fought."

"Look, Dwyer, why don't you tell me what's going on?"

"The cablegram I got from home?"

"Yeah, I figured it wasn't good news."

"My brother wrote that a constable from Ballinasloe by the name of Graves O'Brien sailed to Boston. He's coming to arrest me and take me back."

"Do you know this O'Brien? Wait, he's the guy that placed the notice in the newspaper that Coppenrath was waving around."

"Yeah, he's the one, got that Calvinist way about him."

"A self-righteous bastard, heh?"

"Yeah, but I wonder why he came all the way to America?"

"So, how did you vote?"

"I wanted to support the boys—I voted not to strike."

"Well—" George started with a giggle and ended in a steering-wheel slapping, obscenity laced huzzah. "Let's get the fuck outta here. You and

I are going out for beers, nickel shots and maybe some eight ball. And you can tell me your story." Nolan turned the cruiser away from the curb, but stopped before he pulled away. "What's the charge?"

"Unlawful homicide."

"Murder? Did you do it?"

"No, but I was there."

"That's all I need to hear. Hang on." George pulled out and sped down Washington Street under the elevated railway. A train raced above them as the cruiser flicked in and out of the trestle's iron legs, the train leaving a trail of sparks as it applied its brakes and squeezed the curve of the track just before it entered the Dudley Street Station. The cruiser turned and slid onto Roxbury Street and started for the Crossing.

ON BEACON HILL, Governor Coolidge and Commissioner Curtis drank hot tea and waited for Mayor Peters.

"How was the ride from Greenfield, Governor?" Curtis said.

"It was fine, fine." Coolidge placed his cup and saucer into his lap. "A little wet on the Mohawk Trail, but other than that, fine." He cleared his throat with a short cough. "I've given your situation some thought, Commissioner, and wonder if some moderation might be appropriate to bring the police dispute to a quick and successful closure."

The little color remaining in Curtis' face disappeared and the air wheezing from his lips escaped like steam squeezing out of a radiator. "Attorney Parker continues to give me good counsel regarding the legalities of my position and believes that my decisions will stand up in the courts. There will be no negotiations; there will be no compromise. The patrolmen were given a written directive and they chose not to obey it. That is insubordination. My commanders have told me that most of the patrolmen will report for duty whether they voted to strike or not. And that only some of them will refuse to report to work. If there is a shortage of manpower, we have assembled a solid group of volunteers who will keep the city safe until we can replace the strikers."

Coolidge nodded his head. "So be it then."

"I will inform the Mayor of my decision as soon as he arrives," Curtis said.

The Governor's man entered the room and waited for the Commissioner to finish speaking. "Your Excellency, Mayor Peters has arrived. I've seated him in the waiting room."

"Show him in, please."

Before the attendant could step aside to allow Peter's entrance, the Mayor brushed past him and stood between the two seated officials. "Governor," he said nodding with a jerk of his head. Then he faced Curtis. "Commissioner."

"Mayor Peters," said Coolidge. "Please, sit down."

But Peters didn't sit down and didn't wait for an introduction into the conversation, but immediately began to articulate his concerns for the city and its citizens in the event of a strike. "For whatever reason, which is unclear to me, Commissioner Curtis has chosen not to consider the recommendations of the Storrow Committee. So, I demand to know what preparations are being made to ensure that the public peace is maintained."

Coolidge sat back with a smug look on his face, turned and faced Curtis.

The Commissioner started slowly and deliberately, measuring each word as if he was pouring it into a test tube. "The commissioner of police is appointed by the governor and I was appointed by Governor McCall and am—" He raised his voice. "Answerable to Governor Coolidge. And I have reported to the Governor that I have a solid handpicked volunteer force, but I don't presently see any reason to use them as things are under control."

"Yes, yes, I am aware who appoints the police commissioner, but I am—"

"I don't," Curtis said, "need your advice or consent. Nor do I need any assistance from the Office of the Mayor."

Peters wheeled around and addressed Coolidge. "Have any provisions been made to place the Guard on alert?"

"Calling out the Guard is not necessary," Curtis said from behind Peters.

The Mayor looked back and spit out his reply. "Right now, I am addressing the Governor about his executive powers that don't fall within the purview of the police commissioner."

"Please, Mr. Peters, sit down," Coolidge said.

The Mayor reluctantly pulled his tails up and sat down rigid in a chair across from Curtis.

"I understand your frustrations and your concern for the welfare of the city," Coolidge said. "If you are really that concerned, why don't *you* call out the Guard."

"What? Well, if I—"

"You realize that you are empowered under statute to mobilize the State Guard during a time of emergency."

"Ah—"

"In fact, I will call them out on your behalf if you would like," the Governor said.

"Well, I only want to ensure that there will be three to four thousand troops ready if we need them to keep the peace."

"If we need them, they will be mobilized," Coolidge said. "In the meantime, you could also call the city council into emergency session to vote pay raises for the police, rearrange their work hours and renovate those old stations."

One corner of Peters' mouth turned up into a simple grin. "You must take me for a fool. We are in the throes of a post-war economy, thousands are out of work and you want me to try and run pay raises and other expenditures through the council in the next twenty-four hours, the same council that has for the past two years sat on a request by Mr. Curtis' predecessor to build new and renovate older station houses. I don't need to remind you that the council can't even fund ordinary expenditures because it has not received adequate monies from the Massachusetts Legislature."

The Mayor stood. "The city's Police Department has been used by both Republicans and Democrats in a dirty little political game that could only take place in Boston. You sit there like Solomon, a monument to wisdom, when, in fact, your only motivation is to be reelected two months from now. Thank you for your time."

Coolidge watched Peters storm out of the parlor with curious interest until he was out of sight. Then he reached into his box of cigars, removed one and lit it.

CATHERINE LIMPED shoeless on an unlit and desolate country road where she couldn't see her hand in front of her face. She had separated herself from Greenfield as quickly as she could and stayed to the less traveled roads to avoid being found by Hump, McCarthy or their friends. She guessed that they hadn't gone far when they left her trapped in the room with Rankin, hoping that Dandy Jim would do their dirty work for them. Groping on the dark road, she snapped her head to the sound of the wind and the crack of the pine trees and moved to the center of the road when a dry twig snapped. For hours, there was nothing but the blackness of the country night, and then she saw a light at the bottom of a hill and the ghostly outline of a tiny village with two buildings, a church and a store with a gasoline pump. And an opportunity. A produce truck was parked next to the store with its motor running. She shivered and crawled in the back and waited for the driver and about scared the "living bejesus" out of him after he got behind the wheel. She told a partially accurate tale of being abandoned by her boyfriend, squirted a few, and got a ride to Boston.

ON MISSION HILL, Albert tripped on the top step of the porch and stumbled at the side door of his father-in-law's house, his helmet jarring loose and bouncing across the porch until it rolled under the glider. He recaptured it, straightened himself up, and started up the inside stairs. By the time he reached the top step, Emily was waiting for him."

"Sshhh, you'll wake the baby."

"Sorry, dear," he said like he was squeezing oatmeal through his teeth, "it's been a long day."

"I thought you were getting off duty this afternoon? It's after midnight."

Albert held his hands out. "I did, but afterwards I went to Fay Hall and voted." He dropped his keys onto the kitchen table and placed his helmet on a chair. "Then I went out with a few of the fellas from the station to discuss the strike."

"Have you had anything to eat?"

"No."

"So, the patrolmen did vote to strike." Emily broke two eggs on the edge of a bowl and began to beat them.

"The evening and day shifts did. The night shift votes in the morning." Albert sat down and removed his shoes. "It's almost unanimous." He dropped his shoes in the pantry. "Hey, you know who voted not to strike?"

"It would have been nice if you had come home and told me." She placed the eggs and a cup of coffee on the table in front of him and then walked out of the kitchen.

"Emily?" When she didn't respond, Albert followed her into their bedroom and found her sitting on the edge of the bed and staring into the darkness outside the window. "What's the matter?"

She didn't respond at first. After several moments, she said, "Did you ever consider that I may have an interest in whether you have a job or not?" She lifted a tissue to the corners of her eyes and wiped the end of her nose.

Albert sat down beside her and saw that she looked desperate and unanchored. "Hey, we're going to be fine," he said, the words hanging there in front of them like a cobweb. "Curtis isn't crazy enough to fire all of us. Besides, the people are behind us. Complete strangers have stopped me and told me how much they support us. They know that no working man would stand—" He took her hand and held it, but she continued to stare out the window. "With your father's Central Labor Union behind us, hell, I wouldn't be surprised if the Commissioner calls it off before we actually go out."

She stared into her lap. "Do you really believe that?"

"I have to—"

Emily removed the comb from her hair and pulled it back and twisted it into concentric circles until it was piled on top of her head. "It's Willie—"

"What?"

"Willie voted not to strike, didn't he?"

"Yes."

She replaced the comb and wiped her hands on her apron. "I think I'm pregnant," she said.

In the News

LABOR'S SUPPORT STRONG

Police situation discussed at Central Labor Union meeting and reports of many unions heard. Business Agent Jennings, in reporting on the situation, said that the committee of seventeen from the Central Labor Union had visited Mayor Peters Saturday and asked him as chief executive of the city to use all the power at his command to force a settlement of the trouble, before the "worst situation in the history of the city breaks."

THE BOSTON EVENING TRANSCRIPT

Tuesday, September 8, 1919

EXPECT POLICE STRIKE THIS AFTERNOON

(Boston)

Vote overwhelmingly in favor of walkout at 5:45 P.M.
Harvard organizing force for police duty in Boston

THE BOSTON DAILY GLOBE

Tuesday, September 9, 1919

GOVERNOR SAYS ALL MUST SUPPORT POLICE COMMISSIONER

(Boston)

Boston's protection arranged: plenty of men to supplant strikers
Many present and former college athletes and ex-servicemen volunteer

THE BOSTON EVENING TRANSCRIPT

Tuesday, September 9, 1919

Chapter Twenty-two

~

Tuesday, 9 September 1919
Dawn

When the drizzle stopped and the dawn arrived in gray smoke, a flotilla of ragtag fishing boats and row boats carrying Brodsky's hidden gang of strikebreakers and security guards pushed off from a remote and uninhabited island in Boston Harbor, navigated the lazy swells around Grey's Lighthouse, and made its way into the flat waters of the harbor and a dock where Salvatore Rossini waited.

And while Pearlie's Number One noble watched his finks disembark from the boats, on the other side of the city Catherine slept in the produce truck as it rumbled under the archway at Brookline Village. Her stockings were ripped, the silk dress was ruined and she smelled like dirty laundry. The last time she moved was in Hadley when the driver put his jacket over her and closed the door.

The driver drove onto Huntington Avenue and pulled over to the curb. "Hey, Miss," he said as he shook her shoulder, "isn't this where you wanted me to stop?" He shook her again.

She rolled away from the door and rubbed the back of her neck. "Hmm—"

"You're home."

"Whew." She looked up at her apartment window and thought she saw someone move behind the curtains. "Say, can you do me a favor? I forgot my key and a friend of mine at the diner up the street has a spare."

"Sure, kid, no problem."

The truck entered Brigham Circle and at Catherine's direction, the driver slowed down as he passed the diner. "Are you in some kind of trouble, Miss?" he said. "Not that it's any of my business."

Catherine leaned back and peeked out just far enough so that she could get a view of the inside. "Old boyfriend." Two thugs, strange and queer-looking guys, sat in a booth with the kind of expressions that suggested that pain didn't register with them any longer. Even from a distance, she knew they were not part of the usual crowd. "Can I ask one more favor?" she said. "My new boyfriend lives a couple of streets away. Can you take me there?"

"Yeah, I guess so, but then I gotta get going."

"That's swell. Just let me out there." After they had passed the diner, she sat up and made a rotating motion with her hand. "You gotta make a turn here and go up Tremont." As the truck navigated Brigham Circle, she got a glimpse of the Shawmut Bank and a car parked in front of it. "Hump."

"What?" the truck driver said. "Say, I ain't gonna get into any trouble here, am I, Miss?"

"Yeah, that's it right up there," she said as the truck turned up Tremont Street. "Nah, no trouble. My new boyfriend is a copper. You got no worries."

"Well, that's good."

"Turn here on Iroquois. It's a couple of doors up." When the truck reached Willie's rooming house, she said, "This is it. Gee, thanks a lot. I don't know what I woulda done without you."

Catherine gave the driver directions out of Mission Hill and walked to the front door. It opened before she reached it and a middle aged woman stepped out, holding a scrubbing brush in her hand. "Don't be bringing any funny business to my doorstep, you," she said. "I run a respectable house here, so keep moving."

"I'm a friend of William Dwyer's," Catherine said. "Is he in?"

"No, he is not." The woman started to turn away.

"Wait. I know I look terrible. It's just, I got caught in the rain and—" She dug into her bag, found her bank book and held it up. "I've got money."

"Hmm—" The woman read the deposit entry. "Come on." The landlady opened the door. "Are you looking for a room?"

"Yeah, just for a couple of days."

"You say you're a friend of Mr. Dwyer."

"Yes."

"I'm Mrs. Gerhardt, the owner. If I find you're lying or you can't pay for the room, you'll be out of here a lot faster than you came in."

"Oh, I can pay. Is he working?"

"Yes. He told me when he stopped at the house last night that he can be reached at the station."

"I need to get in touch with him."

Mrs. Gerhardt took a key down from a board of keys and said, "I've got a small room at the end of the hall on the first floor. It's not much, but it's clean. You can use the bath in the hallway." She unlocked the door to the room and gave Catherine the key. She stood back and took a long look. "I don't know what you're doing here, but if Mr. Dwyer vouches for you—"

"As soon as I can get to the bank, I'll pay you."

"Yes, you will. I have a dress I can lend you. Probably not your style, but it's clean. Besides, if the police go on strike like the newspapers are saying, the banks may close. But we'll cross that bridge when we come to it."

FULTON QUIGLEY stood in the Crossing's protective police booth at the intersection of the three converging streets, skillfully signaling and directing the traffic. He moved his hands with dramatic flair and, under his breath, spoke to the motorists in a strange and alien language that suggested unpleasant places where they could go or physically limiting places where they might deposit their horns. And while the motorists could sometimes hear his colorful language as they passed him in the booth, they ignored the vulgar references to their family lineage or a particular part of their anatomy because they appreciated his ability to turn the chaos of Roxbury Crossing into a paradigm of order and discipline. But this morning, he interrupted their normally efficient passing to allow the Bradley boys time to hawk their papers in the stalled traffic and spread the news of the pending police strike. Any complaints from the annoyed drivers, he handled by suggesting the confusion that lay ahead of them once the volunteers took over.

Between one of his sprints to the cars, Frank Bradley stopped at the police booth and rested his bundle of newspapers on the shelf while Fulton waved his arms in a windmill motion. "Officer Quigley, how long do you coppers think you'll be gone?"

"Hopefully, not too long."

"Well, I just want you to know that me and Johnny will miss you. You've always been square with us and our mother, and you tried to help Charlie."

"Thanks, Frankie. How is your brother doing these days?"

"Not so good. He's back to his old self, hitting the sauce hard. He spends most of his time mooching money or lifting it so he can buy more booze. Fenwood Road dried him out—" Frank turned to a passing car. "Hey watch it, Mister. You almost hit my brother." He replaced the stack of newspapers under his arm. "Charlie looked real good after that, but he can't stay away from the stuff."

"I'll tell you what," Quigley said. "If he gets real bad after we strike, you call me at home. You still got the number?"

"Yeah, I keep it in a safe place."

"I'll tell you who to see at the station. You don't want to talk to any of those volunteers. They'll have a hard enough time just finding their way to work each day. And a guy like Charlie can really get on someone's nerves."

"Okay, Mr. Quigley. Thanks."

"Don't worry. With the other unions backing us, the strike isn't going to last very long." Fulton raised his hand up and stopped the traffic. "Go ahead, go get 'em."

"Hey, Globes here!" Frank hollered. "Cops going out!"

Quigley watched the boys run between the cars, excitedly carrying the news to the citizens of Boston. "It won't be long," he said. "It can't be."

THE ELEVATED TRAIN pulled into the Dover Street station and the woman sitting across from Graves O'Brien nodded. He got off and walked down the long set of stairs and followed the directions he was given for 45 Leroy Street. Outside of the two-family home, he checked his .22, climbed the stairs and rang the bell. When he received no reply after his third try, he rapped his knuckles on the outside door. When he still received no response, he stepped into the foyer and knocked on the first floor apartment and then knocked again. O'Brien heard a woman's muted voice and after a few moments, he heard a bolt slide on the inside of the door. It opened just enough so that he could see a slice of an old crooked woman who looked him up and down.

"I heard you the first time. I'm not interested in whatever you're selling."

"I'm not selling anything," O'Brien said. "I'm looking for a man who might live here."

"Why are you looking for him?"

"Why do you ask?"

"Because depending on your answer, I may or may not want to tell you anything."

A man with an unpleasant odor and the face of a mutt stepped up behind her with a scowl and a look like he was trying to find a nice soft spot to stick a knife. "What do you want?"

"He says he's looking for someone who used to live here, Gordon," the woman said.

"I just arrived from Galway and I'm trying to find an old friend from my town." O'Brien turned away from the man and directed his gaze at the woman, hoping that he would have a better chance of success with her.

"Sure you are, 'old friend' my arse. Shut the door, Ma." Gordon turned away and disappeared into another room.

As the woman began to close the door, Graves slid his foot against the bottom. "Wait. William Dwyer, a fella probably about twenty-six years old? This was the last address I had for him. Look—" He reached into his pocket and produced several coins bearing the image of King George. When the woman hesitated, he reached inside his suit jacket and pulled out the papers for his trans-Atlantic crossing and held them up. "Do you see the date of arrival at the top of the page? It's yesterday's date."

She slammed the door in his face and screamed from behind it. "He don't live here no more."

O'Brien rapped on the door again and heard the heavy thud of steps that could only belong to the son. He reached into his jacket pocket, slid his hand around the Remington and directed it belt high.

The door opened fully and Gordon pointed to the street. "Get your arse off my property or I'm going to rip your goddam head off."

"I'm sorry, I don't mean to bother you. It's just that I don't have any other information except the address, 45 Leroy Street."

"That's your problem, not ours. Now, get lost." Gordon slammed the door and O'Brien stood there because he didn't know what to do next. He turned to leave when he heard the son yell to his mother, "Why should I help that bum? Comes around asking about a copper?"

"A copper?" Graves punched the door repeatedly until he heard heavy steps again accompanied by loud ranting. He hung the two-shot behind his leg and when the door slung open and Gordon lunged, O'Brien met him midflight, grabbing his hair with one hand and sticking the derringer up his nose with the other. "Now listen you cock breath you tell me everything you know about Dwyer or I'm going to clean out your fucking sinuses."

"Ma!"

"Shut up. That figures, you'd be crying for your Ma. She comes out here or even gets up from her chair, I'll blow your nose clean off your face."

"You can't—" Gordon twisted and squirmed.

"Now, tell me everything you know about Dwyer."

Gordon continued squirming and grunting in protest when O'Brien delivered a knee to his groin and reduced Gordon's legs to gelatin. He fell in the doorway with his hands between his legs.

"Last time," O'Brien sang. "Tell me everything you know about Dwyer."

Gordon rocked back and forth in the fetal position and tried to talk, but all that came out were grunts and sniffles.

"Hurry up," O'Brien said.

"Boston copper—I don't want any trouble with him." Gordon wiped his eyes with the back of his hand. "He moved out of here a couple of years ago, when his aunt died."

"How come his mail still comes here?"

"I don't know. Gets mail here and we give it back to the postman."

"Where is he assigned?"

"What? I don't know what you're talking about."

"Where does he work as a copper, you dumb shit?"

"Ah, Roxbury, last I knew."

"Anything else?"

"No."

"See how easy that was, Gordon." O'Brien helped him up and stuffed a couple of English pounds into his hand. "Thanks for your trouble."

Graves looked at his watch. "Almost nine thirty. A copper, eh? I wonder if those hot shot Special Agents know that." He jumped off the top step and ran back to the Dover Street station.

Tuesday, September 9, 1919
1600 hours

Rossini waited for his boss to signal the 'okay' while several pickup trucks sat idling behind him, ready to transport groups of armed finks to various businesses. Pearlie Brodsky and Bradford Henshaw stood in the doorway to Henshaw's building and watched the men board the trucks.

"I'm sure they are feeling better now that they're off that pile of sand in the harbor," the boss of the strikebreakers said.

"I couldn't take any more chances with those cops sniffing around," Henshaw said. "I don't need any of this getting into the papers."

Brodsky watched Rossini direct several men to a boat tied up at the pier where two of his lieutenants handed them guns and ammunition from a hidden stash. "Give the heavy ammo to the store guards and have Jew Cohen drive the last truck," he called before he and Henshaw stepped into the office.

"How did things go in the Indiana strike, Mr. Brodsky?"

"Okay, but it cost me two seasoned sluggers and a half dozen finks because I was undermanned in a battle with a thousand strikers. Five of them were killed. Maybe, if I had a few of these guys who were tied up here, that wouldn't have happened. But I understand your situation. You weren't really sure when the police would walk and my boys had to be ready to go into action."

"That's correct."

"I told you that we are the best in the business." Pearlie rapped his knuckles on the window glass to get Rossini's attention and when he turned around, Brodsky held up a stubby index finger and mouthed the word 'wait.' "And that's why I'm going to need an additional fifty thousand dollars before my men go anywhere."

"Fifty?"

"I learned something after Indiana, Mr. Henshaw. Never underestimate the probability that things can go wrong, very quickly."

"We agreed to pay you twenty-five thousand on the day the police walked out, not fifty."

Brodsky's bottom lip crushed his upper lip. "On behalf of my men, I take offense to that. What are you trying to pull here anyways? Gyp me out of money that's due me and my men or something?"

"Whoa, wait a minute now—"

"You can hire some other guy to break a dressmakers strike," Brodsky said, "but when it comes to steel workers or cops, I'm the guy you call." Pearlie walked to the door and pointed at Henshaw with his straw hat in his hand. "Don't try and get cute with me," he roared. "I don't like games or politics."

"Wait, Mr. Brodsky, it's just that we had expected to pay you twenty-five now and the rest when the strike was over."

"I already set you guys up beautiful, as smooth as silk except for a couple skirmishes Rossini had with those two persistent cops. You haven't heard from them lately, have you?" The corner of his mouth began to jerk in a nervous tic. "You got intelligence on all the major players. The biggest Union in the state is pulling its support. And, you got one hundred of my men sitting around here, on a fucking island no less, when I could 'a used them in Indiana. Who do you think is feeding and paying these guys while they're sitting on their asses?" He opened the office door. "What's it going to be? Either I get my money or I load these guys up and you're left with the mess."

Henshaw reached into his desk and took out his checkbook. "You get your money, but not another dime until this is over."

"Fair enough, but the minute the strike ends, I'm going to be at your door with a bill for time and materials." Brodsky was distracted by the loud voices of the men in the street and walked to the window and leaned his head out. "Hey, shut the fuck up out there." He pulled his head back inside and said, "I'm sorry if I got a little rough with you, but without me, those poor devils would be starving. If I don't watch out for them, they go home to their families empty handed and I don't have an army any longer."

"I understand things are difficult these days." Henshaw wrote a check for forty-five thousand and handed it to Pearlie.

"You're missing five grand."

"The girl has your other five." Henshaw pulled out a bottle of whiskey and two glasses. "I have been informed that Rankin decided, on his own, not to support the police with a strike. So, there really is no reason to pay her." He wiped the inside of the glasses with a rag and poured two short drinks.

"I'm way ahead of you, Mr. Henshaw. The boys are looking for her as we speak. You know, we should throw her a little cash to make it easy on her. Let's say a few hundred because after all she did do her part. Who knows, she might want to join our little family. I could use a broad like that."

"Okay, but no rough stuff. Just enough persuasion so that she turns over the money."

Pearlie gulped down the whiskey and opened the door. "We'll take care of it." On the dock, he ordered the guards to report to the largest businesses in the downtown district, like Jordan Marsh, Filenes, Whites and Chandlers. He directed five of his best men, armed with rifles and shotguns, to protect the Jewelers Building because the jewelers paid the highest security rates of all the Washington Street merchants and five men each to the Shawmut Bank and the First National Bank of Boston.

He formed two teams and had them report to Rossini, one team to root themselves with the radical Italians from the North End and another team to pass out newsletters and support the Letts in Roxbury. "Rossini, make sure they connect with the moles that are already in place."

"You got it."

Brodsky dispersed a third team of gamblers, sluggers and borderline crazies to instigate looting, fights and crap games and generally create chaos.

One of the finks stood up and said, "Hey boss, do we get to keep anything we find?" He snickered at his suggestion.

Brodsky jumped up on the back of one of the trucks. "All of you guys listen up. This job ain't no fucking Christmas dinner. I don't mind if something is lying right in front of you. But if you bums get pinched, you're on your own and you can kiss your scratch good-by."

"What do you mean?" the fink said. "The cops are the ones going on strike, ain't they?"

"Not all of them. Their commanders are still around, plus they deputized a gang of volunteers. And listen, stay out of the cops' way. We might have to work with them someday." Brodsky pulled back his long coat and stuck one hand in its pocket. "If the militia or the troops are called in, you guys working the streets, get the fuck out of the city pronto. But check out with the noble that you're working with if you expect to get paid. You guards at the stores and the banks stay at your assignments until relieved by the store owner or manager. And keep track of your hours; they're paying until you are told they no longer need you."

He put a foot up on the side of the truck and was about to jump down when he said, "One more thing, you punks, running with the Bolsheviks. We ain't fucking Reds. If I had my way, I'd shoot every one of those bastards on the spot. We're being paid to stir them up a little, that's all. You got it?"

The convoy moved in single file along the waterfront until it turned onto Commercial Street where the vehicles separated and disappeared. Pearlie sat down on the truck's bumper with pride and watched his boys, his army, ride off into battle.

WHILE PEARLIE'S GUARDS took up positions at the major downtown businesses in full view of the pedestrians on Washington Street, Constable O'Brien walked from the elevated railway station in Dudley Square to a telephone booth and called Station 9.

"Hello? Is this the Boston Police in Roxbury?"

"This is Station 9, sir. What can I do for you?"

"Ah, thank you, sir. I'd like to leave a message for Officer William Dwyer."

"Dwyer? What's his first name again?"

"William."

"There's no William Dwyer assigned to Station 9."

O'Brien hung up and picked up the receiver again. "Hello, operator? Can you put me through to the police in Roxbury?"

"Do you want Station 9 or 10?"

"Ah, '10' please."

"Boston Police, Station 10, Patrolman Cratty."

"Can I speak with Patrolman Dwyer, William Dwyer?"

"Don't you read the papers? We're all just a little busy right now. He's not available."

"Oh—"

"Leave me your name and a message and I'll pass it on to him. Hello, are you still there? Hello—"

The telephone receiver swung back and forth in an arc and the door to the booth hung open as O'Brien raced across the street to hitch a ride to Roxbury Crossing.

DRISCOLL, WILLIAM J.,			RANK	DIV.
Appointed G.O.1227,	Feb'y 4,1918,		Reserve.	6
Trans. G.O.1260,	April 18,1918,			15
Prom. G.O.1329,	Sept. 5,1918,		Patrol.	

Abandoned His Duty Sept. 9, 1919

Boston Police Department Roster Card

Chapter Twenty-three

~

Tuesday, 9 September 1919
1745 hours

In the moments before the Boston Patrolmen reported to roll call, the city wrapped itself in a quilted mantle of anticipated mourning and idle curiosity. Boston's quaint haphazard streets that normally were slogged down with trucks and automobiles looked like vacant roads to nowhere. Some streetcars and elevated trains ran almost empty as businesses closed early and workers abandoned the city and left it in a state of absence. Even the bars, the legal establishments that sold the watered-down Near beer and the hide-away holes-in-the-wall that offered the real stuff, catered mostly to the despondent and the lonely. But tavern owners knew that given time, their establishments would come alive again with customers who came to argue the situation over a pint of lager because everyone had an opinion.

Strangeness was in the air and it stuck to everything like the humidity that hung heavy over State Street and Milk Street, Huntington Avenue and Commonwealth Avenue and it arrived in the neighborhoods just before dusk. People, oblivious to the conflict between the police and their commissioner, awakened as if from a coma, entered the discussion and expressed their concerns like casual acquaintances at the wake of a neighbor. And in Roxbury and the North End, angry young men and a few bold women demanded change and readied themselves to make it.

At Station 10, it began with the veneration of the curious. A few unemployed men and boys, who always had time, milled about and hung over the picket fence, standing like spectators outside a tall building because they couldn't resist the man on the ledge. They huddled and waited for the death knoll to ring over the grave of the Boston Police and wondered aloud how the cops could quit their jobs when men like them couldn't find one. Their opinions about the idea of the police being workers and members of a Labor Union differed as greatly as the New England weather. A card-carrying Teamster applauded their strike as the only move that the cops could make in a game that tipped heavily towards the employer. Others sympathized with the patrolmen, but they could never support a walk-out. "For Criss' sakes, it's like being in the army," they said. "You don't abandon your post." And some considered the police, any police, an objectionable necessity in a free and democratic America.

With one hand on a picket and the other one in his pocket, Charlie Bradley stared at the station door and waited for the strikers to appear. His face screamed out in a wordless tirade, an angry message trapped in the capillaries under his skin. Everything about him screamed 'turmoil' as he danced on rubbery legs, moving one way and then the other in convulsive spasms. Acutely aware of who was around him, he looked for perceived insults and raged at imaginary foes. The younger boys understood that to make eye contact with the 'crazy' redhead was an invitation to do battle. But an older group of rival gang members moved closer to prey on the intoxicated teen and settle old scores, like jackals surrounding, pushing and jarring him, until they were threatened by some of the veterans in the crowd.

Like an onion, the mob grew, layer by layer with as many reasons for being there as there were people, some to witness the event, some to show support and some to walk to the edge and look over. Trolleys brought the laborers, office workers and starch-collared professionals at the end of their day and they joined the original few in clusters behind them. They spoke in whispers and argued in murmurs and waited for the show to begin. Some of the boys at the front climbed the fence and stood in mud left from the previous night's rain. They peeked in the windows, turning every few minutes to report to the crowd. Other boys picked up the mud and slapped it into patties, stacking them like snowballs next to the fence.

Inside the station, Captain Keveney moved the roll call into the kitchen at the back of the building and out of sight. He addressed the patrolmen about the seriousness of their decision, speaking to them as a father with a hint of disappointment. He made his final pitch before he called out the roster and reminded them that whatever their decision, they had the burden of carrying the Department's good reputation with them. As the captain stood before the shift, it was obvious to him that there would be many more strikers than Curtis had anticipated and it was just as obvious which patrolmen would strike and who would remain. Rubber boots, rubber raincoats, short clubs and other personal gear sat on the floor next to the majority of the patrolmen, who stood in civilian clothing. Except for a few younger patrolmen, most of the non-strikers were the gray-hairs, close to pension. And a couple of the undecided called in sick.

Keveney stood before them at a time when he would normally be home, puttering in his garden or finishing his dinner, but because the Commissioner had requested that all of the captains be present, he stood before them and conducted the evening roll call. "I know that some of you didn't always agree with me," he said, "and others never agreed with me." He squeezed a smile out of his fleshy mouth that made him resemble a caricature of Humpty Dumpty. "But fellas, we are all in this together because the citizens will judge us the same. If you leave and don't continue to act in a highly professional manner, we who are left to protect the city will be treated with contempt and disrespect. And with the depleted shifts, some of your fellow coppers may be hurt or killed."

The patrolmen who stood with their gear shifted their weight and shuffled their feet, anxious to get on with it. They knew that a crowd had assembled outside and could tell by the raised voices that the mood had changed from passive to active and that some of the curious had an agenda.

They half listened to their commander who had always maintained a certain aloof distance from them and had difficulty understanding them. Melancholy and anxiety played into their emotions and they looked about and knew in their bones that it would never be the same—that the men whom they had served with and lived with were more brothers than brothers. And they understood that they were partially responsible for dividing their own family, some to remain on duty and most to go home alone.

"Lastly, men," the captain said, "know that those of us who are left behind hold no malice towards you and understand that what you have taken on will eventually benefit all of us. Good luck and God speed."

Keveney received the names of the men who were scheduled to report for duty from Sergeant McGuiness and began to read. "Allen, Martin."

"On strike, sir."

"Did you place all your issued gear on the table with your name?"

"Yes, sir."

"Okay, Allen. Leave the premises."

"If I may make a suggestion, captain," McGuiness said. "That crowd has grown significantly. I'd guess five hundred to a thousand people. The men who are leaving should walk out together."

"Good idea. Browne, Thomas."

"On strike, sir."

Keveney continued through the list until he reached Nolan and Dwyer, pausing with a wry smile when he read their names.

"Reporting for duty, sir," Nolan said.

Willie hesitated before answering and looked over at Quigley as he picked up his belongings.

"Well, Dwyer. What is your status?"

Willie turned back to the captain. "Reporting for duty, sir."

"I see that your uniform still fits you, Nolan. I'm surprised you even found it."

"Yes, sir."

"I'm pairing you two up in the wagon. See the sergeant and he'll issue you two shotguns. As soon as the ghouls outside go home, take those two Reds who are taking up space in our lockup and drop them at the Charles Street Jail. We don't need any distractions tonight."

"Yes, sir."

"Coppenrath, Albert." Captain Keveney scanned the Roll Call line and stretched himself tall and looked over and between the cops. "Coppenrath," he repeated. When no one answered, he marked AWOL on the roster.

Willie leaned back, looked down one side and then the other and then turned his head straight.

"Hurley, Dennis."

"On strike, sir."

When Keveney came to the name that had given him more heartburn in the last three years than he had suffered in his entire career, he read it with an almost sigh of relief. "Quigley, Fulton."

The patrolman who the station nicknamed the 'wreck' answered in a voice two or three octaves higher than his ordinary baritone and with Douglas Fairbanks' flair. "On strike, captain, sir."

"I never thought the day would come, Quigley, when I would actually miss the sound of that voice and when I would hesitate to say, 'leave the premises.' Try and stay in one piece, will you?"

"Ha, I've got the missus for that, sir."

When he had completed his reading of the roster, Keveney ordered Nolan and Dwyer to go out first and stand on either side of the door. Other non-striking patrolmen he ordered to circle behind the spectators and, if they got out of control, to use the shotguns that were issued to them. "Our job is different tonight, men," he said. "No use being heroes. Because we're so badly undermanned, our objective tonight is to keep order and the peace at any cost. Separate the combatants, treat the injured and send them on their way. Get enough information to criminally summons them if you think it necessary, but don't arrest anyone unless the crime is a capital offense."

In the twenty-two minutes that it took Captain Keveney to conduct roll call, the crowd of the benign, orderly and curious had been infected with a spirit of high-minded self-interest and radicalism and the strangeness that had found its way into the city now hung heavy in Roxbury Crossing. Flag carrying veterans and God-fearing nationalists who rejected Wilson's League of Nations, embraced Isolationism and lived by the motto to 'Stay in Step' shadowed the atheistic and the antimilitaristic Bolsheviks and a few wealthy Socialistic Parlor Reds, each special interest calling for its own agenda and each directing its slogans toward the police. Sandwiched between these two odd groups, the Ordinary Joe stood stunned, spiritually fatigued and disillusioned, no longer understanding what the goal was and longing for a nostalgic past.

With assistance from Brodsky's nobles and finks, the Letts marched into the Crossing two hundred strong with resurrected power and the financial support of the newly organized Communist Party in New York. They planted themselves in the crowd, distributing copies of *The New England Worker*, called the cops comrades and asked them to join their crusade. They orchestrated chants to free Fraina and Sturgis, shouting protests against their illegal arrest and detainment. This was the day of the proletariat's deliverance, the period when historians would mark as the 'people's hour' and the beginning of a new world order when the laborer and the capitalist sat at the same table.

Just before he left the station, Willie reached over to Quigley. "No hard feelings, Fulton?"

"None, Willie. Be careful, it may get rough for you fellas." He moved to the front of the strikers. "Make a hole, big man coming through."

Nolan threw open the doors and stepped onto the landing with Fulton right behind him. The crowd filled up the bowl that was the Crossing and then some. Like sand, it defined itself, shaping and adapting to every cutaway, every setback, every yard of space, and it quivered like gelatin, moving one way and then the other, slipping into an open cavity and filling it to the brim. The shouts and chants and incessant tom-tom slogans of the Reds ceased and the crowd fell menacingly silent like the vacuum of sound just before an explosion rips the air in two. Dwyer joined Nolan and Quigley on the landing and held his shotgun at port arms while he scanned the thousand and more faces, trying to read them, trying to interpret whether what he saw was anger or carnival amusement. He slid his thumb up along the stock of the shotgun and pushed the safety into the off position with a click that Nolan answered with an approving nod. Other strikers exited the building and soon the stairs were filled with men in suits, carrying clothing and other paraphernalia.

"Where the fuck is the cavalry when you need them?" Quigley said. "Oh, that's right, the pony jockeys are on strike with the rest of us."

"Bend over, Fulton," Nolan said. "And I'll ride you into the mob myself."

"Ha, you fuckin eejit, I'm going to miss you too, George."

A buzz rose up in the crowd like a jungle full of insects. Those with agendas quickly assessed who were strikers and who were cops and realized that Station 10 was ripe for a siege. The younger boys eyed their mud pies and then each other, but when they saw one of the armed patrolmen glaring at them, they looked away.

Charlie Bradley leaned against the fence where it began at the walkway and was lost in a cobweb of intoxication and delirium. Gibberish spilled out of him like a foreign language as he carried on a three-way conversation with himself. He jumped back and hollered to no one in particular, "Fuck you." As Nolan and Dwyer passed him, he screamed to an imaginary foe, "Oh, yeah. You think so, huh." One of the younger boys picked up a watery mud pie and handed it to him. He tried to follow the flight of it in his hand, moving it back and forth in an attempt to focus on it, but he became impatient, grunted and threw the mud away.

Muck hit Quigley in the face and chest as he passed. Small clumps of brown dirt marked his cheek and ear and the juices stained the front of his suit coat. Stunned, his immediate reaction was to dislodge the culprit's head with his club, but when he saw Bradley looking about like he was trying to determine what planet he was on, Quigley wiped his face, brushed his jacket and walked away. The older boys took the cue, singling out certain coppers for particular revenge, by flinging mud and arming their slingshots with stones, striking the patrolmen as they sought cover and distance away from the onslaught. Quigley threatened some of the boys and described to them in detail the punishment he would administer on his first day back to duty and, in doing so, received the greatest number of hits from the tormentors, including a stone that opened a gash in the soft tissue above his eye. An adolescent boy got up in the face of one of the on-duty cops and yelled "scab." Others picked up on it, and within a few calls, the crowd was alive with the epithet.

Commuters and the curious extricated themselves from the mob, fled the area and surrendered the belly of the Crossing to the radical elements. They were closely followed by Brodsky's agitators who had accomplished their mission and left to join the Boston front. Traffic backed up on all of the intersecting streets and operators blew their horns and were rewarded for their impatience with mud and stones. Rival gangs produced chains and saps and personalized war clubs and swung away at each other with abandon, exacting revenge or establishing territory, lashing at anyone who wasn't one of their own. Chuckers and stone throwers stood behind larger gang members, protected by ash barrel covers, and picked off their enemies with rocks. Younger stringy boys climbed up the bricks at the corner of the police station like monkeys, ripped at the ivy and pulled it off the building, while others broke the fence or threw a hailstorm of mud and rocks at the front door. Communists chanted, "This place is unfair to organized labor," and encouraged the mob to destroy the station and "tear it down." Gang members rolled a buggy onto the sidewalk and set it on fire. Veterans and nationalists moved into sections of the crowd, carved out the entrenched Reds and attacked them, swinging lengths of belts, ax handles and rubber hoses, and indiscriminately whacked any male or female who wore crimson or carried the Lettish banners.

As the level of violence rose, the more passive souls looked for an escape. The wealthy intellectuals and the socially offended Parlor Reds quit first, discarded their placards and cut the shortest route to a trolley stop or train station with the veterans and nationalists in close pursuit. The battling rioters clogged the paths of the strikers, denying them an escape route and closing them off from their protection. Nolan, Dwyer and the other on-duty patrolmen rushed to their aid and formed a skirmish line between the strikers and the crowd. Captain Keveney, Sergeant McGuiness and one of the lieutenants pulled out of the backyard in a Model-T Ford convertible with an air-cooled machine gun mounted on the back and took up a position at the entrance to the police station. On orders of the captain, Nolan fired two rounds of his shotgun into the air. Echoes of the discharges reverberated off the police station and sounded across the plaza, as the police pushed and slashed the rioters and steered them out of the Crossing.

When they reached the opposite side, the cops reversed the skirmish line and swept the area again, collecting any weapons left behind and attending to the badly injured. Willie moved through the trash and kicked at what appeared to be newspapers and a bundle of rags caught in the fence at the front of the station. But when the bundle didn't move, he reached down, pulled it back and discovered Charlie Bradley, beaten and unconscious. His clothing was caught on the bottom of the fence and he was frozen in an act of escape with his head turned up to one side, sand, grit and blood matted into his red hair. His face was red-black and swollen and blood trickled out of his mouth and one of his ears. He wore a short-sleeve shirt that exposed his dirty white, paper-thin skin. At the age of nineteen, Charles Bradley, alcoholic, died against the fence.

After placing a sheet over the body, Dwyer knelt down on one knee, blessed himself and began to say an Our Father when he jolted upright, stepped through a hole in the pickets, bent over and began to vomit into the mud. He continued to throw even after his stomach had emptied, spitting up strings of yellow bile and dry-heaving himself sore. He looked back at Bradley's body and remembered the barn in Ballinasloe and the mask of death that Bernie McLean wore on the day he forever became seventeen.

He sat on the steps of the police station and watched the last few stragglers as they limped or were carried out of the Crossing, saw the wave of young thugs rolling up Tremont Street towards Mission Hill and leaving a path of destruction behind them.

The houseman joined him on the step and lit a cigarette. "After you and Nolan catch your breath, the captain wants you to load up the two Reds and get them out of here."

"What's his rush? That's going to leave you guys really out-numbered."

"I think he'll shoot those two assholes right in the cells if he has to listen to them any longer. Besides, if they're not here, the Bolsheviks will take the fight somewhere else."

"Yeah, they can get to you after a while. Worse than a drunk in the wagon." Willie glanced at the box of cigarettes in the houseman's hand. "Give me one of those nails, will you?"

"I never seen you smoke before."

"I'm not much of a drinking man either, but I think today that all changed."

"It was a close one, Willie."

"Yeah. With all the radicals and hoodlums that were gathered here, it was the unconscious action of a delirious drunk that set the mob off. Would you call the Southern Mortuary, Fred, and tell them we have a body?"

"Sure, kid." The telephone rang inside and, for a minute, the houseman didn't move. He looked back through the window to see if someone was going to answer it and when no one did, he begrudgingly stood, flicked the cigarette into the mud and walked inside. “Station 10, Patrolman Cratty speaking.”

“What?” the houseman said. “No, I don’t have a story for the *Boston Herald*.”

Chapter Twenty-four

~

Standing under the railroad overpass, Graves O'Brien watched the fighting and tried to understand who was at war with whom. He was familiar with the anxiety of policing a mob after being assigned to keep the peace at some of Ireland's monster rallies. They attracted larger crowds for sure than the one he saw in the plaza. But he didn't remember the level of savagery that he had seen today.

He wondered whether Willie Dwyer was one of the strikers trying to escape, or one of the few patrolmen who cleared the plaza. If he was one of the coppers who stood up against that dangerous mob, he had to give him grudging respect. A striker, though, fit his preconceived characterization of someone who fled his country to avoid justice.

In the twilight, men and women stampeded past him. They had panicked and pushed and shoved anyone in their path, regardless of age, sex or cause. The well-dressed men and the woman in ankle-length dresses banded with the red ribbons, he thought were particularly wild in beating a route of escape. Dropping their banners, signs and newsletters in their wake, they pushed their way past slower moving or injured members of the crowd, tearing away the ribbons as soon as they cleared the railroad bridge. Just behind them, men in khaki woolen shirts drove them like cattle.

Boys of all ages ran next, some to keep pace with the veterans and some to pursue other boys. They were faster and deadlier than the adults and dispensed their violence with swift gleeful savagery, kicking and beating their victims with feet, fists and clubs.

Lastly, groups of men, carrying clothing and canvas bags shuffled closely together in clusters until they reached the bridge. O'Brien watched as they shook hands, agreed to meet on a different day, and laughed in a restrained and hesitant way before breaking off into smaller groups of two's and three's. He studied the strikers' faces, looking for the familiar and wondering if any of them might be Dwyer. Ten years is a long time, he admitted to himself, and realized that he was going to need some assistance. He trailed a couple of the strikers and they stared back defensively.

"Excuse me, gents," he said. "Can ye tell me if ye know Patrolman Dwyer, William Dwyer? From Ballinasloe Ireland?"

They turned away without answering and left.

O'Brien began to trek up the hill and saw boys who had fought in the plaza jump the back of a trolley and pull the cable to stop it. They threw the operator overboard, cleared it of passengers and filled the car with their friends. The trolley started up, went a short distance, stopped, rolled back and started again, hiccupping its way up the hill. The gang who occupied it hung out the windows and doors and challenged other boys on the sidewalk. Some of them threw strawberries at the derrieres of passing woman and chestnuts at the men who accompanied them, then threatened anyone who complained.

The constable stopped at a store that had remained open in spite of the disturbance and inquired about 'Patrolman Dwyer.' The adolescent clerk knew a patrolman named Dwyer, but wasn't sure whether his first name was William. The store owner called him 'Officer Dwyer' and said that he walked a regular beat in the neighborhood, but didn't know whether he was a striker or not. O'Brien sat down on a half wall and tried to imagine what resources he would use if he was at home. He watched the commandeered trolley until it was out of sight and canvassed the street and realized that he saw familiarity everywhere. The neighborhood was a larger composite of the little hamlets of West Ireland with the same buildings and same businesses. The village had a food store, a hardware store, a stable and a garage. There were churches and several gathering places like the one that stood across the street. O'Brien slipped past the back end of the crowd and entered O'Neil's, the pub that was filled to capacity.

On the other side of the Crossing at Station 10, Dwyer and Nolan loaded Bradley's body into the back of the wagon and chained Fraina and Sturgis, stripped to their underwear, on either side of him.

"This is a good place for you two because, like Charlie, you might as well be dead," Nolan said.

"You won't get away with this," Fraina said.

"One word from either of you, if you even think about shouting for help, I'll drive to the closest body of water and dump you in, handcuffs, chains and all. Give you a chance to see if you're as good at escape as that Houdini fella."

"It's too late, copper. By tomorrow night, we will own the streets," Fraina said. "The people are ready. What happened here is just the opening act. You will—"

"Shut the fuck up and remember what I said. One thing Boston has is plenty of deep water." Nolan produced a canvas tarp to put over them. "Gag 'em and cover them up, Willie."

"Which way?" Dwyer asked as he drove out of the backyard.

"Take the Golden Highway. We haven't received any reports of gathering crowds in the South End yet. Evidently, the savages only reside in Mission Hill." George lit up a cigar and blew the smoke into the cab. "There, that'll make Bradley a little more tolerable." He put his hands behind his head and looked up at the sky. "Rain, you bastard."

"Who we dropping off first?"

"The two revolutionists. Charlie's not going anywhere."

They avoided Boston proper and traveled along the quiet and unlit Charles River with their headlamps extinguished until they arrived at the County Jail where they were met by several guards. "End of the line, boys," Nolan said. "Have a nice trip back to Europe."

"Why do you think the Reds didn't try and bust them out during the riot?" Dwyer asked.

"Ah, who knows? They're a lot of yapping mouths. Besides, I think they realize by now that all we have to do is step aside and let the veterans tear into them. Some of those guys will gladly crush their Bolshevik skulls."

As they drove away from the jail, they heard the fractured echoes of disorder rattling between the downtown buildings, the sound piercing Boston's placid and tidy streets, shouts and screams interrupted by drunken laughter and breaking glass, and occasionally the pop, pop, of small arms fire.

"Do you hear that, Willie? It's like the goddam influenza—one kid in Jamaica Plain coughs and, within minutes, a hundred drop dead in East Boston. It's the same with this rioting. It's a fuckin epidemic."

"Shouldn't we go up there?"

"Any ordinary time I would, but these are not ordinary times. Keveney will tell us where he wants us to go."

"Which roads should I take?"

"Take the same route we came and backtrack to the mortuary. We want to avoid the city proper for now."

IN THE NORTH END, Rossini joined up with his embedded moles who had attached themselves to a large crowd outside the Hanover Street police station. The moles had recruited unemployed immigrants to The moles had recruited unemployed immigrants to rally their neighborhood and the Italian Socialists and the Italian Socialists from the back of a truck with a call for action to take up the cause of the just. And when Rossini received word that the patrolmen had refused to report for duty and that rioting had begun in Roxbury, he ordered his recruited finks to move to the front of the crowd and lead the march to the center of the city.

Moles walked side-by-side the North End leaders and met up with other groups like the underground libertarian anarchists, the black cats, the radical of radicals who traveled from strike to strike like Christian Evangelists to preach their dogma and walk the picket line of the oppressed, and the affluent gender-conscious feminists who campaigned for sexual and familial freedom.

They crossed the great divide that segregated the squalor of the Italian neighborhood from the streets of gold where money was made and lost in the blink of an eye. In an orderly procession, the crowd passed the businesses in the financial district along State, Federal and Milk Streets where guards stood in the windows with shotguns. They entered Scollay Square and were met by even larger crowds that could have grown anywhere—the young hoodlums, the pickpockets, the gamblers, thugs, certified cuckoos and the bored, like the sailors who later joined in the looting and destruction because they drank too much and stirred up those jungle passions that lay just beneath the surface of every human being. Automobiles filled with thieves rode up and down Tremont and Washington Streets, circling the most vulnerable of stores like vultures waiting to pick the bones of the dead. Crapshooters appeared out of nowhere and games began like spontaneous combustion, the dice shaking and rattling in the gutter after striking the curb. All of them seemed to be waiting for that one belligerent act that would free them of their collective conscience.

It arrived simply enough with a solitary brick that was thrown by an unknown person, smashing through the plate glass window at the United Cigar Store on Washington Street. At that moment the crowds that had formed for different reasons became a single-minded mob, intent on freeing itself from its stringent inhibitions. They moved as if on cue, tossing rocks, full rubbish barrels and anything with weight, including a six-foot chandelier, through the windows of businesses that didn't have someone standing with a gun behind the glass. The looters snatched and grabbed anything of value and denuded mannequins outfitted in the latest designs—taffeta dresses, Bolivia Afternoon coats, satin envelope chemises, leather shoes and Mallory hats.

Hundreds of young men and a handful of girls roamed down dimly lit Washington Street on a door-to-door smash and grab, picked out armfuls of clothing and shoes, and carried their wares into the middle of the street where they stripped down to their underwear and tried on the new duds. On Tremont Street, they sat on curbs and tried on shoes from the Walk-Over Shoe store and fired the rejected ones back through the broken store windows. Then, the ragtag army, drunk on their newfound power, strutted down the street and prepared an attack on the next unprotected small business.

Some of the more aggressive mob members sniffed around the fronts of the large department stores, looking for a soft spot, but were greeted by Brodsky's guards, standing with hairy fingers wrapped around their triggers. At Jordan Marsh, a couple of foolhardy souls busted the door, entered and were greeted by a host of weaponry. They trampled over each other and fled in a hail of birdshot and the threat of a nine-ball barrage. Wounded, burning and bleeding, they collapsed into the middle of the street, hung onto their asses and bellowed for assistance from the police.

Other rioters removed tires and other resalable parts from automobiles. And in their escape, they rolled the rubber like Wellesley College girls roll their hoops while others stacked tires over their bodies like rings tossed over a peg. The automobile thieves and the black market garment dealers counted their profits and departed the city as quickly as they had arrived, laden with goods like refugees. Thugs from as far away as New York rode with guns drawn on the running boards of cars filled to the brim with stolen goods.

Voyeuristic gangs of curious boys ran back and forth and shadowed the criminals so they could say they had rubbed elbows with the dangerous. The youthful spectators tracked the rioting, looting, gambling and robberies like attendees at a carnival, followed the thieves into stores and gambled with their lives when shots rang out.

THE WAGON SLIPPED into the yard at the Southern Mortuary where Nolan and Dwyer met one of the pathologists. "What can you tell me about this guy, detective?"

"Old Charlie, here? Nineteen years old, alcoholic at fifteen, lived by violence, died by violence, dead before he was born."

The doctor removed the sheet and lifted his lantern over his face. "What happened?"

"We found him after the riot at Roxbury Crossing."

"What riot?"

"The first of many, I'm afraid," Nolan said. "Rival gangs got mixed up in the mob and they took advantage of the craziness to settle old scores."

"Bring him inside," the pathologist said. "How many cops are on strike?"

"Patrolmen," Nolan said. "Most of the patrolmen walked off." He and Dwyer rolled the body on a gurney into the building. "You got a stall I can use, doc?"

"Next to the office over there."

The pathologist completed the notes on the death certificate and handed it to Willie. "You're the first delivery, but we may be overrun with bodies if this continues. I'm going to forego the autopsy. The cause of death seems pretty obvious. You can sign as the witness."

Nolan returned from the bathroom and took the certificate out of

Willie's hands. "As long as you're ready to put your mark on the certificate, it's your call, doc. But if you get scrupulous, pull his liver. He was dead long before a boot ever touched him."

"Next of kin?" the doctor said.

"His mother and brothers. We'll notify them." The two cops walked out to the wagon. "If you've got any questions," Nolan said, "give us a call at Station 10. By the way, keep the sheet."

Willie drove through the gate. "Back to Roxbury?"

"No, go over to the City." A couple of large drops of rain fell on the wagon's hood. "Come on—rain. We need a break, just a little something to cool the natives off."

"Why are we going to City Hospital?"

"They'll know better than us how bad it is."

They avoided downtown and the crowds and made their way to Albany Street and City Hospital. Willie shut off the engine and sat there.

Nolan turned the handle of the door, started to step out, but paused and looked back at him. "So, how does it feel?"

"How does what feel?"

"I'm watching you beat yourself up and that's a battle you can only lose." Nolan sat back in the seat and closed the door. "You made the right decision."

"It doesn't feel right to be only one of two patrolmen to vote against the strike."

"I'm the only one who held out, not you. And I told you why. The whole thing is a bag job and the more we learn and the closer we get to the end, the more obvious it seems. The boys have been snookered into a game they can't win. Those Yankee assholes aren't going to beat me. I'll be the last cop standing, if necessary. And as I said, these volunteers they are recruiting are going to need some direction." He interlaced his fingers and bent them until his knuckles cracked. "Now you, Mr. Dwyer, the Ballinasloe felon, you had no choice at all. If you had walked, your friend, O'Brien, would have swooped down on you, citizen, and who knows where you'd be now. At least by being a cop, you have some leverage and he has to keep his distance until this strike is over."

"You're probably right."

"I am right. Say, didn't you tell me that you thought one of de Valera's guards was one of the men in the barn?"

"Yeah, built like a fireplug. You know how you don't remember someone at first, but something about them, the way they talk or move gives you the clue."

"Yeah."

"Well, this guy has a ritual where he bends down and picks up some dirt and gravel. Starts shaking his hand until all he's got left is stone."

"And this is what one of these killers did?"

"Yeah, just before the smaller weasel shot McLean. Jesus, it was supposed to be a warning to anyone who talked to the constabulary, not a fucking execution."

"There you go. When a judge hears that one of the guys who pulled the trigger is one of de Valera's bodyguards and he goes free because of political considerations, I think Mr. O'Brien will be sent packing."

"I don't know if I want to depend on the court."

"Why don't you take it one step at a time?"

"I can't believe the R.I.C. paid his passage to America," Willie said. "But that's who he is. There's only one way to stop him—"

"And that's why you need to stay among friends. Come on, I want to check in with a doctor I know. He'll tell us what's going on in the rest of the city." Nolan waited for Willie to walk around the wagon and patted him on the back. "Then I'll buy you one of the famous City Hospital hot dogs before we leave."

Nolan and Dwyer got an immediate idea of the scope of the rioting and its impact on the city upon entering the emergency ward. The concussed, the wounded, the fractured and the confused occupied nearly all of the examining stations, and the sprains, the bruises and the lacerations most of the stretchers that hugged the hallway walls. Nurses and aides prepped, washed and comforted the injured before sending them to physicians who looked too young and harried to be wearing white coats.

"Have we heard from Doctors Wiggins and Haughton?" one of the physicians yelled to a nurse who sat at the admitting counter.

"They're on their way," she said.

"Oh swell, Willie," Nolan said in a loud voice. "They finally realized that they need some real medical doctors with genuine licenses in here."

"I don't need to turn around to identify that loudmouth," the doctor said. "Just what I need. A real pain in the ass to make things crazier than they already are. Shouldn't you be out keeping the peace, Nolan?"

The detective put one hand on Dwyer's shoulder and the other he held out in the direction of the doctor. "Willie, the estimable Doctor Shutt, as in 'Shut the hell up, I'm the one with the college degree here.'"

"Why, Nolan?" the doctor said.

"Why what, doc?"

"Why couldn't you have been one of the strikers? There wouldn't have been a mob, no violence, just an overindulgence of alcohol while the citizens celebrated your early retirement."

"Ha, I love you too, doc. So, what do you have to report? Has the entire city gone mad like our beloved Mission Hill?"

Shutt turned around and leaned on the counter. "Not all of it, thank God. There are a few neighborhoods that exemplify the discipline and order of our Yankee forefathers."

"Oh, so you're telling me that the neighborhoods where civil order has been tossed out with the dirty dishpan water are only those that are inhabited by the Irish."

"If the rioting occurred only in Mission Hill, Roxbury, South Boston and sections of Dorchester, you would be accurate, but, from what I have been informed by a colleague at Massachusetts General, other areas of the city have produced their own mobs, including the North End.

Nolan turned to Dwyer. "Yeah, we heard some of that paesano music on our way over here. I'm sure our boy, Rossini, played a role in that."

"Who?" Shutt asked.

"A bum we're looking for—"

"So why aren't you out there, detective?"

"Strictly a defensive posture. Let them beat the shit out of each other and then we come in and pick up what's left, like garbage men. Even you have to realize that we are a little bit outnumbered."

"Well, one note of encouragement," the doctor said. "The number of injured has fallen off dramatically as the night has worn on. So, hopefully, they are getting tired or bored and going home."

"Yeah, that would be nice, or they may be just a little more careful when smashing and bashing." Nolan stepped behind the counter. "Do you mind if I make a telephone call to let the station know we're still alive?"

"Go ahead, just don't tie it up long."

"Will do."

Fifteen minutes later, Nolan jumped into the wagon and handed Willie a hot dog. "The house mouse tells me that things have quieted down quite a bit over there. Shutt was right." He took a bite out of the hot dog and spoke with his mouth stuffed. "See what I mean about going to the source?"

Willie wiped mustard from the corner of his mouth. "On the way back to the station, can I make a quick stop at the rooming house?"

"Sure, but we're not going back to the station right away. We've been ordered to report to Superintendent Crowley at HQ to assist in the downtown area."

Nolan removed his revolver from its holster, opened the cylinder and snapped it shut. "Six ready to go," he said. He holstered the weapon and sat back. "So what do you think? Are these the best dogs in Boston or what?"

Chapter Twenty-five

Before the striking police had made their way home or gathered at Fay Hall, reports of looting, fighting and robberies began to come into the office of Harvard's president, A. Lawrence Lowell. "My God. This is what happens when police unionize." He tossed the reports on his desk and continued his dictation to his secretary. "Therefore, I call upon all Harvard students to prepare themselves to assist in the preservation of order in the city of Boston."

He took four measured steps across the carpeted floor, turned and stopped. "Would you read that back, please?"

"It is at times like these when the men of Harvard need to demonstrate the leadership for which this University is known," the secretary read. "The University has received a discouraging report of violence and a breakdown of social order in the city from the Governor's Office. Governor Coolidge is asking for volunteers for police duty to report to retired Police Superintendent Pierce at the Chamber of Commerce building in the morning. Therefore, I call upon all Harvard students to prepare themselves to assist in the preservation of order in the city of Boston."

"That's fine," Lowell said. "Please have it printed and posted around the campus and prepare a release for the newspapers."

"Yes, Doctor Lowell."

In the university's gymnasium, Coach Fisher spoke with several newspaper reporters. "The entire football squad of one hundred and twenty-five students is scheduled to do police work."

"What will that do to your season?" one of the reporters asked.

"To hell with football. If the men are needed, they will report for duty."

"Does that mean you have suspended practices, Coach?"

"I never said that."

THE CARDINAL RULE for any Brodsky venture dictated that Labor may lose or Management may lose, but the strikebreaker always made his money, and while one of his knuckle dusters could get worked over for skimming, the boss didn't mind if his assortment of whacko finks, moles and stoolpigeons supplemented their ten to fifteen dollar-per-week stipend by stealing anything not nailed down from the place they were hired to protect. With this in mind, Rossini and his finks broke off from the mob once the rioting began and met to plan their own selective looting. They targeted unprotected or under-protected businesses that specialized in jewelry, silverware, guns and cash and took particular interest in pawnshops.

"Now listen, you big pricks," Rossini said to his finks and moles outside the Park Street subway station. "You don't take nothing you can't easily carry, you don't get arrested and you cough up twenty-five percent of your stash to me. You got that?"

When some of his crew greeted his instructions with confused screwed-up faces, he pulled aside one of his Italian recruits. "You speak English?"

"A little," the man said.

"Did you understand what the fuck I just said, especially about the twenty-five percent?"

"Si."

"Well, make sure that these dagoes understand." He returned to the group and pulled them close to him. "I want all of you back here in one hour."

Rossini and his goons melded with the rudderless crowds that wandered in one direction and then another, the looters busting into stores like they were tearing into boxes of Cracker Jack, searching for that one special prize. Brodsky's chief slugger found his special prize in the Studio Jewelry store with access from an alley so dark that he never saw the back door, just guessed that it had to be there.

And while he jimmied the lock, Nolan and Dwyer quickstepped in time to a gun shop two doors down with a small contingent of cops and volunteers led by Superintendent Crowley. They charged up the stunted little street known as Temple Place and were greeted with bottles, broken-up furniture and shards of window glass. The belligerent rioters refused to move and chanted, "To hell with the cops." And when the police made their second charge, the mob unleashed a string of fireworks and one of those quarter sticks that boxes your ears and cleans out your sinuses in one concussive clap. Crowley ordered two shotgun volleys fired over the rioters' heads, the deafening blasts roaring in the narrow stone street, the pellets skipping off the brick buildings, fire escapes and business signage, producing a maelstrom of flying shrapnel that sent the terrorized looters stampeding towards Boston Common.

The superintendent ordered Nolan and Dwyer to secure the gun shop while the rest of the detail cleared the street and inspected the other businesses. Just as the two cops entered the front door, they heard a bottle drop and roll along the floor somewhere in the back of the store. They took cover by the counter until they could see enough to move. Shoes shifted on the wooden floor behind the curtain that separated the public store from the workshop in the rear. They waited and the shoes shifted again. Willie could see that the glass at the end of the display case had been broken and that there were two revolvers lying on the end of the counter. The shoes shifted a third time, accompanied by a sigh and an inhale of air. And another sigh. Nolan signaled for Willie to wait.

Dwyer squinted his eyes to see into the darkness, when he heard the first sniffle and looked over at the detective. Nolan heard it too. The sniffle became longer and louder and the shoes shuffled impatiently like their owner was doing a jig outside an occupied toilet. Then another sigh and a small grunt.

When he heard the metallic click, Willie thought he saw movement. Nolan directed him to the right of the curtain. From his new position, Dwyer could see an open box of bullets sitting on the counter next to the revolvers.

The detective jacked a round into the shotgun's chamber and a spent shell went skidding across the floor. "Come out with your hands up!"

The sniffling gave way to several long breaths and sorrowful moans.

"Did you hear me? Come out or we're coming in," Nolan said. "What's it going to be?"

The curtain moved partially away and Willie could see the lower half of a pair of legs that he thought were from a small person. "No one is going to hurt you," he said. "Just come out."

“Come on,” Nolan said. “Get out here.”

The curtain lifted higher and Willie relaxed when he saw a boy about twelve step out from behind it, sniffling and wiping one of his eyes with the knuckles of his hand. Dwyer stood up, walked out from behind the display case and switched on the light.

“Watch it, Willie,” Nolan said.

“Alright, it’s alright,” Willie said to the boy. He stepped toward the curtain and the boy lifted a pistol that was hidden behind it, pointing the weapon at Dwyer’s chest.

“Put it down,” Nolan said as he raised his shotgun to his shoulder. “Watch it, Willie.”

Tears streamed down the boy’s face and he sobbed openly. His hand shook as he continued to direct the revolver at Willie’s chest.

“Come on, boy.” Willie slid his boot closer and raised an empty trigger hand. “See—we’re not going to hurt you. Just drop the gun on the floor.”

The boy shook his head.

“Drop the gun,” Nolan said.

“Look, I’m not going to hurt you.” Willie placed his shotgun against a cabinet. “Now you put yours down.”

“What are you doing, Dwyer?”

“Come on, boy.” Willie slid closer, three arm’s lengths away, saw the revolver’s cocked hammer, the boy’s dirty finger pressed against the trigger, the pin a heartbeat from falling. He held up his arms.

The front door burst open and two volunteers stood at the entrance. “The super wants to know what’s taking you so long—.”

“Get outta here,” Nolan yelled.

They saw the boy with the gun and charged into the store with their pistols drawn. “Hey you, drop it,” one of them yelled. “Or I’ll—”

“No—” The boy screamed.

“Ah—” Willie cringed and felt every muscle in his body lock up frozen with his hands thrown up in a plea, the bullet passing just under his raised arm and lodging in the wall behind him.

“Jesus—” Dwyer pulled his head in like a turtle while the boy stood stunned by the sound of the weapon. Nolan jumped him and slapped the revolver out of his hand.

The twelve-year old cowered into a squat, bringing his arm up over his head to avoid an anticipated blow, exposing bite marks and skin where the flesh had been torn away. Willie stooped down next to him and took his arm away, saw swelling under one of his eyes and digital bruises on his neck.

"Leave me alone," the boy cried.

"What happened to you?" Dwyer said. He placed his hand on the boy's shoulder, felt his body trembling. "I'm trying to help you."

The boy raised his shoulder and pulled it away. He jerked his head and looked back towards the curtain.

"Who's back there?" Willie asked.

The boy tilted his head up, stabbing Dwyer with his stare.

"Someone with you?" Willie made eye contact with Nolan.

The boy wiped his eyes again with the back of his hand and nodded his head.

Nolan raised his shotgun and pulled the curtain aside and let it go as he disappeared behind it, the canvas slapping the doorjamb and shuttering against it. He found the light switch, turned it on and then lifted the curtain again. "Willie, come in here and leave him out there."

The man looked perfect in every way, sitting in a chair still holding a rifle across his lap. A fifth of whiskey lay on the floor and a puddle of the caramel liquid pooled at his feet. His head was bent forward in a sleeping position like he had passed out in the act of doing what he did best. Drool still leaked out of the corner of his mouth. And a small black ring encircled a hole at the bottom of his hairline.

Willie returned to the front of the shop and found the boy huddled in a corner. "Is that your father?" he asked.

He curled into himself and whimpered like a small animal, lowered his head down and shook it. "Stepfather—" He whimpered more loudly and began to rock back and forth. "I didn't want to come."

Dwyer sat down next to him. "Nobody is going to hurt you."

Nolan returned to the front room, leaned against the counter and lit a cigarette. He glanced at the young patrolman and the boy and turned away, spit a piece of tobacco that was stuck to his lip and drew another long drag. He ran his fingers across his forehead and exhaled.

"Well, it looks like we got here just in the nick of time, wouldn't you say, patrolman?" one of the volunteers said as he stood by the door.

"Get the fuck outta here," Nolan said.

Outside the shop, Superintendent Crowley instructed the detail to check the alley behind the stores. He poked his head in the door. "You alright in there, boys?"

"Yes, sir," Nolan said. George looked over at Willie and the boy. "When you're ready, take him out to the wagon." He picked up the revolver from the floor. "Put him in the front seat."

WHILE THE COPS battled the looters on Temple Place, Rossini pried off the hasp and padlock of the jewelry store's display case. He selectively picked out certain pieces that he knew had value and dropped them into a brown paper bag. He dumped several trays of expensive diamond rings into the bag and then stooped down and rearranged the cases so they appeared to be undisturbed.

The front door rattled and he heard voices just outside. He leaned out from the display case and could see two cops peering in between shards of hanging glass. They opened the door and Rossini slipped into the back room and flipped open his blade. One of the cops entered, but stopped when he heard the sound of a single pistol shot. Then they both disappeared. He waited and listened for a few minutes and then closed the cases and took the time to screw the hasp and lock back into place. He stuffed newspaper into the brown bag on top of the jewelry and then covered the gems with fruit that he took from his pockets. He took his time to secure the alley door and then walked the narrow space between the buildings with his bag of oranges like he had made a stop at Haymarket on his way home from work.

The rain fell hard like needles and, like the shower, the spontaneous destruction and looting that had erupted a few hours earlier ceased as quickly as it had begun. The mob and its confusion had left and now real cops and make-believe cops filled the downtown and stalked its streets and alleyways, their voices growing louder and bolder as they reclaimed the battlefield. Rossini heard them. He jumped the fire escape on the side of the building and climbed to the roof where he could see the destruction, could see the cops on Temple Place. He watched two of them place a young boy into a police wagon and then he made his way across the roofs to the last building that faced Tremont Street and vaulted down the fire escape with his bag of oranges. Brodsky's Number One entered the subway station as the voice of the mob became more giddy than violent, echoing in the bowl of Scollay Square and across Boston Common.

CATHERINE WOKE in darkness and stepped out of her room disoriented. "Hello?" she called out. "Is anyone here?"

"Quiet, girl," said Mrs. Gerhardt from the corner of the unlit living room. "I don't want those savages taking out their frustrations on me and my home."

Light from a street lamp bled in and around the window curtains and she was able to see the landlady. "What's going on?"

"The police have gone out on strike and left the city to the criminals and hooligans. There was a riot in the Crossing right outside the police station, if you can imagine that, and a man was killed."

"Oh, God."

Those damn coppers! I'd give them a piece of my mind if I was to run into them."

"Have you heard from Mr. Dwyer?"

"I have not!"

"I think you told me earlier that he said he could be reached at the station."

"Oh. That's right, he did."

"May I use the telephone to call him?"

"I don't think you'll be able to get out on it; it's been busy all night."

"Then I'll walk to the station to speak with him."

"You don't even know if he's there. Don't be foolish; it's three o'clock in the morning."

"But it seems quiet out there now."

"Are you listening to me? Decent women don't walk around in the middle of the night. My neighbor next door told me that earlier this evening her niece, a schoolgirl mind you, was fondled and touched in inappropriate places by those hoodlums."

"I'll be alright."

Light swept around the room in a band as a vehicle turned in the street in front of the home and stopped. Mrs. Gerhardt pulled the curtain away from the window. "It's a police wagon. It looks like Officer Dwyer and there's another policeman in the vehicle." She waited until she heard the doorknob rattle before she unlocked the door. Turn on the lamp near you," she said.

Willie entered the parlor with a confused expression when he saw Catherine. Then the corner of his mouth turned up in a crooked smile. "What are you doing here?"

"I had to make a change in my accommodations." She turned away from the landlady. "Too many roughnecks hanging around. The neighborhood isn't what it used to be."

"Uh-huh."

"It's a disgrace," the landlady said.

"Well, the worst of it seems to be over," Willie said with his eyes still on Catherine. "It is starting to quiet down."

"Miss Loftus tells me that you can vouch for her, Mr. Dwyer," the landlady said. "You know that I run a reputable house here."

"I can speak for her." He walked past the two women and started up the stairs to his room. "She won't be here very long—"

"Yes, he's right," Catherine said.

"I'm just picking up a change of clothes and leaving for the station house." He stopped half way up the stairs. "I haven't had anyone inquiring about me, have I?"

"No, no one except Miss Loftus here. Were you expecting someone else?"

"No, no." He continued up the stairs and entered his room.

"Do you have family close by?" Mrs. Gerhardt asked Catherine.

"Family?" Catherine giggled and shook her head. "No."

"And what about Mr. Dwyer, I thought you were—"

"Friends, we're friends."

"All set," Willie said as he came down the stairs. "I'm not sure when I'll be back. Probably when the strike is over, I guess."

Mrs. Gerhardt turned on another light. "Would you like a cup of tea before you leave?"

"Thank you, but I don't have time right now. Detective Nolan is waiting for me in the wagon."

"Well, let me fix a cup for Miss Loftus, at least." She disappeared past the swinging door into the kitchen.

"Okay, so what the heck are you doing here?" Willie asked Catherine.

"I'm sorry, Willie—"

"Save it, will you." He glanced at the kitchen door. "You didn't even have the common courtesy—If you didn't want to see me anymore, you could have just told me."

She glanced at the kitchen door. "I need to talk to you." She stepped toward him and spoke in a lowered voice, leaned into him to whisper and anchored her hand to his arm.

"Is this another game?" he asked.

"I can't go home right now."

"Why?"

"Some guys are looking for me and if they find me, you're liable to be fishing me out of the harbor."

"What did you get yourself into?"

"A couple of tough guys came into the diner one night, wanted to pay me a lot of money to set up Ran—this guy."

"How did they know where to find you?"

"They'd been tailing me."

"Do you know the names of these guys?"

"Oh, I don't know— Hump did most of the talking."

"Who was the guy you set up, Catherine?"

"I'd rather not say."

"Suit yourself." The wagon horn tooted and Willie turned the doorknob.

"Wait—" She looked away. "Jim Rankin."

"Rankin?" Willie turned away from the door. "You're the girl?"

"It isn't like you think."

"It isn't?" His voice jumped. "What do you mean, set up?"

"A photograph—"

"Stop." He took hold of her shoulders. "So full of life—" He touched her lightly in the center of her chest— "But here, you're a graveyard."

"These guys will kill me if I show my face—"

"This is about the strike and Rankin's support— What about the cops who were counting on him?"

"They didn't tell me—"

"Do you think I'm getting involved with this?"

She felt the strength of his hands soften and dribble away from her shoulders, saw the mood change in his face. "It's too late for the cops."

"What do you mean?"

"Rankin told me he won't support a police strike."

"Did he tell you that?"

"Not exactly. He said that striking cops serve no one and that he's done something."

"Jesus. But why are they after you?" His face hardened. "You were already paid, weren't you?"

"Yes."

"And the thugs want their money back?"

"Yes." Catherine sat down in a parlor chair with her hands between her knees. "These guys are everywhere. I can't go home right now."

Mrs. Gerhardt came in from the kitchen and saw the expressions on their faces. "Oh—I'm sorry." She stepped back through the door.

The wagon's horn tooted again and Willie opened the door and then closed it. "Did you say Hump?"

"Yeah."

"Did he ever mention a guy by the name of Rossini?"

"No, I don't think so. But I know he's got a boss."

He reached into his pocket and removed the list of Brodsky's strike-breakers. "Do you know any other names?"

"Jack, he was the younger one, a real nut case. I think his last name is McCarthy."

Willie glanced at the list again and put it in his pocket. "I'll help you under one condition."

"Whatever you want."

"You set aside one third of the money for me."

"I thought you didn't want any part of this."

"I don't, but it would give a couple of brothers a chance, maybe a new start. Maybe, one decent thing can—"

"You've got a deal." Catherine stood, reached up and kissed him on the cheek. "Don't be sore."

"Don't."

Mrs. Gerhardt entered the room again, carrying a tray. "Oh, I'm glad that you stayed, Mr. Dwyer. I've got enough for you and your friend."

"Thanks, but we have to go. I'll be back when things settle down," he said and walked out the door.

Willie jumped into the wagon next to Nolan while Catherine stood behind the curtain and watched. As it pulled away from the curb, he leaned towards the detective and said something and the detective nodded. The wagon passed by the front door. And then Willie looked back.

When the wagon turned the corner at the end of the block and went out of view, Constable O'Brien stepped out of the darkness of the parking lot across the street and wrote down the address of the rooming house.

O'BRIEN LEFT the parking lot and walked down the hill to the telephone booth across from the Mission Church. Rainwater trickled out of the booth when he opened the door and pieces of splintered wood ground under his shoe. The telephone's receiver hung off the hook, but the equipment appeared intact. He tapped the receiver cradle a few times and listened for the operator. The only other people on the street were four adolescent boys who sat idly on the church stairs, passing a cigarette back and forth among them.

"Hello, operator," O'Brien said. "I'd like to make a collect call to the following number in western Massachusetts?"

When he made his connection, he said, "I got your message to call. Yeah, I know it's the middle of the night, but I've located Dwyer." He glanced up to watch the boys on the church steps. "When were you going to tell me that he's a copper?

"No, I haven't made contact yet, but I was going to file the arrest warrant with his headquarters—Why? What do you mean, stay away? When are you going to tell me what the fuck is going on?

"You're returning to Boston?" the constable said. "Good, where?" He pinned the receiver between his cheek and his shoulder and wrote down the directions.

"Okay, I've got it," The boys crossed the street towards him. "I've got to go."

When they reached the telephone booth, O'Brien was gone.

In the News

MOBS SMASH WINDOWS, LOOT STORES
Wild Night Follows Strike of Police
Washington Street stores sacked; hoodlums roam South Boston;
Scores volunteer for police duty; bystanders must assist officers;
Coolidge won't oust Curtis
THE BOSTON DAILY GLOBE
Wednesday, September 10, 1919

MAYOR COMMANDS POLICE
Takes over guardianship of city under almost forgotten statute;
State Guard to patrol streets; blames the Governor and Curtis;
says city received no cooperation from either when police deserted;
Mayor wants public to know that he granted only request for
increased salary made by police

MASS MEETING AT SYMPHONY HALL POSTPONED
Meeting tonight in opposition to League of Nations,
on account of policemen's strike
THE BOSTON EVENING TRANSCRIPT
Wednesday, September 10, 1919

Chapter Twenty-six

Wednesday, 10 September 1919
0920 hours

The double doors of Fay Hall were pinned open and the singing that could be heard a block away from the corner of Washington and Dover Streets continued in spite of John McInnes' attempts to call the meeting to order. For the third time, he rapped the gavel on the block of wood and for the third time the membership ignored him, singing at the top of their voices "Hail, Hail, the Gang's All Here" after fifty-eight suspended members of the Metropolitan Park Police showed up to announce that they wouldn't "scab" the patrolmen's strike. McInnes smiled at their enthusiasm because he understood. For most of the past year, they had struggled with the idea of going in a way that was contrary to their oaths, traditions and their personal codes of honor. Yet even now, while they knew that their logic was right and that they had taken the only path given them, in their hearts, the battle raged. It was the camaraderie that helped them get through it, that helped them believe, a special bond between men who stood separate from the society that they served, who enforced its laws and kept it civil. And so they broke into spontaneous song.

McInnes looked down at the table, saw the signatures of nine additional patrolmen who joined the Union that morning, and the pledges of support from other Boston Locals. He put down the gavel and smiled.

THE BATH WATER wasn't hot enough to satisfy him. Willie sank as low as the tub would allow and tried to steam the aches and pains and memories from his body. One of the few benefits of the strike was the lack of competition from fifty or more patrolmen, all vying for the same sink, the same toilet and the one bathtub. The station was quiet since he and Detective Nolan had returned from downtown and during the additional four-hour shift of perimeter guard watch. He had sat in the window with a shotgun, hungry, exhausted and rank, poised to send the first asshole to hell stupid enough to storm the door.

He closed his eyes under the washcloth and watched the images race by like lighted windows of a passing train—the boy who, in a desperate act for peace, murdered his abusive stepfather with surgical detachment; Frank and Johnny Bradley freed from their maniacal brother by a random act of savagery; the mob and its nihilistic solution to injustice; and the indelible memory of Bernie McLean gone to eternity for the sins of his father. The windows flashed by faster and faster while Willie sought the strength to rise another day.

A rumble of voices and movement on the stairs reached him on the third floor. He jumped out of the tub, dried off with one rub of a towel and ran to his locker. He heard men's voices getting louder and closer, talking in such a way that he knew they weren't familiar with the building. The door at the head of the stairs slapped open and banged against the locker behind it. He drew his revolver.

"This must be it," said the first man through the door.

He was a few years younger than Dwyer, with an athletic build and dressed in a tailored suit and a soft hat. Behind him were several other young men in similar attire. They entered the darkened dormitory without seeing Willie, and stood looking at the rows of unmade beds, abandoned lockers and the small dimly lit bathroom.

"Say, no wonder these cops went on strike," the first man said.

"Maybe they don't deserve anything more. No one forced them, after all," said another.

"Who the hell are you?" Willie said.

"You don't have to point that pistol at us," said the first man with an air of cultured authority. "We're the special police volunteers, here to make sure there will be no repeat of yesterday's destruction and disorderliness."

"You don't say," Nolan said from a bed in the corner of the room. "What's your name?"

"Maxwell Henshaw, captain of Harvard's football team and team leader for the police volunteers assigned to Station 10." Max leaned one way and then the other in an attempt to see into the corner of the room and the person who asked the question.

"Is your father Bradford Henshaw?"

"Why yes, do you know my father?"

"You might say we've heard of him."

"Class of Ninety-four, owner of Patriot Realty and Henshaw Industries—"

"Yeah, we heard." Nolan raised his hand high so the volunteers could see it and pointed to the door behind them. "Why don't you and your friends go back downstairs and try and keep it quiet so we can get some rest."

"Captain Keveney told us to look around and make ourselves comfortable," Maxwell said.

"I'm sure he did. Now, shut the door behind you." When the last of the volunteers left, he said, "Going to be an interesting day, Willie."

Dwyer removed the sheets on one of the beds and replaced them with sheets that he had brought from the rooming house. "We should have given them the old Station 10 initiation and made them sleep in one of the bug beds."

Nolan pulled the cover up to his shoulder and turned to the wall. "Something to remember their days with the Boston Police."

A FEW HOURS LATER, Nolan entered the kitchen as Willie fried a couple of eggs. "Just spoke to the captain. We've got a few hours to clean up our reports before we have to report to HQ again. He's going to keep his volunteers close to the house, give 'em foot patrols of Tremont Street so they won't get into any trouble."

"Or get the crap kicked out of 'em," Willie said.

"Exactly. So far, there doesn't seem to be a lot of interest in raising Cain around the Hill when there's all that fun in the city." Nolan sat down at the table and opened the newspaper. “I hope you’re not going to feed just yourself.”

“You know, I was thinking about what Catherine told me last night.” Willie slid one of the eggs onto a dish for the detective.

“About Rankin tipping her that the BCLU won’t strike?”

“Yeah, so before you got up, I took a walk and saw two characters sitting in a car outside the Shawmut Bank.”

“Rossini’s boys?”

“Probably. If they’ve checked her room and the diner—”

“And all else fails,” George said.

“Right.” Willie sat down on the opposite side of the table.

“So, she’s the ‘It’ girl.” Nolan scoffed. “And now they want their money back. What moxie.”

A couple of volunteers came into the kitchen and when they saw Nolan and Dwyer, one of them said, “Just getting a cup of coffee.”

Nolan pointed to the container with his thumb. “Go ahead.”

After they left, Willie leaned across the table. “So, what do you think?”

“What do I think? Everybody’s fucking everybody, that’s what I think.” He sprinkled salt on his egg. “So, she wants us to take Rossini’s goons out while she grabs the money?”

“Yeah.”

“I don’t know.”

Willie pulled the Brodsky list from his pocket. “If the two dopes are Schultz and McCarthy, we got warrants for both of them.”

“Hmm, and maybe they tell us where Rossini is holed up.”

“Yeah—”

“I still owe that asshole.”

Willie jumped up from the table. “Civvies or uniform?”

“I didn’t want to do reports, anyways. Hey, wait a minute. You’ll have to excuse an old suspicious cop. What are you getting out of this?”

“Nothing.” He met Nolan’s stare and dropped his eyes. “I told her that I wanted a third for the Bradley family. I wish I could have helped that kid from last night too.”

“You missed your calling, William. You should’ve been a priest. Don’t try and save the world; it’ll come back and bite you in the ass.” He walked to the sink, rinsed his mouth and hands and dried them on a towel. "Well, what are we waiting for?"

Just about noon, when the natives on Mission Hill were behaving themselves and crowds were starting to form again in Scollay Square, Catherine sashayed bold as brass into Brigham Circle in a tan business suit that Dandy Jim had bought for her at an exclusive New York store because seeing her in that suit made a statement about power and gave the little stump an opportunity to advertise the size of his pecker.

She walked right up on Hump and Jack McCarthy where they sat, parked across the street from the bank. Pushed her delicious head into their window and gave them a wink. "Say, boys, what brings you into the neighborhood?"

"Miss Loftus, nice to see you too," Hump said. "I assume, Jack, that she's here to make a withdrawal. That's great. And afterwards we can all go for a ride."

"Gee, I don't think so. The last time you were supposed to give me a ride you left me with Rankin in a hotel room, hoping he would do your dirty work for you."

McCarthy grabbed her wrist. "What if I just rip your fucking head off right here, Missy?"

"Easy, Jack. Let's not get unpleasant." Hump pulled McCarthy's hand away. "No reason we can't all be friends."

Catherine rubbed her wrist and backed away from the car.

"Now look, Miss Loftus, you know that you didn't earn the money."

"How would you know?"

"Listen here. My boss is a generous man and wants to compensate you, just not at the rate that you were paid."

"Let me have her right now, Hump, and I'll stove her fucking head in and then she'll be happy to give us the money."

"See, I only have so much control over young McCarthy here."

"I want to meet your boss to discuss my fair share," she said.

"You know, I think that can be arranged. He likes your style and may offer you a place on our team. So what say that first you withdraw the cash?"

"Nothing doing." She moved closer to the car again. "I want assurances that I'm going to walk away with all my fingers and toes."

"Like what?"

"Like the money stays put until I have a deal with your boss."

Hump leaned his head partially out the window. "That's fine, but don't get cute with me or I'll make Jack here seem like Santa Claus."

"Fine."

"And your assurances, Miss Loftus, better not include the cops."

"What cops? They're all on strike."

Hump opened the rear door. "Get in."

Nolan and Dwyer watched Catherine climb into the car and followed it a couple of car lengths behind. George looked out from under a women's wide-brimmed hat and saw her head and slender neck move bird-like as she glanced around the interior of the car and out the rear window.

"Don't get too hopped up, toots, or your ride could come to a disastrous end," Nolan said. "Say Willie, do you think she's going to be able to pull this off?"

"She's a pretty gritty customer and gets her way a lot, but that's with the orderlies from the hospital and some other diner regulars," he said from the floor behind the seat.

"And young Irish coppers."

Dwyer poked his head up behind Nolan. "Nah, she's got too many goblins in her closet."

"And you don't?"

"Where are they heading?"

"I don't know, but stay down." Nolan followed them into the city and South Station. "Okay, I'm going to have to watch myself here. Lots of dopes from Southie on their way uptown."

Groups of fifteen to twenty crossed in front of them on their way up Federal Street—men followed by boys on their way to crap games, some to shoot the bones and others to knock off the winners, followed by excited boys small enough to shinny up poles to pull the fire boxes, followed by scavenger boys to pick up treasures left behind by the others.

Dwyer lifted his head so he could see. "We're back to the channel near Henshaw's warehouse."

"Right," Nolan said. "I wonder what little Prince Maxwell would say if he knew Daddy was playing for the other team." He stopped the car.

"Come on. The three of them are on foot and look like they are walking to a yacht. No wonder Mulvey and Byrne couldn't find these assholes; they keep moving around."

Nolan and Dwyer left the car by a loading dock and ran from building to building until they reached the yacht where they climbed down a ladder to a ledge that ran under the length of the pier.

"I hope she's alright," Willie whispered.

"She volunteered," Nolan said. "Besides, they want the money so she's safe for now."

A car pulled up and the cops heard footsteps overhead. Nolan leaned out far enough to see, turned back to Willie and mouthed the word, "Rossini." They crept along the ledge until they were almost directly under the gangway to the boat.

"Why did you bring her here?" Rossini screamed

"I thought the boss wanted to offer her a deal," Hump said. "She's still got—"

"You two are really stupid. Do you know that?" Rossini jumped onto the gangway, ran up the pier to the street, turning one way and then the other, and then ran back to the yacht. "You two dopes get out there and check any and every car on the street and, if any of them don't look right, torch it."

"No one followed us," McCarthy said. "And who you calling stupid?"

"Shut the fuck up, you moron. Get out there, now."

The two nobles emerged from the cabin and walked over Nolan and Dwyer with their guns drawn. McCarthy carried a can of gasoline. "Something is getting lit up," he said.

"Sit down," Rossini said to Catherine, "and make yourself comfortable."

"Say listen, pal, are you the boss that these two stiffs have been telling me about or are you wasting my time?"

Rossini wheeled around, slapped her and knocked her down.

"You don't have to get rough, mister. It was your boys who brought me here. I just want to make a deal with you on the money you already paid me and be on my way."

"Shut up—"

An explosion rattled between two of the buildings a short distance from the boat. Rossini pulled out a gun with one hand and grabbed Catherine with the other.

Nolan ran along the ledge and climbed the ladder, hung there for a moment, and then ran back to Willie. "Come on. They're fire-bombing vehicles on the street."

The yacht seemed too quiet as they hit the door to the cabin and plunged into an empty room. "Where the fuck is he?" Nolan said.

"You two assholes will not go away." Rossini stepped from behind the door with his arm around Catherine, holding a gun to her head. "You dopes should have gone on strike with the other cops. Drop your guns or I'll blow her head off."

Willie dropped his pistol to the floor, but Nolan continued to hold a shotgun.

"Drop it, asshole," Rossini said.

George raised the shotgun. "I don't think so and I'll tell you why—simple mathematics. You shoot her and I blow your fucking head all the way to Quincy. You know, one for one, tit for tat."

Catherine struggled in Rossini's grip until he cocked the pistol and then she stiffened with her arms out rigid, digging her hand into her sleeve.

"Stand still, bitch," Rossini said. "We're almost there, copper. You continue to play the hero." He pulled Catherine tighter. "But heroes end up like everyone else, dead in a box of maggots dining on them for lunch."

"You're not going to shoot her because you're a fucking yellow coward, Rossini. You're lord and master over these dumb shits who are unemployable or cons in between stretches—"

"Shut up!" Rossini pulled Catherine towards the door.

She shook her arm and felt the handle in her sleeve.

"You don't put your own ass on the line," Nolan said. "You're a timid little first floor B&E man. Go on, shoot her!"

"Don't push him," Willie said.

"Listen to your young friend, you old fool."

Catherine wiggled in Rossini's arm and he short poked her in the head with the barrel of the gun. She slipped in his hold and the letter opener fell out of her sleeve into her hand.

"What's it going to be, copper?"

She shifted her hips and drove the blade into Rossini's scrotum. He screamed, jerked up, the gun discharging a bullet into the cabin's ceiling, and folded over with the letter opener impaled into his groin. Nolan jumped him and drove the butt of the shotgun into his head, knocking him to the floor, and then stomped the hand that held the gun. "Put the handcuffs on him, Willie," Nolan said as he collapsed on the stairs. After a few moments, he pointed to Catherine. "That's a neat little trick you got there. Who taught you that?"

"Joan of Arc." She held up the handle of the letter opener. "A girl's protector."

"I'd ask you if you're okay, but that doesn't seem to be necessary." Nolan watched Willie finish cuffing Rossini. "Stuff his mouth with a rag and, if he so much as grunts, light it."

They heard footsteps on the dock above them, but then they stopped. There was shuffling and Hump called out Rossini's name and then silence. Nolan held the shotgun in one corner of the room and Willie and Catherine stood in the other. The footsteps moved away from the boat. Then they heard more running and a car starting.

Nolan poked his head out and saw Hump and McCarthy driving off. "Your boys may be stupid, Rossini, but they're no fools." The detective took him under the arm. "You made a tactical error when you drove that truck into me. You made it personal."

THE MORE THEY discussed it, the more they sensed a problem. The delegates at the A.F. of L. convention in Greenfield had argued over the police strike for days now, whether to support the cops with a general strike or just claim to support them in their press releases. In the end, they had blinked and settled nothing. So they delivered a mixed message to the newspapers: "We voted to table a resolution to strike and agreed to meet later in the week to vote again."

They gladly surrendered the floor to Eamon de Valera who urged them to rally their Union members in support of the Irish cause for freedom. He reminded them of the special relationship between the United States and Ireland and the contributions of the Irish to America.

For over an hour, he regaled them with stories of the Gaelic League and suggested that those in the crowd who could call Ireland their birth place first discovered their cultural identity because of the League's educational programs and its campaign for national self-reliance.

He told them he had joined the Irish Republican Brotherhood as a Volunteer and fought side-by-side Patrick Pearse and Thomas MacDonagh and had been sentenced to death after the Easter rebellion. He spoke of Ireland's desperation after years of frustration in dealing with the British Government. That nothing less than self-government would quench the thirst of their mother country, and that he intended to take the battle to Parliament itself, to demand justice and to negotiate a treaty with Lloyd George for the creation of a free and independent state.

And while his supporters raced through the room, soliciting funds from the A.F. of L. officials, the newly elected president of the Irish parliament left the podium and prepared for his return to Boston.

State Guard Rounds up Hoodlums on Boston Common

Chapter Twenty-seven

~

Wednesday, 10 September 1919
Late Afternoon

All through the day, small groups of men strolled through Roxbury Crossing like mourners paying their last respects to a fallen icon, and paused just long enough to tour the place where it all began, when Boston lost its reputation as the civilized cornerstone of America. While the rioting raged on in South Boston and the heart of the city, a somber and stunned Mission Hill remained quiet. Rubbish littered its streets and discarded newspaper hung like old wallpaper on the metal grates that secured some of the shops. And all that remained of the Bolshevik revolution smoldered in piles of wet ashes. Alien police volunteers dressed in civilian clothing, wearing newly stamped badges pinned to their chests, exercised their authority with swagger and patrolled the neighborhood in twos and threes, speaking a different language than the natives and ignorant of their customs.

It was to a different station house that Fulton Quigley returned on the late afternoon of his second day of separation from the job that he loved. Hanging around Fay Hall was good for a while, but enough was enough. He had kissed his wife and six rambunctious children and informed them that he needed to return to work. The twenty year man left his apartment near Fields Corner, boarded the elevated, carrying his boots, raincoat and billy, and arrived at Station 10 prepared to right the wrong and return the city to its former self. No admission of fault from him, instead Fulton remained committed to the Union cause and even more convinced that the strikers and their families were the aggrieved parties. No, he placed the blame for the strike and the subsequent destruction in the city at the feet of their commissioner. But he couldn't stand by any longer and watch his beloved Boston fall into the hands of anarchists, thieves and hoodlums.

So, he stood under the stone arch and took a backwards step into the Crossing, reading the graffiti that was painted on the bridge and examining the places where smoke and flames had discolored the stone black. He slowly turned and scrutinized the intersection, disgusted by the debris and rubbish, the broken shop windows and torn awnings.

The ravaged station house particularly galled him where he saw more paint, more damage, more broken glass. Splatters of brown mud stuck to the front of the building in spite of the rain, indicating the siege that the station had endured. On one side of the façade, the ivy that gave Station 10 its New England identity hung free. "Goddam animals," he said. He stepped up to the double wooden doors and ran his hand over the scuffmarks, dents and chips before pushing one of them open and stepping inside.

The houseman greeted him at the door with a warning. No one disliked the old patrolman who looked more like a librarian than a cop, wearing an old cardigan sweater while he flitted around the station doing odd jobs, running errands, answering the telephone or performing some special project for the captain. Close to retirement, he surprised no one when he wished the striking fellas luck and announced that he would be remaining on duty so he wouldn't lose his pension. "You'd better be going, Fulton, before the sergeant sees you in here," he said.

"What are you talking about?" Quigley dropped his rubber boots onto the floor. "I should think that he will be glad to see me. If I come back, how many more do you think will be right behind me? And from the looks of the plaza, he can use all the help he can get."

"He doesn't have a say in the matter," the houseman said. "That's coming straight from headquarters."

"Ah, go on. I've been a member of this Department for as long as he has and we've known each other for years.'

"Okay, I told you so and that's all I have to do," the old patrolman said. He walked to the front doors and closed the open side. "I didn't realize that it was raining."

"It wasn't when I came—Hey, what do you mean 'I told you so'? Do you mean to tell me that if one of the boys returns to the station you're supposed to tell us, to what, get lost?"

The houseman looked away and was attracted to the sounds of someone coming up the stairs from the garage below.

"Lefty, you didn't tell me the rest of that story." Sergeant McGuiness reached the top of the stairs. "I'll bet you've got a great finish—" He stepped into the room, but paused and turned his back on the two men and quietly closed the door. "Quigley," he said with his hand still on the knob, "you'd better be gone by the time I turn around."

"Mugs, how many years have we known each other? Are you going to throw me out of the station that has been my second home?"

"I don't have a say in the matter." McGuiness turned and faced him. "I can't even invite you in for a cup of coffee."

Two of the volunteers, a former local politician and Maxwell Henshaw, entered the station through the front door. They stomped their feet at the entry and shook their lapels to rid the rain from their clothing. They glanced at the raincoat and boots at Quigley's feet and passed him on their way to the duty desk, nodding a high sign to each other.

The ex-politician stopped a few feet away from Fulton and turned so both Quigley and McGuiness were his audience. "That prowler on Parker Street was just the woman's husband arriving home, a little earlier than she expected." He gave the report with exaggerated flair as if he had been rehearsing the line since he left the woman's home. Then he pulled back his trench coat, exposing a six-inch revolver hooked in his belt.

"What's the matter, Sport?" Quigley asked. "Couldn't you figure out how to open the signal box to make that report over the telephone rather than coming all the way to the station to show what a dickhead you are?"

"That will be all, Quigley," McGuiness said.

"While you're at it, Sport, you might want to get a holster for that gun before you shoot your little dick off."

The sergeant stepped between the volunteers and Quigley. "Leave, now."

Fulton bent over and picked up his gear. "I hope you don't have to rely on your new force, Mugs, if the shit really hits the fan."

"Get out."

Quigley threw his raincoat over his shoulder, carried his boots in one hand and his billy in the other. He opened the door and stepped down the walk, twirling his short stick in small tight circles and humming, "I'll Take You Home Again Kathleen." He strode across the Crossing with an exaggerated step and entered O'Neil's Tavern with an overwhelming desire for a drink.

On the other side of Tremont Street from O'Neil's, Carlo Venezia stood in the rain and swept the glass on the sidewalk in front of his tailor shop and home. He paid no attention to Quigley as he cleared the stone bridge on the opposite side of the street, stopped and entered the only establishment on the block with all of its glass intact. The tailor mumbled to himself as he swept the glass onto a coal shovel and dumped it into a barrel. Bricks and other missiles lay in the window box and ethnic slurs and threats were scrawled across the front of the building. A poster, encouraging the purchase of Liberty Bonds, still hung on the inside of the window and at the top of the poster were the words: *You want no Bolsheviki.*

His wife called her husband for the second time from where she and their young son huddled at the back of the store. "Come in out of the rain, Carlo."

He never looked up, but continued to clean the remaining glass from the sidewalk. *Lasciami in pace.* Venezia emptied the last of the glass into his barrel and pulled it through the narrow space between the buildings to the backyard.

When he returned to the front of the building, he looked up and down Tremont Street, pushed his hands into the pockets of his apron. "No more!" he said.

AT PEMBERTON SQUARE, a reporter stepped aside for the police superintendent and held the door for him as he entered HQ. "Sir, can I ask you whether you think the strikers will be allowed to return to work if they give up their charter?"

"I can't answer that," Crowley said, "You'll have to speak with the Commissioner. Right now, crowds have already formed in the Square and on the Common and I'm just trying to keep the city in one piece."

"One last question, superintendent."

"You'll have to excuse me—"

"Is there any truth to the rumors that the strikers are being supported by New York Communists?"

"Sergeant Newell," Crowley said as he passed through the communications area, "remove all non-police personnel from the premises." When he reached his office, Crowley extended his hand to the State Guard officer who stood waiting outside his door. "General Parker, I'm sorry. I got tied up. Please come in. You can set up your command post in here."

"Thank you, superintendent. I've assigned platoons to Scollay Square and I want to get the rest of my men on the streets as quickly as I can." The Brigadier General placed his gear on a chair. "So, before I get too comfortable, I'd like to take a tour of the trouble spots. Can you assign one of your men?"

"I'll show you myself."

As they left the building, the same reporter stepped in front of Parker. "Ah, General, Roberts from the Boston Herald. Is the city under martial law?"

Parker adjusted his campaign hat and stretched himself tall. "Boston is not under martial law. The troops are assisting the Mayor in maintaining order and are under the direction of Commissioner Curtis and Superintendent Crowley."

"General, there are conflicting reports as to who called out the State Guard, the Mayor or Governor Coolidge—"

Crowley and Parker brushed past the reporter and walked between two platoons of Guardsmen in the plaza. They climbed into Parker's vehicle and drove through Pemberton Square past trucks loaded with additional troops and turned down Court Street. The Superintendent looked back towards his headquarters. Soldiers in khaki uniforms, puttees and campaign hats stood in formation at parade rest, their rifles an arm's length away. Others entered and exited the headquarters and a few of them stood off to the side in small tight circles, lighting up smokes and laughing over a shared story. He turned forward as they passed Scollay Square and saw more Guards running to their posts. Gangs of boys and young men walked back and forth in the middle of the street, pushing and shoving each other, as they made their way up State Street past banks and other financial institutions wrapped in barb wire. The superintendent felt the stress that wrapped him up tight. "It's not our war any longer," he said.

FULTON QUIGLEY sat on a stool in front of the large mirror that hung behind the bar at O'Neil's and stared at his image. He saw his life without the 'job,' hollow and without meaning. Two of the tavern regulars were on either side of him, one with his hand draped on Quigley's shoulder. The two men were talking back and forth to each other like next-door neighbors over a fence in the same conversation they had started three hours earlier when he first came in and sat down.

The first man with his hand on his shoulder said, "You're right as rain, Mr. Quigley, you coppers are the ones taking the fucking, working for peanuts in run-down stations. And for how many hours a week? Shit, even the girls working the sweatshops get better benefits than that. And don't you mind those urchins who pelted you with mud, we'll take care of them. Give them a boot in the arse, we will. And who do these Harvard punks think they are, coming into Roxbury, telling us we got to move along? On Mission Hill? Pity them if they try to fuck around with us. We'll bury 'em. Hit 'em on the side of the head with a good one, if you know what we mean."

The second man leaned over the bar and turned his head to his friend. "One of those make-believe cops says to me, 'get going now or you'll answer to me.' And I says, oh yeah, well you better go get those army boys because you're gonna need them."

"Yeah, well I grabbed one of these tight waists by the throat and banged his fucking squash against the brick and told him if I ever saw him around my neighborhood again, I'd kill him. Gave him a taste of the sap just to get my point across."

"That's right," the second man said. "So you don't have to worry, Mr. Quigley, we'll keep things on the up and up 'til you get back."

"Fucking right, we will," said the first.

The second man stabbed his finger into the top of the bar. "And don't you worry, you fellas will be back before the week is out. When Jim

Rankin and his Union boys get through with those Yankees, they'll wish they never started this fight."

"Shut this fucking city right down," said the first.

"City, shit, they'll shut the whole state of Massachusetts down."

The first man with his hand on Quigley's shoulder reached inside his pocket. "And how is the Quigley brood doing? Do you need a finif until you can get on your feet?"

"Finif, you cheap prick?" the second said. "Give him a sawbuck."

"A sawbuck? Who you calling a cheap prick? You never saw a sawbuck on your best day."

"Sure I did. Remember when I worked for Local 25, running wagons of beer from the breweries, right down Columbus Ave into Boston?"

"Yeah and for how long was that, a fucking day and a half?"

"What the fuck do you know?"

"I'll tell you what I know. I can kick your arse from a sick bed at the Peter Bent Brigham."

"You think so, huh?"

"I know so—Hey, Mr. Quigley where you going? See what you did, you drove him out of here with your talk."

"What are you talking about? You didn't even buy the poor man a beer."

"Well, I tried. He wouldn't take my money."

"Yeah, mine either. He's a good man."

"Aye, he is."

NIGHT LAID ON the Crossing with a vengeance and left little to celebrate. Few of the street lights continued to burn yellow because most of them had been broken in the first, and really, only night of rioting in Roxbury. The rain came and went without sense or order and without warning. On Terrace Street, not a window in the Letts headquarters remained intact and the pungent odor of wet charred wood drifted away from the building into the darkness.

At the corner of the street, the finality of hammer-striking-nail announced the end of one thing and the beginning of another, the struggle to keep a story alive. The tailor drove the hammer into the nail with particular anger as he boarded up his store with wood panels to salvage his little business and to comply with the Mayor's directive. He wasn't really sure about the issues between the police and their commissioner, didn't have an opinion as to who was the villain and who was the hero. His hate was limited to the faceless mob that stole his future and raped his dream, who terrorized his family and stripped away his peace.

Quigley stepped out into the night from the tavern with a tremble, paused and glanced across the street when he heard the sharp rap of the hammer and that unmistakable musical note when a nail pierces the wood and borrows deep into its grain. He watched the shadow of the younger man on the dimly lit sidewalk draw the hammer back and drive it hard, saw him bend down and struggle with the wood, stumble with it above his shoulders until he slapped it into place beside the last piece, saw him hold his hammer against it while he fished in his apron for a couple of nails. For a few minutes, Fulton watched the tailor make the repairs and then finally began to walk to the trolley stop at the top of the hill. But for some reason even foreign to himself, he shifted the raincoat and boots in his arms, turned around and took an exaggerated step towards the Crossing.

In front of Mission Church, the boys eyed the two volunteer policemen when the would-be coppers paused in their foot patrol and glanced back. And from across the street, other neighborhood residents also suspended their end-of-the-day comings and goings to view the unusual pair. Neither respectful nor belligerent, the boys just watched. No cheers or jeers, no calls of 'scabs' or 'heroes,' they just stared and sized them up, expecting to experience 'something' of what they weren't sure, so they walked in anticipation behind them. The two men wore suits under raincoats and soft hats on their heads and, except for the bright shiny badges, could have been a couple of businessmen on their way home from work. They smiled at the boys and nodded to the spectators on the opposite sidewalk and resumed their patrol of Tremont Street. The neighborhood kids fell in behind them and continued to dog them on the way to the Crossing.

When the volunteers reached the opposite side of the street from the tailor shop, they heard the loud hammering. And paused again. The boys paused with them, shuffling in small spaces like a herd of animals, watching and waiting for that 'something.' A young guardsman, not much older than the boys, ran across the intersection, holding onto his campaign hat with one hand and his rifle with the other and asked for directions to Brigham Circle.

One of the volunteers pointed to the top of the hill. "Just continue to walk down the other side and you'll come right into it."

The younger of the two volunteers put out his hand. "Max Henshaw, how are things in the city?"

The guardsman breathed heavy and thrust out his hand with nervous excitement. "A lot more disorderly than here," he said. "Boy, that's where the action is, but I'm glad I was assigned— They need the troops with the bayonets in there. Groups of five hundred to a thousand, mostly boys and men are everywhere just looking for trouble. Crap games are in play in Scollay Square and on the Common. But I hear that there hasn't been the damage they had the first night, just a lot of idle men waiting for something to happen."

"What is the Guard doing about it?" the politician volunteer asked.

"Oh, General Parker is in charge and he won't take no nonsense from them. And the cavalry, why they'll chew them up, that's for sure."

"Should have seen what happened that first night," a boy of fifteen said from the back of the pack. "A crowd of kids, hundreds I'd say, broke into a bunch of stores and cleaned them out good. Took coats, shoes and ties and traded them or sold them right on the sidewalk. And nobody was older than twenty-two."

"How do you know so much?" the politician asked.

"Because—" The boy backed away a little. "I was there."

"Were any of them arrested?" Henshaw asked.

The boy hooked his thumbs under his suspenders. "Naw, everyone was just having fun."

Another boy yelled from the back of the crowd. "Yeah, I was there too and I saw you sub police run chicken when the crowds came to pummel you."

"Well, we're not running now," Henshaw said.

The guardsman separated from the volunteers and the two men continued their patrol, walked by O'Neil's tavern, glancing in the open door as they passed, and under the stone bridge before they entered the Crossing.

In front of the police station, Quigley leaned against the broken fence and looked through the window. He gibbered to himself and kicked at the soft mud under the pickets. Inside, several recently arrived volunteers stood in a loose formation as Captain Keveney and Sergeant McGuiness welcomed them to the Roxbury Station and gave them some general guidelines when on patrol.

Quigley closed his eyes and hung his head, took a short breath and blew the air out of his nose in a snort. His head felt like it was half full of water and the liquid shifted from one side to the other as he moved, making him feel lopsided like some great hand was trying to push him over, like he was walking in the tilted room of a fun house. His tongue tasted like sandpaper and it kept sticking to the roof of his mouth. He wiped his lips with it with the little bit of spittle that he could conjure up. Restless and aggravated from an afternoon of drinking, he leaned on the fence and simmered.

"I'd love to give them a backhand," he said. "Those boys at O'Neil's are right. Who the fuck do these tight waisted assholes think they are coming into a working man's neighborhood? For what, so they can grind our noses into the horse shit once again. Show us that they're the boss."

He bent over to pick up his gear, but stumbled and grabbed onto the fence, held on while he tried to find his bearings. "Woo—"

"Hey, what are you doing there, feller?" someone said behind him.

Quigley let go of the fence and spun around. "What's it to you?"

Max Henshaw glanced at the boys behind him and then his partner. He stepped closer. "I said I want to know what you're doing here. Is that a problem with you?" Before Fulton could answer, Henshaw moved closer again and stuck his head out, turtle like, and said, "Say, you're that striker that was here earlier."

"Sergeant McGuiness told you to get off the premises," the politician said without moving.

"You and those other strikers are the cause of the anarchy and rioting that is plaguing the city," Maxwell said. "What do you have to say for yourself?"

A light drizzle started and the boys began to stir and shuffle in the wet sand on the street in anticipation of 'something' happening. Some of the older boys circled around Quigley and Henshaw, closed the distance to hear the exchange.

Quigley mumbled incoherently under his breath and reached into his back pocket.

Henshaw put his hands on his hips and moved within Quigley's reach. "What did you say?"

"Maybe I should go in and get the sergeant, Max?" the older volunteer said as he slipped past the combatants and started up the walk.

The crowd of boys buzzed in anticipation that they might be onto 'something.'

"That's a good idea," Max said. "And maybe—"

Quigley hit the football player with a short left hook that stunned him. But it was the second blow that caused Henshaw to pee blood for a couple of weeks and would keep him out of the first two games on Harvard's schedule, the blow that dropped him to his knees and onto his side in a gasping ball of spasm and caused those sucking sounds like the last of the dishpan water being swallowed by a sink, the blow from the end of Quigley's billy when he drove it up and into Henshaw's solar plexus.

"Give it to 'em, Mr. Quigley," one of the boys yelled. "And tell him to get out of Mission Hill."

"Shut your yap," said another.

"Yeah, Monahan, shut your yap," said a third. "Come on, Mister, get up and fight. Give the old copper a good one for all the boots in the arse he's given me."

"Fight," more of them yelled. The following crowd of boys pulled the circle tighter and some of them bounced on their toes and shadow boxed. "Come on, give 'em a good one," they said.

Henshaw moaned and rolled himself into a tighter ball, one of his legs kicking involuntarily, the rain falling steady now.

Quigley stood over him. "You won't be taking my job anytime soon."

"Stop right there, Quigley," Sergeant McGuiness yelled from the station door. Behind him were Henshaw's partner and other volunteers. "You're under arrest for assaulting a police officer."

Fulton turned to his sergeant's voice, stunned and confused. He looked down at Henshaw and then at the boys.

"Ah, that ain't right, Mr. Quigley," one of them said.

Fulton looked back at McGuiness who was struggling with his raincoat.

"Stay right there," the sergeant said.

For the first time, he could moisten his lips as he captured drops of rain on his tongue and ran it around his mouth. He saw McGuiness move out of the door and into the night. He looked down at the fallen volunteer and the boys. And he ran.

He lumbered across the Crossing, dodging automobiles until he reached the bridge. Excited encouragement raced alongside of him as the boys kept up, stride for stride, no longer with him or against him but lost in the euphoria of 'something' happening.

"Get out of the way, boys," another one of the volunteer football players yelled from behind them.

Nearly out of breath and lugging at the back of the temporary patrolmen, McGuiness yelled to the volunteers, "Stop him before he gets to the back streets."

Quigley ran past O'Neil's, heard the laughter and loud voices inside, turned and raced across to the other side of the street. The boys shadowed each of his moves close behind him, and he could hear their light rapid breaths under his deep suffocating gasps. He was drenched in rain, his clothes heavy and wet, when he entered the narrow alley between the buildings at the corner of Terrace Street.

He slipped and stumbled on the pea stone as he entered the darkened alley and placed his hands on the sides of the tall buildings to keep his balance. The boys whooped and hollered and slapped the buildings behind him, their voices cracking with excitement. The men followed with deeper and louder voices, men who shouted and blew whistles, and filled the street with noise.

Behind his tailor shop, Carlo Venezia sat under a single lamp and ate a late supper at his kitchen table while his wife put their children to bed. His head dropped in sleep and the fork fell from his hand, struck the dish and fell to the floor. He woke in a jerk and heard the screams and sounds of many people running at the front of his shop, their voices rising above the patter of rain on the house. Jumping up, he turned and heard them enter the alley, the faceless crowd charging down the narrow passageway, stomping and kicking the stones beneath them, laughing and pounding the outside of his home.

"Get him," he heard the crowd yell. "Don't let him get away!"

"Carlo?" his wife cried to him from the door of the bedroom.

He ran to the pantry, pushed a chair against the counter, climbed up and seized the pistol on the top of the cabinet, jumped down and ran to the back of the house.

Out of breath, Quigley slumped against the tailor's house, doubled over with his hands on his knees, trying to catch his breath, spun upright at the shouts of the men, his elbow striking the side of the house again, the boys slowed to a walk, keeping their distance, watching, the volunteers in civilian clothing with the new badges just arriving at the end of the alley. Quigley coughed in fits and chugged each breath. He began to jog, slipping on the stone, correcting himself and sliding his feet, lifting and stumbling and falling against one building and then the other.

"Come on, Mr. Quigley, tallyho," one of the older boys yelled. "Don't let them get you."

They walked fast at first to keep their separation from him, cheering him on and pushing him forward. "Here they come, Mr. Quigley. Here come the phony coppers."

Quigley reached the end of the alley, paused and imagined himself hidden away in the maze of darkened streets, darkened houses and fenced-in yards, gnarly old chestnut trees and six-foot hedges where he patrolled, his place, his jungle. He surprised himself when he giggled. "Okay," he said and he giggled again when he thought of the Harvard volunteer. He exited the alley, turned and looked back for the others, blew the air out of his lungs and started. He laughed at the absurdity of his situation. "Fuck 'em all." His laughter exploded into the night. He started—

Cautious and curious, the boys stopped. They watched him begin to run and bottled up the alley. The men behind them ordered the boys to clear the passageway, yelling and blowing their whistles.

"Get out of the way," they screamed with exasperation. One of the men fired his pistol into the air, the explosion ricocheting between the buildings, the alley now thick with smoke, rain and the acrid smell of lead.

The tailor pressed himself against the back of the house.

"Carlo?" his wife called from the back door.

"Get in, and lock the door." He took two long steps into the rain and the angry night. And fired the pistol.

Quigley emerged from the alley separated from the boys and the make-believe cops, free to run alone. He glanced over his shoulder, turned, laughing and bellowing at the absurdity of it all, and ran—felt his chest cave in. And he ran—a holocaust raging within him—

And he ran no more.

The boys stood back and shifted from foot to foot in the rain that pelted them as they stirred in silence, curious and absent of emotion. Fulton Quigley lay in the rain and the volunteers stood guard as Sergeant McGuiness knelt beside him. The rain ran down the back of the policeman's neck. And it filled the empty boots that stood at the broken fence in Roxbury Crossing.

In the News

STATE GUARD POURS INTO CITY ARMORIES
Nine of crowd wounded in South Boston
Soldiers shoot in air in Dorchester
Cavalry drives mob, crap shooting halted
Infantry draws dead lines around shopping district
Vigilante committee formed in Dorchester
Busy day in Municipal Court, stiff sentences given
Curtis to build up police force by provisional appointments
Appointment of War veterans already authorized
BOSTON EVENING TRANSCRIPT
Thursday, September 11, 1919

BOSTON'S RELAPSE INTO SAVAGERY
Police Strike as Outsiders See It
Boston points to Soviet: Victory of police here means disaster
Police of other cities will unionize
Strikes and disorders sure to follow
Situation Reviewed in United States Senate
U.S Senator Henry Meyers, Montana Democrat,
striking policemen, false to their oaths, wholly responsible
for rioting, looting, killing
New York Times
New York World
New York Herald
Special to BOSTON EVENING TRANSCRIPT
Thursday, September 11, 1919

PRESIDENT CALLS STRIKE A "CRIME"
Says police strike, leaving Boston to mercy of thugs,
a crime against civilization
BOSTON EVENING TRANSCRIPT
Thursday, September 12, 1919

Chapter Twenty-eight

~

Thursday, 11 September 1919
0900 hours

Governor Coolidge took his usual stroll up Beacon Hill on his way to the State House, walked through the debris of the previous night's rioting unfazed by the litter, the destruction or the leftover men stumbling home after a night of drinking and unbridled debauchery. He never noticed the boarded up buildings on Washington Street or the wooden barricades with Open for Business posters tacked to them on Tremont Street or the gamblers already huddled on the Common, stooped in the play of craps at the bottom of the stairs across the street from the State House. Nothing dissuaded the man from his routine. He seemed locked in his own thoughts, closed off to the world and the stuff of life that continually swirled around him.

I waited and marked my course, patient to the 'nth degree. Disciplined myself from taking chances and let the Mayor spin in his own sweat. Some say I am methodical or even mechanical, and that I have no ability to forecast the events as they may play out. But I waited my turn and would never think of interfering with the Mayor's indecision. Should I take responsibility for his lack of leadership or his ignorance of the law that caused his hesitancy to call out the Guard? And when he finally acted and asked for additional guardsmen, I issued no statement, made no sign, but granted his request.

I stood by my Commissioner and refused to undercut him and remained stubbornly principled. Loyalty is a lost quality in today's politics. Perhaps, I should have called out the Guard. But no one knew the extent of the policeman's role in a society of good citizens, a void that was quickly filled by the outrageous conduct of those who discarded their civility and forgot their human intelligence, who became a mob of animals, loud, obnoxious and irresponsible. The people had to experience the chaos, had to live in a world where their public servants, their police, did not strike but deserted them.

Now, a dangerous moment festers and threatens the city and I am ready to go forward, straight to the heart.

He sidestepped the frenetic activity under the dome, the reporters and their questions, the legislators, hedging their advice, and the opportunistic Labor leaders, seizing the day for a little hard bargaining, and slipped away to his office.

Coolidge held the newspaper up as he read it so that the day's headlines could be easily seen by Commissioner Curtis who sat on the other side of the desk—*Mayor Assumes Command of Police, Takes over Guardianship of City; South Boston Crowd Sobers after Two killed by Guard; Cavalry Sweeps Scollay Square.*

"Peters, the Democrat, is now in control and you're out." Coolidge snapped the newspaper until he removed the inside wrinkles and read the article that raised the first signs of emotion from the depths of his cool and calculating self.

"That incompetent," he said. "I gave him the citation in the statutes to allow him to act. Otherwise, he would still be twisting in the wind and running around like a whirling dervish."

"What does he say?" Curtis asked.

"He claims that his committee made suggestions that would have avoided the strike, but that he received no cooperation from you, nor assistance from me." The Governor flipped the page over. "He is charging us with interfering with his authority to act and with grossly underestimating the readiness of the city to provide protection."

The Commissioner sat there dry and brittle, like every ounce of fluid had been sucked out of him. The bottled-up anxieties that filled his days and nights now shriveled him, stole his swagger and his command of all things. "Peters cannot win this battle. I'll resign first."

"No, he can't because he'll allow the police to return to duty and that will result in catastrophic consequences; you will no longer control them. And, there *will* be a next time. Politically, it will be devastating for us in November."

"But people are afraid and they will call for a compromise," the Commissioner said. "And he'll succumb because he'll try to appease everyone. He'll submit the police grievances to arbitration."

"Not on my watch," Coolidge said.

"None of these strikers should ever return to the force." The Commissioner curled himself into the corner of his chair.

"It is not over yet," the Governor said. "The tide is turning, you can feel it. The newspapers, Wilson, Congress hold the police responsible. Every day, I am receiving letters and telephone calls encouraging us to hold fast. Even some of their own kind are embarrassed by this strike, the rioting and destruction." Coolidge dropped the newspaper on the desk. "Go back to police headquarters and run your Department. It is time that I enter the fray and call on old friends in the Press to help us right the ship."

THEY CAME TO pay respects to Fulton Quigley and his family. They began at the threshold to the third floor apartment on Mather Street, wound down the stairs of the triple-decker and out into the night until the line disappeared beyond the rise of Dorchester Avenue, just before the church. Street cops, young cops, old retired cops, cops on strike. In Nomine Patris, et Filii, et Spiritus Sancti. George Nolan and Willie Dwyer were there, and shuffled with the rest, a few stairs, a few steps, a few wartime stories every couple of ten minutes. 'Remember when that crazy bastard.' Confiteor Deo. 'First one in the door.' Death—the common denominator, the final arbitrator. So drink up boys and leave your politics, bitches, and personal problems on the sidewalk. 'I'd follow that son-of-a-bitch anywhere.' Rally round boys, and forget your petty differences; huddle up, you mugs. Lift him up. Dust to dust, eternal rest grant unto him, O Lord. 'We'll make things right by God.'

Slainte. 'We'll do it right.' Promises, promises. 'I promise.' They're all together now.

WILLIE STOOD under a street lamp and read the note. "O'Brien wants to meet."

"Where?" Nolan said.

"O'Neil's—"

"A constable picked O'Neil's?"

"Yeah.

"That's convenient. What is he going to do, buy you a bucket of suds before he arrests you?"

They started through the Crossing and stopped at the police stand while a couple of cars passed.

"Did he say anything to Mrs. Gerhardt?" Nolan said.

"Nah, just said he was an old friend from Ballinasloe."

Nolan looked down Columbus Avenue, turned around and scanned Tremont and then Roxbury Street. "This place looks a lot better at night than during the day. You can't see the filth and the damage, almost quaint you know." They ran to the station where several doughboys hung around the front steps with their campaign hats curled up in front and tipped back like rough riders, smoking and swapping stories of their time in France. The two cops nodded to them as they walked past and the soldiers stopped their conversation and stared back.

Half way up the stairs to the second floor, Nolan whispered, "You know, I've been working and living here for eighteen years and I feel like a goddam stranger in my own station. First the bowtie Harvard fraternity boys and now the Guard."

They reached the office and Nolan shut the door. "So, what are you going to do?"

"I'm going to meet him. I've been living with this for ten years and it's time that I face up to it."

"And if he tells you to surrender?"

"I'm not surrendering." Willie said. "To him, anyways."

"Well, worst comes to worst, he's going to need an extradition warrant," Nolan said. "And that gives you time. When is the meeting?"

"Tomorrow at three. I should be able to make it as long as the natives remain civil."

"Ah, don't worry about them. They realize now that the Guard will shoot them a lot sooner than we will." George lit the stub of a cigar. "You know, there's something else going on with this guy, O'Brien."

"Like what?" Willie asked

"I'm not sure, but I'm going with you to the meeting." Nolan put his foot up on the desk. "Well, not exactly, but I'll be around."

In the News

GOVERNOR TAKES OVER COMMAND IN BOSTON

In charge of governing Boston, will maintain Law and Order at any cost; puts Curtis back in charge as commissioner; issues Executive Orders—calls out entire State Guard and takes command of the police; issues General Order directing all police to obey commissioner; announces no reinstatement of strikers

BOSTON EVENING TRANSCRIPT

Friday, September 12, 1919

DISORDER VANISHES BEFORE MILITARY

State Guard puts an end to rioting and hoodlumism

THE BOSTON DAILY GLOBE

Friday, September 12, 1919

CARMEN'S VOTE IS AGAINST STRIKING

At least three Bay State Locals favor delay

FIREMEN ARE ON JOB

Misunderstanding about joining strikers

"GO BACK," SAYS GOMPERS

A.F. of L. head appeals to Boston policemen; "No man or group of men genuinely regrets the present Boston situation than do the American Federation of Labor and I."

BOSTON EVENING TRANSCRIPT

Friday, September 12, 1919

Chapter Twenty-nine

~

Friday, 12 September 1919
1512 hours

Three o'clock came and went and Willie sat in a privacy booth alone at the back of O'Neil's Tavern. Graves O'Brien, he had decided, was playing a little stunt, a game, to give him the screws. He faced the bar so he could see into the kitchen where Nolan was pretending to be a cook. George had a quizzical look on his face and pointed to his pocket watch, which Willie answered with a raise of his eyebrows and a slight shrug. From where he sat, he could smell the sugar sweet odor of the supper meal cooking, ham and squash he guessed and maybe boiled potatoes. The tavern was filling up with laborers from the Baptist who continued to work on the hospital's new wing at the top of the Hill in spite of the events of the past few days. Francis O'Neil dispensed the lager and liquor freely from the bar without concern that a depleted police force or the doughboys would enter his premises to enforce an unenforceable Massachusetts Dry Law.

Willie drank his beer and scanned the room for a face that looked vaguely familiar, a face with a hawkish nose and an ugly scar that divided the left side of his face in two. It's funny, Dwyer thought, that while his father had had his battles with the local constable, he never had any encounters with him and, in fact, even aspired as a young boy to be a R.I.C. man like him. All that changed and blew away like road dust in a stiff wind when his family joined up with the I.R.B. Many times since his escape to America, he considered the path that he might have taken had he stayed and faced his accusers. But as the son of Tommy Dwyer, he assumed that he would have been on the run or sentenced to prison.

O'Brien set on him before he realized that the constable had entered the tavern, standing over him like a disapproving father, arms folded across his chest and a bowler cocked to one side of his head, looking like an out-of-place shit kicker. He wore a high starched collar with no tie and a light gray vest under a worn tweed suit that was a few pounds lighter than his body weight. The distinctive nose, moustache and scar were still there and a toughness that Willie remembered as being earned and not given. O'Brien reached into his suit jacket, removed a photograph and placed it on the table, pushing it in front of him. "Do you remember him, Dwyer?" He eased into the opposite side of the booth.

Willie shifted his eyes from the constable to the photograph. It wasn't what he expected, thinking he would see a partially decomposed body, stained with the dark brown juices of the bog. But instead a youthful and smiling Bernie McLean stared back, his eyes wide with anticipated success and the curve of his mouth turned up into a dimple of smugness with the knowledge that the joke was on you. Willie guessed that the picture was taken shortly before he died and thought that the expression captured him well. In that moment, he realized that the memory that had haunted him all of these years contained a powerless victim frozen in terror, stripped of his life and his destiny. He picked up the picture and stood it on its edge, tapped it once on the table and looked into McLean's eyes, heard the laughter of their youth, the calls at the back door and the walks to school and Sunday Mass.

But the longer he stared into those eyes, the more he was reminded of the person he last knew, conniving and ambitious, the person responsible for his father's and uncle's imprisonment, his mother's death and his own banishment. He laid the photograph down, placed his fingers against its edge and pushed it across the table, sat back and waited for the constable to make his move.

O'Brien raised two fingers to the tavern girl. "Two tall ones and two small glasses of whiskey, please."

Willie folded his hands on the table and stretched his legs, staring at the older man who no longer produced the fear and anxiety of his youth.

"You've filled out nicely, Dwyer," O'Brien said. "I recall a slender youth, like a young thoroughbred, sinewy and not an extra gram of weight."

Dwyer sat silent.

"You know, I've never been to America before." He twisted in his seat and looked around the room. "It's an interesting place with so many different kinds of people. But, of course, this city is full of the Irish, each one with a story to tell." He rubbed his hands together, picked up the photograph, returned it to the envelope and placed it inside his jacket. "And then, you've got your police strike. Ah, we've got them back home as well. But it didn't turn out too well for the boys in London. Hopefully, it'll go a little better for you coppers here."

The girl brought the glasses of beer and the whiskeys. "Slainte," O'Brien said and emptied one of the short glasses.

Willie tipped back his own glass of beer, placed it empty on the table and refolded his hands.

O'Brien looked toward the door to the street. "Someone is meeting us here."

An awkward lapse of conversation settled in between them. Willie looked into the reflection of the large mirror over the bar, saw the workmen sitting on the stools, sharing stories and laughing, saw the tavern girl running between the tables, taking orders amongst a sea of caps. He turned away from the mirror and caught the constable staring at him. "I am not going back, O'Brien."

"And why should you?" He took out a pair of spectacles. "You're an American now and a peace officer as well. Only one of two who didn't vote to strike, no less. I wonder why?"

"How do you know that?"

"Oh, you know how fellas talk when you buy them a round or two. But don't worry, they don't hold any animosity towards you." He placed the spectacles on the end of his nose.

He reached inside his jacket again and Willie slid one of his hands inside his own. "Easy, Dwyer, I just want to show you something." He took out a folded piece of paper, smoothed it out on the table and slid it across.

A chill ran through Willie as he read the King's warrant, commanding 'Constable Graves O'Brien to bring the charged person, William J. Dwyer also known as William J. O'Dwyer, formerly of Ballinasloe,

County Galway, Ireland and now of the city of Boston, Massachusetts in the United States of America to the court of jurisdiction for purposes of extradition and to bring him without delay before the Court of the United Kingdom of Great Britain and Ireland.'

"A shame really when you think about it, Catholic against Catholic. I mean if you can't trust your own kind."

"If you've got nothing further to say—"

"Is that the way it is?" O'Brien reached inside his jacket again and removed another folded piece of paper. "Have you ever read a pathology report, Dwyer? What am I saying, you're a copper. Of course, you have." He slid it across the table.

Willie picked up the document and began to read it.

"It can all get pretty technical, mumble jumble medical stuff," the constable said. "Turn the report over to the back page and skip two-thirds of the way down, right where it says, 'Conclusion.'" He waited for Willie to follow his directions and then said, "Yeah, that's it. It says that although the victim suffered a gunshot wound to the forehead, the trauma caused by the bullet was not the cause of death." O'Brien pointed his finger at the section Willie was reading. "Death by asphyxiation, caused by drowning—" He jabbed his finger into the table. "Now, that's the cause of death."

He slid back in his seat, took a long drink and emptied his glass. "The boys must have brought their secret recipes over from the old country. This is as good as you'll find at home, hey Dwyer." He waved his hand in the air until he caught the attention of the girl and then put two fingers up. "Two more tall ones, will ye, dear." He removed a box of cigarettes from his pocket, lit one and sucked on it deeply.

Willie wished the word, 'Conclusion,' the ink and the paper that it was printed on, the goddam medical report would somehow disappear, evaporate, burn right up in his hands. He did what he was told, faithful to his father, with never a thought of consequence—

Scare the hell out of the bastard. Give them a taste of it. The Regimental boys will know what to do with him, teach him a lesson. I saw a death mask that night, the hole in his forehead and the black ring. And his eyes, I remember his eyes—rolled back in his head like he had seen something wonderful and frightful at the same time. His face, whitewashed except for the blood smears. Blue lips, I know his lips were full blue. There was no life in him, goddam it, collapsed like a marionette, dead weight. Jesus, he was heavy. But the water. Oh, for fucks sake, McLean was dead. I know he was dead.

He flipped the pathology report back to O'Brien and picked up the other short glass of whiskey, emptied it and cracked the tumbler into the middle of the table.

"Dr. Mary McKeigue, the pathologist? She's a pretty clever lady," O'Brien said. "Can tell you all kinds of things about a body and what happened to it before it ceased to be.

"Let's see if this sounds familiar, Dwyer. You and your cousins kidnap McLean on the road from his house to the bank. I mean, who could blame you. Your father and uncle are rotting in Kilmainham and the pub has been stolen from the family. Two battalion heads show up and because Bernie is a tattler and because of what he and his father done to a Brotherhood family—they shoot him. And then for good measure, they cut out his tongue and nail it to the door of Tohers' to send a message to the good citizens of Ballinasloe and the surrounding towns. So what say ye, my fellow policeman? Is that pretty much how it happened?"

"An interesting story—"

"Why did they leave you holding the bag, Dwyer? And why did they insist that you and your cousins help them dispose of the body?" O'Brien paused. "Because they didn't trust you."

The crowd grew louder as more laborers stopped at the pub on their way home. Some played darts at the back of the room and some broke out in card games. One of the laborers who knew Willie stopped by the table and asked him about the strike and when the rest of the police would be back to work. He entertained the workman longer than he might have ordinarily and Graves watched with admiration how he handled the man, pleasantly and efficiently, giving him the time so has not to insult him, but not so much time as to make him comfortable enough to take a seat.

When the laborer walked away, the constable said, "You handle yourself well, Patrolman Dwyer. It'd be a shame to lose all of this."

Willie remained silent.

O'Brien removed his bowler and placed it on the table. "I've been working this case for ten years while you fled Ireland, moved to Boston, grew from a boy into a man and became a patrolman in one of America's cosmopolitan cities. You separated yourself from Bernie's murder, maybe not entirely, but I lived it every day. Became friendly with his family. They're not bad folks, probably not much different from your own—"

"Not much different from my own? My father and uncle are in jail and my cousin is dead. My mother is dead, her family ripped apart, couldn't even attend her—" Willie tipped forward and leaned on the table. "Whatever happened to McLean and his family was tragic, but it doesn't cheapen what happened to mine."

One end of O'Brien's moustache was wet from beer and it rose up with his lip as he grinned on one side of his face. "As I started to say, I've worked this case for ten years and have followed every clue, interviewed half the populations of three towns and never let that family feel for one moment that their son's death would be forgotten."

"Do you know what I think, O'Brien?"

"No, what?"

Willie jabbed his finger at the constable. "I think you've wasted a lot of time and money coming to America."

Nolan noticed a change in Willie, saw him fidget in the booth and become flushed and angry. He guessed that things were not going well or had taken a turn for the worse. "Come on, Dwyer, keep your composure."

"The fact of the matter is," Graves said, "if you had run from the barn and never looked back, I probably wouldn't be here talking to you today. But you and your cousins stayed with the Republican men, wrapped McLean in a horse blanket and buried him in the bog by staking his body to the earth." O'Brien crushed his cigarette with the heel of his shoe. "And that made you more, what's the word, culpable."

O'Brien leaned to one side and looked through the crowd. He put his hand in the air and waved someone to the table. "McLean was still alive when you buried him that night and that makes you an accomplice to murder."

Willie slid along the bench and started to separate himself from the booth. "Enjoy your sail home."

"Wait, Dwyer," O'Brien said. "I've got someone for you to meet."

"The fuck, you do."

Nolan pushed open the door to the kitchen wider and caught the attention of Francis O'Neil who reached for a club under the beer taps. But the detective put his hand up when he saw Willie sit back down and a third man join them.

If he had to put two more unlikely people together, Willie couldn't have found a less compatible pair even though they greeted each other like old friends. Aiden Fahey, Eamon de Valera's bodyguard, ordered three more beers from the girl as she passed. He sat down next to Willie, trying to find room for his long legs in the close confines of the booth, his angular body looking uncomfortable and compacted like a folded yardstick. Willie's eyes bounced back and forth between the two of them.

"You look a little confused, Dwyer," Fahey said.

"I'm just having a little trouble putting you two at the same table." He shook his head. "But it doesn't make any difference to me because I am about to leave."

"I told you he was a tough one," O'Brien said.

"Yeah, I got that when we last met, right, Dwyer? By the bye, how's your friend, Coppenrath?"

"Have a nice day, gentlemen." Willie slid against Fahey.

"Why don't you listen to what I have to say before you leave?" Fahey said. "You didn't come here to walk away or because you were curious. You came here to face your demons."

"There isn't anything you can say that will interest me." Willie sat back against the wall. "But go ahead, Fahey. I'll give you two minutes."

Fahey pushed fresh glasses of beer around the table. "Now, drink up, fellas."

"Come on, get on with it," Willie said.

"Okay, after we met that night at Fenway Park, Quinn told me—he gets a little mouthy after a few as you might have noticed. Anyway, he guessed that you might have been one of the boys in the barn that night McLean was killed even though you denied any knowledge of the murder. I assume that you guessed that Quinn was one of the I.R.B. men in the barn that night, right?"

Willie drummed his fingers on the table.

"I thought it queer that you wouldn't have heard something about it in a small farming town where everybody knows everybody," Fahey said. "And the fact that you left for America about the time of the murder, I decided to do a little research, which eventually led me to the inspector here."

"Is that it? Who are you?"

"R.I.C. on special assignment with His Majesty's Secret Police."

"You're an agent against your own people?" Willie turned on O'Brien. "Is this who you wanted me to meet, a fucking spy?"

"Listen to what he has to say, Dwyer. It might be beneficial to you, a way for you to put Bernie McLean out of your life for good and give you a chance to finally be free."

"Tell me, Fahey, what makes me so interesting to the British Secret Police?"

"You're a Boston copper. And luckily for us, one of only two who didn't go out on strike and is still on the job, someone who could be valuable to us. And someone who might be interested in negotiating a settlement."

"Settlement?"

"Inspector O'Brien, since he's been in America, has learned a lot about William Dwyer. He's learned that he is a man of character and a man of his word and O'Brien guesses that this ten-year old unfortunate circumstance has probably eaten away at him every day since it happened. And he guesses that he's a man who is ready to take advantage of an opportunity. Is he guessing right, Willie?"

"Since the day we found McLean's body," O'Brien said, "things sort of fell into place, beginning with the cooperation of one of the I.R.B. men who shot him and is now sitting in a prison of his choice."

"You've got about a minute left," Willie said.

O'Brien reached across the table and grabbed Dwyer. "Listen to me, I didn't want to do this settlement. I wanted to bring you back to

Ballinasloe and show those hick farmers that not even a Yank copper from America is above the law. They need to know that even after ten years, the R.I.C. will hunt you down—"

Willie pulled his wrist free and shot his hand into O'Brien's throat, knocking his spectacles to the table top. "Put your fucking hands on me again and it will be the last thing you remember. Those 'hick farmers' were my neighbors, my friends and my family. Understand that, you bastard."

"Easy now, no use losing our tempers," Fahey said.

O'Brien leaned back and slapped Willie's hand away and fell against the bench, his neck flushed and spotted white with the impressions of Dwyer's fingerprints. "I understand that you're a fool." He felt his throat. "I would listen to him if I were you because you're not going to like the alternative." He slid out of the booth. "This was your idea, Fahey. See if you can talk some sense into him, because otherwise I'm ready to take him back."

"Go fuck yourself," Willie said. "It will take more than you to bring me back."

O'Brien walked to the bar and sat on one of the stools.

Fahey moved to the opposite side of the booth from Willie. "Everyone has their price, Dwyer, even one of your cousins. He cooperated because his brother is dead and he thought you were safe in America. He confirmed that you were inside the barn that night and that you helped him and his brother kidnap McLean and bury his body in the bog. His price? Transfer from Kilmainham to a local prison and an early release.

Willie sucked his lips inward.

"And you, we saved the best for you, a chance to rid yourself of this thing forever without doing a day behind bars."

"What are you talking about?"

"I'm sure you have been following the events at home. The guerilla war over Ireland's independence—cold-blooded assassinations, ambushes and bombings. The locals call it the 'Troubles' like it was some kind of feckin' debating contest. The Volunteers or I.R.B. or I.R.A or whatever they're calling themselves are responsible"

"And what about the R.I.C. and the British Auxiliary? The great and powerful British Empire. Does it fear that it no longer can keep its boot on the throat of its bloody peasants?"

"I was hoping that I could appeal to you as one policeman to another. O'Brien and I know several fellas who have been targeted and killed in ambushes, policemen with families. We're trying to maintain order just like you. Let's leave the politics to the politicians."

Willie picked out O'Brien at the bar, sitting between several workmen. He was sulking into his glass and still running his fingers around his neck. "I'm not saying that I'll go along with—" Dwyer brought his eyes back to the agent. "Talk."

"Fair enough." Fahey looked around the tavern and slid to the edge of his seat. "Michael Collins and the I.R.B. need money to finance their war. Without it, it withers away. Lop off the head of the beast, the devil dies."

"What are you talking about?" Dwyer tried to read Fahey's face. "Money—de Valera?"

"Yes, the Long Fellow, Eamon de Valera, an escaped prisoner sentenced by a British court of law. The president of the Dáil Eireann, who publically supports a 'state of war with England' and financially supports the murderous attacks on the R.I.C." He stuck his long legs out the end of the table. "Eliminate the money raised by de Valera in America and Michael Collins cannot buy guns or pay his rag-tag army in Ireland. Eliminate the donated American guns and ammunition and the I.R.B. can't ambush and murder innocent constables."

"The man you've protected since his arrival in the States? You're the snake in the grass."

"He's your hero, not mine."

"Why do you think the Irish in America support the rebels, Fahey?"

"What trash are you giving me now?"

"They're exiles. The lucky ones who escaped."

"Yes, yes," he said, "I understand."

"No, you don't. No one in your family was forced out of his home and not allowed to work. Your people sold out and live a good life."

"For Criss sakes, Dwyer, you've been an American for ten years. This is a chance for you to remain a Boston copper and to finally live your life without waiting for the knock on the door in the middle of the night, a bloody chance to end it all."

"I intend to—"

O'Brien slid back in next to Fahey. "If you walk out of here and try to fight extradition with the evidence we have against you—" He paused. "But for argument's sake, supposing you win. We can't take you back for trial and you remain a Boston Patrolman. You will never return home. You will look over your shoulder forever. And you know why? Because I'll never quit. If you ever step off a boat," he tapped the table with his finger, "I'll be waiting for you at the end of the gangway."

Fahey sniffed and shook his head. "I don't think you will win, Dwyer, not in this town, not the way things are going right now. Been following the stories about your police strike in the newspapers? Things are not going well for your boys. The tide has turned against them, and they're branded as Reds. What kind of support do you think you'll get when we make public the facts of your case? Your commissioner and governor have already said that under no conditions will they take back any of the strikers. They'll dump you like old ashes when they discover you're charged with murder."

Willie caught the attention of the bartender and put up three fingers.

"Eventually, Dwyer," Fahey said, "all things come to an end, even this. What are you going to do?"

The crowd in the tavern began to thin out as some of the laborers left and the remaining workers lingered around tables in small clusters. And with the departure of the crowd, the stale smoke-laden air began to move. Willie felt the change and stared into the mirror behind the bar. He didn't see McLean, the barn or feel the cold damp night in the bog. He pictured himself standing alone by the rail of a ship, felt the moisture rising off the water, lifting him up, drifting in and out of him like he was porous. And for the first time since he ran from the bog, he saw himself free.

"I know what kind of man you are, Dwyer," O'Brien said. "You're a stubborn son of a bitch, but a solid man, a man of quality. You want to make everything right before you get on with your life, maybe marry, have children. I couldn't have made this pitch to someone else, but let me assure you—"

"You can't assure me of anything."

Fahey turned to the constable and said, "Didn't go as we had planned, did it."

O'Brien leaned closer to Dwyer. "You help us and we'll help you. That's how it works."

The bartender placed three short whiskeys on the table in front of the three men. "Francis," Willie said, "I'd like to introduce two men from the old place, Aiden Fahey and Graves O'Brien."

"Pleased to meet you, fellas," O'Neil said as he shook their hands. "The whiskeys are on the house."

After O'Neil returned to the bar, Willie propped his elbows on the table, interlaced his fingers and looked across at Fahey. "I've listened to all your old shit. Now, I'll tell you what I want—an immediate release for my father and uncle."

"Are you crazy, Dwyer?" O'Brien said. "Hasn't it sunk in yet that you have no chips on the table? Not on your life—"

"Anything goes wrong, Fahey, you still have me. Without their release, I don't care what you're offering."

The agent covered his mouth with his hand for a moment and then withdrew it. "Alright, you've got it."

"What?" O'Brien said.

"In writing," Willie said.

"Aiden, I'm not having anything to do with releasing those two."

Fahey shook his head as if to confirm his answer. "In writing."

Willie took out a piece of paper and slapped it on the table in front of him. "And I want the Order for their release sent to this solicitor in Dublin before I do whatever it is that you want me to do."

"I don't know if I can do that on such short—"

"That's your problem. Release them or I don't assist you in whatever you have planned."

Fahey read the name and address of the solicitor and put the paper into his pocket. "You came prepared, didn't you?"

Willie rested his forearms on the table. "Now, tell me exactly what you think I'm going to do."

The R.I.C. agent took out an envelope and laid it on the table. "In here, I have two documents, a King's Warrant for the arrest of Eamon de Valera for Escape and Sedition."

"Why now?" Dwyer said. "You've had access to him for months."

"Two reasons. We didn't have permission until now. The British Government has declared the Dáil Eireann illegal and its president a fugitive. We finally received our orders yesterday, a few hours before Constable O'Brien left you the note. You can imagine the politics in all of this."

"In Boston?" Dwyer said. "He's got more supporters here than anywhere in America."

"Yes, he does." Fahey looked around the tavern. "He has thousands of supporters in America, but he also has his share of enemies, some who are sympathetic to Ireland, but are appalled by the guerrilla killing. So there is mounting political pressure to stop the slaughter and negotiate a settlement with the new Irish parliament. But first the guerilla warfare must stop."

"What kind of settlement, the same one that you bastards have been offering for years? You want the advantage in any negotiations to dictate your terms, that's what you want."

"You can look at it that way, but it allows the Crown to negotiate towards a realistic objective, a shared government in which Ireland remains part of the United Kingdom, not the idealistic and radical total separation that de Valera and the Sinn Fein government want." Foley removed the warrant from the envelope and opened it on the table. "Here it is, Dwyer, your opportunity."

"And what is the second reason for doing this now?"

"The second reason?" Fahey slumped back into the seat. "The police strike—the chaos in the streets. What better timing? A gift of sorts." He snickered. "The timing is perfect."

"Timing to do what?" Willie caught O'Brien looking away from the agent, taking a sudden interest in a group of men at a nearby table.

"Ships sail from Boston to England regularly," Fahey said.

"Yeah, so?" Dwyer turned to O'Brien who continued to look about the room with a purposeful disinterest in the conversation. "You need my assistance because you're planning a kidnapping. That's what you're talking about, isn't it?"

"Come on, Dwyer, what success are we going to have if we try and bring him before a local magistrate? When he arrives in England, he will be formally charged." Fahey pushed aside an empty beer glass that was between them. "Sunday night, de Valera is accepting an award and a donation from the Ancient Order of Hibernians at Memorial Hall, a short distance from your barracks in Roxbury Crossing. As soon as the presentation is over, we need you on the detail to get us out of Roxbury quickly and bring us to our destination. You'll be with us the moment he leaves the stage and will get us to where we are going without any problems."

"Why wait?" Willie said.

"What?"

"Why wait 'til Sunday?"

"If de Valera doesn't make his last public appearance, his supporters, the Press, your politicians will make inquiries. This way he accepts his award and quietly disappears. And nobody knows the difference until he's back in London."

"And what do you think Quinn and the other guards will do, just step aside?"

"Don't worry about them, that's our problem," Fahey said. "When we come out of Memorial Hall, I'll tell you where we're going."

"And by the by," O'Brien said, "Quinn will be arrested at the same time as de Valera for the murder of Bernie McLean. So, there you are, Dwyer, everyone wins."

The tavern girl delivered two beers to the laborers in the booth behind them, her skirt brushing Fahey's arm as she passed. He watched her walk across the floor as she flirted with another table of laborers and talked them into buying another round of drinks.

"And what about de Valera?" Willie said.

"For Criss' sakes, Dwyer, he'll be a political prisoner," Fahey said. "Probably be in the top class on the boat ride home and be held at one of the best hotels in London during the negotiations. Once they're completed and the treaty written, he'll walk away a free man and, who knows, maybe become the real president of Ireland. " He removed the second document from the envelope and pushed it across the table. "This is the most important piece of paper as far as you're concerned, the King's Pardon. It grants you full immunity from any further investigation and prosecution." He started to read—"Into the events associated with the death of Bernard McLean in Ballinasloe on or about the

9th of March 1909 in exchange for your cooperation in the apprehension of Eamon de Valera."

Willie picked up the glass of whiskey and sucked it down. "I'll think about it."

"I need to know today," Fahey said.

"If I decide to do this, I'll want another man to work the detail with me."

"If you have any ideas about fucking us—" O'Brien said.

"I'll be sure and ask for two men when I talk to your superior," Fahey said, "but when we leave the hall, the other patrolman stays behind. I don't want any funny business."

Willie slid out of the booth. "As you said, Special Agent, I'm a man of my word."

"Good, then we have a deal?"

"Give me your telephone number and I'll call you later tonight."

"Seven," Fahey said.

"Seven o'clock. And only if I hear from my father by Sunday afternoon." Willie jammed the paper with the number into his pocket and walked out the tavern door.

The pub had cleared out and there were only a few patrons left besides the two R.I.C. men. A State Guardsman came in and sat down at one of the tables and asked the tavern girl about the night's supper.

"Give us a chance to clean up first, will you, fella?" O'Neil said to him. "Start cleaning the tables in the booths," he said to the girl. "We'll use them first."

She cleared the table next to Fahey and O'Brien. As she passed them on her way to the bar, she said, "Will you be staying for the ham, boys?"

"Yeah, I think we will," Fahey said. "In the meantime, bring us a couple of tall ones."

"Sure thing. Just let me clear your table." She picked up their empties as they went back to their conversation and brought the glasses to the bar.

O'Brien stood and watched Willie through the large window until he disappeared from view and then sat down across from the special agent. "What do you think?"

"I think he wants McLean out of his life. And I suspect that he would like to see his family."

"But does he want it bad enough to turn on de Valera?"

"He's a Boston Yank now." Fahey took the two full glasses from the girl.

"And a dreamer," O'Brien said.

"That's right, and dreamers rarely get what they want."

Graves waited for the girl to walk away. "What about the guns?"

"We'll take those at the same time."

The girl returned to the table and put her hand on Fahey's shoulder. "The bartender said the first drink is on the house for patrons who buy the ham supper."

"Is it that bad?" Fahey could feel her hip up against his arm.

"Nah, it's actually pretty good, a tradition at O'Neil's."

"What other traditions do you have to make a customer feel welcome?"

"Oh, you'd be surprised," she said. "Will there be anything more?"

"No, that'll be fine." Fahey caught her wrist as she started to walk away. "Does the hospitality include having the tavern girl join us for a drink?"

"Aren't we the bold one?" She pushed his hand away. "The ham will be out in a few minutes."

"Swell," he said as he watched her walk away.

NOLAN DUG in his pocket for the office key. "Your little friend, Catherine, played her part well."

"Yeah, a regular Mary Pickford," Willie said. "Hope she learned a few things."

Nolan opened the door and scaled his hat like a horseshoe and it landed on the tree stand. "British Secret Agents, here in Boston? What do you know?"

"Now I understand why the R.I. C. sent O'Brien to America."

"So, the plan is to capture de Valera and bring him back to Mother England. You give them an escort out of the city and in exchange, you walk on McLean."

"Yeah—"

"Hmm. The war in Europe changed everything for Ireland. I wouldn't be surprised if there is a deal in place between Washington and London." Nolan watched Willie pace in front of his desk. "Sit down, will you? You're making me nervous." He put his hands behind his head. "The Limeys do their dirty deed and America looks the other way."

"Yeah."

"Big catch for those two R.I.C. boys. I can see why they're willing to take a chance on you. No accidental outside interference, and with the strike—"

Willie was up and pacing again.

"You're going to wear the floor out."

"Never mind that," Willie said. "I've got to get an answer back to them by seven."

"Do you trust them?"

"Would you?"

"That makes it unanimous. So, what are you thinking?"

"About their offer?"

"Yeah."

"I'll tell you what I'm thinking. I'm thinking about getting my father and uncle out of prison."

Nolan ripped a wooden match across the sole of his shoe and stared at the flame. "I like a challenge." He lit a cigar, and walked to the door. "I need to talk to the fellas with the rifles."

"The Guard?"

"Yeah. Them too—"

"Hold on, George." Willie leaned his hand against the door. "I've got to do this myself, even if —"

Nolan removed Willie's hand. "Do you want to get your father out of jail?"

"Of course, but I don't want to be known as the guy who set up the Irish president either."

"Then do what they want."

"What?"

"Do what they want." Nolan started out, but then came back inside. "Say, you can tell me to mind my own business, but how serious are you about Catherine?"

"Huh?"

"Don't play dumb with me, Dwyer. It's pretty obvious that she thinks you're hot stuff. Why else would she stick her neck out and play in our little charade?"

"She likes to act?" Willie laughed at his own joke. "You'll have to ask her. We're friends—"

"Sure, friends." Nolan stepped into the hallway with his hand still on the doorknob. "I know one thing, she's got more balls than you and I put together. You better watch out, Dwyer, or as old as I am—"

Willie waited for the door to close. "Ah, go on you old lizard before you hurt yourself."

"I heard that," the voice from the hallway said.

"PATROLMAN DWYER, it's for you." The volunteer handed Willie the telephone as he passed the desk. "She sounds nice."

"Don't you have something to do in the kitchen like help the houseman with the dishes?"

"All right, I get the hint."

Willie waited until the volunteer was out of the room. "Hello?"

"Is this the famous Patrolman Dwyer, the one whom every girl pines for?" Catherine asked.

"Where are you? I can hear people talking."

"O'Neil's."

"Still there?"

"Just sent those two off. Tall one thought that I came with his suds."

Willie listened for the volunteer and heard him bending the ear of the houseman behind the closed kitchen door. "What did you find out?"

"What, no foreplay, no enticements? Just spit it out, sister."

"You're a pip. Hurry it up, will you? That volunteer is nosy and will be back any minute."

"Oh, alright. The tall one? I heard him say something about your loyalty to your father and uncle, and that you're a dreamer."

"Did he say anything about where I'm supposed to bring them?"

"I heard them say something about a boat, Dorchester and a boat."

Willie turned to laughter in the kitchen.

"Actually a shlip—a ship." Catherine giggled into the receiver.

"What are you laughing about?"

"I had a few glasses with those two and—"

"Ah, Jeez."

"You know, pick up a thing or two. "

"And?"

"That's all I heard, but the kid in the booth—"

"What kid, how much did you drink?"

"I'm not bolloxed, Willie. O'Neil put one of his runners under your seat, just large enough for him, the little shit."

"He was right under my arse?"

"Hope you were kind to him?" Catherine giggled.

"Did they mention de Valera's bodyguards?"

"Would that be the same as a squad?"

"They said, 'squad'?"

"That's what the kid told me. He said 'squad' like the squad was in charge."

"Shi—squad? Thanks, Catherine. I really—"

"The kid also told me that they mentioned the moon and the water several times."

"The moon?" Willie saw the kitchen door open and the young volunteer, coming out. "The tide?" He turned his back to him. "Thanks again, Catherine. I appreciate you doing this."

"You can thank me when I see you."

"And a good day to you, madam," he said and handed the telephone to the volunteer.

WILLIE MADE the call to Fahey from a telephone booth at a half past seven, just to give him the screws, and then trudged the couple of blocks to his rooming house, hauling the police strike, O'Brien, Fahey and Bernie McLean up the hill. Before he could put the key into the lock, the door to his room fanned open. He removed his revolver and pushed on the door with the end of the barrel. The bed was made and, except for the clean sheets on the end of the bureau, the room looked in the same condition as when he left it. A sweet light odor bubbled in the room, penetrated him and lifted him like helium.

"What took you so long, Buster?" Catherine said from the dark end of the bedroom. "You really don't need the gun." She sat with her legs crossed in a chair in a corner close to the bed.

"Just a little jumpy with all of this business." He took a look out into the hall and closed the door. "How did you get in here?" He lit the light on the bureau.

"I found your key on Mrs. Gerhardt's board."

"If she finds you in here, we'll both be out on the street."

"If you'd rather I leave—"

"No."

"She's gone out for the evening," Catherine said. "With the soldier boys running the show, she thinks the world is safe again."

Willie hung his coat on a hook and placed the revolver in the top drawer of the bureau. "Even the captain thinks it's safe. He gave Nolan and me the night off." He sat down on the edge of the bed. "Say, how did you know I would be home?"

"I called the station again. The young volunteer asked me if I wanted to leave a message. One thing led to another and—" She shrugged her shoulders. "He told me what I wanted to know."

"Cocky kid, thinks he knows everything." He bent over and untied his boots while her legs uncrossed in front of his face, caught a flash of white stocking and consumed her sweet aroma. "What's that perfume you're wearing?"

"It's coconut oil beauty soap. Do you like it?"

"It's—"

"Stimulating?"

He smiled. "Like a punch in the face, you are."

"Why beat around the bush?" She sat down next to him on the edge of the bed, began to walk her fingers up his back. "How about I go with you to Memorial Hall when Mr. de Valera receives his award?"

"Ah, I don't think that's a good idea."

"Why not? I can get into a lot of places you can't. Besides, who made you the big cheese?"

"What if you run into Jim Rankin? He's probably going to be there."

"You afraid I can't handle that windbag?"

"No—"

"Ah, I've got other plans anyway." She ran both of her hands up the sides of his neck and down into his shoulders. "A lot of tension there."

"I don't trust those Peelers. But they're right, what choice do I have?" Willie dropped his boots onto the floor. "A Boston copper charged with murder, after these riots. Wait—other plans?"

"I picked up an odd job from Francis O'Neil while I was at the tavern." She ran her hands into his hairline, pulsating his temples with the tips of her fingers. "If you had your druthers, tell me what you would want?"

"I wish—I'd like another chance to make things right."

"I'm talking about now, silly." She traced his cheekbones and his jaw line. "You can only do what the moment asks for. So what about right now, Mr. Dwyer. What do you want?"

He pulled her into him and closed his eyes, felt for her lips, just barely touching her flesh. "You," he said. "I just want you."

Catherine turned her head away, opened her neck to him, inviting him into her long slender landscape. Willie brushed her cheek with his lips and settled into the soft gentle curve under her jaw. He held her face and admired the flush of her cheeks, the freckles scattered across the bridge of her nose, the promise in her eyes.

"Are you blushing with excitement for me or the uncertainty of what may come?" he said.

"Both. But right now, it is for you."

"When did Mrs. Gerhardt say she would return?"

"Late. She said that she would be very late."

Chapter Thirty

~

Sunday, 14 September 1919
Early Evening

Willie Dwyer stood in the street outside Memorial Hall and fidgeted. He adjusted his helmet and tugged on his white traffic gloves. The darkness of the previous night bullied and taunted him, and by the time dawn crept under his bedroom door, the demons had torn the confidence out of his chest. He directed traffic and watched the Roxbury Irish; freed from the quarantine of their homes, they came to the meeting house to see Ireland's national hero, indifferent to the fact that boys in khakis now patrolled their neighborhood instead of men in blue.

A brand new Buick caught Willie's attention as it stopped at the entrance to let out its passengers. Jim Rankin emerged from the automobile with the ever present red carnation in his lapel, removed his low black topper and waved to his constituents, pointing out certain spectators for special recognition. When he saw Willie standing in the street, he pumped his fist and yelled, "Good job, Dwyer." Willie returned the greeting with a plastic smile and a vulgar word whispered under his breath.

Virginia Rankin sat sidesaddle with her legs out the car door. She interrupted her husband's politicking for assistance in standing. The Boston socialite waved from a distance with as little effort as it took to rock her hand back and forth twice. She stretched herself tall as the diminutive Dandy Jim slipped his arm under hers and escorted her to the roped-off area to greet neighbors, union members and a few of his loyal campaign workers. After they completed their hobnobbing, she looked around and caught Willie looking back. The thin line of her lips cracked slightly as she gave him a controlled purposeful smile, turned and walked into the hall with her husband in tow.

As the last of the invited guests disappeared through the long narrow doors, the automobile carrying Eamon de Valera crested the hill and the crowd of well-wishers broke into enthusiastic applause. Peter Quinn and Aiden Fahey rode the running boards and another younger guard drove the vehicle. De Valera stepped out, his long sloping shoulders, bent nose, goose-like neck and gold circular glasses in unmistakable profile.

"Chief, this is the policeman I have been telling you about," Fahey said, "a Ballinasloe man. His father and uncle were early Republicans."

The Irish president walked into the street and extended his hand. "From Ballinasloe?"

"Yes, sir." Dwyer shook his hand and felt the press of Peter Quinn against him on one side and the younger guard on his other.

"That area of Galway was not a stronghold of support back then. What happened to them?"

"Sir?"

"Your father and uncle?"

"Kilmainham."

"Ah."

Fahey approached the group. "We should be going inside. The ceremony is about to begin."

Willie stole a look at the two bodyguards and then between the bodyguards and Aiden Fahey, tried to recognize unspoken words between them—a nod, a shrug, the flash of an eye blink, some kind of visual signal to a plan. *What's the plan?* Together, they conducted their business as if they were working on one of Henry Ford's production lines, one more fund-raiser, one more speech, one more ceremony. But individually, he saw them edgy like rodents, heads down-eyes up, snatching jerky hesitant glances, sizing each other up, looking for the sweet spot.

De Valera hesitated, broke from his protection and cuffed Dwyer under the arm, then moved him away from the group with Fahey trailing a few feet behind. He turned Willie into the sun and stood beside him. "I understand that you are providing an escort after the ceremony."

"That's correct, sir."

"Thank you for your assistance." De Valera removed his glasses and wiped the lenses with his handkerchief. "I knew your father in the early days. And I wanted you to know that you come from good stock."

"Thank you, sir."

"If you ever have a mind."

"Thank you, maybe someday—"

"The invitation is always there." He tucked his handkerchief into his breast pocket and turned. "Okay, Aiden."

As Fahey and Peter Quinn led him away, Willie heard Quinn say, "It's good to see one of our Galway men become successful here."

"Yes, it is." De Valera placed his hand on Quinn's shoulder and stepped towards the spectators behind the ropes. He thanked a few of them for coming and walked into the hall.

Dwyer looked around and thought about escape routes out of Massachusetts and then he thought that maybe surrendering was the ultimate escape. He blew out a long breath and massaged his forehead as he walked off the street unsure of anything any longer, especially of himself. If he only knew how Fahey and O'Brien intended to remove Quinn and the other bodyguard.

Where is O'Brien? He no longer believed that the R.I.C. had sent an inspector to America to bring him back home. There were too many Irish stories of retribution and revenge lying about the ports of the American East Coast. The constable could have filled an ocean liner with fugitives like him. Nolan was right—kidnapping the charismatic Irish leader from within the borders of England's closest ally must have had the blessings at the highest levels of both governments. This operation had the stink of international politics draped all over it.

Have the car by the back door and be standing beside it when the president completes his speech. That's it? And if de Valera and his bodyguards decide to be uncooperative? Not for you to worry. What about the 'squad?'

Engrossed in his thoughts, he walked off the street and slipped between Rankin's Buick and another car to get to the front of the hall when Peter Quinn stepped into his path.

"Ah, Dwyer, we meet for a third time, I believe."

"A third time?"

"Oh, I see the charade continues. I guess we're not counting that time in the old barn. Okay, a second time, it is."

The guard stepped closer and Dwyer turned away from the odors of tobacco breath and the dangerous combination of liquor and the stink of survival.

"Do you think that night will just go away, Dwyer?" Quinn turned and saw Nolan coming up the alley. "Do you want to disavow our common thread, the one irrefutable link between us, our penchant for vengeance and violence? It runs in the blood, you know. Or do you think that we leave it behind when we sail to a new land?"

"I think you've been drinking and need to move away, Quinn. Now that I know who you are, it will take nothing for me to club you into mincemeat."

"Ah, that's the Dwyer I remember, the genuine article, chip off the old block." Quinn pounded his fist into the palm of his hand. "Young and hot-headed, vigilant and righteous. Not the American imposter in the blue costume that stands in front of me. Got everyone fooled haven't you?"

"I was all those things, but I wasn't a murderer."

A murderer, a revolutionary, a Republican Brother, it's all in interpretation."

"Not for me, it isn't."

"Civilized, are you?" He slapped Willie's chest with an open hand and laughed. "It's too fucking late, William. You took an oath, a blood oath. You and I, trapped in that barn forever." He removed his pipe from his coat pocket and tapped out the remains of his last bowl. "An eye for an eye, that's what it was."

"I didn't pull the trigger."

Quinn flinched when he saw Nolan emerge from the alley, turned his face up, close enough that Dwyer could see that his eyes were yellow-grey. "I've been hearing things—" He smiled at Willie, a short crooked smile. "Remember, you brought McLean to the barn. You covered his head with a blanket. Whether you like it or not, we are bound—" He looked back. "I wouldn't be too scrupulous, might get you into serious trouble."

"Are you threatening me?"

"Let's say that I have concern for any foolish decision on your part to rid yourself of your problem at my expense."

"You're being played for a fool, Quinn—"

As Nolan approached them, the I.R.B. man jabbed his hand into Dwyer's stomach. "Take it, you lug." He grabbed Willie's hand, tugged him closer and began to shake it. "McLean was a casualty of a just war. You get that? De Valera understands that, your father understands that."

"My father?"

"You leave what happened in that barn—bury it, or so help me God, I don't give a fuck if you are a copper."

When Nolan reached them, Quinn was pumping Dwyer's hand like a long lost friend and Willie was standing there with his face hanging hollow.

"We'll have to get together for some drinks afterwards, Yank," Quinn said. "But no arguments this time, I'm buying." He turned on his heel and put his hand out to Nolan as he passed him. "Peter Quinn, got to get inside, you know how it is."

"Yeah, sure," the detective said, "George Nolan—"

Quinn swallowed George's hand with his own, stamp pressed it and then he was gone. "You never know with the boss," he said over his shoulder, "could speak for five minutes or five hours."

Willie watched him enter the alley. "Wait." Dwyer followed him. 'Quinn!"

Just before he got to the rear door of the hall, Quinn stopped and looked back, framed by buildings on both sides. The bodyguard paused in the shadow of the narrow alley like he was at the end of something. Willie saw the desperation of a man standing on the edge, and said nothing.

"I'll see you later, Dwyer." He entered the hall and disappeared.

"What's going on?" Nolan asked as he caught up to him.

Willie stared down the alley, pulled off his gloves and shoved them into his pocket. "I think I smell a double-cross—he's been warned about me."

"Keep an eye on him at all times." Nolan removed his own traffic gloves and they walked back to the square. "Didn't you tell me that Fahey said they were sailing with de Valera?"

"Yeah, first class."

"No ships sailing from Boston to England for two weeks."

"So, how do Fahey and O'Brien expect to get de Valera on a ship tonight?"

"I don't know. Maybe they've got a private yacht or something."

"Catherine told me that, after I left O'Neil's, they mentioned Dorchester and a ship."

"A pickup point?" Nolan said.

"And that kid I told you about, under the seat?"

"Yeah."

"He heard them say something about the moon. I would guess they were talking about the tides."

"Do you want to call it quits, Willie?

"No."

"Because I wouldn't blame you if you did—"

"No. It's just the 'or something' that bothers me."

THE DRIVER WATCHED the two men struggle with the last wooden box before they placed it into the back of the truck. They covered the boxes with a tarp and then shoveled sand on top of the canvas, mounding it up, until the sand completely covered the boxes. "Leave the shovels on the back," the driver said, then reached into a jacket on the front seat and removed several bills, counted them and gave them to the men.

"This is more than what I made in a couple of weeks as a copper," one of them said.

"Yeah, thanks," said the second man. "The missus will be delighted." He shoved the money into his trousers. "Is there anything else we can do?"

"No, this is the last shipment, but you were very helpful," the driver said and climbed up behind the wheel. "I wouldn't have been able to move them by myself. But keep this to yourselves, would you, fellas? I don't have a lot of work, but when I do—"

"Oh, you don't have to worry about us," said the first man. "No one wants to hire us right now, we're like pariahs."

"No, we won't say nothing," said the second.

The driver gathered her hair together and clipped it with a bobby pin. "Good men are hard to find," she said and pulled on a cap.

"Say," the second one started. "You know how to get in touch with us, don't you?"

Catherine waved at them, put on the headlamps and moved the stick into gear.

"Just like this time," the man shouted as the truck passed them in the drive. "Leave a message at O'Neil's."

RAUCOUS APPLAUSE and whistles erupted and rolled out of the hall, cheers that were picked up by the crowd outside. Willie backed the car down the alley and parked it by the back door and in front of de Valera's car. Nolan came down the alley and stood with one foot up on the running board as Fahey exited out the back door of the hall, closely followed by the Irish president, Quinn and the other guard.

Nolan looked back and watched de Valera climb into the back seat of the touring car. The young guard drove and Quinn stood on the running board with the front door ajar. "If this turns to shit," George said to Willie. He saw Fahey running up the alley. "Ah, you'll be fine." He walked to the street and held back the spectators from blocking the alley.

The agent climbed in next to Dwyer. "Okay, let's go."

"Where are we going?" Willie said. A door shut in de Valera's car behind him and he looked back. Quinn motioned to him to get going.

"Start driving towards Quincy and the water," Fahey said.

Black dust rose up from the cinder drive as both vehicles climbed out of the alley. The cars reached the street, paused while Nolan held up the traffic, turned left and disappeared.

GRAVES O'BRIEN stooped down in the sand at the end of the narrow causeway that connected Quincy's Squantum Neck to Boston's Moon Island where four enormous granite storage tanks held the municipality's raw sewage that the city jettisoned into the harbor at high water. A light wind lifted off the bay and stroked the island as intermittent rain fell like ball bearings. A repugnant stench filled his nostrils until he thought the heavy raindrops must be carrying the dung itself. Light from his car's headlamps illuminated the apron where he carved out a hole in the sand large enough to accommodate a device, topped off with a blanket of nails. He covered it over, stood and brushed the sand from his knees, removed his bowler and began to shake the rain from its brim, but stopped.

"Is that you, Myles?" he said. He spun around and faced the island. "I thought you fellas were going to stay on the other side."

He didn't receive an answer and he jerked his head and lifted it to a noise that he didn't actually hear, but intuitively imagined as the sound of a metallic click. Turning his good ear towards the island and its field of tall grass, he sorted out the meaningless background and searched in the acoustic darkness for the scratch of underbrush against a pair of trousers, an absent-minded sniff or maybe a cough, the crack of a human joint or the snap of a dry twig. He pulled out his pistol and swept the tree line, listening for something that didn't belong, something that caused his apprehensive tic.

"Getting feckin' jumpy. I'll be seeing goblins next." The constable turned away from the island and saw the last bit of evening light and then looked down the long narrow causeway back to Squantum Neck, watched the waves crawling and writhing to the berm and slapping against the makeshift road. "Hurry up, will you, Fahey. Let's get this over with."

He heard it again. Or at least he thought he did. The wind picked up and it raced to the island in short sprints, skidded between the holding tanks, then into the field where it bent over the tall grass. It distorted his selective hearing and he waited for it to subside before turning back to the island's blackness, squinting and straining to see something he could not see with his eyes, but rather with his mind—to make known out of the unknown, to give a name to the nameless. He stooped down, making himself smaller, and crawled on his hands and knees to the driver's open door. The wind rose off the water again as he sat in the car and breathed a sigh of relief. He looked to the bay and saw the lights of a ship just as a single dum-dum bullet that he never did hear entered his brain in the shape of a mushroom just above his temple.

RIFLES, long brown coats and campaign hats—Willie saw them first as rain began to splatter against the windshield. The four Guardsmen had stationed themselves on either side of the drawbridge that spanned the Neponset River, the boundary line between the city of Boston and the city of Quincy, discouraging out-of-town hoodlums from coming in, and tossing vehicles for contraband going out. Cars merged from the adjoining streets and funneled in a procession to the foot of the bridge where they were stopped by the first soldier.

"Watch what you say, Dwyer," Fahey said. "Were you expecting this?"

"How the hell can I control what the Guard does?"

"Evening, gents," the Guardsman said. "Oh, sorry, patrolman, I didn't see the uniform. But we got orders to search every single vehicle."

"Go ahead," Willie said. "You've got your orders."

The Guardsman held the back door open and stuck his head inside and checked the interior. "Sorry for the inconvenience."

Fahey jerked a look at Dwyer, snapped straight ahead and then looked back. "Is this because of the riots, soldier?"

"Yes, sir."

"Damn strikers, caused a lot of aggravation for us working cops."

The soldier closed the door, looked up to the bridge and raised his rifle over his head. "Okay, have a good night."

"Let's go, Dwyer."

"You look like you're going to shit yourself, Fahey."

As they reached the top of the bridge, another soldier on the inbound side stepped into the road and signaled them to stop.

"Now what?" the agent said.

"Not too calm when you're in the line of fire, are you?" Willie said.

"Shut up."

"He's making a car turn around and he's sending it back to Quincy."

The soldier waved them on. When they reached the other side, Willie looked back and saw de Valera's car cresting the top of the bridge.

HEAT LIGHTENING skipped across the sky over Boston Harbor as Willie turned the wheel and drove onto the long neck of filled-in land. "Why couldn't you have just said, 'Squantum' instead of all this secret shit?"

"Relax, Dwyer, your part in this is almost over. Besides, I am a man of my word, am I not? Have you heard from your father or your uncle?"

"I heard from the solicitor this afternoon. He assured me that they were released."

"Okay then, there's nothing for you to worry about."

The rain was steady now and drummed incessantly on the car's steel hood. The single wiper couldn't keep the windshield clear and caused momentary periods of blindness when Willie couldn't see the medallion at the front of the vehicle, let alone the road. He eased up on the gas pedal and moved cautiously along the causeway. The other vehicle rode in tandem with them and its headlamps shown into the back of the car so bright that they lit up the interior. He watched Fahey's head swivel from side to side.

"How did you get de Valera to come out to this God forsaken place?" he said.

"Good question, but I didn't have to convince him to come."

"What do you mean?"

"There's a shipment—" Fahey looked out the window to the causeway. "If this thing was any narrower." He sat back and rolled his head to look at Willie. "I guess we had you pegged pretty well."

"What are you talking about?" Willie said. The steering wheel jerked in his hand.

"Your cooperation. You're an idealist."

"Don't you mean 'a dreamer?'"

The agent grinned. "Yeah, I did say 'dreamer,' but you weren't there to hear it." He snickered. "The tavern girl—good one, Dwyer. Tried to get her back to my hotel room, almost had her." He watched Willie's jaw harden. "A friend of yours?"

"Shut up."

Fahey sniffed and looked out the windshield. "Yank."

The wind blew in a high-pitched whistle as the two vehicles inched across the causeway and high water on the ocean side rushed at the embankment in three-foot black and white swells, exploding against the berm into spray and soapy foam. The broken waves slipped over the roadway and rolled in to the point.

Sea water slapped against the side of the car and it wobbled back and forth as it bumped along on top of the stone road. "Jesus, Mary and Joseph," Fahey said as the car chattered. "Take it easy, will you, Dwyer? Goddam water is going to pitch us into the bay."

"Shit." Willie jerked the wheel towards the point and then compensated and pulled it back to the ocean side to keep the vehicle from ditching into the water. "What the hell are we doing out here, Fahey? There are no ships to England—"

"Just do your part and shut up!" Fahey braced his hand against the roof of the car. Another wave, larger than the others, crashed into his passenger door and bay water seeped into the car. Willie stepped on the gas and made a short bumpy run.

They crawled along the causeway in silence, sprinting between the waves, until Willie could feel a change in the steering wheel. "I'm not fighting the wind as much." For the first time since they started their crossing, he could hear his voice clearly and noticed that the battering from the wind and the surf had diminished. He could hear the windshield wiper and the whine of the car's engine. "We must be getting close."

"There it is," Fahey said.

Moon Island rose up in front of them like an apparition. Scattered high black-green trees stood silhouetted at the edge of the island like sentries. They swayed at the tops, bending with the wind, and the vegetation and tall grasses below them flitted around the gnarly giants like a woman's skirt. The rain slowed to a drizzle as Willie drove the last couple of feet on the causeway.

He covered his hand over his nose and mouth. "Ah, Jesus, the tanks must be full."

"Not a very cheerful place, is it?" the agent said.

Willie stopped the car in a jerk at the end of the causeway. "Okay, how about you tell me just what the fuck is going on here." The second vehicle drove right up behind them, but at the last instant turned away. He could hear Quinn and the other guard yelling at him.

"Don't be stupid, Dwyer." Fahey pushed open the passenger door and looked down at the wheels. "Move before we're both killed."

"What?"

"Move!" Fahey pushed a pistol into Dwyer's ribs, reached over with his foot and stepped on the accelerator, the rear wheels jumping on the stones and the car jolting off the causeway.

"Get that fucking gun—" Willie slapped at the agent, but Fahey rolled out of the passenger door.

The car leaped forward onto the island and then rolled back to the apron. Dwyer heard a 'click' and saw a brilliant white flash—the power of the blast driving up through the bottom of the car near the engine block and lifting the front end off the ground. He felt the force of it pass through his feet and legs and expand into him, filling every void in his cavity and pushing the air out of him. He yanked on the steering wheel and felt himself tumbling and collapsing like a deflating balloon, gasped and felt the stab of pain in his back and legs, tried not to panic—thought of his father and his family, thought of his dead mother, and Catherine—disoriented and confused, his heart drumming uncontrollably like it would vibrate out of his chest, heard rapid gunfire, some of it striking the overturned vehicle, hoping that one of those stray bullets would find him.

Saw McLean just like the photo that O'Brien showed him, cocky and no remorse, threatening even when they covered his head, never believing it would end the way it did. *You've done it now, Dwyer. You and your old man will rot in the gaol.*

He began to gag and turned his head, retched forward and vomited against the firewall, his head and shoulders trapped between the steering wheel and the door, one leg folded underneath him as the car seemed to be pinning him down. He pawed with his free foot and tried to move himself from his contorted position, but just flailed away at empty space, tried to lift his head, but sunk back dizzy and unbalanced.

The little island echoed with distant gunshots and shouting and a last and final muffled explosion before the battle gave way to the natural quiet of rustling leaves, chafing grass and water lapping the sand at the island's edge. Willie remained pinned in the car, stunned in a distorted world of ringing and partial blindness. Then the passenger door opened and he smelled the salty air and tasted the raw sewage. A familiar voice said, "Here, get him out of there and try not to mess him up any worse than he already is."

He could hear several voices, some that had, in his present condition, a distorted familiarity to them. Outside of the car, he sat on the moist sand and hung his head. People moved around him in definite patterns and he guessed that they were organized into some kind of work force—heard a hammer and the squeak of nails releasing their hold in wood and men passing back and forth in front of him, carrying something, walking toward the sound of steam escaping and the rhythmic chug of an engine.

"Lay back so I can wash your eyes out," the voice said.

Water ran from the top of Willie's forehead down his face. "George?"

"Yeah, tilt your head back and open your eyes."

Willie saw a hazy Nolan kneeling beside him, felt a solution enter his eyes and winced.

"Saline," the detective said. "Here, dry your face." He handed Willie a towel. "Do you think you've got anything broken?"

Willie heard Nolan's words like a ham radio broadcast, interrupted by a lot of static. "What?"

"Broken bones, do you have any broken bones?"

"I don't know, don't think so." Willie pulled his legs up. "Oh—what happened?"

"That's good, no broken bones," Nolan said. "Now, first things first. We won't be able to bring you to a hospital in your present condition, especially while you're wearing your uniform."

"What? Why?"

"But we've got some pretty good medical people here who can take care of you if you need it." Nolan unbuttoned Willie's tunic and pulled his arms out of it. "Once you're on your feet, I'll explain everything to you, but for the time being—what happened here tonight, on Moon Island, never happened. You got it?" He put a canteen up to Willie's mouth. "Here, drink this."

"Oh, that's good," Dwyer said. "Pour some in my hands." He wet his ears and neck and dried them with the towel. "You're as bad as Fahey with all the— Say, what happened to him?"

"Dead."

"And the others? Quinn? O'Brien?"

"Same."

"Jesus." Willie took another drink. "Where are they?"

Nolan glanced at the granite storage tanks. "They're already buried." He sat down on the sand next to Dwyer. "If anyone ever asks you about tonight, tell them that you heard that some kids were shooting off fireworks out here." He cut an apple in half and gave it to him. "I'm sorry you had to get hit with the concussion mine, but that was the ideal place to disable the vehicles and separate Fahey from his hit squad. It was supposed to go off in front of the vehicle. But when your car jerked forward and then rolled back, you stopped on top of it."

"Great, almost killed by my own partner."

Nolan took a bite out of the apple. "Look at the bright side. Your friend, O'Brien, buried a real nasty ball breaker there, topped off with nails. It was planted to rip de Valera and his bodyguards to shreds if we hadn't removed it."

"Fahey must have known."

"Their plan didn't include you walking out of here, Willie. You can thank Catherine and that kid, hiding in the booth at O'Neil's." Nolan threw his apple core into the water. "I still can't believe the shit luck of O'Brien picking O'Neil's for a meeting place."

A shortened one-two toot from a boat echoed in the bay. Willie turned towards the sound. "Is that a ship?"

"It is," Nolan said, "on its way to Ireland."

"De Valera?"

"Never here."

"What's it here for?"

"467 Tommy guns."

Willie turned to a hazy blurred version of the cop that he had come to respect and admire. "Tell me, George, who the hell are you? And what the hell went on here tonight?"

"Let's just say that the British Secret Agents came up short in a contest with our own Hit Squad."

"Our?"

"I.R.B."

Willie buried his head in his hands and talked down between his legs. "Oh—"

"Can you stand?" Nolan said.

"Who else was involved? Damn, I don't think I know my own name right now."

"When you have a clear head, I'll tell you everything there is to know." Nolan lifted him under his arm and helped him up. "Come on, let's get you off this island."

They began to walk to a truck that was partially filled with sand. "How did you get here?" Willie asked.

Nolan nodded to the truck. "A switch at the Guards' roadblock."

They heard the rhythmic drumming of a turbine engine and the heavy clanging of steel slapping stone. Willie stopped and turned in the direction of the noise.

Nolan paused with him. "The gates are opening."

"Ugh—" Willie said. "Boston's shit, a gift to the world."

"It's more than a gift, Willie. It's a resolution."

In the News

POLICE UNION VOTE TO GO BACK—
CURTIS REFUSES THE STRIKERS
Gompers' suggestion accepted by strikers, in request to Governor–ready to work pending adjustment; Coolidge announces cannot see way to reinstate men whom he calls "deserters"
THE BOSTON DAILY GLOBE
Saturday, September 13, 1919

DISCHARGES UNION'S OFFICERS—
CURTIS TO MEET LABOR LEADERS
Positions of strikers declared vacant, Commissioner takes steps to fill their places; Governor says pay and hours should be revised–Peters plans for increase; Gompers asks for cool consideration, appeals again to Governor Coolidge
THE BOSTON SUNDAY GLOBE
Sunday, September 14, 1919

OFFICIAL WASHINGTON BACKS COOLIDGE
On Capitol Hill, at the departments, in the clubs and hotels, indeed wherever public men gather, only commendation for the chief executive of the Bay State is heard
WASHINGTON—SPECIAL TO TRANSCRIPT
Monday, September 15, 1919

EDITORIAL PAGE—THE REPUBLIC
Impasse on negotiations, looks like none will be rehired; we agree with President Wilson, obligation of policeman sacred as soldier; police should have been patient little longer, faithful to noblest traditions; blame rests on arrogant Commissioner Curtis, might have averted strike
THE REPUBLIC
Saturday, September 20, 1919

Chapter Thirty-one

Monday, 15 September 1919

Bradford Henshaw had his feet up on the desk with the morning newspaper collapsed in his lap as he stared out the office window that faced the harbor, the waterfront coming alive with barges, gangways and dock-wallopers. A stiff ocean breeze pressed into the shore and rippled the water like aged skin while a lone seagull sat perched on a pole, huddled with his wings tucked up and out of sight, the underside of his body lit up bright by the water's reflection. Light and warmth filled Henshaw's office and, for the first time in a week, he surrendered to sleep. His head dropped onto his chest and he began to doze.

The slamming of an automobile door in the driveway startled him and he swiveled in his chair to look out the side window. By the time he collected himself and had his feet on the floor, Pearlie Brodsky stood at his door in the outside hallway.

The strikebreaker knocked once and blustered into the room, full of himself and dressed to the nines. "Well, it looks like it's going to finally be a good day, Mr. Henshaw, after all that humidity and rain." He removed his bowler and held it by the brim.

"It is a good day, Mr. Brodsky, but for other reasons," Henshaw said with the newspaper still in his hands. "Have you seen these headlines?"

"They're pretty good, huh," Pearlie said. "It looks like things are turning your way."

"Pretty good, are you kidding? They're wonderful." Henshaw read the headlines from page one—*Police Strike Denounced by Wilson*; *Police Strike, Civic Treason, says New York World*; *Police Desertion Condemned by City's Poor*—and this one's the best— *Gompers Not Coming, Does Not Want General Strike.*

"It's a total condemnation of those Mick cops. The national press is onboard—they're linking the police strike to the Bolshevik Movement." He rapped the newspaper in the palm of his hand. "They're dead. They'll never work in this city again." He opened his bottom drawer and took out a bottle of sherry. "I know it's a little early in the day, but this news isn't just pretty good, it's the best news we could have expected. It's a day for true Americans to stand up and be proud." He filled two water glasses a third full and handed one of them to Brodsky. "We've just rid Boston of that goddam Labor Movement for who knows how long, maybe in my lifetime. Cheers to a job well done."

"Cheers." Brodsky drank down the sherry. "We might have used different tactics in this strike, but the results were the same. Like I told you before, you want to bust 'em—" He held out his glass as Henshaw poured him another round— "We're the guys to call. I can assume that your partners are also satisfied?"

"We couldn't have asked for a better outcome." Henshaw opened the safe behind his desk and removed an envelope. "The Guard has control of the streets while the Commissioner recruits a new police force, businesses are open and the damage—well, that's why we have insurance." He handed Brodsky the envelope. "That should balance the books. We will not need any further services."

Pearlie opened the envelope. "Do you mind?" he said as he removed a wad of bills.

"No, go ahead. I hope you don't mind the cash, but sometimes it's just better to pay in currency. Makes for a cleaner transaction."

"Cash is fine." Pearlie piled the bills into neat little stacks until he tabulated the total payment. "Perfect, Mr. Henshaw."

"Where are you headed next?"

"Home. I haven't seen the little woman in quite some time." Brodsky stuffed the envelope into the inside pocket of his suit jacket. "Although it could be a short stay. I'm getting calls about the steel union. And if those boys go out, it will make this strike seem like an afternoon tea with some society dames. I already sent my new Number One ahead."

"Yes," Henshaw said. "That's too bad about Rossini."

"Yeah, I'm going to miss him. He was like a son."

Henshaw rubbed his hands together. "Ah—he wouldn't say anything? You know, mention who he was working for."

"Nah, he knows the game." Brodsky flinched towards his client with his hand out, but when Henshaw stood stiff and didn't react, Pearlie took his hat with both hands and placed it on his head.

"Well, good luck," Henshaw said.

"You too. Nice doing business with you."

JIM RANKIN approached the double doors to the large hall, turned and faced the District Reps of the BCLU. He adjusted his carnation and tugged on the ends of his bow tie. "Are we ready?"

The District Reps murmured and nodded, a few of them said, "Yes."

"We need to show them that they are not mistaken in their sympathies for the police," he said. "But, while they are to be commended for their willingness to toe the line, we need to keep control in there and make them realize that now is not the time for a general strike. That card should only be played when it benefits us all, and this is not the time to play it."

He turned back to the doors and allowed his sergeant-at-arms to step in front of him. The man held the doorknobs and waited for Jim's order. Rankin heard the delegates' chatter in the packed hall quiet to a buzz of whispers in anticipation of the doors opening.

He looked back again. "One last thing. There are several representatives of the police union in there. We are not going to be intimidated into making a decision that is not in our best interests. Remember, the whole country is watching what we do." He gave a last tug on his lapels. "We'll give moral and some financial support, that's all."

Rankin reached up and placed one of his hands on his man's shoulder. "Okay, Sam, let's go." The two enormous doors swung open and the president and his Board marched in.

EVEN JOHN MCINNES was having trouble believing what he said any longer. He had told them that the A.F. of L., BCLU and the other unions were just waiting for the word. "They will stand beside us and support us to the bitter end of this." The veteran policeman believed that no one in their right mind could fail to understand their position, couldn't say that they had bargained without good faith—there was a strike because they could not get anyone to honestly address their grievances.

Voices echoed at the back of the dimly lit and nearly empty Fay Hall. Random patches of shadow fell across the floor near the stage where McInnes sat in a folding wooden chair.

"John, do you want me to wait for you?" his vice president called from the exit.

"Thanks, no, I think I'll sit here for a few minutes."

McInnes stretched out his legs, tipped his chin down and closed his eyes, realizing that the coppers were the last to know that they were expendable. "Nolan was right," he said. "It was a stacked deck."

But the slightest glimmer of hope existed. The courts hadn't heard the arguments yet and McInnes resolved himself to continue to fight even when things looked so bleak.

Chapter Thirty-two

~

Sunday, 19 October 1919

The landlady opened the door before the visitor reached it. "You've got company, Mr. Dwyer."

"Thanks, Mrs. Gerhardt." He continued to read the editorial in *The Pilot.*

"Come in, Mr. Nolan," she said. "You look handsome in your new uniform. More like, what am I trying to say? Like an army officer, that's it, especially the hat. No more helmets, yuh?"

George held out his arms and turned all the way around. "New uniform, same old— "

"What?"

"Yes, no more helmets, Mrs. Gerhardt, and I didn't have to pay for the uniform. Do you mind if I smoke?"

"No, come sit down." The landlady handed him an ashtray.

He sat in the parlor across from Willie and waited until the landlady walked out of the room. "You'll never believe why I'm here."

"Not one word. Not one—" Willie dropped the paper and looked for Mrs. Gerhardt.

"She's in the kitchen," Nolan said.

"Not one goddam word about the strike, like it never happened. The Cardinal must have glued their mouths shut and threatened excommunication for any mention of it."

"What did you expect, Willie? Half the country now believes that the police strike was the start of America's second revolution."

"Bullshit."

"I know it and most of the city knows it, but the men with the money are back in control of everything, including Information."

"I'll tell you what I do expect from my Catholic Church. I expect them to direct some of that fire and brimstone at Curtis and the politicians, all those bastards who are responsible for the strike, the savagery, Quigley. What happened to the 'Noble and Honorable Working Man?' The Church has no problem supporting other strikes."

"I don't know." George flicked his cigarette over the ashtray. "But I do know, if the strike demonstrated anything it showed that if there are three people left on this earth, one of them better be a copper."

Willie folded the newspaper and put it back into the stand. "You started to say something when you came in."

"Yeah, me and a couple of the other 'scabs' have been ordered by the captain to go to the homes of the Station 10 strikers and collect their uniform brass. Useless Curtis has determined that it's Department property."

"You've got to be kidding!"

"I wish I were, Willie."

"Does he want my long johns too?"

"To be honest with you, some of the fellas are having a hard time finding the brass buttons, if you know what I mean." Nolan crushed the cigarette into the ashtray. "How are you doing for cash?"

"I had a little put aside, one of the benefits of living like a hermit for ten years." Willie looked out the window like he was alone with his thoughts. "Catherine's friends offered a loan until I get back on my feet."

"A loan? The Brotherhood's got money. De Valera's Government is greasing the Washington politicians to get them to officially recognize Ireland as a republic. They couldn't have just given you something to tide you over, or for Criss' sakes, rewarded you for helping them save their president's arse?"

"The only money I took was part of the money she scammed from Brodsky's thugs. That went to the Bradley boys and their mother."

"You and her?"

"Still friends, but she's busy, picking up the odd job at O'Neil's." Willie rubbed the stubble on his face. "It would mean sharing her, and I'm not ready to do that."

"She's not willing to give it up?"

"Not right now."

"What about de Valera? He needs new men for protection."

"I don't think all of his compatriots completely trust me."

"What the hell do they know? We controlled the whole thing. He was never in any danger, never set foot on Moon Island. He was switched at the Guards' roadblock."

"It's yesterday's newspaper, George."

Mrs. Gerhardt entered with a tray and two cups of coffee. "I think I remembered how you like it, Mr. Nolan."

"I'm sure it's perfect." George waited until she left the room. "Fahey was under suspicion for a time, but we needed you and Bernie McLean, and the strike. We got that assassination squad to a place where we could dictate the terms of the fight. And the best part? No one is the wiser—no press, no inquiring politicians. And the Limeys? They're not going to say one bloody word."

"I'm just about ready to start working with Bill Driscoll anyways. You know him, right?"

"Oh, sure, builds houses, used to work out of '15.'"

"Yeah, he's put a few of the fellas to work." Willie pulled himself up and stood. "I'll get those buttons for you."

"I'm going to talk to O'Neil," Nolan said when Willie reentered the room. "Have him straighten those bastards out."

"Don't bother. I don't care what they think."

"If that's what you want."

"Yeah." Willie handed the brass buttons to Nolan. "I kept one for myself."

"A little memento." Nolan shoveled the buttons into his pockets. "It's going to be awfully dull without you, Dwyer. You're like an asshole magnet. Some cops will walk right by a couple of stiffs up to no good because they can't see shit. But you, you're like a big pile of dung. The flies just can't resist you."

"I'll miss it," Willie said. "Every time I walk past a copper or when I see a cruiser barreling down the street, I'll second-guess myself.

"I know you will." Nolan started to turn. "Oh, guess who I saw in Harvard Square a few weeks ago?"

"Who?"

"Joseph."

"Kursh?"

"Yeah, still passing out the Socialist drivel."

"Well, no one can say that he isn't dedicated."

"Say, Willie. Why now?"

"Strike?"

"Yeah."

"Because now I can." He sat down easy into the chair. "Maybe if I had as much time on the job as you, George, I'd think differently."

"Well, you're free to make your own decisions now."

"Free, hmm. Not sure if I know what that is yet."

"With time, Willie. Before you know it, one day will fall into another and you'll just live." Nolan turned and opened the door. He held his cap up. "I don't think I'll ever get used to this thing." He placed it on his head, cocked to one side. "You realize that you fellas, you strikers, will never be cops in this city again."

"Yeah, I know—" Willie leaned on his elbow. "But maybe it doesn't deserve us."

Eamon de Valera inspects I.R.A. Troops at Sixmilebridge, County Clare, Ireland

The Last Word . . .

~

Pasadena, California

Rose Bowl Results
1 January 1920
Harvard 7
Oregon 6

Beacon Hill, Boston

"Congratulations, Governor, even the President has publically stepped forward and commended you." Frank Stearns, his closest confidant, stood by the overstuffed couch where Coolidge sat slight and straight in a natty dark wool suit.

"He has, hasn't he," Coolidge said. He put down his glass of Bourbon whiskey and turned to face his guests. "So what should the theme be for the November election?" He grinned, the gaze from his robin-blue eyes sliding off the tip of his nose.

Stearns took the seat across from him. "You are the 'Law and Order' candidate, the country has already knighted you. So why not take advantage of it?"

"Hmm, you think so?"

"'There is no right to strike against the public safety by anybody, anywhere, anytime.' Brilliant, just the right response to Gompers." The successful businessman and fellow Amherst alumnus placed his glass on the end table. "That admonition is on the front page of every newspaper in the country and on the lips of every Washington politician who wishes he had thought of it first."

"Listen to him, Governor," Herbert Parker said, "he is right on target. If the police strikers had any lingering support, those words put an end to it. Right now you're standing as a beacon of common sense and old-fashioned American values at a time when the country is being torn apart by radicalism. People want stability and they want a return to decency."

Coolidge reached into his vest pocket and removed his grandfather's watch. He opened it and cupped it in his hand, admiring the picture of his mother that was encased inside the cover. "And what about the unions, how are we going to appease them?"

"In your address at the Republican state convention," Parker said, "you'll emphasize that you would never resist the lawful action of organized Labor. Cite examples where your administration has supported the trade unions. Justify your actions during the strike by emphasizing the chaos that the police would have created had they won. You could not give aid and comfort to their deliberate intention to intimidate and coerce the Commonwealth."

"Do you have a meeting, Governor?" Stearns said when Coolidge continued to look at his watch.

Coolidge ignored the remark and the two men waited for him to reenter the discussion. He remained detached several additional moments before he folded the watch cover closed, returned it to its pocket and lifted his face to Stearns. "So, you think we should frame the campaign around the police strike?"

"Yes," Stearns said. "The question before the voters should be—'Shall the state of Massachusetts be governed by law or mob rule?'"

"And you agree with that, Mr. Parker?"

"Yes, Governor, I do. The stage is yours."

The attendant entered, carrying a tray with a box of cigars on it. He presented it to the Governor and his two guests, and once they had made their choice, he lit the cigars for the three men and left the room.

"The road can travel all the way to Washington," Stearns said. "The Amherst College Board of Trustees met recently. And afterwards the chairman, Malcolm Burrows, called. Are you acquainted with him?"

Coolidge released the smoke into the room and nodded. "How is Mr. Burrows? We are classmates."

"He's well. He called to say that the Amherst Board will consider backing one of their own in next year's national election."

Coolidge turned toward Stearns, the melancholic finish of his face softening into a child's impish grin. "And who would that be?"

"They will support a national campaign for vice president if you decide to run."

"Hmm," Coolidge said, "seems like there is a lot to do."

Boston Police Headquarters

Albert sat ramrod straight, his hands at rest on the tops of his thighs as the three captains hovered in a cluster above his personnel folder that lay open on the table. The captain on the right—*Jeremiah Sullivan, Headquarters, will make it difficult for you, known as By-the-Book Sullivan, answer his questions directly, unemotionally and professionally*—leaned closer to the other two, whispered something that was unintelligible, turned and glanced at him, scratched the top of his ear and then turned back to the others while they continued to confer in a low murmur.

After what seemed like an eternity to Coppenrath, the officers broke off their discussion and sat back in their chairs. The captain in the middle, the chairman of the Review Board, closed the folder and breathed heavily before he spoke. "Coppenrath, I called Captain Keveney at Station 10 before we convened this morning and he said you were a good patrolman, always well groomed, disciplined, diligent in your duties, no citizen complaints and timely when submitting your reports, which," he raised his voice and spoke in a lilting cadence, "will always keep you in good stead with your commander." The chairman snuffled a short laugh. "Right?"

"Yes, sir."

The chairman resumed the dispassionate business of the hearing. "Do we have any questions of Coppenrath?"

"Yes, I do," Captain Sullivan said. He stared directly at Albert across the bridge of his hands. "You are aware that Station 10 and the Roxbury Crossing neighborhood suffered one of the most violent riots of the strike?"

"Yes, sir. I am aware of that."

"Damage to homes and businesses and at least two men killed during the rioting?"

"Yes."

"And the task of defending the station and quelling the fighting and malicious destruction left to a handful of older senior police officers and volunteers." He picked up the personnel folder. "I must be honest with you Coppenrath. If I had my way, not one of you strikers—"

"Sir, if I may—"

"This isn't a debate, Coppenrath." Sullivan opened the file. "There would be no need for these hearings or this Board because none of you would be even considered for reinstatement." He removed a single sheet of paper from the folder. "In your letter of appeal, you state that you were incapacitated with influenza and unable to report for duty."

"That's correct, sir."

"But, Coppenrath, there is no record in the Daily Log of you calling in sick. How do you rectify that?"

"I don't, sir."

The chairman wiggled in his chair. "But you did call in? Is that correct?"

"Yes, sir."

The captain on the left—*Don't worry about Howell, he's on board*—began to tap his fingers together. "Whom did you speak with?"

"Patrolman Quigley."

"Fulton Quigley?" Howell stopped drumming his fingers. "The striker that was killed?"

"Yes, sir."

"A dead man is your alibi?" Sullivan said.

"Sir?"

"You're going to have to come up with better proof that you reported in sick than enlisting the name of a dead man, if you expect this Board to take your appeal seriously."

"Ah, Captain Sullivan," the chairman said. "Would you mind if I ask a few questions?"

"Yes, that would be fine."

"Okay. First of all, we need to establish that you were sick. Did you bring some proof of your bout with influenza, Coppenrath?"

"Yes, sir." Albert reached inside his suit jacket and removed a sealed envelope. "May I," he said as he offered it.

"Yes, bring it forward," the chairman said.

Coppenrath handed over the envelope.

After reading the letter inside, the chairman passed it to the other Board members. "Dr. Paul Epstein, a reputable and distinguished physician."

Sullivan dropped the doctor's letter on the table. "Okay, Coppenrath, you had the flu."

"When did you call in?" the chairman said.

Albert resumed his military position with his back pressed against the chair. *They know you voted to strike.* "The evening before the strike I went to Fay Hall and voted."

"We know about that," Sullivan said. "You voted to strike, didn't you?"

"Yes."

"Yes, you did, Coppenrath." He held up several sheets of paper. "This is the list of patrolmen who voted to strike and your name is on it." He passed the evidence to the chairman and Captain Howell. "And when did you decide not to strike and conveniently become incapacitated with the flu?"

"Sir, if I may—"

Sullivan raised his voice. "When did you get the flu and when did you report your illness to Station 10?"

"I—"

"Captain, let's give him a chance to speak," the chairman said. "Go ahead, Coppenrath."

Tell it the way we rehearsed it. "I wrestled with the decision to strike," Albert said. "I have a family, one child and another on the way. But the grievances, they're legitimate."

"Go on, Coppenrath," the chairman said.

"I came down with the flu earlier in the day."

"What day was that?" Howell said.

"Ah, before I went to Fay Hall," Albert answered. "It was Monday when I got the fever, the day before the strike. When I returned home, I decided not to walk out, but by that time, I was vomiting every few minutes and I couldn't keep anything down—" He looked down at the floor. "—couldn't get out of bed."

Captain Howell poured a glass of water.

"My wife, Emily, actually called in, early Tuesday morning. She spoke to Fulton."

"And did he say that he would make an entry into the log?" the chairman asked.

Albert shrugged his shoulders. "She told me that he just laughed and said, 'Covering all his bases, is he?'"

The chairman glanced at the other captains and then pointed to the door. "Wait outside, Coppenrath."

After a few minutes, Albert was called back into the room and resumed his seat in front of the Board.

The chairman held his personnel folder. "Ordinarily Coppenrath, we would have notified you by mail in about ten days." He signed the bottom of the Order and passed it to the other Board members for their signatures. "But the Department can use some experienced men right now." Before he slid the Order into the folder, he wrote at the bottom of the page—'Not to be given to the Press.'

"Thank you, sir."

"Don't thank me, Coppenrath. Commissioner Curtis will have the last say. But I suspect that you will be reinstated on a technicality. We made our decision based on the evidence, that's all." The chairman stood and pushed back his chair. "A lot of good men got swept up in that strike business, including men with twenty and more years and the Department is poorer for it. You're one of the few lucky ones who retained his position." He picked up his papers and stepped from behind the table. "Make the most of it."

Albert waited for the three Board members to leave the room.

Captain Sullivan, the last to exit, paused as he passed him. "There was something in the newspapers recently."

"Sir?"

"Didn't Dr. Epstein recently open a clinic on Whitney Street?"

"Ah, I believe he did," Albert said.

"In fact, I think he had tried to raise funds for several years for that clinic." Sullivan adjusted the file under his arm. "Wasn't it fortuitous that he received that anonymous donation?"

"Yes, sir."

"I spoke to Captain Keveney and he thinks you have some talent for the administrative side of the business. So, coupled with your reinstatement, you will be transferred to my section here at HQ. We will be introducing some new technology to the Department and a sophisticated reporting system that will track cases and create modern intelligence files. And we will be acquiring the Teletype machine for better and faster communications. I will need someone to become proficient on it and be able to train other officers." Sullivan placed his cover on his head. "It will keep you out of harm's way for the time being."

"Thank you, captain."

When Sullivan reached the door, he turned around. "Say hello to your father-in-law. We go back a long way."

"I will, sir."

"And tell Jim that the vote was unanimous to reinstate."

Albert stepped outside the double doors and onto the platform that faced Pemberton Square. He removed a cigarette from his pocket, twisted the paper on one end and lit it. As he exhaled, a steamship blew its horn several times in the harbor as it moved away from the wharf, the sound resonating between the close waterfront buildings and rising up Beacon Hill. He could hear the pulse of the city and listened to its slow purposeful breathing. And knew that it was alive and well.

Station Ten, Roxbury Crossing

So, he's gone, huh."

"Died alone in his home." The houseman placed a cup of coffee on the desk in front of the sergeant. "Refused assistance until he was out of the public eye. Just made it in the door, from what I hear."

The sergeant rolled his chair away from the typewriter. "He was a tough old bird, Fred, but I can't say that I'm going to miss him. While he modernized the Department, I can't ever forgive him for not coming to some kind of settlement with the fellas and firing all of those good Irish coppers."

"Not to mention what their families went through," the houseman said.

"They loved the job," the sergeant said. "And then being blackballed in the city, so no one would hire them."

"Just wasn't right."

The two men put their feet up on the desk.

"These new cops don't have the stuff, you know. All they want to do is whine about the hours they have to work."

"Fucking eejits."

"Or they're bitching that they don't make enough money. They should have been on the job when we worked eighty hours a week for 1200 bucks a year."

"I got to tell you," the houseman said, "when Willie Dwyer joined the strikers, why that knocked the shit right out of me." He held the coffee cup with both hands and sipped the hot liquid. "I thought at that stage of the game, who is next?"

"I think it was a matter of principle," the sergeant said.

The two men sat quietly and they could hear the floorboards squeak above them. Someone started the paddy wagon in the backyard.

"I hear he is working as a carpenter," Fred said.

"You ask most of these kids about Willie Dwyer or—" The sergeant paused. "Poor old Fulton Quigley."

"Or John McInnes."

"That's right, John McInnes, the man who led the fight for the benefits and pay that these guys enjoy today. You mention those names to them and they don't have the first idea who you're talking about."

"That's because when you're gone, sergeant, you're gone."

Boston Harbor

Willie looked down at his shoes and saw the dust that had collected on the toes during his walk from the Park Street Station to Long Wharf. He lifted one foot and wiped it on the back of his trousers and then the other. He had moved through the streets like an apparition observing the remaining vestiges of the police strike that memorialized 'the battle fought in defending America in the war against anarchy.' A copper's billy hung from an electric light pole, and small businesses with the boarded-up windows still waited for insurance adjustors to respond. Merchants' handwritten signs offered 'Correct-size Exchanges for looted goods, No Questions Asked' or declared that they were 'Robbed but Open for Business.' Spent brass cartridge cases and discarded shotgun shells still lay here and there, hidden under cast iron sewer covers or tucked away in the gutter. Political signs from the previous year's election peeled away from the sides of buildings—

Remember September the 9th
Don't Let It Happen Again
Vote for the Law & Order Candidate
Vote for Coolidge

A late winter chill drifted across the near empty deck of the *Pontia* as the steamer escaped the dark grey shadows of the shoreline and withdrew from the protection of the inner harbor. A crew member stood watch at the bow of the ship, looking for obstructions while the steamer navigated through the flat translucent water before it reached the deeper darker waters of the frosty Atlantic. Willie turned around and leaned his back against the rail, pulled the collar of his peacoat up around his ears and adjusted his cap, stood there rubbing his hands together, and scanned the grizzled waterfront as the steamer rode into the day's early brilliance, chugging past the first of the harbor islands.

A young woman stepped onto the deck and glided to the rail near the covered promenade. She wore slacks and was fashionably wrapped in a long winter coat that was tied at her waist, and on her head, a brimless Cloche hat that resembled a helmet covered her forehead and rested on her eyebrows. She placed her gloved hands on the rail, inhaled herself tall and breathed in the warmth of the sun and the ocean air. On the open deck, Willie continued to stand with his back against the rail, noted her presence, but watched the city grow smaller in the distance.

They stood in the privacy of their own wishful dreams while the ship cleared the last outer island and broke for the sea. The woman stepped away from the rail first and sat down on one of the lounge chairs under the cover of the promenade. Willie turned away from the Boston skyline, rolled his shoulders forward and jammed his hands into his pockets as he started for the stairs. Before he reached the hatchway, a steward stepped out of the door and announced that breakfast was being served in the main dining room. Then he approached the woman.

"Miss Malone, your brother wanted you to know that he will not be joining you in the dining room."

"Thank you," she said without turning to acknowledge him.

As Willie approached, the steward held the hatchway door open. "Mr. Dwyer, you have a message in the wireless room."

"Thanks," Willie said. "Can you tell me where the wireless room is located?"

The steward stepped away from the door. "I'll show you, sir." The two men walked to the beginning of the promenade. "Mr. Dwyer, if you go this way here and enter the hallway about halfway down, the first room on the left is the wireless."

"Thanks again," Dwyer said. "I'll pick it up after breakfast."

The steward left and Willie chanced a glance at the woman whose elbow rested on the arm of her chair with her hand supporting her chin. Her face was tilted back toward him with a familiar expression of educated coyness.

"Mr. Dwyer," she said. "What a pleasant day for a trip."

"Miss Malone? Hmm, I am acquainted with a woman whom I dare say looks remarkably like you."

"Really."

"A very attractive woman if I may add, but her name is Catherine Loftus."

"Ah, what a coincidence, same first name."

"Malone, and a brother?"

"You should meet Dudley," she said. "A visionary. I think you would find that you've had some common experiences. Probably get along smashingly."

He nodded in understanding. "You and Dudley?"

"The odd job, Willie—"

"Ah." Willie gestured to the chair next to hers. "May I?"

"Please do."

He stretched out his legs and rested his head against the bulkhead wall. "Let me see. The *Pontia* is bound for Ireland with no stops in between." He rolled his head in the direction of Catherine. "On holiday? Or is it better that I don't ask?"

"Something like that."

"Like what? On holiday or don't ask?"

"You realize," she said, "that the more you know, the more you are expected to know." She undid the button on one of her gloves pulled it by the tips of her fingers and slid the glove off. "And you, why are you returning?"

"Because—now I can."

"Yes." She nodded and took his hand. "Your skin is cold. You really should wear gloves."

"I have to say, Miss Malone, that I'm a little bit concerned."

"And why is that?" Her fingers slipped under his palm. "Calluses, the hands of a laborer."

"During that last encounter that involved your *brother*, I was, for the lack of a better term, recruited and damn near killed. And here we are, you and I and your *brother*, coincidentally sailing on the same ship on the same day. And last I knew the Crown still had unfinished business with—what was his name, 'Dudley'?"

"But this is a different day, Willie." Catherine held his hand to her face. "This time, the president returns for the birth of a new republic and a promise of a treaty with England. And you and I are going home."

"Ah," he said.

Acknowledgments

The Rising at Roxbury Crossing is a work of fiction. It takes place somewhere between my imaginary world and historic reality. The Boston police strike was an actual event, a Shakespearean tragedy of sorts, with real players and recorded results. It is embedded in the psyche of the city. However, all scenes, incidents and characters are intended to be fictional and any semblance to actual events or persons is coincidental.

With deepest respect, I remember my late father-in-law, William E. Mulvey, who once asked me, "Can you do some research on my father, William J. Mulvey? He was a Boston Police officer." The Boston Police Department record for Patrolman William J. Mulvey reads: "Mulvey, William J., ABANDONED HIS DUTY, September 9, 1919."

To my children and grandchildren who patiently asked, "When?"

To Bonnie and Scott Dittrich who kept the faith even when I doubted. I am forever grateful.

During my seven-year sojourn back to 1919 Boston, I had the good fortune to be assisted and counseled. I am the grateful recipient of the generosity of the following who made this story breathe: Ann and Gerry O'Connor, daughter and son-in-law of police striker, Malachy McGrath; John Driscoll, son of striker, William J. Driscoll; Donna Wells and Margaret Sullivan, Records Managers & Archivists of the Boston Police Department; Michael Finn, Shannonbridge, County Offaly, who has dug more than his share of peat at the Poolboy Bog; The Massachusetts State Police Bomb Squad; Damien Murray, Assistant Professor of History, Elms College; Maxine Rodburg, mentor, friend and Director of The Crimson Summer Academy at Harvard; Beth Bruno and Linda Sperling, editors extraordinaire, Maggie Lichtenberg, Kathi Dunn, Hobie Hobart, Dorie McClelland and Bobbye Middendorf who helped me get it done.

THIS STORY would not have risen without the source material here:

Sacco & Vanzetti: The Anarchist Background by Paul Avrich; *American*

Decades,1920–1929 edited by Judith S. Baughman; "Boston's Labor Movement: An Oral History of Work and Union Organizing" by The Boston 200 Corporation, Kevin White, Mayor; "Louis C. Fraina/Lewis Corey and The Crisis of the Middle Class" by Paul Buhle; "Crowd was Not with Police," *Boston Evening Transcript*, Last Edition, 10 September 1919; "De Valera Hidden if He is in Ireland, May Not be Seized," *The New York Times*, 1 January 1921; "Red May Day in Prison," Martha Foley's account of the May Day riot in *The Revolutionary Age*, 17 May 1919; "General Order No. 178," Report of Trial Board, 14 November 1919, Boston Police Archives; "Great Irish Leader Honored by Boston," *The Pilot*, 5 July 1919; *Boston's Immigrants 1790–1880* by Oscar Handlin; *Police Administration in Boston* by Leonard V. Harrison; "People of the Boglands" by the Irish Peatland Conservation Council 2000; *The American Irish: A History* by Kevin Kenny; *I Break Strikes* by Edward Levinson; *Ballinasloe: A Story of a Community over the Past 300 Years* by Tadhg MacLochlainin; *Anarchist Women 1870–1920* by Margaret S. Marsh; "From Parnell to Pearse (1891–1921)," in *The Course of Irish History* by Donal McCartney; *Calvin Coolidge: The Quiet President* by Donald R. McCoy; "Go Forth as a Missionary to Fight It: Catholic Anti-socialism and Irish American Nationalism in Post–World War I Boston," by Damien Murray; *Red Scare: A Study in National Hysteria, 1919–1920* by Robert K. Murray; "Island Facts: Moon Island," by National Park Service, U.S. Dept. of the Interior; *Bibles, Brahmins, and Bosses: A Short History of Boston* by Thomas H. O'Connor; *The Boston Irish* by Thomas H. O'Connor; "Obituary of John F. McInnes," *Boston Globe*, 17 May 1924; "The Perfect Corpse: Bog Bodies in the Iron Age," Nova, PBS, Ch 2, Boston, 7 Feb. 2006; *Police in America*, "The Boston Police Strike: Two Reports, Boston 1919–1920: 'Report of Citizen's Committee Appointed by Mayor Peters to Consider the Police Situation' and 'Fourteenth Annual Report of the Police Commissioner for the City of Boston,'" by Arno Press and *New York Times*; *Dark Tide: The Great Boston Molasses Flood of 1919* by Stephen Puleo; *Twentieth Century Teen Culture by the Decades* by Lucy Rollin; *A City in Terror* by Francis Russell; "Nineteen Nineteen: The Boston Police Strike in the Context of American Labor" by Zachary M. Schrag; "Sidis Gets Year and Half in Jail," *Boston Herald*

14 May 1919; "Calvin Coolidge: A Study in Inertia" in *They Also Ran* by Irving Stone; *Images of America: Boston Police Department* by Donna M. Wells; *A Puritan in Babylon: The Story of Calvin Coolidge* by William Allen White; *Boston: A Topographical History* by Walter Muir Whitehill and Lawrence W. Kennedy.

ALSO: News accounts of International, National and Massachusetts events occurring in 1919, including the Boston Police Strike: *Boston Evening Transcript, Boston Globe, Boston Herald, Boston Labor World, New York Times, The Pilot and The Republic.*

CPSIA information can be obtained at www.ICGtesting.com
Printed in the USA
LVOW061546060213

318956LV00007B/890/P